Appalachian Gateway

Appalachian Gateway

An Anthology of Contemporary Stories and Poetry

Editors: George Brosi and Kate Egerton
Student Editors: Samantha Cole and Morgan Cottrell

The University of Tennessee Press · Knoxville

First Edition.

The paper in this book meets the requirements of American National Standards Institute / National Information Standards Organization specification Z39.48–1992 (Permanence of Paper). It contains 30 percent post-consumer waste and is certified by the Forest Stewardship Council.

Library of Congress Cataloging-in-Publication Data

Appalachian gateway: an anthology of contemporary stories and poetry / editors, George Brosi and Kate Egerton; student editors, Samantha Cole and Morgan Cottrell. — First edition.
pages cm
Includes bibliographical references.
ISBN-13: 978-1-57233-944-6 (pbk.)
ISBN-10: 1-57233-944-6 (pbk.)
1. American literature—Appalachian Region—Bio-bibliography.
2. Appalachian Region—Literary collections.
I. Brosi, George.
II. Egerton, Katherine E.

PS537.A67 2013
810.8'097569—dc23 2013001460

This book is dedicated by George Brosi to:

his wife, Connie Brosi, and to their children:
Brook Emmanuel, Berry Justice, Blossom Katrina, Sunshine Liberty,
Sky Harmony, Glade Blythe, and Eagle Valiant
and to their grandchildren:
Daisy, Summer, Fox, Lily, Iris, Harlan, Clay, Aviva, and Wendell

It is dedicated by Kate Egerton to:

her husband, Edmund Pendleton, and their son Malcolm

It is dedicated by Samantha Lynn Cole to:

her parents, John David Cole and Deborah Cole; her two sisters, Rachel Leanne Cole
and Anita Marie Cole; and to her Granny and Papaw Charles

It is dedicated by Morgan Cottrell to:

her partner, Luke; her son, Pheonix; her sister, Megan; her parents,
Mark and Chris and her Nana and Papaw Richard

Contents

Part 2: The People

Part 3: Work and the Economy

Part 4: Cultural Traditions

Part 5: Institutions

Acknowledgments

by George Brosi

Appalachian literature is an important field of literary studies. We are indebted to all those whose hard work helped establish and gain recognition for this subgenre of American literature. Regional literature has been viewed as an important part of Appalachian Studies from its beginnings as a distinct field of academic inquiry in the 1960s. Cratis Williams (1911–85), widely considered the "father" of Appalachian Studies, titled his 1961 PhD dissertation for New York University "The Southern Mountaineer in Fact and Fiction," dramatically establishing the primacy of fiction as well as nonfiction in this fledgling academic field. Among the visible early promoters of regional literature were Wilma Dykeman (1920–2006), Jim Wayne Miller (1936–96), and Gurney Norman. These efforts burgeoned in the early 1970s as an infrastructure for Appalachian literature was created. Loyal Jones, the first director of the Appalachian Center at Berea College, began holding a summer institute on regional literature, music, and history. Grace Toney Edwards initiated the Highland Summer Conference at Radford University in Virginia. Albert Stewart (1914–2001) founded *Appalachian Heritage* magazine and the Appalachian Writers Workshop in Hindman, Kentucky. The magazine, the workshop, and the conference are still flourishing. *Voices from the Hills* was published by Robert J. Higgs and Ambrose N. Manning, professors at East Tennessee State University, in 1975. We are indebted to all of them, along with countless others who played important roles in the establishment of this significant academic enterprise.

After a June 2009 panel discussion celebrating the contributions of author Jim Wayne Miller, Laura Sutton, then an acquisitions editor with the University Press of Kentucky, repeated her entreaties to George Brosi, the editor of *Appalachian Heritage* and proprietor of Appalachian Mountain Books, to utilize his extensive experience promoting regional literature to prepare an anthology. Kate Egerton, whose course load at Berea College included Appalachian literature, reinforced Laura's view of the need for such a book and expressed her willingness to participate. She suggested the possibility that

Berea College students could be involved. We are grateful to Laura Sutton for her initial encouragement and also to Kerry Eileen Webb from the University of Tennessee Press for shepherding the book through all the developing stages to reality.

Subsequently, Berea College's Undergraduate Research and Creative Projects Program provided financial support that allowed two student editors—Samantha Cole of Beattyville, Kentucky, and Morgan Cottrell of Spencer, West Virginia—to work full-time on this book in the summer of 2010 and part-time afterwards. Their perspectives and their diligence have been essential to whatever success we have achieved. During the final stages of preparation for the press, we involved two additional Berea College students. We extend our deep thanks to Stephanie Mullins of Clintwood, Virginia, and to Sarah McLewin of Norfolk, Virginia. The Berea College Hutchins Library, including director Ann Chase and reference librarian Edward Poston, provided help with research on the authors.

We are deeply indebted to the authors represented here. One unique aspect of this book is that almost all authors approved, and often improved, their biographical sketches, all of which were prepared and written by George Brosi. We also appreciate permissions provided by both authors and publishers to use the stories and poems included in this collection; permissions statements appear immediately after the selections.

Finally we'd like to express our appreciation for family and friends who have helped and sustained us during this effort, especially to Connie Brosi, whose deep involvement throughout has been invaluable.

Foreword

by George Brosi

We enthusiastically welcome you to a book that we hope you will find delightful, thought-provoking, and insightful. This is a collection of stories and poems by authors with strong ties to the Southern Appalachian region. At the time this book was prepared for publication, all the authors represented were contemporary, very much alive and engaged in regional life. These writings thus illustrate regional life around the time of the turn of the twenty-first century.

This book does not present a complete sample of Appalachian literature partly because we have not included any novel excerpts. Some of the region's most outstanding authors—for example, Charles Frazier and Cormac McCarthy—are thus not included. We wanted to limit the book to what writers designed to be read as a whole. However, we do include mention of important regional novelists in our overview of Southern Appalachian literature.

Our selections are organized into the same categories that appear in the *Encyclopedia of Appalachia*, edited by Rudy Abramson and Jean Haskell Spears and published by the University of Tennessee Press in 2006. We feel that these stories and poems illuminate regional life and are thus useful to informal students of the region as well as to those who teach and learn in educational institutions.

We view this book as a gateway to Appalachian literature, which is why we have included rather extensive bibliographic information. This book shows simply the tip of the iceberg, not only in terms of the work of the individual authors, but also in regard to the literary output of the region. The editors do not mean in any way to imply that these are the twenty-five best writers working today or that our selections represent their finest work. Rather, we have made very difficult decisions about inclusion based on achieving a variety of balances.

We hope this book will be popular with a wide general audience, but we have designed it to be particularly useful for courses in creative writing, Appalachian Studies, and Appalachian literature. For these uses, we feel that one of its most outstanding attributes is that, throughout the four years it has taken to prepare this book for publication, our student coeditors from the region, Samantha Cole and Morgan Cottrell, have been actively involved in making the selections and monitoring the writing involved. We feel that student input has been crucial to making this a book that other students will find both enjoyable and meaningful and that instructors can thus assign confidently. George Brosi has taught courses in creative writing, Appalachian Studies, and Appalachian literature. Kate Egerton has taught a variety of English classes, including Appalachian literature. This book has been edited by students who have taken creative writing, Appalachian Studies, and Appalachian literature courses, and by teachers who have taught these classes as well. The editors and student editors all participated in choosing the authors and their selections and preparing the bibliographies. Kate Egerton and Morgan Cottrell prepared the afterword, and George Brosi wrote the introductory material and wrote the biographical sketches of the authors.

An Overview of Appalachian Literature

by George Brosi

Appalachian literature begins with the stories told by those who first settled our region. The stories of the Cherokees, as well as those brought to America from Europe and Africa, form a rich tradition that not only propelled Appalachian literature to an auspicious beginning but that continue to infuse regional writing. The literature of Europeans who immigrated and settled into these mountains began with travel accounts and then fiction by visitors to the area. Among the first Appalachian authors in the pre–Civil War era was David Hunter Strother (1816–88) of Martinsburg, Virginia, now West Virginia, who wrote under the pen name "Porte Crayon." At about that same time, Hardin Taliaferro of Surry County, North Carolina, was transcribing the oral traditions of the European settlers in the region in his book *Fisher's River Scenes and Characters* (1859). George Washington Harris (1814–69) of Knoxville, Tennessee, published *Sut Lovingood's Yarns* in 1867. In their important essay introducing the "Literature" section of *The Encyclopedia of Appalachia,* Grace Toney Edwards and Theresa Lloyd call Harris's character, Sut Lovingood, "an archetypal hillbilly trickster, akin to the medieval fool in his ability to mock the foibles of polite society."

The Civil War was catastrophic to this region, resulting in a breakdown of law and order and sometimes pitting kinfolks against each other. The aftermath of the war was particularly devastating to the region, partly because many mountain areas followed their war allegiances and voted Republican in traditionally Democratic states, thus positioning themselves poorly for infrastructure improvements, including public spending on education. For more than fifty years after the Civil War, practically no books by people born and raised in the region were published.

Nevertheless, in the 1880s, outsiders put Appalachia in the forefront of the local color movement in American literature. Mary Noailles Murfree (1850–1922) of Murfreesboro, Tennessee, was a sickly lady who spent months at Beersheba Springs and Montvale Springs, spas up in the mountains not far from her Middle Tennessee home. She created many archetypal mountain characters who have been found in regional literature ever since, including the cranky crone, the flirtatious fiddler, and the patronizing preacher. Her motifs, including the romance between the mountaineer and the outsider, have also become standards. At the turn of the century, when the local color movement began to fade—superseded by literary romanticism—John Fox, Jr. (1862–1919), kept the region in the limelight. He had grown up in the Kentucky bluegrass, but his brother was in the coal business in the mountains, and Fox followed him there, setting his novels, including his huge best sellers, *The Little Shepherd of Kingdom Come* (1903) and *The Trail of the Lonesome Pine* (1908), in the mountains. Eventually, he settled in Big Stone Gap, Virginia. Lucy Furman (1869–1958) was another popular writer who came to Appalachia from outside—in her case western Kentucky—but lived at the Hindman Settlement School in eastern Kentucky for seventeen years. Her best-known novel, *The Quare Women* (1923), took its name from the designation that some local people gave to the missionaries from outside who taught their children at school.

One can draw an interesting parallel between the literary history of the region and its economic history, which was very early dominated by the hospitality industry for lowlanders, like Mary Noailles Murfree, and then by extractive industries, which led John Fox, Jr., to the area. The establishment of charitable organizations, like the Hindman Settlement School, which drew Lucy Furman to the area, was a subsequent economic development.

An important transition took place in the 1910s and 1920s, led by two fascinating feminists who, though outsiders, identified closely with the local people. At the age of fourteen, Olive Tilford Dargan (1869–1968) taught at a one-room school where she was responsible for forty students ranging in age from six to twenty. She won a scholarship to Peabody College by earning the highest score in the state of Arkansas on a competitive examination. While in Nashville, she traveled with schoolmates to the North Carolina mountains and vowed, "If I ever own a home of my own, it will be in these mountains." Her first published works were dramas written in verse, and in 1906 she realized her dream and moved to a farm in Swain County, North Carolina. She published three proletarian novels in the 1930s under the pen name "Fielding Burke."When she died in Asheville at the age of ninety-nine, her publishing career had spanned fifty-eight years, and she had also authored short stories and poetry as well as nonfiction, most of it set in Appalachia. Emma Bell Miles (1879–1919) was born in Rabbit Hash, Kentucky, along the Ohio River west of Cincinnati, but her schoolteacher parents moved to Signal Mountain above the city of Chattanooga when she was a young girl. Miles was an artist and naturalist, and she married a local man, Frank Miles, who was ill-equipped to support what became a burgeoning family. In 1905 a New York publisher brought out her book, *The Spirit of the Mountains,* the first study to systematically portray mountain life as a distinct culture. Desperately trying to support her family, she often sold her individual poems illustrated by her drawings. In 1912 she published a book of poetry, *Chords from a Dulcimore.* Miles is widely viewed as one of the most compelling figures in Appalachian Studies as well as regional art and literature.

The life of a third feminist writer of this era took a path opposite that of Dargan and Miles. Willa Cather (1873–1947) was born on her maternal grandmother's farm in the Back Creek Valley of the Gore community west of Winchester, Virginia. Soon her family moved to a farm that had been in her father's family for six generations. However, when she was ten years old, Cather moved to Nebraska, the state that claims her important literary legacy, which includes a Pulitzer Prize. In 1940 she published *Sapphira and the Slave Girl,* her only novel set in the moutains of Virginia where she lived as a child.

Because only a very few mountain writers were active earlier, not until the 1920s did the first continuous generation of writers with deep mountain roots enter the national literary scene, but their impact was huge. Many in this generation were born in the first decade of the new century, had come of age in the relatively prosperous 1920s, and began publishing in the 1930s, a tumultuous decade receptive to writing about folks of humble origins. In 1926 Elizabeth Madox Roberts (1881–1941), a native of the hill and holler country on the western edge of the region in Washington County, Kentucky, published *The Time of Man,* a pioneering portrayal in novel form of the rural poor. In his 1935 book *Creating the Modern American Novel,* Harlan Hatcher wrote, "Its success was arresting because of the poetic mood she had created out of materials that were starkly realistic" (250). Before the end of the decade, Thomas Wolfe (1900–1938), the son of a Pennsylvania father and a mother from the mountains of Yancey County, North Carolina, published novels and stories and even plays often set in Asheville where he grew up, including *Look Homeward, Angel* (1929). W. D. Weatherford and Wilma Dykeman, in their seminal essay on Appalachian literature in the important 1962 book *The Southern Appalachian Region: A Survey,* claim, "Wolfe's roots are in the mountain soil, but his vision includes the world. He is at once the most specific and the most universal of mountain writers. Wolfe, the mountain boy, the American singer, the lost and seeking man, has spoken not only to other mountain people, or to American readers, but to men everywhere." Wolfe received considerably more national and international attention than any previous Appalachian writer.

Three of this first continuous generation of mountain writers—Jesse Stuart (1906–84), James Still (1906–2001), and Don West (1906–92)—all graduated from little Lincoln Memorial University at Cumberland Gap, Tennessee, in the class of 1929. This university was founded by Union General Oliver O. Howard in honor of the mountaineers who fought for the Union. Howard, who headed the Freedmen's Bureau after the war, also created a university for black students that bears his name in Washington, DC. The three classmates, of what can easily still be considered the greatest literary class the region has ever produced, all went on to study at Vanderbilt University, where they encountered the Southern Agrarians. Although these LMU grads did have deep roots in southern soil, and they benefitted from the perspective of these professors, they didn't share a love for the plantation South and never became identified with this group. Despite these similar starting points, and a similar kind of Jeffersonian ethic, each of the three went on to very different lives and careers. Jesse Stuart was raised in W-Hollow in northeastern Kentucky, the son of an illiterate sharecropper. He was a prolific writer in a variety of genres including poetry, story, novel, and autobiography, as well as a lifelong Republican and occasional conservative spokesperson. Eventually, he would own all the land that his father ever farmed for shares. His novel *Taps for Private Tussie* (1943) told the story of a family that was notified their son had died in World War II, only to learn—after they had spent the compensation money—that he was merely the victim of army bungling. Don West's maternal uncle, Kim Mulkey, was not only a Union sympathizer in North Georgia during the Civil War but also a Civil War–era radical Republican. He helped inspire Don West to fight for labor and civil rights. West's militant poetry book, *Clods of Southern Earth* (1946), articulates his radical agenda. In contrast, James Still was a liberal intellectual from Alabama whose sparse output of books, including his only novel, *River of Earth* (1940), won the admiration of literary critics. Weatherford and Dykeman claim, "No writer of the mountains has captured more faithfully the distinctive idiom of the people than James Still."

James Agee (1909–55) was awarded a Pulitzer Prize, posthumously, for his novel *A Death in the Family* (1957). Like Thomas Wolfe before him, he was a Harvard graduate who achieved a national and international following, in his case as a screenwriter, essayist, critic, and the author of *Let Us Now Praise Famous Men* (1941), a powerful illumination of the lives of southern tenant farmers. The writing of Harriette Arnow (1908–86) is characterized by strong female protagonists, who are up against an oppressive industrial system and repressive sex roles. She is best known for her novel *The Dollmaker* (1954), which tells the story of a mountain family that moves to Detroit. Weatherford and Dykeman call it "a memorable portrait of a woman and a group of people who are trying to adapt to a strange environment and new customs." This book was made into a Tony Award–winning television drama starring Jane Fonda in

1984. Janice Holt Giles (1905–79) was one of the most popular regional writers of this generation. Her writing career began at the age of forty, after she entered into her second marriage with a man from the Kentucky hill country. Her first three novels, *The Enduring Hills* (1950), *Miss Willie* (1951), and *Tara's Healing* (1951), comprise a trilogy of books about outsiders who come to the hills to "do good" for the local people, but who find that the locals are able to help them overcome their own problems.

The second continuous generation of Southern Appalachian authors can be viewed as the World War II generation, as they mostly came of age during that conflict. In sharp contrast to the first generation of mountain writers who were born into relative prosperity and came of age at a time of great turmoil, this generation was born into the Depression and lived as adults at a time of great national consensus. Interestingly, this generation excelled in historical fiction.

Two prominent authors in this generation, Wilma Dykeman (1920–2006) and John Ehle (b. 1925) have careers that mirror each other across the Smoky Mountains. Dykeman served as the Tennessee state historian and wrote nonfiction books and historical novels that illuminated her concerns about environmental issues and discrimination on the basis of social class, sex, and race. She was a popular public speaker best known for her novel *The Tall Woman* (1962). On the other side of the mountains, John Ehle of Asheville also was involved in state government and wrote historical novels and nonfiction books dealing with civil rights as well as other topics. Like Wilma Dykeman, whose famous husband was James Stokely of the canning company family, John Ehle married fame and fortune in the person of Rosemary Harris, one of the finest actresses in the English-speaking world. Five of John Ehle's novels depict the King family from 1779 when it settles in western North Carolina—*The Land Breakers* (1965)—until the Great Depression in Asheville—*Last One Home* (1984).

In contrast to Wilma Dykeman and John Ehle, who both played significant roles encouraging racial integration in the South, was a talented writer who was a promoter of racial segregation. He wrote the words, "Segregation now; Segregation tomorrow; Segregation forever" as Alabama Governor George Wallace's speechwriter. Asa Carter (1925–79) chose the pen name Forrest Carter to celebrate the founder of the Ku Klux Klan, Nathan Bedford Forrest. His novel *The Education of Little Tree* (1976) won the very first Abbey Award for the book that booksellers most enjoyed recommending when it was reprinted by the University of New Mexico Press in 1990. Soon after that, it became widely known that its author was a white man with no discernible Indian blood whose book was not "*A True Story*," as the subtitle of the first edition proclaimed, but a compelling work of fiction that depicted positive human values that Carter attributed to Native Americans.

Mary Lee Settle (1918–2005) served in the armed forces in England during World War II and researched the history of her native West Virginia in the British Museum. Five of her novels tell the story of her state, from its precursors in Cromwell's army—*Prisons* (1973)—to Charleston in the twentieth century—*The Killing Ground* (1982). The very first book that her fellow West Virginian David Grubb (1919–80) published, *The Night of the Hunter* (1953), is widely viewed as his very best, although it was followed by a dozen more from major publishers. The screenplay for the movie *The Night of the Hunter* was written by James Agee. Mildred Haun (1911–66) is one of the most enigmatic and fascinating writers of this period. Born on Old Christmas, January 6, she was thought to have been from Cocke County, Tennessee, but undergraduate researchers in one of Jeff Daniel Marion's classes at Carson-Newman College in Tennessee discovered that Hoot Owl Holler, where she was raised, is actually in neighboring Hamblen County. Her grave still reads "Dr. Mildred Haun," despite the fact that she never held a doctorate. She did, however, as a young woman, aspire to be a midwife, and a midwife is the central character in her only book, *The Hawk's Done Gone* (1940). Weatherford and Dykeman said of it, "Perhaps no novel of the mountains has drawn deeper on the legendary folk qualities of speech and character, the brooding atmosphere and terror of the old ballads." Byron Herbert Reece (1917–58) was born in the Choestoe Valley of Union County, Georgia, in the shadow of Blood Mountain and Slaughter Mountain, on a small farm served, at the time, only by a footpath. His haunting poetry, replete with language and images from the King James Bible, is often considered the quintessential folk poetry of the region. Earl Hamner (b. 1923) published *Spencer's Mountain* (1961) after service in World War II and an auspicious career in radio. Two years later, the novel became a movie by the same name, and in 1971 it became the basis for a television pilot. The resulting TV series, *The Waltons,* ran from 1972 until 1981.A native of Virginia's Blue Ridge Mountains, Hamner is one of the most beloved literary figures ever to emerge from southern Appalachia.

Two authors, born in the thirties, Fred Chappell and Charles Wright, are represented in this anthology and thus will not be considered in this "Overview of Appalachian Literature." Those born in this decade may be considered part of the World War II generation because of the continuing impact of the war on their lives. Two important writers of this period have Appalachian credentials yet are seldom associated with this region. Born in 1933 Cormac McCarthy is widely viewed as one of the preeminent working authors in the world today.

McCarthy has written so powerfully about the West that few realize he mostly lived in and around Knoxville, Tennessee, from the time of his birth until he was almost fifty years old. His first four novels are set in East Tennessee: *The Orchard Keeper* (1965), *Outer Dark* (1965), *Child of God* (1974), and *Suttree* (1979). However, he has received the most recognition for his books set out west. *All the Pretty Horses* (1992) won not only the National Book Award but also the National Book Critics Circle Award. McCarthy received the Pulitzer Prize for *The Road* (2006), a postapocalyptic novel with what most consider a universal setting, though it can be easily traced to travel through East Tennessee. Wendell Berry (b. 1934) has lived and worked on a hillside farm on the Kentucky River for decades, near the small town where he was raised. The area where he lives appears very similar to many parts of Appalachia, and it is in one of our region's most important watersheds, but lies to the west of the Kentucky bluegrass. Berry's fictional characters appear in more than a dozen story collections and novels, including *The Memory of Old Jack* (1974). They live interconnected lives in and around the same fictional small town, Port William. Berry is also well known for this essays pleading for a return to strong connections to and reverence for the land, as well as for his more than two dozen poetry collections and for his activism, which includes advocating civil disobedience as a tactic in the struggle against mountaintop removal mining. He has received numerous awards, perhaps most notably the National Humanities Medal and the Cleanth Brooks Medal for Lifetime Achievement from the Fellowship of Southern Writers. In 2012 he delivered the Jefferson Lecture in the Humanities at the behest of the National Endowment for the Humanities.

The next generation of writers with roots in Appalachia can be considered the Vietnam War generation. Many of the parents of this generation left the region during World War II and, upon their return, embraced more mainstream values, including a desire for their children to enjoy good educations. As the consensus engendered by World War II evaporated into distrust and dissent over the Vietnam War, some of this generation questioned their parents' lifestyles and yearned for the old-fashioned mountain ways of life that their grandparents best symbolized. Ten authors with birthdays in the 1940s are represented in this anthology, namely Lisa Alther, Kathryn Stripling Byer, Robert J. Conley, Elizabeth Cox, Nikki Giovanni, Jeff Daniel Marion, Sharyn McCrumb, Robert Morgan, Lee Smith, and Meredith Sue Willis.

Divine Right Davenport, the protagonist of *Divine Right's Trip* (1972) by Gurney Norman (b. 1937), is often considered an archetypal 1960s character. This novel turns the tradition of westward movement novels inside out as it depicts hippies traveling from California back home to Kentucky where they will raise rabbits whose manure, they hope, can reclaim strip mines. Norman was raised in eastern Kentucky and southwestern Virginia, and, after graduating from the University of Kentucky, became one of a string of four UK graduates, including Wendell Berry, who earned Stegner Fellowships at Stanford University in California. *Divine Right's Trip* was first printed in the margins of *The Last Whole Earth Catalog* (1971) before it saw print as a hardback and then as a paperback.

Jim Wayne Miller (1936–96) traveled around the region promoting its literature so much that when President Jimmy Carter lowered the speed limit, Miller published a book of poems titled *Nostalgia for 70* (1986). His influence is so great that at the Appalachian Writers Workshop at Hindman Settlement School in Kentucky there is an annual tradition of taking turns reading aloud his long poem "The Brier Sermon." Lee Maynard (b. 1936) grew up in Wayne County, West Virginia, and received a journalism degree from West Virginia University. That propelled him to magazine editing jobs and then a variety of leadership positions in both business and nonprofit organizations involved in outdoor recreation. A writer for *Readers Digest* for a couple of decades, his coming-of-age novel, named for one of his hometowns, *Crum* (1988), shocked some and delighted others with its frank bad-boy protagonist. David Huddle (b. 1942) grew up in Ivanhoe, Virginia, in Wythe County. After retiring from a long career at the University of Vermont, he has accepted temporary teaching assignments at Hollins University in his native Virginia and at Austin-Peay State University in Tennessee. Huddle is the author of six poetry books, six story collections, and two novels, set in a variety of locales. He is clearly one of the most accomplished mountain writers of his generation. Donald McCaig (b. 1940) grew up in Montana, but has lived for decades now on a western Virginia sheep farm. His novel *Nop's Trials* (1984), the story of a sheepdog, was a best seller. Two important contemporary writers with deep Appalachian roots and a large following are typically viewed as southern writers. Gail Godwin (b.1937) was born in Birmingham and raised in Asheville, but now lives in New York State. Five of her novels have landed on *New York Times* best-seller lists. Dorothy Allison (b. 1949) grew up in Greenville, South Carolina, first with a single mother and then with a stepfather who abused her. Her novel *Bastard out of Carolina* (1972) created quite a stir in the literary community and beyond. Subsequently, Allison has continued to write both fiction and nonfiction. When called upon to give speeches, her disarmingly frank delivery of commonsense wisdom and openness about her sexuality enthralls her audiences. In 2010

Jaimy Gordon (b. 1944) won the National Book Award for her novel, *Lord of Misrule,* set in the northern panhandle of West Virginia. She is a West Virginia native who currently teaches at Western Michigan University.

A consideration of the writers born in the 1950s includes several represented in this anthology: Darnell Arnoult, Barbara Kingsolver, Jayne Anne Phillips, and Ron Rash. A discussion of other authors born in the 1950s may begin, sadly, with Breece Pancake (1952–79) of Milton, West Virginia, who took his own life at the age of twenty-six. His only book is *The Stories of Breece D'J Pancake* (1983), published posthumously. It has remained in print since its publication and is widely considered a cult classic. Like Thomas Wolfe, James Agee, and Jim Wayne Miller, Pancake was one of those men who lived at a deep, sometimes self-destructive, level. He loved to hunt and explore the back roads in his Volkswagen, often ending up at roadside dives playing pinball or shooting pool and drinking beer. Intense, hard-drinking, hard-working, diligent both at introspection and at observing the world around, he shared with the world, through his stories, what he learned at the cutting edge. Denise Giardina (b. 1951) was a student at West Virginia Wesleyan at the same time as Breece Pancake. Her dad was a bookkeeper for Pageton Coal until the company mined out their holdings, laid off their workers, evicted them from their homes, and bulldozed Black Hawk, the McDowell County coal camp where she had lived the first twelve years of her life. Her novels *Storming Heaven* (1987) and *The Unquiet Earth* (1992) reflect her interpretation of the impact of coal on her home state. Her European novels, which are more numerous, reflect her cosmopolitan interests and experiences. A committed activist, Giardina was a third-party candidate for governor of West Virginia in 2000. Another important writer of this generation who is not represented in this anthology is Charles Frazier (b. 1950) whose novel *Cold Mountain* (1997) won the National Book Award and was adapted into a Hollywood film in 2003. Frazier grew up mostly in Andrews, North Carolina, and enjoyed an academic career until writing a best-selling novel allowed him to devote full time to his craft. Frazier's novel *Thirteen Moons* (2006) is loosely based on the life of William Holland Thomas (1805–93), the Indian trader whose efforts were largely responsible for some Cherokees being allowed to stay in their North Carolina homeland instead of being moved to Oklahoma on the Trail of Tears in the 1830s. *Nightwoods* (2011) is a novel set in western North Carolina during the 1960s.

At this time, an even younger generation is emerging. Authors in this anthology born in the 1960s are Pinckney Benedict, Chris Holbrook, Maurice Manning, Ann Pancake, Frank X Walker, and Crystal Wilkinson. Pamela Duncan

(b. 1961) teaches at Western Carolina University and has written three novels that have pushed her to the forefront of regional literature. *The Big Beautiful* (2007) is a hilarious novel that enthusiastic readers don't soon forget.

Two authors in this anthology were born in the 1970s, Silas House and Mark Powell. When Silas House emerged as an important regional writer, many assumed that he would be the last Appalachian writer who had lived in his home county until he was almost forty years old. However, in 2009 Alfred A. Knopf, one of the most prestigious New York publishers, released *Bloodroot,* a novel by Amy Greene (1975). Not only does she still live in Hamblen County, Tennessee, where she was born and raised, but, unlike House, she never even commuted away from her home county for school or work. Among the many other young and promising regional authors born during this decade is Jesse Graves (1973), who was raised on a farm at Sharp's Chapel in Union County, Tennessee. His poetry collection, *Tennessee Landscape with Blighted Pine,* was published by Texas Review Press in 2011.

For five years in a row around the turn of the twenty-first century, Appalachian novels were on the *New York Times* best-seller lists: *Cold Mountain* by Charles Frazier in 1997 and 1998, *Gap Creek* by Robert Morgan in 1999, and *Prodigal Summer* by Barbara Kingsolver in 2000 and 2001. Then, in 2010, Barbara Kingsolver won the Orange Prize for her novel *The Lacuna,* and Ron Rash won the Frank O'Conner Award for his short-story collection *Burning Bright,* both international awards for works in the English language. Despite, or maybe even because of, the region's reputation for being old-fashioned, Appalachian literature is clearly a dynamic force with very strong prospects for the future.

Works on Appalachian Literature

by George Brosi

Ballard, Sandra, and Patricia L. Hudson, eds. *Listen Here: Women Writing in Appalachia.* Lexington: UP of Kentucky, 2004.

Brosi, George. "Appalachian Literature." In *The Companion to Southern Literature: Themes, Genres, Places, People, Movements, and Motifs.* Ed. Joseph M. and Lucinda Hardwick Mackethan. Baton Rouge: Louisiana State UP, 2002. 43-8.

———. *The Literature of the Appalachian South.* Berea, KY: self-published, 1992.

Dyer, Joyce, ed. *Bloodroot: Reflections on Place by Appalachian Women Writers.* Lexington: UP of Kentucky, 2000.

Edwards, Grace Toney, and Theresa Lloyd. "Literature." In *The Encyclopedia of Appalachia.* Ed. Rudy Abramson and Jean Haskell Spears, Knoxville: U of Tennessee P, 2006. 1035–39.

Higgs, Robert J., and Ambrose N. Manning. *Voices from the Hills: Selected Readings of Southern Appalachia.* New York: Frederick Ungar Publishing Company, 1975.

———, and Jim Wayne Miller. *Appalachia Inside Out: A Sequel to Voices from the Hills.* 2 vols. Knoxville: U of Tennessee P, 1995.

Lang, John, ed. *Appalachia and Beyond: Conversations with Writers from the Mountain South.* Knoxville: U of Tennessee P, 2006.

Miller, Danny L. *Wingless Flights: Appalachian Women in Fiction.* Madison: UP of Wisconsin / Popular Press, 1996.

———, Sharon Hatfield, and Gurney Norman. *An American Vein: Critical Readings in Appalachian Literature.* Athens: Ohio UP, 2005.

Mitchel, Felicia, ed. *Her Words: Diverse Voices in Contemporary Appalachian Women's Poetry.* Knoxville: U of Tennessee P, 2002.

Weatherford, W. D., and Wilma Dykeman. "Literature since 1900." In *The Southern Appalachian Region: A Survey.* Ed. Thomas R. Ford. Lexington: UP of Kentucky. 1962. 259–70.

White, Charles Dodd, and Page Seay, eds. *Degrees of Elevation: Short Stories of Contemporary Appalachia.* Huron, OH: Bottom Dog Press, 2010.

Williams, Cratis Dearl. *The Southern Mountaineer in Fact and Fiction.* Diss. New York U, 1961. Ann Arbor: University Microfilms, 1961.

Wright, William, Jesse Graves, and Paul Ruffin, eds. *Contemporary Southern Poetry.* Vol. 3. *Contemporary Appalachia.* Huntsville: Texas Review Press, 2011.

Part 1

The Landscape

Lisa Alther

The Fox Hunt

The jeep shuddered along the dirt road, its hood bobbing like a duck decoy on rough waters.

Sunlight danced through the rust and mustard foliage. Palmer felt like a kid laying out of school. Even if he did own the company. But he was, after all, out here on business. Julius was an expensive dog. His ancestors had been lead hounds for the best hunts in Virginia, right back to the beginning of the nineteenth century. But Lucas had implied on the phone this morning that Julius might not make it.

He and Lucas rode away from the clearing, Julius hanging across Lucas's saddle, his neck ripped open and oozing black blood.

"We'll take him to the vet in Beulah," said Palmer, who had raised Julius from a puppy and helped Lucas train him.

Lucas shrugged. "Ain't no use."

Palmer sighed. Lucas always turned as fatalistic as a European peasant in the face of a crisis. "Don't be ridiculous. He'll be fine."

Reaching the top of the rise, Palmer surveyed Red Hatcher's bottom land, spread out below like an old burlap feed sack. That soil there along the riverbank used to be pretty rich, but you couldn't say much for it now. Looked like he'd sown winter oats, just sprouting. Red drove his land as hard as the antique tractor he worked it with.

The Jeep jolted down the hill, the power lift on the back clanking. Palmer spotted some fresh stumps and brush piles in a woods Red was leveling for more pasture. That man razed rather than cleared. He didn't plow, he gouged.

Four boys in bib overalls marched up Rollers's valley, tobacco-stake rifles on their shoulders. Palmer was leading, his Confederate great-grandfather's sword hanging from his waist, scabbard tip etching the earth.

"Halt-two-three-four!" barked Palmer. "All you men down in that trench on your bellies!"

The boys peered into the drainage ditch by the rosa multiflora hedgerow as the enemy closed in.

"On the double!"

They jumped in, sinking to their knees in mud. Palmer crawled beneath the hedge to inspect the advancing Yankees.

Red's carrot-colored crew cut appeared above the lip of the ditch. "Ain't you comin' down here too, Palmer?"

"Head down, soldier! Do you want it blown off?"

Red leapt out of the ditch. Twisting Palmer's arm into a hammerlock, he forced him to the edge. "Palmer—sir, I ain't playing at your goddam game no more." He hurled Palmer face-first into the slime and stalked off down the valley, swinging at grasshoppers with his tobacco stake.

Gazing at Palmer with vacant blue eyes, Lucas Bledsoe helped him out of the mud. But he didn't reply when Palmer asked, "Why'd he do that for?"

Red's fencing needed help fast. A couple of posts had rotted, dragging the barbed wire to the ground. Last week Red had come up to him by the tobacco barn, struggling to sound amiable, despite the stubborn jut to his red-bristled jaw. "Y'all right today, Palmer?"

"Fine, thanks, Red. And you?"

"Tell you the truth, I got me some problems." He slipped a kitchen matchstick between his lips and began to chew it.

"What's up?" asked Palmer, even though he already knew, since he went to Rotary meetings with every banker in town.

"Reckon you could make me a loan? Through the winter? Whatever interest you think's fair." Red gazed at the ancient oaks on the far hillside. He was humiliated. But it was his own damn fault.

"I'm sorry, Red." He had been too, even though he could see how much better off Red would be in the end. "But I'm no banker. Have you tried Beulah Savings and Loan?"

"Hell, they's a mortgage on ever last one of my damn cows." His bony face began to twitch.

Palmer shifted his own gaze to the oaks on the hill. "My offer still holds: I cover the bills. We split the profits. Cash for your land. Fair market value. Same as my father did with Lucas's father."

"Thanks all the same." Red hurled his matchstick at the ground and strode away.

The fence posts flashed white as Palmer passed from Red's land onto his own. To the right was a field at rest. To the left Lucas's hired man was disking a newly cleared cornfield. Directly ahead was the barn, freshly whitewashed, and three shiny indigo silos.

Palmer had to confess that he loved his work. He'd turned an abandoned textile mill in town into a shopping mall. Once he'd finished salvaging these forlorn little foothill farms, he'd use part of the land for a golf course, a lake, and a vacation home development for retirees with a taste for country living. At cocktail parties he often quipped that, like Napoleon, his only ambition was to own all the land that adjoined his.

Rounding the bend, Palmer eyed Lucas's maroon-shingled house, which clashed with the orange clay of his yard. Pulling his Jeep alongside Lucas's battered pickup, he cut the ignition and studied the truck, which was rusting away like a junkyard soup can.

Palmer walked over to the garage. As his eyes adjusted to the gloom, he spotted snarled rope, rolls of chicken wire, rusted equipment parts, empty oil cans, all tangled up together.

Palmer and his father had stood in front of this same garage, newly painted then. Inside on pegs hung coils of rope and wire. Paint cans and rotor blades were neatly arranged on shelves.

"Mr. Bledsoe, this is my son Palmer," said his father.

"Pleased to make your acquaintance, Palmer."Mr. Bledsoe nodded toward a skinny boy in overalls nearly white from washing. "This here's my boy Lucas."

Palmer and Lucas studied each other. Palmer held out his hand. Lucas just looked at it. Feeling foolish, Palmer dropped it to his side.

Palmer's father said, "Well, I'm sure the boys will have fun playing together when we come out here on weekends."

"Luke here, he don't generally have him a whole lot of play time. But I reckon we can make him some."

"Mr. Bledsoe, we're pleased to know you, sir. You and your boy."

"Yessir, Mr. Claiborne, and I'm right proud to be working for you'uns."

Last month Palmer had ribbed Lucas, "Looks like you just take a pitch fork and heave anything running around loose into that garage there."

Palmer smiled, but Lucas just gave him his numb blue stare."Ain't ourn no more. Don't make no never mind to me what hit look like."

"But you and I are in this together."

Lucas glanced at him sideways, then lowered his gaze to the ground.

Palmer shook his head as though clearing the din from his ears after target practice. Then he walked toward the house, whose top-floor windows lacked several panes of glass. He'd let Lucas stay on in the house as though he still owned it, so he supposed how Lucas kept it up was his own business.

"Lucas!" he called.

A bald truck tire hanging from a mulberry limb in the front yard swayed silently. He started down the road toward the cinder block milking parlor. The gravel had long since washed off, and gullies had formed which Lucas had filled with trash.

The hounds began yapping and hurling themselves against the chicken wire of their pen. Palmer put his palms against the wire and let the hounds lick them, scanning the pack for Julius. Somehow he'd believed Lucas would have come up with a remedy by now.

That morning of the hunt the riders in their blue and buff coats had gathered in the field beside Palmer's house at the foot of the valley. Sitting on their horses, they sipped wine from plastic cups.

Alvin Ferris called to Palmer, "Where's your better half at, son?"

"Marge refuses to have anything to do with us ever since she broke her leg last September on that jump across Dead Creek. She says we're out of our minds."

"Well, she's correct about that!"

Palmer actually suspected that Marge, who'd put on fifty pounds since college, didn't like to watch how some of their women friends looked at him in his tight buff jodhpurs, the same ones he'd always worn. She seemed to hold it against him that he hadn't gone to pot along with her. Well, let the old girl sulk in solitude. He couldn't help it that he had some life left in him yet. Raising the antique silver hunting horn he'd bought in England, he played the tattoo that signaled the start of the hunt.

"Let's get on with this circus," he muttered to Mindy Ferris with the rueful smile she'd found irresistible for a brief period a couple of years ago.

"It *is* a circus." She was struggling to rein in her snorting bay, thighs gripping the saddle as tightly as they had recently gripped his hips. "That's what makes it so much fun. If we took this stuff seriously, we'd be dreadful."

"You don't take much of anything seriously, do you, Mindy?" he murmured with a mock-doleful smile.

"Nope, I just take life and love as they come. Lucky for you, I might add." She shot him a coy smile.

A couple of riders finished checking girths and adjusting stirrups in the drizzle of the wet fall dawn. As they mounted, the hounds were released from their cages to scurry around the paddock, sniffing milkweed pods, manure piles, and each other's rear ends. The whips kept rounding them up, only to have them break away again.

"This is as hopeless as herding cats!" Jimmy Bransom called to Palmer, his whip dangling dejectedly.

Palmer spotted Lucas in the doorway of the tobacco barn. He had trained the hounds and liked to watch them work. Bunches of drying burley tobacco leaves hung from poles along the rafters behind him. Lucas's wife had driven a steel spike used to string the leaves on the stakes through the palm of her hand during the harvest last month. She merely wrapped the wound with a rag and kept on working. And Marge thought *she* had problems when their swimming pool pump broke.

As though an electrical switch had been thrown, the hounds headed through the gate, followed by the whips. They raced across the field toward the West Woods, one swelling and contracting mass, a cell about to divide. Palmer loosened his reins and his gelding Colonel pranced through the gate behind them.

Alvin took a practice jump over the chicken coop in the fence, his horse's hooves thumping the wood. Someone who'd had too many stirrup cups let loose with a rebel yell. Leather squeaked and metal clanked. Horses whinnied and tossed their handsome heads. A couple of riders charged across the soggy field, reining in to one side of Palmer. The cortege glided toward the skeletal woods as though in a disorderly death march behind some distant hearse.

Colonel tiptoed through the damp fescue, fighting the tight reins. Palmer sat easily in the smooth curve of the saddle, not unaware that he looked pretty good sitting straight and tall in his blue jacket, high black boots, and top hat. He inhaled deeply, pleased by the prospect of a morning of hard riding with his friends from Beulah, with whom he'd grown up and gone to UT, with whom he now did business deals and attended church services, parties, weddings and funerals. Spotting Lucas by the barn, gazing at him with that bizarre blue stare, Palmer squared his shoulders and angled Colonel to exclude Lucas from his line of vision.

Mixed in among the caws of crows and muted conversations of riders, Palmer detected Julius's howl. They'd barely started. Wasn't it too soon to have picked up a scent? He waited for Julius to recognize his mistake. Colonel tensed his muscles for the chase.

Soon Julius was joined by the rest of the pack, howling like air-raid sirens. There was no question they were in serious pursuit of something.

Palmer slackened his reins, and Colonel surged forward, nearly catching him off balance. They cantered toward the West Woods.

Taking the fence, Colonel careened across a carpet of leaf mold, weaving among the tree trunks like a slalom skier. Palmer lay alongside Colonel's neck as branches swatted at his hardhat.

As they paralleled the fence line, Palmer could see old man Partridge sitting by his pond, casting his fishing line into the murky water, not so much as glancing up at the racket going on in the woods alongside him. Palmer had tried several times to buy his place after his wife died. He figured the old man might like to move into Beulah near his daughter Anna, who was married to Dr. Roller. But each time, the old man acted as though he hadn't even heard Palmer's offer.

Leaving the woods behind, Colonel and he reached the red clay rise to the plateau. Without a moment's hesitation, Colonel scrambled up it, arcing again and again like a salmon leaping upriver. Upon reaching the flat shelf up top, he broke into a gallop, throwing up a spray of red clay and staining his graceful white forelegs burnt orange.

They'd been locked up all week; Palmer in his office and Colonel in his stall. Both craved this illusion of freedom and flight. Palmer knew there were limits to his ability to play the solid citizen. These moments of folly and terror were his drug of choice. In the valley below, he caught glimpses of the streaking hounds, intent on their scent, wherever it was leading them.

Reaching the far side of the ridge, Colonel didn't so much as slow down. He plunged off the edge like a diver, nearly pitching them both forward into somersaults. Just in time his front legs locked, and he skidded down the face of the bluff, hooves plowing furrows in the sticky clay.

When they arrived in the valley, Palmer could hear other riders behind and above him, whooping with delight or shrieking with fear. Marge was a smart woman: This country was too precipitous for hunting. It was a miracle someone hadn't been killed yet.

Palmer heard the hounds not far ahead. They weren't sounding frustrated and bewildered, as when they'd lost the scent. But it wasn't the chilling bay of success either. It was a sound Palmer had never before heard from them. They were yipping almost like pups taken too soon from their bitch.

Palmer wove through the trees, Colonel dancing two steps sideways for every unwilling one forward. Frowning, Palmer forced the horse ahead, kicking him in the flanks as he rarely had to do. What the hell was going on?

Parting their way through a curtain of tangled grapevines, they entered a narrow clearing fenced in by bare grey saplings, ghostly sentinels, like branches that loom up out of the mist in nightmares about moonlit midnight pursuits. Julius crouched off to one side, trembling and whimpering. The other hounds had formed a tight semi-circle. They inched forward, then scooted back, whining and yelping.

The object of their hysteria was a motheaten red fox. It was shuddering like a baby with convulsions, palsied head bobbing. Spittle oozed from its mouth to fleck its mangy coat and the mat of dead leaves below. Its burning eyes seemed to focus on Palmer.

Grabbing his silver horn from his waistband, Palmer played the tattoo he and Lucas had worked out to signal trouble. He climbed down from Colonel. The horse shied dramatically and bolted off into the trees, where he stood with his reins tangled around one fetlock, tossing his head and rolling his eyes back to reveal the whites, like a silent movie actress.

Palmer walked over to Julius, who was shivering in spasms. A chunk was missing from his neck, and his fine fawn coat was caked with blood. Stooping to pat him, Palmer remembered buying him as a pup from a stable near Charlottesville, seduced by the shape of his head, which had promised unusual intelligence. And this promise had been fulfilled.

Looking up, he saw Lucas, mounted on his fastest mare, fighting his way through the web of tangled vines. His mare was hopping in place, reluctant to move forward. Lucas slid off her and walked over to Palmer. He studied the hound and the fox. The fox, snarling weakly, dragged itself across the clearing. With a final backward glance, it disappeared into a maze of brambles and briars.

The fox seemed to have had hypnotic powers. The mesmerized movements of the other animals continued for several moments before all hell broke loose. Horses snorted, reared and lunged. Hounds raced around the clearing, baying boldly now. The blue coats and black hats of other riders began to appear among the grey saplings.

Lucas turned to stare at Palmer with his annoying blue gaze. Palmer averted his eyes, feeling guilty. But what in God's name was he guilty of? By the time he realized that the fox should be destroyed, it was long gone.

Palmer surveyed the new milking parlor and the freshly whitewashed hay barn. Regardless of how Lucas maintained his house, Palmer insisted that the farm buildings be in mint condition, and they were. The Holsteins were lined up awaiting relief for their bulging udders. A few heads turned to look at him with eyes of melted chocolate. There was never any question who got milked when. Lucas said he always knew which cow would be through the door next.

When Palmer reached the parlor, he heard voices raised above the hiss of the machines that passed milk from the udders through cooling coils into the refrigerated tank.

"Lord, Lucas, that man is just as cold as a walk-in freezer. Don't leave you nothing but a living."

Palmer recognized Red's voice.

"Can't a small farm do nothing no more," replied Lucas.

"Not when his neighbors gang up on him."

"He helped us when we was whipped."

"Helped you? Didn't leave you no choice but to sell out. That, or turn on him, one."

As Red's words sank in, Palmer felt anger sweep over him like a blast from a furnace on a dog day afternoon. You knocked yourself out trying to help these people, but all you harvested was resentment. He'd taken a bunch of run-down dirt farms and turned them into the best dairy operation in the state. The butterfat content of his herd's milk had broken regional records. Without him half a dozen families would have starved to death in winter or moved to factory jobs in town. Kudzu would have buried their shacks without a trace.

Lucas appeared in the doorway. He looked like a boy, but the lines around his mouth and across his forehead showed his age. Hands stuffed in his overall pockets, he squirted a stream of tobacco juice through the gap between his front teeth. It splattered on the gravel. Turning to go back in, he spotted Palmer. His face flushed."Howdy, Palmer. Didn't know you was out today."

"Just got here. How're you today?"

Neither looked at the other. Palmer knew his own face must still be crimson.

"Fine, I reckon." Lucas ambled over.

"Came out to see how Julius is doing." Palmer tried to sound hearty despite feeling as though an arrow was twanging in his chest.

"I done told you this morning that he ain't doing so good."

Palmer and Lucas strolled toward the barn.

"All these modern wonder drugs will fix him up in no time flat."

"Seem like the spirit flowed plumb outen him after that fox ripped him up like that."

Palmer glanced at Lucas ironically. This was one of his typical Old Testament pronouncements.

They stopped before a cage against the barn. Inside lay Julius, head between his paws. Both men squatted and studied him. His panting was the gasps of a drowning man about to sink for good.

"Hey, Julius," called Palmer. The dog lifted his lids to reveal watery crimson eyes. He turned toward Palmer with a plaintive whimper.

"See what I'm telling you?"

Palmer nodded. Until now he hadn't seriously entertained the possibility that Julius might not recover. "Did you tell Red and the others that we have to find that fox and make sure it's dead?"

"Yeah, I told Red. But he says he ain't helping."

"Why the hell not?"

"He says it ain't his concern." Lucas was giving Palmer his blank blue gaze.

"But it can get after his cows just as easy as ours."

"He says he ain't helping 'cause you done turned that fox crazy."

"Me? It's rabies. From bats."

Lucas shrugged. "Could be Red knows some things you don't."

Reprinted with permission of Lisa Alther. Published in *Appalachian Heritage* 32.1 (Winter 2004) and reprinted in *Stormy Weather and Other Stories* (Mercer UP, 2012).

Lisa Alther: A Biographical Sketch

Lisa Alther is one of those rare writers who can create absolutely hilarious scenes, yet the overall impact of her writing is anything but frivolous. Rather she is an author of great depth whose books address a wide range of important contemporary issues. Together, her first five novels sold over six million copies and have been translated into seventeen different languages. Her first three books were Book-of-the-Month Club featured selections. This kind of success runs in her family. Her father and grandfather were esteemed surgeons. Her mother was a Phi Beta Kappa and high school English teacher who taught her children to love books, reading, and writing. Of Alther's four siblings, three are third-generation physicians, and the other is John Shelton Reed, an illustrious nonfiction author and sociologist of the South.

Lisa Alther was born in Kingsport, Tennessee, in 1944 and graduated from Wellesley College in 1966. That same year she married and moved to New York, where she worked for a publisher. Two years later she moved to rural Vermont to raise her daughter. There, Lisa (who pronounces her name, Lie-za) actively participated in feminist groups and consciously identified with the "back to the land movement." She continued writing during this nine-year period, despite collecting over two hundred rejection slips from publishers.

Then, in 1975, Alfred A. Knopf published *Kinflicks,* a wildly successful, hilarious, coming-of-age first novel, set in a fictional version of Kingsport. Her second book, *Original Sins* (1981), was another East Tennessee novel, which portrays five young characters who choose different paths to personal identity in the 1970s. By the time Alther published her third novel, she had lived in New England for almost two decades, and that provided the setting for *Other Women* (1984).

Following her divorce, Lisa Alther lived in London, Paris, and New York as well as Vermont. Her 1990 novel, *Bedrock,* is set in Vermont, but her next novel, *Five Minutes in Heaven* (1995), follows a Tennessee-born woman to Paris. It reflects additional time Alther spent in Tennessee as a visiting professor and caring for her aging parents. Lisa Alther is now happy splitting her time between her parents' farm south of Kingsport, her New York apartment, and her condo in Burlington, Vermont. She claims she has "as many ex's as Elizabeth Taylor." Currently, she is in a long-term relationship with a woman who shares her Tennessee heritage.

In 2007 Lisa Alther published her first nonfiction book, *Kinfolks: Falling Off the Family Tree.* It grew out of Alther's discovery that a third cousin had written about the mysterious Melungeons of East Tennessee and claimed to be related to them. Her considerable research revealed that the Melungeons were only one of what were likely many groups of Europeans who ventured into the American wilderness. There many intermarried with natives and escaped slaves. The result is that multitudes of Americans have a mixed ethnic and class heritage. The novel about the Melungeons, *Washed in the Blood*, which she started before the related nonfiction work, was published in 2011.

In 2012, Alther published another nonfiction book inspired by her genealogy: *Blood Feud: The Hatfields and the McCoys: The Epic Story of Murder and Vengeance.* She is related to the McCoys through her father. The book became a national best-seller. Remarkably in that same year, her final story collection, *Stormy Weather and Other Stories* was published. As with all her work, she is trying to get at the human reality behind the cultural stereotypes. She considers herself lucky to have "been able to do what I love to do, which is to write for my own reasons."

Lisa Alther: A Selective Bibliography

INTERNET RESOURCES

Alther has a website that features an autobiographical essay, a bibliography, interviews, and reviews.

BOOKS

Blood Feud: The Hatfields and the McCoys: The Epic Story of Murder and Vengeance. Guilford, CT: Lyons Press, 2012.

Stormy Weather and Other Stories. Macon, GA: Mercer UP, 2012.

Washed in the Blood. Macon, GA: Mercer UP, 2011.

Kinfolks: Falling Off the Family Tree. New York: Arcade, 2007.

Five Minutes in Heaven. New York: Dutton, 1995.

Bedrock. New York: Alfred A. Knopf, 1990.

Other Women. New York: Alfred A. Knopf, 1984.

Original Sins. New York: Alfred A. Knopf, 1981.

Kinflicks. New York: Alfred A. Knopf, 1976.

PROFILES/INTERVIEWS

Alther, Lisa. "Lisa Alther Goes Back to East Tennessee." *Women's Review of Books* 16.10/11 (1999): 6–7.

Edwards, Carol E. W. "Interview with Lisa Alther." *Turnstile* 4.1 (1993): 34–50.

LITERARY CRITICISM

Brosi, George, ed. *Appalachian Heritage* 32.1 (2004). Features Lisa Alther.

Dever, Carolyn. "The Feminist Abject: Death and the Constitution of Theory." *Studies in the Novel* 32.2 (2000): 185–206.

Hart, Vada. "Woebegone Dykes: The Novels of Lisa Alther." In *Beyond Sex and Romance? The Politics of Contemporary Lesbian Fiction.* Ed. Elaine Hutton. London: Women's Press, 1998. 46–59.

Lang, John, ed. *Iron Mountain Review* 17 (2001). Features Lisa Alther.

Fred Chappell

The Gentrifiers Are in Pursuit

of Rafer Barnstable born according
to any account he ever heard
in Haint Holler by Hellfire Creek
in "Bloody" Harbison County in 1932

now come the real estaters
and their minion politicos and
it is no more Haint Holler
no more Hellfire Creek but Sweetwater Brook
in Castle Glen yonder in "Sunny" Harbison

it is like that all over
Snakeden shed its name to become
Laurel Dell and Frying Pan Gap
is now Crown Summit and Rafer lives
in trepidation he'll wake up tomorrow as Sir
Cholmondeley ffyfe-Gordon, Bart

they are gentrifying the Bible too
no more Sodom and Gomorrah but
Gay Land Meadows and Happytyme Acres
and Senator Fairchild plans to redevelop Hell
as a theme park celebrating Redevelopment

as soon as he gets his hands on the money

Reprinted with permission of Fred Chappell. Published in *Appalachian Heritage* 31.3 (Summer 2003) and reprinted in *Backsass* (LSU Press, 2004).

❁ ❁ ❁

The Critic

I can tell you what is wrong
with anything everything

your scientific theories have holes
I spotted immediately and even if
you are proven correct I will pronounce
the results trivial

your painting is so deathly static
so lacking in dynamic
so academic   so literary: save
your money   don't buy a ticket
to New York

your novel makes no sense
your soufflé has already fallen
your face has lobsterlike tendencies
your car was plucked from a citrus tree
your team is an eternal cellar dweller
your poetry let's not go there
your kids are strong arguments for abortion rights
your wine needs more paint thinner

your wife is passable I suppose
when Total Dowdy is all the fashion rage

as for God what a domineering old codger
and carelessly indiscreet gossip

I hear some of the things
He has been saying about me and
they always put me in an ugly mood

Reprinted with permission of Fred Chappell. Published in *Backsass* (LSU Press, 2004).

❁ ❁ ❁

Editor's note: This selection is presented in the novel I Am One of You Forever, *before chapter 1, and thus we do not consider it a novel excerpt.*

The Overspill

Then there was one brief time when we didn't live in the big brick house with my grandmother but in a neat two-storey green-shingled white house in the holler below. It was two stories if you stood at the front door; on the other side it was three stories, the ground floor a tall basement garage.

The house was surrounded by hills to the north and east and south. Directly above us lay the family farm and my grandmother's house. Two miles behind the south hill was the town of Tipton, where the Challenger Paper and Fiber Corporation smoked eternally, smudging the Carolina mountain landscape for miles. A small creek ran through our side yard, out of the eastern hills. The volume of the creek flow was controlled by Challenger; they had placed a reservoir up there, and the creek water was regulated by means of the spillway.

At this time my mother was visiting her brother in California. Uncle Luden was in trouble again, with a whole different woman this time. Maybe my mother could help; it was only 5,000 miles round trip by train.

So my father and I had to fumble along as best we could.

Despite the extra chores, I found it exciting. Our friendship took a new and stronger turn, became something of a mild conspiracy. New sets of signals evolved between us. We met now on freshly neutral ground somewhere between my boyhood and his boyishness, and for me it was a heady rise in status. We were clumsy housekeepers, there were lots of minor mishaps, and the tagline we formulated soonest was: "Let's just not tell Mama about this one." I adored that thought.

He was always dreaming up new projects to please her and during her absence came up with one of masterful ambition.

Across the little creek, with its rows of tall willows, was a half-acre of fallow ground considered unusable because of marshiness and the impenetrable clot of blackberry vines in the south corner. My father now planned it as a garden, already planted before she returned.

We struggled heroically. I remember pleasantly the destruction of the vines and the cutting of the drainage ditch neat and straight into the field. The ground was so soft that we could slice down with our spades and bring up squares of dark blue mud and lay them along side by side. They gleamed like tile. Three long afternoons completed the ditch, and then my father brought out the big awkward shoulder scythe and whetted the blade until I could hear it sing on his thumb-ball when he tested it. And then he waded into the thicket of thorny vine and began slashing. For a long time nothing happened, but finally the vines began to fall back, rolling up in tangles like barbarous handwriting. With a pitchfork I worried these tangles into a heap. Best of all was the firing, the clear yellow flame and the sizzle and snap of the vine-ribs and thorns, and the thin black smoke rising above the new-green willows. The delicious smell of it.

After this we prepared the ground in the usual way and planted. Then we stood at the edge of our garden, admiring with a full tired pride the clean furrows and mounded rows of earth.

But this was only a part of the project. It was merely a vegetable garden, however arduously achieved, and we planted a garden every year. My father wanted something else, decorative, elegant in design, something guaranteed to please a lady.

The weather held good and we started next day, hauling two loads of scrap lumber from one of the barns. He measured and we sawed and planed. He hummed and whistled as he worked and I mostly stared at him when not scurrying to and fro, fetching and carrying. He wouldn't, of course, tell me what we were building.

On the second day it became clear. We were constructing a bridge. We were building a small but elaborate bridge across the little creek that divided the yard and the garden, a stream that even I could step over without lengthening my stride. It was ambitious: an arched bridge with handrails and a latticework arch on the garden side enclosing a little picket gate.

He must have been a handy carpenter. To me the completed bridge appeared marvelous. We had dug deep on both sides to sink the locust piers, and the arch above the stream, though not high, was unmistakably a rainbow. When I walked back and forth across the bridge I heard and felt a satisfactory drumming. The gate latch made a solid cluck and the gate arch, pinned together of old plaster lathe, made me feel that in crossing the bridge I was entering a different world, not simply going into the garden.

He had further plans for the latticework. "Right here," he said, "and over here, I'll plant tea roses to climb up the lattice. Then you'll see."

We whitewashed it three times. The raw lumber sparkled. We walked upstream to the road above the yard and looked at it, then walked downstream to the edge of the garden and looked at it. We saw nothing we weren't prideful about.

He went off in our old Pontiac and returned in a half hour. He parked in the driveway and got out. "Come here," he said. We sat in the grass on the shoulder of the culvert at the edge of the road. "I've been to the store," he said. He pulled a brown paper sack from his pocket. Inside I found ten thimble-shaped chocolate mints, my favorite. From another pocket he produced a rolled band of bright red silk.

"Thank you," I said. "What's that?"

"We want her to know it's a present, don't we? So we've got to tie a ribbon on it. We'll put it right there in the middle of the handrail." He spooled off two yards of ribbon and cut it with his pocket knife. "Have to make a big one so she can see it from up here in the road."

I chewed a mint and observed his thick horny fingers with the red silk.

It was not to be. Though I was convinced that my father could design and build whatever he wished—the Brooklyn Bridge, the Taj Mahal—he could not tie a bow in this broad ribbon. The silk crinkled and knotted and slipped loose; it simply would not behave. He growled in low tones like a bear trying to dislodge a groundhog from its hole. "I don't know what's the matter with this stuff," he said.

Over the low mumble of his words I heard a different rumble, a gurgle as of pebbles pouring into a broad still pool. "What's that?" I asked.

"What's what?"

"What's that noise?"

He stopped ruining the ribbon and sat still as the sound grew louder. Then his face darkened and veins stood out in his neck and forehead. His voice was quiet and level now. "Those bastards."

"Who?"

"Those Challenger Paper guys. They've opened the floodgates."

We scrambled up the shoulder into the road. As the sound got louder it discomposed into many sounds: lappings, bubblings, rippings, undersucks and splashovers. Almost as soon as we saw the gray-brown thrust of water emerge from beneath the overhanging plum tree, we felt the tremor as it slammed against the culvert, leaping up the shoulder and rolling back. On the yard side it shot out of the culvert as out of a hose. In a few seconds it had overflowed the low creek banks and streamed gray-green along the edge of the yard, furling white around the willow trunks. Debris—black sticks and leaves and grasses—spun on top of the water, and the gullet of the culvert rattled with rolling pebbles.

Our sparkling white bridge was soiled with mud and slimy grasses. The water driving into it reached a gray arm high into the air and slapped down. My father and I watched the hateful battering of our work, our hands in our pockets. He still held the red ribbon and it trickled out of his pocket down his trouser leg. The little bridge trembled and began to shake. There was one moment when it sat quite still, as if it had gathered resolve and was fighting back.

And then on the yard side it wrenched away from the log piers, and when that side headed downstream the other side tore away too, and we had a brief glimpse of the bridge parallel in the stream like a strange boat and saw the farthest advance of the flood framed in the quaint lattice arch. The bridge twirled about and the corners caught against both banks and it went over on its side, throwing up the naked underside of the planks like a barn door blown shut. Water piled up behind this damming and finally poured over and around it, eating at the borders of the garden and lawn.

My father kept saying over and over, "Bastards bastards bastards. It's against the *law* for them to do that."

Then he fell silent.

I don't know how long we stared downstream before we were aware that my mother had arrived. When we first saw her she had already got out of the taxi, which sat idling in the road. She looked odd to me, wearing a dress I had never seen, and a strange expression—half amused, half vexed—crossed her face. She looked at us as if she'd caught us doing something naughty.

My father turned to her and tried to speak. "*Bastards*" was the only word he got out. He choked and his face and neck went dark again. He gestured toward the swamped bridge and the red ribbon fluttered in his fingers.

She looked where he pointed and, as I watched, understanding came into her face, little by little. When she turned again to face us she looked as if she were in pain. A single tear glistened on her cheek, silver in the cheerful light of midafternoon.

My father dropped his hand and the ribbon fluttered and trailed in the mud.

The tear on my mother's cheek got larger and larger. It detached from her face and became a shiny globe, widening outward like an inflating balloon. At first the tear floated in air between them, but as it expanded it took my mother and father into itself. I saw them suspended, separate but beginning to drift slowly toward one another. Then my mother looked past my father's shoulder, looked through the bright skin of the tear, at me. The tear enlarged until at last it took me in too. It was warm and salt. As soon as I got used to the strange light inside the tear, I began to swim clumsily toward my parents.

Reprinted with permission of Fred Chappell. Published in *I Am One of You Forever* (LSU Press, 1985).

Fred Chappell: A Biographical Sketch

Fred Chappell is widely recognized as one of the nation's preeminent men of letters. The dimension of his work that perhaps most distinguishes it is the way it is layered with meaning, yet completely accessible on the surface. A poem or a story may parallel—or even make fun of—either an obscure or a prominent work of world literature or a mountain folktale, but assuming there are only a few layers of meaning in a seemingly simple Chappell work is always a mistake.

Fred Chappell was born in 1936 and raised on a one-hundred-acre farm three miles from Canton, North Carolina, where he lived with his maternal grandparents and his parents. His father was fired from the local school system—according to many observers for simply being too open-minded—and then established a furniture store. Fred Chappell began writing science fiction in the eighth grade and poetry in the ninth. In 1954 he enrolled at Duke University, but dropped out before earning a degree and returned to Canton where he worked as general manager of the Brown Supply Company for a couple of years and then for a year as credit manager at the Candler Furniture Store. After marrying Susan Nicholls, also from Canton, he returned to Duke in 1960 and graduated the next year. An eleven-hundred-page thesis completed his master's degree in 1964, and by that time his first novel, *It Is Time, Lord,* had been released by Atheneum, a major New York publisher. He was hired to teach English by the University of North Carolina at Greensboro right out of graduate school. In the 1960s the Chappell's son, Heath, was born, and Chappell published two novels. His third, *Dagan* (1968), received the best foreign book award from the *Academie Francaise* after it was published in France in 1971.

In the 1970s Harcourt published another Fred Chappell novel, *The Gaudy Place* (1973), and LSU Press published five books of his poetry, including four named after the four basic elements of life: *River, Bloodfire, Wind Mountain,* and *Earthsleep.* In 1981, the four were published in a single volume called *Midquest,* which was awarded Yale University Library's Bollingen Prize in Poetry. These same elements are incorporated into the Kirkman Tetralogy of novels named for the western North Carolina family they depict and published over a fourteen-year span. *I Am One of You Forever* (1985) represents water; *Brighten the Corner Where You Are* (1989) represents fire; *Farewell, I'm Bound to Leave You* (1996) represents wind; and *Look Back All the Green Valley* (1999) represents earth. During this period, Chappell's first story collection appeared, as did two books of literary criticism, and LSU Press released five more of his poetry books. In 1987 the scope and importance of Chappell's work was recognized when St. Martin's Press released *The Fred Chappell Reader,* and the following year he was awarded an endowed chair at UNC–Greensboro. He was named North Carolina Poet Laureate in 1997 and served until 2002. The first decade of the twenty-first century was also productive for Chappell. In 2009 LSU Press published his third poetry book of the decade, and St. Martin's published another story collection, *Ancestors and Others: New and Selected Stories.*

Outwardly, it is hard to imagine a more conventional life than Fred Chappell's, but he loves to surprise and stimulate his audiences. For example, the one year he was on the faculty at the Appalachian Writers Workshop at Hindman Settlement School, he read a story he had written about a mountain man herding a drove of women through the mountains. His many readings and his written work have combined to make him a reigning elder of Appalachian literature.

Fred Chappell: A Selective Bibliography

INTERNET RESOURCES

The *Poetry Foundation* offers Chappell's poems "Message" and "Narcissus and Echo," and an in-depth biography of Chappell. The *North Carolina Arts Council* posted Chappell's poem "The Attending." The blog *Complete Word* includes Chappell's poem "The Foreseeing." *Turn Row,* the journal of the University of Louisiana at Monroe, features an interview with Chappell by William Nash.

SELECTED BOOKS

Ancestors and Others: New and Selected Stories. New York: St. Martin's, 2009.
Shadow Box. Baton Rouge: Louisiana State UP, 2009.
Look Back All the Green Valley. New York: Picador, 1999.
The Inkling. Baton Rouge: Louisiana State UP, 1998.
Farewell, I'm Bound to Leave You. New York: Picador, 1996.
It Is Time, Lord. Baton Rouge: Louisiana State UP, 1996.
Spring Garden: New and Selected Poems. Baton Rouge: Louisiana State UP, 1995.
Brighten the Corner Where You Are. New York: St. Martin's, 1990.
The Fred Chappell Reader. New York: St. Martin's, 1990.
I Am One of You Forever: A Novel. Baton Rouge: Louisiana State UP, 1987.
Midquest. Baton Rouge: Louisiana State UP, 1981.

PROFILES/INTERVIEWS

Hovis, George. "An Interview with Fred Chappell." *Carolina Quarterly* 52.1 (1999): 67–79.

LITERARY CRITICISM

Bizzaro, Patrick, ed. *More Lights Than One: On the Fiction of Fred Chappell.* Baton Rouge: Louisiana State UP, 2004.

———. *Dream Garden: The Poetic Vision of Fred Chappell.* Baton Rouge: Louisiana State UP, 1997.

Brosi, George, ed. *Appalachian Heritage* 31.3 (2003). Features Fred Chappell.

Lang, John. "Flesh-Tree and Tree of Spirit." In *Six Poets from the Mountain South.* Baton Rouge: Louisiana State UP, 2010. 38–72.

Lang, John. *Understanding Fred Chappell.* Columbia: U of South Carolina P, 2000.

———, ed. *Iron Mountain Review* 2 (1985). Features Fred Chappell.

Shurbutt, Sylvia Bailey. "A Roadmap for Becoming an Artist: 'Unstoppering the Story Jug' in the Poetry and Prose of Fred Chappell and Listening to the Female Voice." *Journal of Kentucky Studies* 23 (2006): 137–46.

Nikki Giovanni

Progress

i'm looking at old men . . . pregnant bellies hanging over worn blue jeans shirts open to expose old dried breasts were they on a woman . . . but since they are on men just fatty useless tissue hanging . . . they are riding yellow machines that shake my house . . . that scatter brittle white hairs that the crows collect for nests . . . that smile stupid toothless smiles . . . because they are once . . . again . . . called to rape the earth . . . though they think of it as work . . . they stop to cool themselves in the shade of my pine trees though if they had their way the trees would be ashes in the wind since construction people always like to burn what they call rubbish but what is actually warmth giving cool giving life giving green . . . one wonders . . . why even so unbright a group as highway and byway constructionists cannot find a way to save something that gives life while they build something that most certainly will take life . . . they call it land development as if somehow the green is undeveloped . . . the old men stand and look and clank their balls together . . . as if some progress . . . is being . . . made

---

Reprinted with permission of HarperCollins. Published in *Blues: For All the Changes: New Poems* (William Morrow and Company, 1999).

❁ ❁ ❁

Serious Poems

(FOR AMIRI BARAKA AND, MOST ESPECIALLY, HIS GENTLE SISTER, KIMAKO)

Poems are not advertisements braying
For the good life
They have serious work to do
Birthing people burying people
Celebrating joy mourning loss
Poems are not beer commercials

Or there to really show you which soap
To use
Poems have serious business to do
They need to bring down presidents who
Start wars they themselves wouldn't go to
They need to expose lies about chemical weapons
They need to raise real questions about who flew the planes
Into the world trade center towers
Last most poems knew about it
Computers fly planes and pilots keep
The stews on their knees and smoke cigarettes
Since the cockpit is the only smoking area of the plane
Poems have serious work to do
Since they can't plant okra or tomatoes
They can't brew a beer
Or properly ferment wine
They have to at least recognize the importance of the people
Who sweat whether it is a fireman
A policeman
Or any number of athletes who bring such pleasure
When our team wins
Poems have to tell the truth
Which is world holding up time
They need to remind people of our sacred duty
To remember the captured people whom we called
Slaves
To remember they believed in tomorrow
They believed in us
They believed in the power of a serious poem
To carry our story forward
Poems are serious business
And only serious people
Should apply

Reprinted with permission of HarperCollins. Published in *Acolytes: Poems* (William Morrow and Company, 2007).

❁ ❁ ❁

All Eyez on U

(for 2Pac Shakur 1971–1996)

as I tossed and turned unable to achieve sleep unable to control
anxiety unable to comprehend why

2Pac is not with us

if those who lived by the sword died by the sword there would be no
white men on earth
if those who lived on hatred died on hatred there would be no KKK
if those who lived by lies died by lies there would be nobody on wall
street in executive suites in academic offices instructing the young
don't tell me he got what he deserved he deserved a chariot and
the accolades of a grateful people

he deserved his life

it is as clear as a mountain stream as defining as a lightning strike
as terrifying as sun to vampires

2Pac told the truth

there were those who called it dirty gangsta rap inciting there were
those who never wanted to be angry at the conditions but angry
at the messenger who reported: *your kitchen has roaches your toilet is overflowing your basement has so much water the rats are in the
living room*
your house is in disorder

and 2Pac told you about it

what a beautiful boy graceful carriage melodic voice sharp wit intellectual breadth what a beautiful boy to lose

not me   never me I do not believe east coast west coast I saw
them murder Emmett Till I saw them murder Malcolm X I saw
them murder Martin Luther King I witnessed them shooting

Rap Brown I saw them beat LeRoi Jones I saw them fill their jails
I see them burning churches not me never me I do not believe
this is some sort of mouth action this is some sort of political
action and they picked well they picked the brightest freshest
fruit from the tallest tree what a beautiful boy

but he will not go away as Malcolm did not go away as Emmett
Till did not go away your shooting him will not take him from us
his spirit will fill our hearts his courage will strengthen us for the
challenge his truth will straighten our backbones

you know, Socrates had a mother she too watched her son drink
hemlock she too asked why but Socrates stood firm and would
not lie to save himself 2Pac has a mother the lovely Afeni had
to bury her son it is not right

it is not right this young warrior is cut down it is not right for
the old to bury the young it is not right

this generation mourns 2Pac as my generation mourned Till as we
all mourn Malcolm this wonderful young warrior
Sonia Sanchez said when she learned of his passing she walked all day
walking the beautiful warrior home to our ancestors I just cried as all
mothers cry for the beautiful boy who said he and Mike Tyson would
never be allowed to be free at the same time who told the truth about
them and who told the truth about us who is our beautiful warrior

there are those who wanted to make *him* the problem who wanted
to believe if they silenced 2Pac all would be quiet on the ghetto
front there are those who testified that the problem wasn't the conditions but the people talking about them

they took away band so the boys started scratching they took away
gym so the boys started break dancing the boys started rapping
cause they gave them the guns and the drugs but not the schools and
libraries

what a beautiful boy to lose

and we mourn 2Pac Shakur and we reach out to his mother and we
hug ourselves in sadness and shame
and we are compelled to ask:
R U Happy, Mz Tucker? 2Pac is gone
R U Happy?

Reprinted with permission of HarperCollins. Published in *Love Poems* (William Morrow and Company, 1997).

❁ ❁ ❁

Crutches

it's not the crutches we decry
it's the need to move forward
though we haven't the strength

women aren't allowed to need
so they develop rituals
since we all know working hands idle
the devil
women aren't supposed to be strong
so they develop social smiles
and secret drinking problems
and female lovers whom they never touch
except in dreams

men are supposed to be strong
so they have heart attacks
and develop other women
who don't know their weaknesses
and hide their fears
behind male lovers
whom they religiously touch
each saturday morning on the basketball court
it's considered a sign of health doncha know
that they take such good care

of their bodies
i'm trying to say something about the human condition
maybe i should try again

if you broke an arm or leg
a crutch would be a sign of courage
people would sign your cast
and you could bravely explain
no it doesn't hurt—it just itches
but if you develop an itch
there are no salves to cover the area
in need of attention
and for whatever guilt may mean
we would feel guilty for trying
to assuage the discomfort
and even worse for needing the aid

i really want to say something about all of us
am i shouting i want you to hear me

emotional falls always are
the worst
and there are no crutches
to swing back on

Reprinted with permission of HarperCollins. Published in *Cotton Candy on a Rainy Day: Poems* (William Morrow and Company, 1978).

❁ ❁ ❁

Knoxville, Tennessee

I always like summer
best
you can eat fresh corn
from daddy's garden
and okra
and greens
and cabbage
and lots of
barbecue
and buttermilk
and homemade ice-cream
at the church picnic
and listen to
gospel music
outside
at the church
homecoming
and go to the mountains with
your grandmother
and go barefooted
and be warm
all the time
not only when you go to bed
and sleep

Reprinted with permission of HarperCollins. Published in *Black Feeling, Black Talk, Black Judgement* (William Morrow and Company, 1978).

Nikki Giovanni: A Biographical Sketch

Nikki Giovanni is one of this country's most widely read poets and one of America's most renowned poets worldwide. Her poem "Knoxville, Tennessee" is arguably the single literary work most often associated with that city.

Nikki Giovanni was born Yolande Cornelia Giovanni, Jr., in Knoxville, Tennessee, in 1943, but her parents moved to the all-black Cincinnati suburb of Lincoln Heights when she was a young girl. She and her sisters spent the summers with their grandparents in Knoxville, and she returned there for her high school years. Then she enrolled at Fisk University, where her grandfather had graduated, but she was "released" in February 1961 because her attitudes were deemed inappropriate for a "Fisk woman." She then came home and took classes at the University of Cincinnati until she returned to Fisk in 1964. At Fisk she reinstituted the school's chapter of the Student Nonviolent Coordinating Committee (SNCC), edited the literary magazine, and graduated magna cum laude in history in 1967. Returning to Cincinnati she directed the city's first Black Arts Festival before enrolling briefly in the University of Pennsylvania's School of Social Work. Recognizing that she was not meant to be a social worker she entered Columbia University's MFA program. In 1968 she self-published her first poetry book, a nineteen-page staple-bound volume titled *Black Feeling Black Talk,* which sold some two thousand copies in its first few months. This allowed Giovanni to self-publish her second book of poetry, *Black Judgement.* William Morrow and Company approached her about publishing her first two volumes together in one book, and *Black Feeling Black Talk / Black Judgement* was published in 1970. She has continued to publish her poetry with Morrow (now an imprint of HarperCollins) since then.

During the late 1960s and early 1970s, Giovanni lived in New York, and after giving birth to her only child, Thomas, she began earning an income through her lectures and poetry readings. Her frequent appearances on the black entertainment show *SOUL!!,* along with her extensive lecture tours, made her one of the most popular and recognizable poets of the black arts movement. In 1971 *Gemini: An Extended Autobiographical Statement on My First Twenty-Five Years of Being a Black Poet* was a finalist for the National Book Award. In that same year she published her first children's book, *Spin a Soft Black Song,* and released the album *Truth Is On Its Way,* on which she read her poetry accompanied by the New York Community Choir. Although she made no money from it, *Truth* was an enormous success, selling some one hundred thousand copies in the first six months of its release.

In 1978 Giovanni's father suffered a stroke, and she and her son returned to Cincinnati to take care of her parents, while she did brief teaching stints at The Ohio State University and the College of Mount St. Joseph. In 1987 Nikki Giovanni began teaching at Virginia Tech, where she was named, in 1999, a University Distinguished Professor. Since she has been at Virginia Tech, she has published two collections of essays; several illustrated children's books, including the award-winning *Rosa;* and five volumes of poetry for adults. In 2005 both her mother and her sister died of lung cancer, for which Giovanni herself had undergone successful surgery some ten years earlier.

Giovanni continues to teach at Virginia Tech and lecture widely to enthusiastic audiences. One of many indications of her national stature was her invitation to read a poem at the dedication of the Martin Luther King Jr. National Memorial in Washington, DC, in 2011.

Nikki Giovanni: A Selective Bibliography

INTERNET RESOURCES

The *Poetry Foundation* offers four of Giovanni's poems and a profile. Giovanni's website offers an excellent range of her poetry, essays, and interviews. HarperCollins Publishing allows users to view inside Giovanni's book *Bicycles* on its website, and *Poets.org* gives a brief biography of Giovanni.

SELECTED BOOKS

Bicycles: Love Poems. New York: William Morrow, 2009.

Acolytes. New York: William Morrow, 2007.

The Collected Poetry of Nikki Giovanni: 1968–1998. New York: William Morrow, 2003.

The Prosaic Soul of Nikki Giovanni. New York: Harper Perennial, 2003.

Quilting the Black-Eyed Pea: Poems and Not Quite Poems. New York: Harper Perennial, 2002.

Blues: For All the Changes: New Poems. New York: William Morrow, 1999.

Love Poems. New York: William Morrow, 1997.

The Selected Poems of Nikki Giovanni. New York: William Morrow, 1996.

PROFILES/INTERVIEWS

Fowler, Virginia C. "Nikki Giovanni's Appalachian Ties." *Appalachian Heritage* 36.3 (2008): 42–50.

———, ed. *Conversations with Nikki Giovanni.* Jackson: U of Mississippi P, 1992.

———. *Nikki Giovanni: A Literary Biography.* New York: Praeger, 2013.

Reid, Chera. "Interview with Nikki Giovanni." *Iris* 42 (2001): 8–10.

LITERARY CRITICISM

Brosi, George, ed. *Appalachian Heritage* 39.4 (2012). Features Nikki Giovanni.

Cook, Martha. "Nikki Giovanni: Place and Sense of Place in Her Poetry." *Southern Women Writers: The New Generation.* Ed. Tonette Bond Inge and Doris Betts. Tuscaloosa: U of Alabama P, 1990. 279–300.

Fowler, Virginia C. "And This Poem Recognizes That: Embracing Contrarities in the Poetry of Nikki Giovanni." *Her Words: Diverse Voices in Contemporary Appalachian Women's Poetry.* Ed. Felicia Mitchel. Knoxville: U of Tennessee P, 2002. 112–35.

———. *Nikki Giovanni.* Twayne's United States Authors Series 613. New York: Twayne, 1992.

Odon, Rochelle A. "'[T]o fight the fight I'm fighting': The Voice of Nikki Giovanni and the Black Arts Movement." *Langston Hughes Review* 22 (Fall 2008): 37–42, 77.

Robert Morgan

Brownfield

The lot that's poisoned by a spill
of toluene or gasoline
and tons of industrial swill
and drops of mercury dispersed
among the bits of asbestos
and rusting nails and tangled coils
with scattered beads of Styrofoam
all tossed among the posts and beams
of rotting wood and toads of grease,
exploded garbage bags and inks
on asphalt floes, and silty sinks,
is touched in one remote spot by
an ironweed's purple mystery.

Reprinted with permission of Broadstone Books and the Captain's Bookshelf. Published in *October Crossing: Poems* (2009).

❁ ❁ ❁

Inspired

The mouths of giant caves are known
to breathe in during winter months
then slowly start to sigh out air
as spring slows into summer heat,
as if the earth itself inhaled
and exhaled once a year in turn
and kept the rhythm but for bats

that swoop outside at twilight, then
return at dawn to roost as drops
of fur. The threshold sings with warm
air whispering toward the summer sky,
then hums as wind that's chilled and shrunk
falls back across the cavern's lip.
The throat between the worlds is thrilled
with constant music of the shifts
no matter how the planet tilts.

Reprinted with permission of Broadstone Books and the Captain's Bookshelf. Published in *October Crossing: Poems* (2009).

❁ ❁ ❁

Vietnam War Memorial

What we see at first seems a shadow
or a retaining wall in the park, like half a giant pool or half
an exposed foundation. The names
start a few to the column at
the shallow ends and grow panel
by deeper panel as though month
by month to the point of opposing
planes. From that pit you can't see much
official Washington, just sky
and trees and names and people on
the Mall and the Capitol like
a fancy urn. For this is a wedge
into the earth, a ramp of names
driven into the nation's green,
a black mirror of names many
as the text of a book published
in stone, beginning almost
imperceptibly in the lawn
on one side and growing on black
pages bigger than any reader

(as you look for your own name in
each chapter) and then thin away
like a ledger into turf again,
with no beginning, no end. As though
the black wall uncovered here a few
rods for sunlight and recognition
runs on and on through the ground in
both directions, with all our names
on the hidden panels, while
these names shine on the open noon.

❁ ❁ ❁

The Bullnoser

"He thinks he's shit on a stick, but he's really just a fart on a splinter," Carlie said. It was a cotton mill saying she'd been repeating for years. She especially liked to say it about T.J.

T.J. was walking back down the hill to his pickup. He had brought her another case of Budweiser, a bottle of pills, and a carton of Winstons.

"He's hoping I will drink myself to death and then he won't never have to pay me," Carlie said as she tore open the carton.

"Whyn't you get the law after him in the first place?" I said.

Carlie lit a cigarette and pulled a can out of the box of beer.

"Give me one of them," I said.

"Get your own beer you lazy pup."

I helped myself to a can and popped the top. The beer tasted a little bit like aluminum, but it was cold, and mighty good on a humid day. It was a taste I craved when we didn't have no money.

"Whyn't you get the law after T.J. in the first place?" I said again. This was a conversation we had at least once a week. I knew all the answers already, but we couldn't resist going through the motions, especially when we had beer. When Carlie was on her pills she liked to listen to rock and roll on the radio and laugh and sometimes dance. She danced by herself in the dark room with a cigarette in her mouth. She circled round and inhaled and laughed. And she didn't want the light on. She didn't want to see the mess on the floor and on all the chairs. She just wanted to turn in circles and smoke and think about when she was a girl working in the cotton mill and had a boyfriend named Grover. That was way before she met Daddy and moved up here to the farm.

"On Saturday nights we'd go dancing at the Teenage Canteen," she'd say. "That was just before he went overseas." Sometimes she'd say Grover was killed in the war and never did come back, and sometimes she'd say he returned and married somebody else. It was hard to know what the truth was in her stories because she made up so much. In fact, I don't think there ever was a Grover. I think that was just a fig leaf of her imagination.

But when Carlie drank beer she liked most to talk how terrible T.J. had done us, and was still doing her.

"Why'd you agree to sell him the place in the first place?" I said.

"Cause your Daddy, bless his poor little dried up soul in hell, borrowed five thousand dollars from T.J. and I couldn't afford to pay it back."

I noticed a speck of dirt on top of my can. "I wonder where T.J. gets such dirty cans," I said.

"Probably at the Salvation Army," Carlie said, and laughed. She laughed so hard she bent over in her chair and the ash from her cigarette fell on the floor.

"The world is my ashtray," she said in falsetto.

"This floor ought to be swept," I said.

"You're a big strong feller, sweep it yourself," Carlie said. "'Stead of sitting around on your fat ass drinking my beer."

"T.J.'s beer."

"It's payment on what he still owes me."

I wiped the top of the can with my sleeve. For some reason I like the top of a can to be dry when I'm drinking from it.

"Why'd Daddy owe him five thousand dollars?" I said.

"Cause your daddy didn't have a mite of sense and he had cancer and couldn't work. The truth was he never did work much. And I was too sick after you was born to go back to the cotton mill."

"So he just borrowed?"

"He borrowed against the place. He was going to inherit this big place. Everybody said Riley's place was the finest place on the creek."

"Give me a cigarette," I said.

She pulled the carton out of my reach. "Get your own cigarettes," she said. "Besides, smoking is bad for you."

"And it's not bad for you?"

"Don't do as I do, do as I say do." She laughed, but the laugh turned into a cough. I took a cigarette from the pack and lit it.

"Next time T.J. comes tell him you'll sue him," I said.

"And he'll say we got to move out."

"We can move out if he'll pay us the rest of the mortgage."

T.J. had built a trailer park on the pasture hill, cutting out level places almost to the top of the ridge. The ridge was called Riley's Knob after my grandpa who kept it clear and grazed cattle on the very top.

"How much does he still owe us?" I said.

"He claims he don't owe us nothing, that we done used it all up in rent for this old house and in the beer and little bits of groceries he brings."

"People say he paid you years ago and you drunk it all up."

"That's a damn lie."

"He tells people he lets you live here out of the goodness of his heart."

"People are dog puke," Carlie said, and opened another can.

"Ain't it about lunch time?" I said.

"No, it's almost time for *Tucson Days.*" That was a soap opera that comes on in the middle of the day which she had been watching for several months. It was all about people in a retirement community and their families and people who work at the center. There was always somebody dying of cancer—or some old guy who turned out to have a second younger family in Phoenix. And then there was somebody with AIDS and somebody impotent, and a young nurse who was to marry an old guy for his money, except the young nurse is really a lesbian.

"Maybe I'll get my gun and go talk to T.J.," I said.

"You ain't gone talk to nobody," Carlie said. "You want to talk to somebody go talk to somebody about a job."

It was a point that always came up in our conversation that I had lost my job. And she knew as well as I did it was impossible to get another one. When I worked in the cotton mill they put me to lifting boxes in the stockroom and I hurt my side. Their crooked doctor wouldn't give me disability and when I stayed out a few days for my side to heal they fired me. Because they fired me no other company would give me a job. All these plants work together against poor people.

Carlie turned the TV on and sat about a yard away from the screen. She kept her lighter in her right hand and a can in the left.

"Ain't you going to fix no lunch?" I said.

"Get out of here," she said below her breath.

You always feel stuffy when you've been drinking in the daytime and go out into the sun. It's like the light presses against you and pushes you around. And you don't feel like doing anything either. Even while the beer makes you feel lighter it pulls you down inside. That's why Carlie likes her pills in the morning, and sometimes even when she's drinking.

I'd grabbed a pack of cigarettes on my way out of the dark house and I lit one, bending over to get out of the bright light and the breeze. The smoke tasted good. It was the only thing interesting out there in the yard.

The pickup still sat where I had jacked it up the week before. "I'll let you have my old pickup," T.J. said. But he'd just use it as another excuse not to pay us the rest of the mortgage. You don't get nothing from T.J. for nothing. The bearings were gone in the left front wheel, but I couldn't afford another set. I could squirt some grease in and drive it to the store if I had to, but the front end shimmied like sixty, and I was afraid it would ruin something else. I had to wait till I got some money from T.J. or from working for the rich people down on the lake. They'd come after me sometimes to help fix a railing on a deck or dig out a ditch along their driveway. But my back had been killing me again, ever since I wrenched it crawling under the truck to get the bearings out.

"You get that damn truck fixed so we can go to town," Carlie said.

There wasn't a thing to do but walk down to the mailbox to see if a letter had come from the unemployment office. I applied for compensation, but they said I couldn't draw anything unless I could prove I was laid off in good standing. They said I'd have to contest the mill's claim I was fired. I filled out another form for them. I said I was as hard a worker as the next man, except when my back was acting up. It was their crooked doctor that wouldn't give me disability.

So they said they would have a hearing about it, and I've been waiting ever since and not drawed a cent from the government.

Used to, Grandpa kept the yard mowed clean in front the house. But after the lawn mower broke down and wouldn't start I couldn't keep up with all the weeds. And then Carlie throwed out her old washing machine in the side yard, and the rusty barbeque grill and about five hundred cans, and it was such a mess you couldn't hardly walk out of the house without stepping on glass or a snake. And the weeds had already grown up around the truck like it had been parked there all summer.

When I was a kid Grandpa kept the driveway neat as a golf course. But T.J. had covered up the old drive and made a road to his trailer park. He was always bringing in trucks and building more spaces for trailers. I could hear a bullnoser somewhere up there grading, way on back of the Knob.

I took T.J.'s road across the little creek and up the hill to the mailbox. Grandpa had a little bridge there, and it was the perfect place for a kid to play, where the mowed grass came right down to the water and you could watch minnows shoot around the pools. I waded there and made little dams, and fished with a stalk of grass. I could slip through the edge of the pasture when the bull was penned up. Grandpa would take me over to the orchard on the bank below the road and peel an apple or pear with his knife and let me eat it. It looked like a little park in there, the way he kept the place, the gate and apple trees, the little bridge over the branch, the boxwoods along the driveway. Carlie sold all the boxwoods right after Daddy died to help pay for the funeral, she said. If she had known what T.J. was going to do she would have sold off everything else too.

One time I went by the barn and pulled all the railings out of the gap. I liked to slide the poles back and forth in their slots and drop the ends on the ground. But they were too heavy for me to lift back into their holders and I left them down when I saw the mailman stop and I ran to the mailbox.

When the bull got back to that end of the pasture he walked out, just stepped right through the bars. And he was a mean bull too. Everybody was afraid of him. Grandpa kept him to breed people's cows, and he made some money for he charged three dollars a time. People were always driving their heifers down when they were spreeing, and bawling along the road. And the bull would hear them and bawl back, and then come running from whatever part of the pasture he was in. People usually brought their cows down late in the day, after they had stopped work in the fields and when they knew Grandpa would be around the barn, milking or watering the stock.

But when the bull got out it took half the people in the valley half the night to find him. I knew I'd done something bad, but Grandpa said nothing. He lit his old barn lantern and went out looking. Carlie smacked me across the mouth with the flat of her hand so hard my lip cracked.

"You'll get somebody killed with that bull and we'll all go to jail," she said.

I followed Grandpa and didn't go back to the house. The men hollered and ran along the fence at Fairfield's place, where the bull had run trying to get in with the cows. Grandpa couldn't hear too well and the men talked about him like he wasn't there.

"Riley's too old to keep a bull," they said.

"And Riley's boy has fouled his nest," they said.

"Now he's got cotton mill trash in on him," another said.

"Got to keep your breeding stock up, otherwise a family will run to ruin in two generations."

Grandpa walked along with his lantern not saying a thing. They followed the bull along the fence up into the holler and cornered him among the poplars. Grandpa snapped a chain to the ring in his nose and they put a halter over his head:

"You want us to lead him back?" they said.

"Much obliged," Grandpa said. "I can handle him."

I walked in front of Grandpa carrying the lantern.

Where the old driveway wound through the apple trees up to the mailbox, T.J. had bullnosed a new road for the trailer park and put in a culvert over the branch. It was all raw dirt. Grass wouldn't seem to grow on anything T.J. made.

"This place is all clay," he said. "I don't see how Riley ever growed a weed on it."

But T.J. knew how to grow trailer sites. They were all over the old pasture, all over Riley's Knob to the very top.

There wasn't no mail except a circular and three bills. I threw the circular in the ditch and stuffed the bills in my pocket. Carlie won't hardly ever pay bills until they cut the electricity off, and then she has to ask T.J. for the money. Of course, if T.J. owns the house like he says he does, the bills should come to him.

I saw I was going to have to have it out with T.J. I couldn't count on what Carlie said. She got mixed up, and she'd stretch anything to suit her, depending on who she was talking to.

I tried to remember if T.J.'s truck had gone up the hill after he left the beer, or if he had turned back toward the road. If he was up on the Knob I could catch him and have some things out. But I couldn't recall. I had been too busy arguing with Carlie about the beer to notice where T.J. went.

You could hear the bullnoser up there, working somewhere on the Knob. And there was always trucks going up there, pulling new trailers and carrying loads of this and that. You would have thought he was building a shopping mall up there for all the stuff they hauled up the mountain.

I hadn't been up on the Knob in years. It was a steep climb and T.J. had cut down all the trees so there was no place to squirrel hunt. And they were always working up there. You could hear the bullnoser going almost every day, and the clank of a well driller, and the shower of gravel being dumped on the road.

I'd just go up there and have a little talk with T.J. There wasn't anything else to do, except go back and watch TV with Carlie. The beer was wearing off and I was starting to sweat.

The old house sat on the only spot of ground that hadn't been bullnosed by T.J. Where the barn and shed stood he had covered up the old boards with dirt and filled in over the culvert. The whole hill behind the barn had been skinned off, with rocks and dirt showing. Where T.J. sowed grass around the trailers it mostly didn't take, and the little bits of shrubbery died. But them people living up there didn't care. They came and went, some working at the cotton mill and some with construction crews. Several trailers had Mexicans in them. They worked in the shrubbery business as diggers and weedcutters. But you almost never saw them. They left before daylight and didn't get back in the rattly pickup until after dark. One time I heard they bought a goat and roasted it for a celebration. But I don't think it was anything voodoo. They just like goat.

My feet kept slipping on the gravel of T.J.'s drive and I was out of breath before I got halfway up the hill. Too many smokes, I thought, and too much beer. Most of the trailers I passed were deserted. Sometimes you could hear the sound of a TV from one or the buzz of an air conditioner. Pretty little wives sitting around in shorts watching television, I thought. That's what you could have if you worked: a pretty little wife in shorts sitting cool at home when you get off from work. The oil tanks on their stands stood like steel cows behind every trailer, and off on the side of each one a satellite dish tilted like a big white flower. I glanced through a window or two but I couldn't see anybody inside.

Up ahead a little kid was peddling his plastic racer around. It was a low tricycle that was meant to look like a motorcycle. The plastic wheels crunched hollow on the gravel.

"Ruddunn, ruddunn," the kid said, revving his engine. The kid was making so much noise with his throat and with the sound of the wheels on gravel, he couldn't hear a truck coming round the switchback above. It was one of those trucks with sideboards, the kind they use to deliver building supplies. The kid kept peddling out into the road, and the truck didn't slow down, but seemed to be gaining speed.

"Hey," I hollered, and tried to run up the hill. I tried to flag the truck driver, but he just kept coming, like he didn't see the tricycle. The kid was peddling right out into the middle of the road, and at the last second the truck swerved and missed him and then passed me in a cloud of dust. I didn't even get a look at the driver. The name on the truck door said something about "Division" but I didn't have a chance to read it.

"Does your Mama know where you are?" I said to the kid. He didn't seem worried by what had almost happened. I felt like I had been electrocuted, and needed to stand still. The dirty little kid had nothing on but a pair of shorts.

"I'll race you down there," he said, and pointed down the road.

"You better get back in your yard," I said. There was no woman in sight around the trailer, and no car neither.

"Better get out of the road," I said.

"You ain't my daddy," the little boy said, and peddled on downhill. It wasn't clear which trailer he belonged to.

Grandpa used to take me for sled rides on the pasture hill. He'd hitch up the stone boat to get wood around the Knob and let me stand on the sled while the horse pulled it up the pasture hill.

"Why don't you use the wagon?" I said to him.

"Because it's too steep here," he said. "A wagon would tip over or run away."

From the Knob you could see all the way down to the river valley, and the lake and cotton mill town. Today all I could see was the superhighway they cut through above the cotton mill. The traffic on it was a steady roar. It was too hazy to see much further.

I heard the bullnoser going around the back of the Knob, and thought that's where T.J. must be working. He must be clearing more woods and cutting out more places for trailers. I'd just go over there and see what he was doing.

The Knob used to be a grassy top where you could sit and look all over the valley. But it had grown up in bushes and briars, right at the summit. The new road T.J. had cut went around to the back, into a kind of holler between Grandpa's and the Casey ridge. What could T.J. be doing back there? It wasn't even part of the place.

Whatever it was, they had been busy, for the road was packed down and dusty. A few ragweeds drooped in the middle, but they didn't have much of a chance against the traffic and dust. Dead roots stuck out of the bank of the road.

The new road went further into the holler, into the trees. I could hear the bullnoser rev up and then quiet down, screech into reverse, lurching and grinding like a tank. That seemed strange. Why would T.J. be making another trailer place further in the woods when he still had space in the pasture?

You could smell the diesel exhaust in the holler. Kudzu had climbed up the oak trees right to the top and then hung over. I don't know how the kudzu got started because it wasn't there in Grandpa's time. The Caseys brought their bottles and cans and dumped them in the holler. Maybe they had brought a sprig of kudzu or a seed of the stuff with their trash.

T.J.'s pickup was parked right in the road, and then there was another big truck beyond it. Republic Industries: Carrier Division was painted on the big truck. It was the kind of truck that had an elevator at the rear, but the bed was empty.

T.J. stood at the edge of the clearing watching the bullnoser work. The whole place had the smell of opened dirt, which always reminds me of mothballs and camphor, and the smoke of hammered rock. There must be some kind of fumes that come up out of the ground. Far above the clearing the kudzu hung from the oak trees in a mournful way.

I couldn't tell what the bullnoser was doing, except there was oil drums and big paint cans on the ground, where they had rolled them off the truck.

You should have seen the look on T.J.'s face when he saw me. Maybe he knew what I'd come to talk to him about.

"You ain't got no business up here," he said. "This is no trespassing land."

"It ain't even your land, yet," I said, sounding madder than I felt because of the heat and being out of breath.

"Don't start that again," he said. "This wasn't never your Grandpa's land. This was Casey land and I bought it from them."

"Just like you bought Grandpa's?" I said.

"Let's go talk in the truck," he said. "It's air conditioned." He practically pushed me toward the truck.

"It's time to settle this," I said, feeling bolder than I ever had before.

"Let's get out of the heat," he said.

T.J.'s pickup was practically new, but the cab was already dusty and piled with bills and invoices, candy wrappers, old cups, a crowbar, and a basketball goal.

"I'm going to put that up for Jerry," he said, pushing the goal to the floor. "When I get time. Just push everything out of the way."

When he started the motor and turned on the air conditioning it was hotter at first, and then the breeze got cold. The sweat made me shiver, and I could see he was hoping to dampen the anger I'd worked up. It's harder to be mad sitting beside somebody than standing up and facing them. I expected him to start in telling me how Carlie had already drunk up half the price of the place, and smoked and borrowed the rest, like he always did. But he didn't.

"Are you hurting for money?" he said. "I knowed you got laid off."

"I'm always hurting for money," I said.

"I could let you have some," he said.

"T.J., it ain't dibs and dabs I'm talking about. This was a big place."

"It's just a rocky mountainside."

"Not when Grandpa had it."

"Your Grandpa killed hisself to make something out of this brush and hardpan."

"You're going to have to pay up," I said.

"Or you'll what?"

"Or I'll go to law."

"If you need a few dollars I can let you have it."

From the cold inside of the truck I could just barely see the bullnoser. But for the first time it occurred to me what the bullnoser was doing. Those oil drums weren't full of fuel. He was covering them up. He was burying the paint cans and barrels.

"What you putting in the ground there, T.J.?" I said.

"Just some trash from the Republic plant." He offered me a cigarette, then put the truck in gear and started backing away. "We can talk better down at the house," he said. "Or better still, we could go down to the highway and get some dinner. How'd you like a hot dog and a Pepsi?"

Nothing T.J. said was what I expected him to say. He didn't get mad and cuss like he usually did. His face was red but he didn't seem mad. He hadn't even claimed the place was paid for a long time ago.

We bounced down the ruts and washes of the road, and the truck whined on the switchbacks as he geared it down. He had a real good air conditioner. It was a funny feeling, looking down on the valley through summer haze from Grandpa's Knob, from a box of chilly air, and winding among the trailers and scraggly bits of shrubbery T.J. had set out.

And then it struck me what the bullnoser was covering up back there, and why T.J. was being so friendly.

"You're burying poisons and chemicals up there," I said. Carlie and me had seen on TV about how it was illegal to put chemicals in the ground. You could be sent to jail for poisoning the water system.

"What you mean?" T.J. said. "I give them permission to put trash from the factory there."

"Them barrels are full of poison," I said. "Now I see."

"You don't see nothing," T.J. said, all his friendliness gone.

"You could be sued."

T.J. was driving faster, banging on the washouts.

"You cotton mill trash will have to get off my land," he said. "Tell Carlie she's got to move."

"We ain't moving," I said. "Not after I tell the law what you're putting up there."

T.J. kept going faster on the switchbacks, sliding on gravel and throwing rocks every which way. I was glad to see the kid on the plastic bike was off the road and waving from the shade of a trailer.

"You tell the law a thing and you're out in the road with your old TV and stinking couch," he said. "And they'll lock Carlie up in the asylum for crazy people and drug addicts."

"And they'll lock you up for poisoning the ground," I said. "Then the place will come back to us."

"Get out," he hollered, and slid to a stop in front of the house.

"You're in trouble," I said and slammed the door. He spun off throwing rocks fifty or sixty feet. The heat felt good after the cold cab.

The screen door scraped on the back porch when I opened it. The bottom of the screen had scratched a curve on the floor boards. I'd meant to fix it for months, but a door is harder to repair than it looks. We'd probably have to replace the whole thing one of these days, because if you unscrew the hinges and put them on again slightly different the door will rub in other places, and the latch won't click, or one of the corners won't fit into the frame. It has to be a complete job or nothing.

Carlie had tied a piece of cloth over the hole in the screen to keep the flies out. It looked like something put there for a charm to keep the bad spirits away.

"Where the hell you been?" she said.

"I've been around," I said, and pulled the bills out of my back pocket to hand to her. She'd had two or three more beers since I'd left and maybe another pill from the jar.

It was so dark in the house I could only see her face reflected in the TV light. The air was filled with smoke. She was so wrecked she couldn't tear open the envelopes, and gave it up and threw them on the table.

"You'll have to pay them," she said. "I'm just an old woman."

"You got years left in you," I said.

"Trifling lard ass," she said, and tossed her head, as she does when drunk, like she was a debutante on TV.

"I seen T.J.," I said. I wouldn't tell her about the chemical dump for a while. It was my little secret.

"You get any money from him?"

"I told him he'd have to pay up."

"You lazy-assed chicken," she said. "I'd rather eat shit with a splinter than beg for money." That was another of the cotton mill sayings she liked to bring out when she was drunk. She lit another cigarette, not touching the flame to the tip until the third try.

I decided I wouldn't tell her at all. The oil drums buried across the Knob would be a secret between T.J. and me. He would keep me in beer and cigs and maybe get the pickup fixed. There was no way he could throw us out, and I didn't need to tell Carlie a thing about it.

"Give me one of them beers," I said.

"Get your own beer."

There was a game show on the TV with a laugh track. I hated game shows as much as Carlie loved them. I popped a beer and headed back outside. I hadn't felt so good since I found a twenty dollar bill in the parking lot of the plant before I was laid off. I sat on the porch looking down at the driveway T.J. had put in where the barn was. The cold beer tasted like both hope and confidence. I'd have the pickup running again by next week.

When Grandpa was old and couldn't really work anymore he piddled around the barn, mowing a few weeds, watering the horse, sharpening his hoes, and talking to hisself. When I was home on leave from the army he took me down to the shed adjoining the barn where he kept his tools. There was an old table with sacks piled on it, and he showed me one by one where he hid his mowing blade and pliers, his hammer and wire cutters, whet rock and file. He said people stole so bad nowadays you had to keep things hid. He wanted me to know where they were in case he died. The tater digger and ax leaned behind some boards in the corner. The good harness for the horse was behind the table with some sacks piled on it.

Reprinted with permission of Robert Morgan. Published in *The Mountains Won't Remember Us* (Peachtree Publishers, 1992).

Robert Morgan: A Biographical Sketch

Robert Morgan is an erudite intellectual and scintillating conversationalist. His mother was a Baptist mill-worker, and his father was a Pentecostal Holiness believer who farmed ten hilly North Carolina acres first settled by his great-grandfather. Attention to Morgan's writing increased dramatically when Oprah Winfrey selected his novel *Gap Creek* for her book club in 2000, but that hasn't changed the trajectory of his career whose roots in poetry are obvious even when he ventures into prose.

Robert Morgan was born in Henderson County, North Carolina, in 1944. His family didn't own a motorized vehicle until 1953, but his worldview widened considerably when a library bookmobile began to come every Monday to the Green River Church near his home. As a result, Morgan's reading expanded gradually to include Laura Ingalls Wilder, Jack London, Charles Dickens, Thomas Wolfe, Leo Tolstoy, and Ernest Hemingway. Morgan wrote his first story in the sixth grade when he had to stay at school while all the other students in his class had the three dollars to go tour the Biltmore Estate in nearby Asheville. Like many in his generation, Morgan was pushed into the study of math and science after *Sputnik*. At the age of sixteen he entered Emory University with the intention of helping America win the space race. He transferred first to North Carolina State University, where his writing teacher, Guy Owen, told Morgan that his story about his great-grandmother had moved him to tears. "That was better praise than I had gotten in math classes," Morgan relates, "and I was hooked on writing." Then he transferred again, this time to the University of North Carolina at Chapel Hill, where he served as fiction editor for the *Carolina Quarterly* and earned a BA in 1965. He then returned to his boyhood farm and supported himself, as his father had often done before him, as a house painter. Soon, however, he enrolled in the MFA program at the University of North Carolina at Greensboro to study under Fred Chappell. After graduating in 1968 Morgan was hired by Salem College in Winston-Salem. In 1969 his first book, *Zirconia Poems,* was published, and his first National Endowment for the Arts grant allowed him to quit teaching and return to the farm. In 1971, after a successful poetry reading there, Cornell University offered Morgan a teaching position. At this time, his wife, Nancy, was able to count twenty houses they, and their son, Ben, had lived in since their marriage in 1965. In the 1970s Morgan published two chapbooks and three poetry collections, Cornell made his job tenure-track, and two daughters were born. In 1977 Morgan saw a Cormac McCarthy play on television, which drew him to fiction writing, but it wasn't until 1989 that his first story collection, *Blue Valleys,* was released after another chapbook and another poetry collection. Morgan's first novel, *Hinterlands,* came out in 1994, and was followed by two more novels, another story collection, two poetry books, and a book of essays by the end of the decade. Then in January 2000 Morgan got a phone call from a woman who had read his novel *Gap Creek* and wanted him to speak to her book club. When she said, "I'm up north, too. I'm in Chicago," it began to dawn on him that he was talking with Oprah Winfrey.

In the first decade of this century Morgan published two poetry collections and a novel, and served as a visiting writer at Appalachian State University, Furman, and Duke. He also published his first biography, *Boone,* in 2007. In 2011 Morgan published *Lions of the West,* telling the stories of early explorers, and *Terroir,* another book of poetry. Robert Morgan has been the recipient of numerous awards, but he says he most values the Arts and Letters Award he received in 2007 from the American Academy of Arts and Letters because it was given by his peers.

Robert Morgan: A Selective Bibliography

INTERNET RESOURCES

Morgan's website offers ten of his poems and seven of his essays. The *Atlantic Monthly* features three poems by Morgan, "Girdling," "Wind from a Waterfall," and "Option." The *Writer's Almanac* has the poem "Great Day in the Morning." The *Poetry Foundation* features poems "Holy Cussing" and "Mountain Dulcimer," as well as a brief biography and bibliography. *Cornell University Chronicle Online* offers the poem "Yellow" and a biographical sketch.

SELECTED BOOKS

Terroir. New York: Penguin, 2011.
Lions of the West. Chapel Hill, NC: Algonquin, 2011.
October Crossing. Frankfort, KY: Broadstone Books, 2009.
Boone: A Biography. Chapel Hill, NC: Algonquin, 2007.
The Strange Attractor. Baton Rouge: Louisiana State UP, 2004.
Brave Enemies. Chapel Hill, NC: Algonquin, 2003.
This Rock. Chapel Hill, NC: Algonquin, 2001.
The Balm of Gilead Tree. Frankfort, KY: Gnomon, 1999.
Gap Creek: The Story of a Marriage. Chapel Hill, NC: Algonquin, 1999.
The Truest Pleasure. Chapel Hill, NC: Algonquin, 1995.

PROFILES/INTERVIEWS

Harmon, William. "Robert Morgan: Imagination, Memory, and Region." In *Appalachia and Beyond: Conversations with Writers from the Mountain South.* Ed. John Lang. Knoxville: U of Tennessee P, 2006. 91–104.

LITERARY CRITICISM

Brosi, George, ed. *Appalachian Heritage* 32.3 (2004). Features Robert Morgan.

Conway, Cecelia. "Robert Morgan's Mountain Voice and Lucid Prose."In *An American Vein: Critical Readings in Appalachian Literature.* Ed. Danny L. Miller, Sharon Hatfield, and Gurney Norman. Athens: Ohio UP, 2005. 275–95. (Reprinted from *Appalachian Journal* 29.1–2 [2001]: 180–99.)

Graves, Jesse, guest ed. *Southern Quarterly: A Journal of the Arts in the South* 47.3 (Spring 2010). Features Robert Morgan.

Lang, John. *Iron Mountain Review* 6 (1990). Features Robert Morgan.

———. "Mountains Speak in Tongues." *Six Poets from the Mountain South.* Baton Rouge: Louisiana State UP, 2010. 73–98.

Villiers, Regina. "Women in Robert Morgan's Short Fiction: A Study of 'The Blue Valleys' and 'The Mountains Won't Remember Us.'" *Pembroke Magazine* 35 (2003): 65–70.

West, Robert. "A Study in Sharpening Contrast: Robert Morgan and the Distinction between Prose and Poetry." *Pembroke Magazine* 35 (2003): 77–81.

Part 2

The People

Robert J. Conley

Plastic Indian

We had driven past it dozens, perhaps hundreds of times, the giant, plastic Indian which stood in front of the motel on Highway 51, and we had almost always cussed it as we went by. It was an insult to us all. One feather in its hair, a pair of moccasins and a flap on its front and back were all the clothes it wore. It stood with one leg straight and the other slightly bent at the knee; it held one hand up against its head as an eye shade. Its hair was long and worn in two braids which dangled on its chest. Perhaps worst of all, its flesh was pink. It stood there, towering over us as we drove from Tahlequah to Tulsa or to any number of smaller towns along the way.

We came to view the big, pink, plastic Indian as a symbol of all that was wrong and all that was evil in our midst. Before 1907, the spot on which the plastic Indian stood had been definitely and unquestionably Cherokee. It had been a part of the Cherokee Nation, a portion of the land that was owned by all Cherokees. But Oklahoma statehood had changed all of that. Before 1907, the Cherokee Nation had produced more college graduates than the states of Arkansas and Texas combined. By 1970, according to the U.S. census, the average adult Cherokee had but four and one-half years of school. Even Will Rogers had said, "We had the greatest territory in the world, and they ruined it when they made a state," or words to that effect. We all agreed with him, and we all further agreed that the plastic Indian was a symbol of all of that.

We had all been out drinking one summer's evening, and we were headed back toward Tahlequah, when we drove past the plastic Indian.

"Look at that ugly son-of-a-bitch," Tom said.

"We've been looking at it for years," said Pat.

"We talk about it every time we drive past here," I said.

"We've talked long enough," said Tom. "Let's do something about it."

"Like what?"

"Let's tear the damn thing down once and for all."

The plastic Indian was already well behind us and long out of sight, but the conversation continued. Perhaps it was all the beer we had consumed. Perhaps the timing was just right. Who knows? But the talk just kept going. It wouldn't stop.

"How are we going to do that?" I asked.

"Drive out to my house," Tom said, "and I'll show you."

By the time we got to Tom's house in the Rocky Ford community on the other side of Tahlequah, Tom had passed out. None of us had any idea what he'd had in mind, so we rolled him out into his front yard and drove off. Nothing was done about the plastic Indian.

It was several days before we all got together again. We were at my house drinking beer, and for some reason, Tom started talking about the plastic Indian again. I don't recall our ever having talked about it before except when we had just driven past it. It was still early in the evening, too. I suspected that something might develop.

"That damn thing," Tom said, "is an insult to all of us. It would be bad enough if a white man put up a tall Indian that really looked like a Cherokee to advertise his business. But that thing doesn't even look like us. If anything, it looks like Longfellow's Hiawatha or maybe Uncas from *The Last of the Mohicans.*"

"It is an ugly bastard," I said, not being possessed of Tom's eloquence. I sipped some more beer from the wet can.

"Those guys think they can do anything right here in our own country," said Pat. "They're surrounded by Indians all the time. Hell, some of their customers are Indians."

"Most of them," said Tom.

"There's the U-Need-Um Tires Company," I said, "and the U-Totem Stores."

"That damn plastic Indian covers it all," said Tom. "Let's go."

Without waiting for an answer, Tom got up and headed out the front door. Pat and I followed, giving one another puzzled looks. Tom had an old pickup parked outside in my driveway, and we piled in. Tom fired the thing up and backed out into the street.

"Where we going?" Pat asked.

"You'll see," said Tom.

"We going out to look at that plastic Indian?" I asked.

"Yeah," Tom said. "That's where we're going."

"What are we going to do?" Asked Pat.

"You'll see."

We were lucky the cops weren't out that night because Tom ran four red lights and drove about ten miles over the speed limit all the way out to where the plastic Indian stood guard over the motel on Highway 51. He pulled over on the shoulder and stopped just across the road from the monstrosity. We all sat there in silence staring at it for several minutes. Then Tom got out of the pickup.

"You drive it, Pat," he said.

Pat had been sitting in the middle of the seat, so he scooted over behind the wheel.

"Okay," he said, "but where are you going?"

"I'll be in the back," Tom said. "Drive on down the road a way. Then turn around and drive back, and when you come up on that plastic Indian, don't slow down."

"What are you going to do?"

"Just drive," said Tom. He climbed into the pickup bed, and Pat gunned the engine. There were no cars coming, so he moved out onto the road in a hurry and drove on down for maybe a mile. Then he made a U-turn, and as he did, I saw Tom fall over in the back of the truck. Pat kept driving, and Tom got back up to his feet. I twisted my head to watch him, and I saw him pick up a coiled rope and pay out a loop. Tom was a frustrated cowboy. He was always talking about chasing wild horses on government land.

Up ahead, the plastic Indian came back in view. Pat roared ahead. In the back of the truck, Tom swung a wide loop over his head. He looked magnificent, standing in the back of the speeding pickup, spinning that loop. We came closer, and Tom threw the loop. I watched fascinated as it arced its way up and over the plastic head, but the fascination turned to horror as I saw the loop tighten, the rope straighten, and Tom go flying out of the back of the pickup.

"Stop," I yelled to Pat.

Pat hit the brakes. "What's wrong?"

"We've lost Tom," I said. "Hell, we might've killed him."

"Damn."

The old pickup came to a stop on the shoulder. Pat shifted into low and made a U-turn. He drove back toward the plastic Indian, and we could see Tom struggling to his feet. Pat pulled up beside him.

"Get in," he said.

I opened the door and moved to the middle of the seat to make room, and Tom slid in with a moan.

"God damn," he said.

"What the hell were you trying to do?" Pat asked.

"I was going to rope that damn thing and pull it over," said Tom.

"Well, you roped it all right," I said.

"Yeah."

Tom moaned again, and I said, "Are you hurt?"

He lifted up his arms, and I could see that his shirt sleeves were in shreds, and even in the dark I could see where his arms had been skinned by the pavement.

"Jesus," I said. "You're lucky you're not dead."

When we got back to my house and in the light, we could see that not only Tom's arms, but also his chest and belly were skinned pretty bad. He was bleeding some. We washed him up and found some kind of salve to rub on the affected spots. His face had a couple of places on it too, but they weren't too bad. To tell the truth, he had been remarkably lucky. If I had tried that fool trick, and I'd been skillful enough to catch anything with the rope, I'd have been killed for sure.

"Son-of-a-bitch," Tom said.

"What?"

"It's starting to hurt now."

It was a couple weeks later when Pat and Tom drove up to my house in the old pickup again. They had a couple of six-packs with them. Actually, they had one six-pack and a part of another. They had already broken into that one. I took one and opened it, drinking fast to catch up with them. We sat in my living room and drank and talked for a while. Then Pat said, "We got it figured out this time."

"What?" I said.

"We figured out how to pull down that plastic Indian."

"Bull shit," I said.

"No. Really."

I looked at Tom. "He's right," he said. "We do have it figured out. You going to go out there with us?"

Well, I wouldn't have missed it for the world. We had to stop for some gas, but in a short while, we were on the way again.

"What's the plan?" I asked.

"It's brilliant," said Pat. "It's all Tom's idea."

"Well, what is it?"

"You'll see," said Tom.

"You're not going to sling something from the back of the truck again, are you?"

"No. Nothing like that."

Tom still had scabs on parts of his body. As he drove through town, I kept wondering what grand scheme he had in mind, but he was in one of those moods. He wouldn't tell me. I would just have to wait and see, so I quit asking about it. I sat in the middle of the pickup seat drinking my beer. We passed one cop, but he was going the other way, and Tom wasn't driving too fast just at that moment. We got out to the plastic Indian unmolested, and Tom, once again, pulled over to the shoulder. I looked at him. He sat staring at the monument to the crass economics of the white conqueror.

"Okay," Tom said at last, "you two take the chain over there and get it ready. Then signal me."

"Come on," Pat said to me.

I got out of the pickup to follow him, even though I still had no idea what we were up to. Pat reached over into the bed of the pickup and hauled out a length of chain, throwing it over his shoulder. He looked both ways down the highway and, seeing no traffic, ran like hell for the plastic Hiawatha. I ran after him. On reaching the big Indian, Pat slung a length of the chain around its ankles, then hooked the short end of the chain back into one of the links.

"Stretch the rest of that out," he said.

I laid the chain out on the ground, trailing it along parallel to the road. I was beginning to get it. I looked up and down the road for any sign of cars. Off to the west I saw some headlights coming our way.

"Hey," I said.

Pat looked and saw them too.

"Just be casual," he said. "They won't notice anything."

The car finally came up and whizzed right past us without slowing down a bit. It was followed by two more, and then a pickup coming from the other direction. No one seemed to notice anything amiss. Pat looked at me.

"Are we ready?" he asked.

"I guess so," I said, still not having been told what we were up to, even though I had guessed it by then.

Suddenly Pat made a noise which I took to be his imitation of a hoot owl, but I couldn't be sure. Across the highway, Tom gunned the old pickup. He ground the gears. The pickup moved forward, made a U-turn and pulled beside us on the opposite shoulder before moving ahead to stop close to the end of the chain. I followed. Pat dropped down on his knees, picked up the chain and started to coil it around some part of the pickup underneath.

"Is it all right?" Asked Tom from the cab.

"I guess so," I said. "He's hitching it up."

I looked nervously from one direction to the other. No one was coming. Finally Pat stood up. "Come on," he said. "Get in the truck."

He was in first, so he was in the middle of the seat this time. I piled in right behind him. All three of us twisted our heads around to look at the big plastic

Indian standing there waiting to meet his doom. Tom gunned the engine. He moved the pickup ahead slowly. The chain tightened. The engine roared. The pickup did not move.

"Damn it," said Tom.

"Back it up," said Pat. "Take a run."

Tom shifted into reverse and backed up more than a car length. Then he shifted back into low. He gunned the engine. He popped the clutch. The pickup leaped forward. The chain straightened. There was a sudden jerk that came near giving us all backlash. There was a terrible noise. Suddenly we broke loose and sort of skidded ahead, sliding off the side of the road. The engine died and would not start again.

"Damn," said Tom.

We got out and looked back behind us to see the whole rear end of the pickup still chained to the plastic Indian. The rest of the vehicle was lying stupidly in the ditch. We had to walk back to Tahlequah. We thought about hitch-hiking, but there was hardly any traffic that late at night, and the few cars that did pass us paid us no attention. The next day, when the cops called Tom about his car, found in two pieces out on Highway 51, one part of it chained to the plastic Indian, Tom said that he knew nothing about it. Someone had taken his car.

Tom disappeared shortly after that, presumably off chasing wild horses on government land. Pat didn't come around much. He didn't have a car, and he lived quite a ways out. I went back to my job at the Cherokee Nation, wondering daily why it seemed so much like a job at some corporation owned and run by white people. In the evenings I found myself thinking about the Cherokee Nation before Oklahoma statehood. Of course, I was imagining. I had never known it. I knew it only through stories told by my grandparents and through books I had read.

And I thought about what happened in those years following 1907. Tahlequah had a Kentucky Fried Chicken with a great big bucket on the end of a pole. The road going from town out to the tribal headquarters was lined with fast food joints and a Walmart. The old, historic railroad depot was a crumbling pile of bricks. Downtown a business called Cherokee Abstracts sported a sign out front which bore a profile of an American Indian wearing a plains-style headdress.

Our Chief was a Republican banker who had grown up in Oklahoma City, and there was one person on the tribal council who could speak Cherokee. There were still some Indian allotments left in Indian hands, but most of the land of the old Cherokee Nation was lost, owned by white people, who fenced it in and put up signs that said, "No Trespassing," "No Hunting," "No Fishing," "Get the Hell Out of Here," and other such things. And way out on Highway 51, the great symbol of it all, the huge pink, plastic Indian, still stood his post.

Reprinted with permission of Robert J. Conley. Published in *Appalachian Heritage* 47.4 (Fall 2009).

Robert J. Conley: A Biographical Sketch

Robert J. Conley, an enrolled member of the Cherokee Nation, is a prolific, popular, and versatile author who has become a dominant voice for the Cherokee people. In 2008 he moved to the North Carolina mountains to become the Sequoyah Distinguished Professor of Cherokee Studies at Western Carolina University. Dwelling in his ancestral homeland carries deep meaning for Conley. While living in Oklahoma he and his wife, Evelyn, had visited Cherokee, North Carolina, many times to do research not only for several of his novels but also for his *Cherokee Encyclopedia* (2007), and for *The Cherokee Nation: A History* (2008), the only history officially endorsed by the Cherokees.

Robert J. Conley's paternal grandparents were teachers in Indian Territory, and Conley was born in Cushing, Oklahoma, in 1940. He attended high school and college in Wichita Falls, Texas, receiving a BA in drama in 1966 and an MA in English in 1968 from Midwestern University. He then embarked on an academic odyssey that provided him with jobs not only in Oklahoma, but also in Illinois, Iowa, Missouri, and Montana. During the early 1970s he published many poems and became coauthor and co-compiler of four academic collections, including *Poems for Comparison and Contrast* (1972) and *The Essay: Structure and Purpose* (1975). Then he answered a call from the Cherokee Nation at their headquarters in Tahlequah, Oklahoma, for trained professionals, quit his academic job, and joined the Cherokee Programs Management team as a writer and administrator. In 1986 his first novel, *Back to Malachi,* was published as a Cherokee-themed Doubleday hardcover western, followed in that decade by seven more popular Cherokee westerns.

Early in his career Conley remembers a New York editor telling him that the country wasn't ready for a western novel with an Indian hero and asking for a book whose Indian character was the sidekick of a white guy. Conley's response was to submit *Strange Company,* a Civil War novel featuring two prisoners chained together: a semiliterate farm boy who thought his name, Ben Franklin, was shared with the first president of the United States, and his sidekick, a Harvard-educated Cherokee. Never again was Conley questioned for submitting a novel with a Cherokee protagonist.

The Western Writers of America first presented Conley a Spur Award for the Best Western Short Story, and then gave him two Best Western Novel awards in the 1990s, ironically for two of his novels set in the Southern Appalachians, considered the "first West" from the perspective of Colonial America. Each year in the 1980s Robert J. Conley published more than one new book and saw multiple titles of his books reprinted, including his very first novel. Conley also wrote the screenplay for the Columbia Pictures 1993 movie *Geronimo: An American Legend.* His very popular *Mountain Windsong: A Novel of the Trail of Tears* (1995) was adapted into a musical drama that premiered in Tahlequah. At the core of his body of fiction is the Real People series, named for a literal translation of *Ani-yunwi-ya,*, a word the Cherokees use for themselves. These twelve books follow Cherokee history from prehistoric times to their arrival in Indian Territory, now Oklahoma, on the notorious Trail of Tears, their removal from the Southern Appalachians by the U.S. Army during the 1930s. Conley's biographical novel, *Sequoyah* (2002), is the final book in the series. Conley remains as productive as ever. In 2011 he published four new books, bringing his book title count up to more than eighty.

Robert J. Conley: A Selective Bibliography

INTERNET RESOURCES

Robert J. Conley's website includes his works "On Holding a Pre-Columbian Clay Figure," "The Caretaker," and "Dlanusi," along with additional information.

SELECTED BOOKS

Cherokee Medicine Man: The Life and Work of a Modern-Day Healer. Norman: U of Oklahoma P, 2011.

The Cherokee Nation: A History. Albuquerque: U of New Mexico P, 2008.

Cherokee Thoughts: Honest and Uncensored. Norman: U of Oklahoma P, 2007.

Mountain Windsong: A Novel of the Trail of Tears. Norman: U of Oklahoma P, 2007.

The Real People series, including *Sequoah, The Way of the Priests, The Dark Way, The White Path, The Way South, The Long Way Home, The Dark Island, The War Trail North, The Peace Chief, Cherokee Dragon,* and *War Woman.* Norman: U of Oklahoma P. 2000-2001.

The Witch of Goingsnake and Other Stories. Norman: U of Oklahoma P, 1991.

PROFILES/INTERVIEWS

Ballard, Sandra. "Backtracking from Oklahoma to North Carolina." *Appalachian Journal* 28.3 (2001): 326–44.

Bruchac, Joseph. "A More Realistic Picture: An Interview with Robert J. Conley." *Wooster Review* 8 (Spring 1988): 106–14.

Teuton, Sean. "Writing Home: An Interview with Robert J. Conley." *Wicazo Sa Review* 16.2 (2001): 115–28.

LITERARY CRITICISM

Brill de Ramírez, Susan Berry. "Before the South Became the South: Pre-colonial and Colonial Geographies of Contact in Robert J. Conley's Cherokee Historical Novels." *Mississippi Quarterly* 60.1 (2006/7): 179–207.

Brosi, George, ed. *Appalachian Heritage* 37.4 (2009). Features Robert J. Conley.

Teuton, Chris. "Interpreting Our World: Authority and the Written Word in Robert J. Conley's Real People Series." *MFS: Modern Fiction Studies* 53.3 (2007): 544–68. (Republished in Teuton, *Deep Waters: The Textual Continuum in American Indian Literature.* Lincoln: U of Nebraska P, 2010.)

Ann Pancake

Redneck Boys

Richard has gone on and died, she thinks when she hears the knuckle on the door. Took two weeks after the accident, he was strong. The other three dead at the scene. She glances at the digital clock on top of Richard's New Testament, then she covers her face with her hands. The yellow stink of the hospital still hangs in her hair. It's 3:07 a.m., and Richard has gone on and died.

She pulls on yesterday's jeans and feels her way through the hall, not ready yet for a light in her eyes. Cusses when she hits barefoot the matchbox cars her son's left lying around. She's so certain it's her brother, who was made messenger back towards the beginning of this mess, she doesn't even pull back the curtain to see. She stops behind the door to steady her breath, which is coming quick and thin even though she's expected the news for days. But when she unbolts the door, it is a boy, a man, she hasn't seen in a few years.

He blows steam in the porch light, straddling the floor frame Richard never had time to finish. Coatless, his arms pork-colored in the cold. He has forced himself into corduroy pants he's outgrown and wears a pair of work boots so mud caked they've doubled in size. He grins. She knew him some time ago. And he grins at her, his face gone swollen, then loose under the chin, the way boys get around here.

"Cam," is what he says.

She draws back to let Splint pass. He unlaces the muddy boots and leaves them on the ground under the porch frame. The surprise she might have felt if he'd shown up before Richard's wreck—and she's not sure she would have felt surprise then—has been wrung out of her by the two-week vigil. Splint walks to the sofa where he wraps himself in an afghan and chafes his upper arms with his palms. He swipes at the runny nose with his shoulder. Cam remembers what she's wearing—just a long-john shirt of Richard's over the jeans, no bra—and for a moment, her face heats with self-consciousness. Then the heat leaves her face for other places in her body. Angry at herself, Cam wills the heat away.

"Where's your boy?" Splint asks. Then, "I heard about Richard."

"Down to Mom's," Cam answers.

“You’re up on this mountain without even a dog at night?”

Splint squats in front of the woodstove, still shawled in the afghan that doesn’t quite fall to his waist. Cam watches the soft lobs between the waistband of the corduroys and the hem of the hiked-up T-shirt. Burrs snagged in his pants cuffs. Cam wonders what he’s done now to end up coatless in the middle of a freezing night. Then she doesn’t wonder. She crouches on the edge of the sofa behind him, her chest clenched, and she waits for what he’ll do next.

What he does is open the stove door and huddle up to it closer, giving Cam a better look at his soft back. Hound-built he was as a boy, a little bow-legged and warped along the spine, the new muscles riding long and taut and rangy right under the skin. Freckle-ticked shoulders. She recalls trailing him one August afternoon up a creek bed where he’d stashed a six-pack of Old Milwaukee in sycamore roots. He’d outgrown that shirt, too, a tank top, and she had watched it ride up, watched the tight small of his back. The muscles coming so soon, too early, on those boys.

“Why don’t you poke up the fire for me?” Splint startles her. She starts to move, then pauses, asks herself who she’s answering to and why. But she’s been raised to obedience. She leans forward and picks up a split chunk on the hearth. Its raw insides tear the skin on her palm, even though it is a hard hand that has handled many stove logs. She shoves the log in the embers, kneels, and blows until the coals flare up. Then, as she reaches to shut the door, Splint’s own hand snakes out of the afghan and grabs her arm. Cam goes icy in the roots of her hair. She yanks away, harder than she needs to. The stove door stays open, the pipe drawing hard and loud. A sizzle and whupping in the flue.

“It’s too bad about Richard,” Splint says. “He was always a good boy.”

Cam can’t tell if he’s mocking her.

“And a hard worker, huh?”

This is funeral talk, and Cam doesn’t answer.

“You never were a big talker,” Splint says. “Guess you don’t got any cigarettes around here?”

He pulls a big splinter from the stove to light the Virginia Slim she gives him. Cam knows he knows Richard is just like the others. Went down off the mountain at five a.m. to meet his ride, traveled two hours to build northern Virginia condominiums all day, traveled the hundred miles back to a six-room house he was putting together on weekends and didn’t finish before the wreck. Celotex walls and the floors unsanded. Yeah, Richard was a hard worker, just like all the other boys. Only Splint wouldn’t work hard, and Splint ended up in jail.

“I still think about you,” he says. He’d been staring into the stove, but now he cocks his head sidewise to look at Cam, kneeling a little behind him. She has her bare feet drawn up under her, and not just for warmth. To be all of a piece like that, pulled together, makes her feel safe from herself. Her eyes drift to his hands in the firelight there, them hanging loose in his lap. It occurs to her she has never seen them so clean although the heat draws an odor from his body, the odor of ground in the woods. But the hands—no grease in the knuckle creases or in the prints, the nails clear and unbroken. Back when she knew him, the hands were all the time dirty. He spent half his time with his head in an engine, the other half under the chassis. Frittered his cash away on parts and auto wrecker junk, and when it still wouldn't run, he'd steal. What've you been into now, buddy? Cam thinks. Splint pulls up the tail of his shirt to stob his running nose.

The last time she and Splint ran, they were seniors in high school. Splint told her to meet him a ways down her road so her parents wouldn't see, and he showed up in a brand-new Camaro, she recognized the car. Sixteenth-birthday present to some lawyer's kid at school, but Splint was playing his own music. Lynryd Skynyrd. Cam got drunk before they hit the paved road, grain alcohol and orange pop, the music thrusting through her stomach and legs, while Splint cussed the car for handling like a piece of shit. She cranked down her window, stuck her head in the wind. Wind, leaves, hills, but no sky. Sky too far overhead to see from a car. Just ground, pounding by on either side. It was spring, and by that time, they knew about the college, the scholarship.

They eventually reached Frawl's Flat, the second straightest piece of road in the county, and they started seeing how fast the Camaro would go. Stupid-drunk like they were, the state police snuck up on them easy. Splint squealed off down the highway, and even though the car was a piece of shit, they might have outrun the cops, or, more likely, could have ditched the car and both run off in the woods. But Splint did something else.

He swerved back a narrow, heavy-wooded road, braked, and screamed at Cam to get out, shoving at her shoulder as he yelled. And Cam did. She tumbled out, the car down to maybe fifteen miles an hour by then, landed on her hip in the ditch, then scrambled up the shale bank into the scrub oak and sumac. The staties were so close they caught Splint where she could watch. Crouched in the brush, cold sober, she saw the three of them moving in and out the headlights and taillights. He'd just turned eighteen, and they put him in jail for a while that time. They didn't know to look for Cam.

"Oh, you were bright," Splint is saying, and she winces at how the gravel has come in his craw. Tobacco voice. "Bright. All that running around you did and they still gave you a scholarship."

Cam doesn't answer back. Splint knows there was one person in their class as bright as Cam, and that was Splint. She knows Splint knows she got a boy instead of a college degree. She realizes she's unnumbed enough to need a drink, and she heads to the kitchen to fetch one. Aware of what Splint will want, she starts to open the refrigerator, then stops. On the door, her boy's drawings, motorcycles and eighteen-wheelers. Instead, she pulls a bottle of Jim Beam and two jelly glasses from the crates they are using until they have money for cabinets. The whiskey she and Richard shared, but the beer in the refrigerator belongs to just Richard.

She even called Splint once or twice during the year she spent at the university in gray Morgantown. Then she left the state and saw a little of the world, ha. Waited tables in Daytona for eight months before she met a boy named Eric, and they went west, that was for six. What she remembers best—or worst—at any rate, what she remembers clearest—is the way this Eric talked. In six months, she never could get used to it. Hardened every consonant, choked up every vowel. Such an awkward, a cramped way to work your words out your mouth. It got to where she couldn't stand to hear him say her name, how he'd clip it off, one syllable. Cam. Like he had no idea about the all of her. Back home, they speak it full. They say it Ca-yum. Back here.

Splint drains his glass, shivers his head and shoulders, stretches. The afghan drops to the floor. He swaggers over to Richard's gun cabinet, and Cam sees how he carries himself like a middle-aged man. Still small in his hips, he is, but big across the belly, and him no more than thirty. Although her eyes stay on Splint, her mind sees her own body at the same time. She knows she's gone in the other direction, a rare way to go around here. Cam knows she's worn rutted and flat. Splint strokes the rifle stocks along their grains, draws one out and pretends to sight it down the hall. It is Richard's, and Cam feels an urge to lift it from Splint's hands. Between his third and fourth fingers, the cigarette smolders, there under the finger playing the trigger. "Pow," Splint says.

She'd known she'd never stay with Eric, but Richard was just something that happened when she came home for Christmas. Fifteen minutes in Richard's dad's pickup behind the Moose, the windows fogged, and then Richard sat up with his jeans around his ankles and printed their names in the steam. Like a twelve-year-old girl, Cam thought at the time. Some little twelve-year-old girl. No, she never felt for Richard what she felt for Splint. She was so fresh back home she was still homesick and she just wanted to hear them talk, talk to her, it could have been any boy who talked that way. She ran into Richard that night. But Richard was a good boy and a hard worker, everybody said so. She could have done way worse; her mom made sure to remind her of this often. After a while, she wrote Eric in Phoenix. (Seventy-five, eighty miles an hour across that flat Oklahoma, Texas, New Mexico. Highways like grooves, and the land. She fixed that land, she remade it every night. She dreamed it green where it was brown, rumpled it where flat.) He wrote back once. Told her he always knew she'd end up with some redneck boy.

The second time she and Splint ran, they were thirteen. They met at the end of her road right around dawn, the hills smoking fog twists and a damp raw in the air. They flagged the Greyhound when it came, the Greyhound would pick you up anywhere back then, but although they'd had their sights set on North Carolina, the money Splint thieved off his older sister got them no farther than middle-of-nowhere Gormania. When the driver realized they'd ridden past how far they could pay, he threw them off at a mountaintop truck stop and told the cook to call the sheriff.

The deputy who showed up had only one ear. He phoned their parents with the receiver flat against the ear hole. It was Cam gave him the numbers, and Splint wouldn't speak to her for four weeks after. She remembers Splint all tough over his black coffee in that drafty restaurant, pretending Cam wasn't there. The waitress locking up the cigarette machine. The deputy told her how his ear got shot off stalking deer poachers, but after he left, the cook said his wife did it with sewing scissors. When Splint's dad appeared, three hours later, he, too, pretended Cam wasn't there. He jerked Splint to his feet and dragged him out behind the building while Cam slunk along the wall to watch. Splint slouched between the Stroehmann bread racks and raw kitchen slop. The scraggly garbage birds in a panic. But his father just looked at him and shook his head, then cussed him without imagination. The same two words, over and over, his voice flat as an idling motor. In the constant wind across the mountaintop, his father's coveralls flapped against his legs, making them look skinnier than they were. Finally he threw a milk crate at Splint. Splint caught it.

"I still think about you," Splint is saying again. He has put away the rifle and settles on the sofa, leaving her room which she doesn't take. He's trying to start something, but this time, she tells herself, she won't follow.

Richard always called it love. Ten years of late suppers and, even on weekends, him asleep in front of the TV by eight p.m. Two hours later, he'd wake and they'd shift to the bed, the brief bucking there. Afterwards, he'd sleep again, as sudden and as deep as if he'd been cold-cocked. Richard was a good boy and a hard worker. And now he's waited for two weeks, in his patient, plodding way, to be killed in a car wreck. That week's driver asleep at the wheel ten miles short of home after a day of dry walling.

Cam feels as tired as if she'd been awake for all her thirty years.

The first time she and Splint had run, they were twelve years old, at 4-H camp. The camp lay five miles back a dirt road where they hauled kids in school buses until the mountains opened into a sudden clearing along the river. Like a secret place. The county had turned 1950s chicken coops into bunkhouses and jammed them mattress to mattress with castoff iron beds, and Cam slept uneasy there under the screenless windows, the barn board flaps propped open for the little air. She had seen Splint at school, but this was the first time she noticed. And as she watched from a distance, she heard what was live in him like a dog might hear it. What was live in him, she heard a high-pitched whine. The beds in the coop were packed so close together she could feel on her cheeks the night breath of the girls on either side. And the whine a hot line from her almost-breasts to her navel.

On the last evening, they had a Sadie Hawkins shotgun wedding, where the girls were supposed to catch the boys. The counselors lined them up, the boys with a fifty-foot head start, then blew a whistle and turned them loose. Cam aimed at Splint. Splint knew she was after him, and he headed towards the river, where they were forbidden to go. All around Cam, big girls seized little squealy boys, older boys faked half-hearted escapes. Splint fled, but at twelve, Cam was his size, and as fast, and as strong. She saw him disappear in the tree line along the river, then she was dodging through trees herself, and she caught up with him on the rock bar there. Panting, but not yet spent, she reached out to grab him, but she scared, then just touched at him like playing tag. Splint was trotting backwards, bent in at the waist, dodging and laughing. They heard others following them to the river, heard them hollering through the trees. "Pretend you ain't caught me yet," Splint said.

He wheeled and sloshed into the river, high stepping until the water hit his hips, then he dropped on his stomach and struck out swimming. Cam, just as strong, as swift, right behind.

The far side had no shore to it, just an eroded mud bank. They hauled themselves up the exposed maple roots, and then they were in woods, they were hidden, alone. Cam was twelve years old, she thought she knew what to do. Splint grappled her back, too much teeth in the kiss, his hands in unlikely places. They rubbed at each other through their soaked clothes, serious and quick, and the threat of the others swimming the river pushed them faster.

Cam was finding her way, so absorbed it was like being asleep, when she realized Splint wasn't doing anything back. He rolled away from her into the weeds and sat up with his face between his knees, his thin back to her. Too naive to feel hurt, Cam crawled closer. She heard a strange little animal noise that made her want to pet. Finally, she understood Splint was crying.

Something taps her feet folded under her. Splint has rolled his jelly glass across the floor.

"Girl, if you don't talk to me, I'm going to do something drastic."

Cam looks at him. "What are you doing up here in the middle of the night without a coat?"

Splint laughs, soft. "Got into it with a girl driving home. She threw me out of her car." He rises off the sofa, leans down to open the stove door, and strips away his T-shirt. He stands fat in front of the fire, soaking heat in his skin.

Cam's all the time finding her own boy sketching pickup trucks and stock cars on notebook paper, oh, he is careful, detailed and neat. Until the very end. Then something breaks in him, unstops, and he turns violent and free. He gouges deep black lines behind the vehicles to show how fast they can go. When he was littler, and they still lived in Richard's parents' basement, he'd ride the back of the couch like a motorcycle, forcing air through his lips for the throttle. That he is not Richard's, she is almost sure, but he seems not Eric's either. Seems mothered and fathered by her and the place. She stands next to Splint now, following his stare in the fire. Without looking at her, Splint lifts her hand and presses it against his naked side.

"I'm not having sex with you," Cam says.

"That's not how come I'm here," says Splint.

He drops her hand and walks to the closet behind the front door. He pulls out a quilted flannel shirt of Richard's and buttons it on. Shoving aside the blaze-orange hunting jacket and coats that belong to Cam, he finally reaches the end of the rack and mutters.

"He's got his good one back in the bedroom," Cam says.

She finds the big Sunday coat. Splint takes it. Cam doesn't think about offering him a ride until after he's gone.

He got mad about the crying, screwed his fists in his eyes and muddied his face. Cam mumbled it didn't matter. By that time, counselors were yelling at them from across the water, how much trouble they were in if they didn't come right back. Cam stood up and Splint followed. They crept out of the trees and climbed down the bank without looking at the grownups. They waded out to thigh-deep and started paddling.

They pulled that water slow, kicked sloppy. They were putting off their punishment. Cam remembers the water still springtime cold a foot under the surface, this was June. The eyeball green of the river, and how you could see current only in the little bubble clusters gliding down its top. She swam a little behind Splint, her head about parallel with his stomach, and when she remembers back, she understands how young he was. Twelve, same as her, yes, but a boy-twelve, and she thinks of her own son and feels sad and shameful for how she did Splint.

Because she was so close to him as they swam, and because she couldn't help but look at him, and because the way they glided along cut the water clean—no foam to speak off, no wave—Cam saw clearly what happened next.

She saw Splint break his stroke to reach out and toss aside a floating stick. His legs frogged behind him. This was about the solstice, it was still very light, she could see. He reached out, not looking too closely, not paying attention. He was just moving a thing in his way. But when Splint grabbed hold the branch, Cam saw it liven in his fist and change shapes. She saw it spill water, jerk curvy in his hand. She saw it uncurl itself upright over Splint's head.

And was it a snake before he grabbed hold, or after he did? Cam used to wonder before she grew up. Now she only wonders why neither of them screamed.

Reprinted with permission of University Press of New England. Published in *Given Ground* (2000).

Ann Pancake: A Biographical Sketch

Ann Pancake is an award-winning writer and teacher with strong roots in West Virginia and a home on the West Coast. Her writing gives voice to an international perspective and a deep commitment to environmental justice.

Pancake was born in Richmond, Virginia, in 1963 while her father, whose family had strong roots in Hampshire County in West Virginia's eastern panhandle, was in seminary. Her mother grew up in Huntington in the northwestern part of the state. When Ann Pancake was three years old, her father was called to a Presbyterian church in Summersville, West Virginia. She remembers the sirens going off when she was five, alerting the community to the Hominy Falls mine disaster. Within a year, she recalls her father telling her that they were taking their last trip to Buck Garden because it was going to be strip mined, and she remembers repercussions from the sermon he preached against the practice. When she was eight years old, the family moved to Hampshire County where her father took a job at a community mental health center. She graduated from the county high school in Romney, by then the big sister to five younger siblings. In an interview with Robert Gipe, which appeared in the Winter/Spring 2011 issue of *Appalachian Journal,* she admits, "[W]e only got one channel on our TV. [. . .] [A]t the time us kids were all angry about it constantly, but in the long run, it definitely helped make me a writer."

In 1985 she graduated magna cum laude from West Virginia University with a BA in English, which yielded her a job as a manager at Wendy's. After teaching English in Japan for a couple of years, she landed in Albuquerque where she worked as a substitute teacher and took a creative writing course. Then she accepted a job at a community college in American Samoa. "Teaching in non-Western countries," Pancake declares, "was the most transformative experience of my life. Only from the perspective of living in a completely different culture was I able to perceive Appalachian culture as a unique culture. And distance from home and homesickness inspired me to start writing seriously about West Virginia."

In 1990 she returned again to the United States, this time to the University of North Carolina at Chapel Hill, where she earned an MA in 1992. She then taught at a college in northeast Thailand until 1993, when she enrolled in the PhD program in English literature at the University of Washington. Upon completing that degree in 1998, she joined the faculty at Penn State Behrend in Erie, Pennsylvania.

While in Pennsylvania, Pancake's first book, the story collection *Given Ground* (2001), was published and won the Bakeless Fiction Prize. Adept at winning writing awards and fellowships, Pancake was able, in 2002, to quit her teaching job. She moved to Charleston, West Virginia, to collaborate with her sister, Catherine, on *Black Diamonds,* a film about mountaintop removal coal mining. Pancake notes that "researching mountaintop removal and its effects on residents for my book and for my sister's film was the second most transformative experience of my life." Pancake was a recipient of a fifty-thousand-dollar Whiting Award in 2003, and, since 2004 she has taught in the low-residency MFA Program at Pacific Lutheran University, located on the southern perimeter of the Seattle metropolitan area. In 2007 Pancake's first novel, *Strange as the Weather Has Been,* appeared. It portrays a West Virginia community devastated by mountaintop removal mining and was a finalist for the Orion Book Award. "West Virginia's storytelling traditions, its rich language, and its bone-deep sense of place all shaped me as a writer," Pancake proclaims, and her readers will likely agree.

Ann Pancake: A Selective Bibliography

INTERNET RESOURCES

Willow Springs features a brief profile and a link to an extensive interview. The *Iowa Review* posted a review on Pancake's book *Strange as this Weather Has Been.* *Appalachian Journal* has an interview and biography titled "Straddling Two Worlds" on Pancake. Her personal blog features a bibliography of reviews. *Orion* posted an article written by Pancake, listing readings she recommends.

SELECTED BOOKS

Strange as This Weather Has Been. Berkeley, CA: Shoemaker and Hoard, 2007.

Given Ground. Hanover, NH: UP of New England, 2001.

LITERARY CRITICISM

Miller, Danny. Review of *Strange as the Weather Has Been,* by Ann Pancake. *Journal of Appalachian Studies* 13.1/2 (2007): 257–59.

Pendarvis, Jack. "Buried Alive." *New York Times Book Review* 14 Oct. 2007: 26.

Mark Powell

The Beauties of This Earth

In his first spring after the war, Walt Berger went home, home to see the old man, and home to rest. He had a bottle of Jim Beam between his thighs and his discharge papers in his sea bag. He sipped the coffee and topped it off with Jim Beam, and by the time he hit I-40, he was thinking of Leigh Ann, but was still sober enough to miss her exit north of Sevierville. He knew the old man was waiting.

Back home, he drove down Main Street, catching the first red light by the new Kawasaki dealership. ATVs, motorcycles, jet-skis, three-wheelers. The place was usually populated by men in caps and jeans, guys in Dickies and bib overalls with long goatees flowering down their throats, heads shaved and bolts driven through their noses. Berger had seen one with a series of three or four silver hoops embedded in his eyebrow, looked like a grizzly catfish with a beard of five-pound test lines. The place was quiet this morning, however, and he watched a giant American flag unfold itself in the breeze, then collapse down onto the pole.

Three blocks down, he passed the Otasco his granddaddy had managed for better than forty years. Town had changed in the last decade, he could see that. With the rich second-homers laying waste to the mountains came stores selling lawn sculptures and blown glass ornaments, solar lights to line walkways, paintings that looked like an infant had slung his peas and carrots against the wall. There was a store that sold nothing but flags, a thousand different flags bearings pineapples and watermelons and UT and ETSU logos. The Otasco had closed right after Home Depot opened on the bypass. There was no diner left, but a place selling hummus wraps. There were Mexican restaurants and three pizza joints, but nowhere besides Hardees to get a decent cup of coffee. A single feed and seed store down near the abandoned railroad tracks. The big fifty-pound bags stacked and plastic-wrapped on pallets. Dog food. Fish food. Sweet feed. He remembered climbing the loading dock as a boy, standing inside the high hangar-like expanse, going with the old man to buy feed or grass seed for whatever his granddaddy was working on at the time.

His granddaddy had been a Marine, joining in January of '42 when he was seventeen years old. By the time he was twenty he had made four amphibious assaults, suffered two Purple Hearts, and earned the Navy Cross. His granny was dead now, and all that was left besides the old man was a cousin living in Charlotte, working for a bank and running for the board of the PTA. His granddaddy, alone for years, drank too much and talked about the way they had died along the cliffs on Okinawa. Then he would pass out to dreams of Jesus Christ wading ashore at Guadalcanal, whisper in his sleep about Tarawa and Siapan, about dead Seabees and the nights sleeping in the cool insect mud. Now and then, he would drag out a box of photographs, gruff children in Marine fatigues, the blush of a three-day beard on a skinny nineteen year old as he shouldered his rifle across on some faraway moonscape.

The beagles bellowed and twisted around Berger's feet when he stepped out of his truck at home. He stood in the living room and imagined his granddaddy waking from his dreams. Christ wading ashore through the early mist off Siapan. His granddaddy's feet would be socked, and he would rise from the musty blankets of the couch to walk out onto the porch, testing the weather and his joints. It would be early, not yet daylight though moonlight might move cloud shadow across the open fields, the pasture land cropped as close as a shaved skull.

Berger saw his granddaddy running one foot forward until his sock caught against the head of an eight-penny nail, half-dreaming. Christ coming ashore at Siapan. Guadalcanal. Tarawa. The old man in the rocker, the thread of his sock pulling free of the nailhead just as a car goes up the road, pushing its lone head lamp so that the world is lit singly, a tree, a parked tractor, a pale footlight pushing a vapor of night fog. The highway ghost-lit and then not.

Berger knew well these solitary offices. The things his granddaddy never said.

Okinawa. Them cliffs above Okinawa, son. It got ugly there.

Berger had waited all his life for war.

He was on the porch when his granddaddy came home. The walls were lined with canning, kraut and green beans, corn and chow-chow, and the room smelled of dirt, cool and metallic. It was almost dusk, and the old man squinted when he looked at him.

"I figured on you flying down," he said. "Been quicker."

"Hey, papa."

"Seen your truck pass the store today. You go over and see Leigh Ann?"

Berger shook his head. "Not yet."

His granddaddy sat down and exhaled, motioned at Berger's glass eye.

"Your granny would be glad of it, that it come out like it did. She would have," he said. "But I ain't gonna sit here and lie to you, son."

They ate Hungry Man dinners heated in the microwave, then watched the last innings of the Braves-Dodgers game.

"I can take you on at the store if you like," his granddaddy said. He cut his country fried steak with his pocket knife. "Could use the help." He chewed, swallowed.

"I'm moving on, papa."

"That the plan, is it?"

"That's the plan, yessir."

In the morning Berger came out of his old room dressed in jeans and Tony Lama boots. His granddaddy was sitting at the kitchen table drinking coffee, looking ancient and veined.

"Getting on?" he asked.

"Soon enough."

"You ain't going over to see her?"

"I don't know," Berger said, though he did.

He left his granddaddy's and drove up Picket Post Road to Main Street, past the café, a squat block building ringed with pickups and sedans, past the new Arbys and the antique stores where old women stood on the sidewalk leaning on push-brooms and squinting against the morning sun that was just beginning to peak over the rust red buildings on the facing street. He took 441 and this time didn't miss the turn.

His house—her house, now—was in a subdivision south of Knoxville, a broad two-story of vinyl siding and new brick. They had hardly moved in before Berger had been deployed, and he saw now that in the intervening months she had done little or nothing in the way of upkeep. The driveway was still gravel, washboarded from over a year of rain and too much hard driving, ruts where tires had spun and slipped betraying her carelessness, betraying those late nights, Berger imagined, drinking margaritas with her boyfriend before driving home buzzed and foggy-headed. The yard was all mud and scattered straw, matted and rotting, up to an apron of dull yellowing grass: the sod Berger had laid just days before shipping out.

He had never understood but did now. Sitting in the driveway and looking at the house that rose from the ground like a tombstone, he understood the house was about *her* future, *her* plans. What happened at Balad, Iraq, had only given her an excuse, cover and commiseration from circles of sympathetic friends drinking Mai Tais in some crowded living room while HBO blared from the tube.

"I don't want the house in Fayetteville," she'd told him over the phone when he was in Walter Reed. They were officially separated by then, divorce in the offing, and he knew she had read a copy of the letter he had left, the one that began *What you see before you is the body of Captain Walter Berger.* He knew, too, that she knew what his granddaddy understood, what everyone understood: that at the moment to which his life had narrowed, the cold barrel at his temple, he had flinched.

"Take it," she told him. "I don't want it. Just leave me the new house. Don't contest anything, and I promise you can see Billy now and then." Walt had stood there in the corridor wearing his paper gown and watching the one-legged men wheel by, giving little nods as they passed. He had made the down payment with his reenlistment money. "Are you there? Walt?"

"I'm here."

"Well?"

"I don't want it either. The house."

"Fine then. We'll sell it."

"I want to see my son again, Leigh Ann."

Her sigh like wind singing along high-tension lines. "Just don't contest anything then and you can see him. Jesus—" It all seemed to amaze her. "Can you imagine if you actually did contest this? Be smart, Walt. Don't make this any worse."

He pulled beside her beige Civic and cut the engine. Beside him sat a Volvo wagon, a deep hunter green, and all-wheel drive, something sensible and middle class. The car belonged to her new boyfriend, Vance something. A schoolteacher, middle school math, if Berger remembered correctly. She had wasted no time moving from Fayetteville, finding a new job, a new body for the bed, a little heft to impress the mattress, someone to crawl onto when the urge struck.

Berger noticed the Christmas wreath was still up, withered and tacked to the front door, closer now to next Christmas than last. No lights were on in the house, though he imagined Billy was downstairs watching cartoons over a bowl of Cocoa-Puffs. They would have heard him grinding up the drive—he would have to tell her either to get it paved or smooth the goddamn thing out, one or the other—but maybe he could have a few minutes with his son.

Last time they had spoken had been on the phone, three weeks prior. His son talking about feeding the beta fish whose tank sat beneath the far window in his first grade classroom. *That's good, son. I'm proud. Now put your mamma on, all right.* She had sold the house in Fayetteville and had a check for him.

"Keep it," he told her.

"All right then. I will."

"Put it away for Billy."

"You don't have to tell me how to raise my child," she said. "Things are good for him right now. We don't have to fuck him up just because we fucked everything else up."

"You, Leigh Ann. I don't know who else you're talking about."

"Jesus—"

"I don't know who else you're talking about fucking things up besides yourself. This is what you wanted."

"I gotta go, Walt."

"I just want you to damn well remember that."

"Walt." This was her schoolteacher voice, the voice of the weary public servant, put-upon but patient. "You know I'm not the one who stood around while they murdered some poor kid."

He said nothing.

"I'm sorry you made me say that," she said.

Berger walked up the front steps to what should have been his house and moved along the windows, cupping his hands to the glass to see inside. No Billy. No one in the living room. The TV was off. No one in the kitchen. By the step sat several ceramic turtles, green and glassy-backed, and he flipped one after another before finding a dull brass key taped to a pale underbelly.

Inside, the house was still as silent prayer. He stood in the foyer looking up at the stairs, dust drifting through a span of light then collecting along the wooden balustrade like drifts of snow. He had hardly lived here long enough to know the place, a few long weekends driving over to check on progress, to bitch at the contractor or argue with Leigh Ann for cheaper bathroom fixtures. Hardware it was called, like it was something beside trinkets to impress the kind of people Berger despised, the safe ones, moderately wealthy and healthily fat, the ones who talked about their dental and whole life policies, the ones with model trains or ping-pong tables in their basements, the weekend joggers and internet pussies.

He walked into the kitchen.

The counters were empty, wiped clean and flashing spirals of silvered moisture. Plates and silverware stacked in the sink, a glass holding a thimble full of diluted red wine—little tremors feathering the surface— balanced atop the pile. Several glasses were cloudy with grainy solutions, one holding a spoon made grotesque, large and misshapen in the opaque liquid. He looked out the window to the eight-foot basketball goal that sat unevenly, the ball beyond it, faded orange and marooned in ankle-deep weeds the color of mustard. His breath spread on the window, silver and expanding, then retreated, faintly, erasing itself like a fingerprint. A little suction cupped thermometer. A potted cactus the size of a child's thumb. Taking stock of things, filing away images to pore over later so that he didn't hear her come in but somehow knew she was there. He was looking at the vague reflection of his face one moment then her figure the next. She stood leaning against the door in socks and a long flannel shirt that hung just above her knees.

"I didn't know you still had a key," she said.

He held up the brass key he'd found. "I don't. You should hide this better."

"Mostly I don't count on people snooping around."

"Well, you should. Married to a son of a bitch like me."

Her arms were crossed, and when she exhaled her body seemed to cave, shoulders collapsing forward, breasts sagging so that they rested on her pale forearms. He could see the hairline cracks fissuring out from her mouth and eyes.

"What are you doing here, Walt?" It was less question than exasperation, already tired, already ready to leave it, to walk. "You want some coffee?" she asked.

He turned back to the window.

"Yard looks like shit."

She opened the cabinet then shut it. "Move," she said, and filled the pot with water. "I don't know why you're here. I thought all this was done. I thought you were in Georgia or something."

"You don't know why I'm here?"

"That's what I just said."

"That statement makes absolutely no sense to me, Leigh Ann. Absolutely none."

She looked at him, those liquid brown eyes he remembered rolling over him once, their first date, taking a canoe down the Pigeon River in the middle of a terrible drought, the way she'd looked at him after they'd dragged the boat over tiny rocks scattered along the riverbed and were drifting in the warm waning light, the sun sinking slowly over the mountains.

"Jesus Christ, Walt. I wish you'd just get on."

He shook his head. "What is it you want here, Leigh Ann?"

"Please, Walt."

"In this house. With him. Just answer me. Why do you want this?"

She poured the water into the filter. "Why do I want this? Because someone had to. Someone had to make a life while you were off jumping out of airplanes and running all over the world. What can I tell you? That I didn't want my son raised by an absent father living out his adolescent fantasies while squatting in some goddamn third world jungle?"

"I squatted in those jungles for you. Every fucking one of them."

"Keep your voice down, please."

"Why?" he asked. He motioned up with his head. "So we won't wake him. What's his name? Vancc, isn't it."

"He's trying to stay out of this," she said quieter.

From upstairs came the sound of footsteps, water rushing through pipes.

"Is that him?" Berger's eyes were still cast up at the ceiling.

"Yeah, that's him."

"The new me."

She shook her head. "No," she said. "That's just the point: he's not you." She took two cups from the sink and rinsed them, shook out the water and filled each with coffee.

"You can't get him to do anything about the yard? Sow some grass or something."

"Drink some coffee, Walt," she said. "And then leave."

He took the cup and sniffed it. "He won't come down?"

"He wants to respect my privacy."

"He's afraid of me. Afraid I'll tear his fat head off."

She looked up from the cup she held with both hands, sleeves having slid almost to her fingertips. "Would you?"

He turned back to the window. He was watching the leaves trembling with the breeze, their undersides translucent and veined. One floated free to drift down, swirling for a moment before coming to rest in the mud yard amid the bits of straw that stirred with the wind, a quiet rustle he imagined but could not hear.

"Billy's at your mother's I take it," he said.

That exasperation in her voice again, beneath the tongue, behind the teeth, veiled poorly as she spoke slowly, as if to a child: "We stayed out later than I planned. He was already over there. He's fine."

"Does Vance sleep over when Billy's home?"

"Sometimes. Sometimes, yes."

"Fuck, Leigh Ann."

"You know I still have a life, Walt. I want to have a life, at least."

"That's the idea is it, a life."

"Generally. Yeah."

He turned from the window. She had approached him but shrank back now, pressing the small of her back against the island centered in the kitchen.

From the window fell clear light, eerily transparent light he felt moving along the bare nape of his neck.

"You know we're still married," he said.

"Walt."

"Technically," he said. "In the eyes of the state of North Carolina we are still technically married, Leigh Ann."

She shook her head slowly and with great attendance. "Oh, Walt," she said. "Poor Walt."

He tossed his coffee into the sink and set his cup there.

"Well, how about you tell Mister Vance I said good morning, why don't you. Tell him I hope he enjoys sleeping under the roof I'm still fucking paying for."

She followed him out of the kitchen into the foyer. "Don't you go over there, Walt. She knows not to let you see him."

He spun on her and she jumped back, a little wave of coffee splashing from her cup onto the hardwood floor in the narrowing space between them.

"Not to let me see my own son, you mean?"

"That's exactly right," she said. "At least—"

"At least what, Leigh Ann?" He was yelling now. "At least fucking what?" Her voice like that whisper of knowing: "At least not until things are better. All right?"

He threw his head into his hands. "Fuck," he said. "Fuck, fuck, fuck."

"Walt—"

"Fuck, Leigh Ann."

A voice floated down from upstairs. "Everything OK, honey?" Berger's eyes flared and Leigh Ann looked at him, shaking her head, willing him to silence there in the laddered sun splitting the blinds. "You tell him—"

She cut him off. "Fine. Everything's fine. Come out here," she said to Berger, hustling him onto the porch where the Christmas wreath still hung.

"My fucking house, Leigh Ann."

"Please."

"My fucking house."

She pulled her shirt tighter around her. "Please, Walt. Just go."

They stood for a moment. The wind gusted and a shudder of leaves showered across the yard, catching against the gutter then sailing free to cyclone down at their feet.

"Please," she said.

He stood there shaking his head. "Yard looks like shit," he said.

"I know."

"Just get him to sow some grass or something, all right? Looks just awful. You want to impress the neighbors, and this won't impress anybody."

"I know. Please just go, Walt."

It was dusk by the time he got back to his granddaddy's.

He took a bottle of J&B and walked onto the porch where moths batted around the porch light. The beagles slept around his feet. He swallowed as much J&B as possible, and then took another drink, not stopping until he felt it hammering through his brain and he was back again.

They had found the boy along a service road beneath a highway overpass in Balad, Iraq. Seven months into his tour. Berger was riding along with a patrol when the call came. Second Platoon had found the boy crawling around under the bridge pilings and chased him out. Now he was by the river, fifteen or so, the sergeant with his flashlight in his face and the boy down on his knees. He wouldn't stop praying. It was almost one a.m., hours after curfew, and Berger could see the pale soles of his bare feet tucked up beneath his legs as he muttered to Allah.

"Said he was headed home, didn't know how late it was," the sergeant said. He shook his head. "It's way too late for that, sir."

"Fucking A," said one of the soldiers, his voice cracking.

Berger looked at the soldier who had spoken and saw that his eyes appeared to be vibrating.

"Shut up, Michaels," said the sergeant.

The Iraqi boy kept praying, prostrate, hands extended and upturned, empty and waiting, as if they might yet be filled with the spirit. Berger could see the rings of hair that grew along the nape of his neck. He followed the boy's motion, the narrow back, the long arms that turned to delicate fingers.

"You find anything under the pilings?" Berger asked. The sergeant shook his head.

"No, sir. Not yet."

"That's the bridge where them fuckers killed Teddy."

"I said to shut it, Michaels."

Berger smelled the water, the tang of mud and diesel, the surface scummed with foam and trash, dark water, dirty sewer water like something out of a childhood nightmare. The boy kept praying.

"He was all up in under the stanchions climbing around, sir. All up in under. There's only one thing you're doing up there."

"Fucking *hajjis* casing the place."

The sergeant told Michaels to shut up.

Berger washed his hands of it, that's what he said: I wash my hands of this, sergeant. You deal with it. Like Pilate, he thought, the decision that is no decision, and was halfway back up to the road when he heard the shot. The splash—he never heard the splash. Just kept walking.

At the inquiry, he had sat in his Class A's, creases sharp and medals shining, looked down to see his warped face in the curve of his leathers, smell the starch in his clothes. Turned over for psychiatric evaluation. Case pending. When they sent him back to his post to collect his things, he took the pistol from behind loose paneling. The letter he had already written. He spread it before him along with his identity card and driver's license and next of kin contact information, and wondered about the boy's body floating down the river, catching somewhere, perhaps, in the reeds, or in some fisherman's tangled net. Then he thought of his wife and son.

You know I'm not the one who stood around while they murdered some poor kid.

In the morning Berger woke early, swallowed five BC headache powders, and struck out into the woods toward Sevenmile Creek. He had heard gunshots just before first light and thought someone might have been firing at one of the black bears that rooted their way through garbage cans. The beagles were already running, so he walked alone, shafts of sunlight falling through the trees and shaping a cathedral of sorts, backlighting the purple ginger and blue bellflowers that bloomed from the decomposing remains of a nurse log. When he met the creek, he followed it downstream, morning light glimmering along its surface, until he found a small cairn of stones balanced delicately atop a rock in the center of a still pool.

It was there he picked up the first swatches of blood, following them into a laurel thicket where bedded in the cool earth he found a buck lying on its side, its back hip blasted open. A gout of blood had dried, crusting the surrounding fur and turning the dirt wine-dark. The deer breathed heavily and slowly, struggling to raise its head and turn one glassy eye on Berger before lowering it again to exhale into the dust. Berger stepped closer and saw a large Wolf Spider legging its way toward the buck's eye.

He walked straight back to his granddaddy's house and found the old man sitting at the kitchen table drinking coffee from the metal cup of a Stanley Thermos. Berger sat across from him and put his hands on the table.

"Looks like I might stay maybe a little longer than I expected," he said. His granddaddy nodded. "I reckoned you'd see her sooner or later." Berger said nothing.

"You own it now," his granddaddy said. "If that hadn't occurred to you yet it will soon enough."

He stood, staggering his way to the cabinet, and Berger saw then he had been staring down at a wallet-sized sepia portrait of Berger's grandmother. He came back to the table with two glasses and a bottle of twelve-year old Macallan's scotch, pouring them each a glass.

"Every time I drink this I start to cry," his granddaddy said after a few minutes. "The beauties of this earth."

"The wonders," Berger said.

His granddaddy took a long swallow. "The goddamn wonders, indeed."

Reprinted with permission of Mark Powell. Published in *Appalachian Heritage* 38.1 (Winter 2010).

Mark Powell: A Biographical Sketch

Mark Powell is a young writer from the "dark corner" of South Carolina where the Blue Ridge Mountains dip down from the north descending spectacularly into the state's northwestern corner. His first three novels have established him as a major contemporary chronicler of mountain life. His work elicits feelings of stark recognition for its verisimilitude to sometimes harsh realities. It has a strong sense of place and great narrative force that does not spare violence, often counterbalanced by redemption. Powell has said, "Life is violent and terrible, but it's also comprised of moments of amazing beauty, and I lack the ability to render it in any other form."

Mark Powell was born in 1976 in Mountain Rest, South Carolina, into a family whose roots in Oconee County go back at least to the early nineteenth century. His family is known for its strong military ties, so the Citadel, South Carolina's military college, was a natural choice for him. There, Powell ran track and cross country and graduated with an English major in 1997. The next year he started an MFA program at the University of South Carolina, graduating in 2001. While there he married Denise Frasier and finished his first novel, *Prodigals,* which was published by the University of Tennessee Press the very next year. This qualified him for visiting writer positions at five different universities over the next six years. In 2004 Powell garnered fellowships from both the prestigious Breadloaf Writers Conference and the National Endowment for the Arts. The next year, his novel *Blood Kin* won the Peter Taylor Prize, judged by distinguished novelist Jill McCorkle, and he was invited for the first time to teach at the Appalachian Writers Workshop at the Hindman Settlement School in eastern Kentucky. Powell credits Silas House and Ron Rash, fellow Hindman faculty, as mentors who have ably assisted his literary career. After a Playwriting Fellowship to Prague in the Czech Republic in 2005, Powell enrolled at Yale's Divinity School. He finished there in 2007 with an MA in religion and literature. In 2008 Powell landed his current job on the faculty at Stetson College in Florida, and his son, Silas, was born. The next year he won the Chaffin Award for Contributions to Appalachian Literature given by Morehead State University in Kentucky, and in 2010 Powell was granted a fellowship to the Collegeville Institute for Ecumenical and Cultural Research. The following year, a daughter, Merritt, arrived. His fourth novel, *The Dark Corner,* published by the University of Tennessee Press in 2012, is set in his home county and chronicles the rise of an extremist right-wing militia group.

Mark Powell is a young man with a strong physique yet a disarming smile and convivial way. He has a penchant for being helpful in any way he can.

Powell is intensely proud of his young family, and has a reputation for being an extraordinary writing teacher. His literary career is certainly off to an auspicious start.

Mark Powell: A Selective Bibliography

INTERNET RESOURCES

Mason's Road, a literary and arts journal, features the short story "The Eye of a Needle." The personal blog of Charles Dodd White features an interview with Powell on themes in his writing, his shift in language style, and his literary influences.

SELECTED BOOKS

The Dark Corner. Knoxville: U of Tennessee P, 2012.
Blood Kin. Knoxville: U of Tennessee P, 2006.
Prodigals. Knoxville: U of Tennessee P, 2002.

LITERARY CRITICISM

Brosi, George, ed. *Appalachian Heritage* 40.1 (2012). Features Mark Powell.
Clabough, Casey. Review of *Blood Kin. Appalachian Heritage* 35.2 (Spring 2007): 91–93.

Lee Smith

Ultima Thule

"You'll remember to get the Thule put on top of the Volvo, then?" On his way over to the university, Jake turns back to ask her. "And make sure the key works?" He hands her this little bitty key.

"Sure," Nova says, rubbing her eyes, wearing a black number three muscle shirt that used to be her brother's, and nothing else. She knows she can get Theron to do it. "The drug boys are coming today," she says, and Jake nods. He is on the board of Agape, the residential drug treatment program which runs the landscaping and lawn care business that comes to work at their little farm outside Charlottesville, which is not really a farm, any more than they are really farmers, or Jake is an average graduate student, or they are a regular young couple just trying to make ends meet.

No. The big surprise is that Jake has turned out to belong to a very rich family, rich enough to own an entire island in Maine, for instance, which is where they are heading tomorrow morning at the crack of dawn in the Volvo with the Thule on top of it like an enormous coffin filled with their clothes because the dogs will be taking up all the space in the car—Thor, Jake's old black lab, in the backseat, and Odin, the big husky pup, in the back-back. Everybody in Jake's family owns big dogs that wear bandannas and go to Maine. Nova has been there once, last year, when she and Jake had just gotten married.

Everybody in Jake's family called her "The Bride" in a tongue-in-cheek way that made her nervous at first, until she figured out that's just how they all talk, like they are putting quotation marks around everything. Nova recognizes irony, which is what Mrs. Stevenson, her senior English teacher, defined as, "Irony is when the fire chief's house burns down." Part of the irony in calling her "The Bride" came from the fact that Nova was already pregnant, she knew this, too.

"No, this is great, this is awesome, this is seriously great." Jake's brother had assured her in Maine. "We always figured he was gay."

Now Jake blows her a kiss from the yard before he drives off in his old truck. Nova has never known a man before who would blow anybody a kiss, ever, under any circumstances. She rubs her flat stomach, fingering the navel ring. Jake took pictures of her pregnancy, every few days. He used rolls and rolls of film. She lost that baby at five and a half months, and it was a girl, they said. Nova had wanted a girl, she would have taken such good care of it, not like her own mother at all. Nova and Jake had already bought a crib, and gotten Agape to paint the extra bedroom tangerine, her idea. Nova has plenty of ideas, she is not dumb at all. Jake has made her realize this. Now they have closed the door to the little tangerine room, until later.

Good thing they've got these two dogs, which keep her busy, sort of. Nova likes the dogs, but she did not like Maine, an entire state that smells like Pine-Sol, especially Blueberry Island, a very cold and foggy place that is far away from everything, especially the grocery store. Nova does like to cook and it drove her crazy not to be able to go to the grocery store every day, which is what she likes to do at home. Also, the water will freeze your ass off, and the grocery store does not even carry grits. Also, there is no TV on Blueberry Island, something Jake forgot to mention in all the times he talked about the island like it was paradise. The only positive thing was that all the Maine women turned out to be big and ugly, almost as if they were doing it on purpose, so this made Nova look like a beauty queen. You should see these women! Nobody wears any makeup or nice clothes. Their hair sticks out on one side and looks awful. This is also true of Jake's mother and sisters, at least in the summertime. Nova does not know if they look any better during the rest of the year or not.

She and Jake did not go up to Connecticut for Christmas, although they were invited, because this is when Nova lost the baby and had to spend several days in the University of Virginia Hospital, very ironic considering that is where she and Jake first met, though Jake was over in Neurosciences and she was working the cash register in the snack bar on the first floor. Jake had been in the hospital for three months when she met him; this is why he had a blue badge and was allowed to come down to the first floor unsupervised. Later he would get a town pass, and still later a day pass that would allow him to take her to the Boars Head Inn and fuck her eyes out. Yes! His brothers would have been so surprised. Nova had never been to the Boars Head Inn before, although she had lived outside Charlottesville all her life. Their room had a sixty-inch TV hidden away inside an antique hutch, she was so surprised. Also a minibar.

Nova had noticed Jake right away because he was so thin. Most of the mental patients are real fat, it is due to their medications. Jake was also sweet, not usually true of doctors or patients either one. The day they met, he was standing patiently in line behind that heavy woman with the big blonde hairdo growing out black at the roots who was so pushy and bought the same thing every day, a cheeseburger and fries and strawberry shortcake, and had a fit whenever they didn't have the strawberry shortcake. That day she forgot her money. When Nova handed her the little piece of paper, she started to cry. The woman had a black mustache, which drove Nova crazy, Nova has got sort of an obsession about facial hair. Maybe she should slip this woman some Nair. "Just go on," Nova told her, looking all around first. "You can pay me tomorrow."

"Oh no . . . I . . ." The woman began to flap her hands.

"Here. Keep the change," Jake said, popping up behind the woman, handing over a ten-dollar bill.

"I'm not allowed to do that," Nova said as the woman started to cry.

"Just add my bill onto hers, then," Jake said.

The woman cried louder, big sobs coming up out of her cleavage.

"Here now, ma'am." He took the woman by the elbow and steered her over to a table, pulling out a chair for her.

Nova rang up the woman's food again, along with three little bowls of macaroni and cheese, and coffee. "That's not a very balanced meal," she said to him when he came back.

"Well." Jake grinned at her. "I'm not a very balanced man. I'm crazy."

"What's your diagnosis?" Nova knew she wasn't supposed to ask.

"Life," he said. "What's your name?"

"Nova," she said. "Named for the car, not the star. My mother got pregnant at a drive-in."

Nova thought he looked like one of those cornhusk dolls her granny used to make, with thin, thin corn silk hair flopping onto his face and a long thin stick nose and big even teeth like a row of corn on the cob and beautiful huge blue eyes like lakes, swimming behind his thick glasses. Or she was swimming in his eyes, that's more like it. Suddenly Nova became very critical of Raymond Crabtree who had given her this job for certain considerations, he had steel blue jaws by five o'clock, and lived for *Monday Night Football*.

"You don't seem very crazy to me," Nova heard herself say, though really he was so thin and pale, he was not her type at all.

"I guess you'll have to get to know me, then," Jake said, and so she did, and still he never did seem very crazy to her, only too sensitive for this world. Jake used to be a rock musician and play in bands, she learned, but now he was a graduate student in American Studies. He used to do a lot of drugs, but now he does oral histories with people such as lobster fishermen in Maine and the drug boys who work for Agape. He has already taped Theron.

The first time Nova went up to visit Jake in the third-floor dayroom in Neurosciences, a skinny blonde woman came over and hugged him and turned to Nova and told her, "You may not know it, but this is Jesus Christ."

"Wow," Nova said.

"All the girls say that," Jake said.

Jake played Pachelbel's "Canon in D Major" and "Bridge over Troubled Water" for Nova on the piano they had brought into the dayroom for him. Nova started to visit him every afternoon when she got off lunch duty, and one time when she was up there, this little old black man went over and leaned against the piano and started scat-singing along when Jake was playing blues. "I was born down in Savannah," he sang, "under an ugly star." Nurses and aides and other patients gathered around to hear him; this little man had not said a single word since he had been admitted to the hospital months before. Nobody knew who he was or where he had come from or anything of his history. They wrote it down as he sang it, accompanied by Jake.

When Jake got out of the hospital, Nova moved out to his weird house in the country with him. Raymond Crabtree was mad at her now, so she couldn't afford her apartment anymore, but she didn't tell Jake that, and it didn't matter anyway, because by then she was pregnant.

"Honey, if I was you I'd make a good thing of this," Nova's mother said, smoking a cigarette, when Nova went to ask her for money at the dry cleaners where she worked. "You're crazy if you don't." Of course Nova's mother didn't have any money anyway.

And really, Jake was so happy when she told him, and so sweet, he was putty in Nova's hands. She told him she didn't believe in abortion. They got married at the big courthouse downtown. Nova wore a beautiful midcalf flowered dress with a low lacy neckline, while Jake wore some old army pants and a tux jacket. By then she was catching on to how rich people will wear just any old thing. The witnesses at their wedding were a courthouse secretary named Alice Robinson and a black prostitute named Shawndra Day who had been sitting out in the hall waiting to see her court-appointed attorney. Then Jake took Nova down to Richmond for a night in the Jefferson Hotel with its crocodile sculpture and its great dome of stained glass in the lobby like a cathedral, the closest Nova has ever been to one.

When they got back to Charlottesville, there was *his* mother, leaning up against her car parked beside the mailbox. Her car was a navy blue Mercedes with smoked windows, you couldn't tell if she had a driver or anybody else in there with her or not. Jake's mother has dyed red hair and anorexia nervosa even at her age, Nova could tell right off. She recognizes a mental illness when she sees one. Jake's mother's name is Barbara.

Jake got out of the car and Barbara ran over to fling her arms around him dramatically, like a person in a movie. "I can't believe you would do this to me," she sobbed. Jake patted her while extricating himself as best he could, motioning for Nova to get out of the Volvo, "Barbara," he said, "here she is. This is Nova." But Barbara cut loose again and would not even look at her. *Well fuck this,* Nova thought, standing there.

Then the driver's side door of the blue Mercedes opened and Jake's father got out, a horsey-looking man in khaki pants and a pale blue denim shirt. He came over and took both of Nova's hands in his, looking into her eyes in a way that made Nova trust him immediately, as well as feel sort of bad about herself. "Welcome to the family, dear," he said.

"Won't you come in?" Nova said.

"No," said Barbara.

"Sure," said Mr. Valentine.

They had ginger ale and stale cookies and strained conversation, with Barbara sniffling on the old truck seat that served as a sofa, looking all around the crazy living room. "Folk art," Jake explained as his mother took in the old signs and homemade art on the walls, and the chain-saw angel, and the barber's chair that Mr. Valentine was sitting in. Nova went along with Barbara on this. She could not understand why anybody wouldn't have nice comfortable furniture if they could afford it. She hates that chainsaw angel. Nova said she wasn't feeling well and excused herself. So they didn't know that she was standing right there in the overgrown grape arbor when they left, that she saw Mr. Valentine poke Jake in the side and say, "Way to go!" as Jake turned to leave, or that she heard Barbara say, "I don't like her," when he was out of earshot. "At least he's not gay," Mr. Valentine said as he got in the car.

Now Jake's parents are already in Maine, on the island, with a cook and a housekeeper and a "man" who live in little log cabins out in the piney woods and do everything for them. Nova stands at the screen door and thinks about everything she has got to do to get ready for the trip, besides getting Theron and his boys to put the Thule on top of the Volvo, that's the least of it. Nova does not see why she can't have decent help instead of drug addicts and crazy people, why they can't have a nice house, why they have to go back to the land. Nova would like to get away from the land! She doesn't understand why they have to go to Maine instead of Hilton Head Island, which is where anybody in their right mind who could afford it would surely go.

But now Nova has got to clean out the refrigerator and wash a load of clothes and go in to town to buy more dog food and sign that little thing in the post office that will cancel their mail delivery while they are gone, though she never gets any mail anyway except stuff from the community college now that Jake has signed her up to take some courses in the fall. She has got to read *The Scarlet Letter* first, which looks awful. Mrs. Stevenson used to want her to go to college too, but then Nova ran off with her mother's boyfriend's brother, a disc jockey from Columbia, South Carolina, ending up in Myrtle Beach doing some things that did not require a degree of any kind. Nova runs her finger along the screen door, she knows she's procrastinating. Actually procrastinating was a word on the GED that Nova just did so well on.

Then beyond the mailbox and the meadow she sees a rising plume of dust so she runs back into their bedroom and pulls on some cutoffs and puts on that red halter top and some red lipstick and ties her hair up into a high swingy ponytail on top of her head. She's back at the screen door by the time Theron jumps out of his jeep, looking like an ad for something. Anything! Theron has gray eyes and the most beautiful legs and a café au lait complexion. He says he is Hawaiian but Nova knows he is not. Theron stands for a minute outside the door, peering in.

"Where is everybody?" Nova asks, meaning the rest of the Agape yard crew.

"Taco Bell." Theron unbuttons his shirt.

Nova is naked by the time they hit the bedroom.

Afterward, they share a joint in the unmade bed. Since hiring Agape, Nova has had them clear the meadow and make a stone path out to the old spring-house in the woods that Jake uses for his photography studio. Now she has just decided to make a rock garden out front, on the side of that little hill by the mailbox. It will be a lot of work. Nova smiles, lying flat on her back with her feet up against the wall.

"What you call that thing you want me to put on the car?" Theron is already up, pulling on his pants.

"Thule," she says.

"Funny name." Theron sits back down on the side of the bed to lace up his work boots.

"I thought it was a brand name, but Jake says it means some mythical northern country;" Nova says dreamily in that dreamy way she always feels after sex, thinking *Thule, Yule, Thor, Odin,* all of these words that Theron does not and will never know. Thule. It sounds like a kingdom of the olden days. Still he's gorgeous, those big brown arms.

"Hey babe, you know something?" Now he turns to look at her, he pinches her nipple.

"What." It's hot in the bedroom. A bee buzzes against the screen.

"Well, I been thinking." Now he seems hesitant, for Theron. Usually Theron is right up front. "You know, it wouldn't be too hard for you and me to, you know, do something about Jake. If that's what you wanted me to do, I mean."

Suddenly the whole room goes completely still, like it has turned into a black and white photograph. The air gets thick and hard to breathe.

Nova sits up. "What did you say?" she says.

"You and me, we could, you know." Theron grins at her.

She looks out the window and down the meadow to the road where she sees the dust, which means that Agape is coming up the hill in that old panel truck.

"Hey now, you know, I didn't mean nothing by it." Theron is on his feet, ready to go, smiling at her.

Nova smiles back. "Well, that's good, then."

Maybe that rock garden is not such a good idea, she thinks later, watching Theron lift the Thule like it's nothing. He and his boys attach it securely to the racks on the top of the Volvo. Then they start up their regular mowing and weed eating like crazy. Nova knows they do a lot of unnecessary work out here because they need the money. She doesn't blame them a bit. While they work, she cleans out the refrigerator and finishes the wash and packs her own suitcase, but he knows she can't leave the farm until Agape leaves first, because they will steal something. Of course they will. And why not? They are the underclass, a word she learned last week when she went over to the university with Jake for the opening of that photography exhibit he's in, "The Mind's Eye."

The next morning Nova has to work like an animal because Jake is so disorganized. He forgot to give her the clothes he wanted her to wash, he forgot to pick up his medicine from the pharmacy or the dogs' heartworm pills from the vet, so she has to drive into town to get all this stuff. When she gets back the clothes are dry. They fold them together and then she climbs up on the stepstool and puts them into the Thule as Jake hands them up to her, one item after another in the blazing midday sun, then his tennis racket and his wet suit and all the books and equipment he will need for his various projects—his tripod, his printer, his tape recorder, whatever. Jake makes a huge production about packing everything just so. Nova feels like hitting him, but instead she smiles brightly and says, "Ready?" and Jake reaches up to hug her and says yes, he guesses so. He whistles for the dogs who have been circling the Volvo warily, like fish. He puts Thor into the backseat and opens the back-back door for Odin who will ride behind the pet gate next to Nova's suitcase. Odin jumps in. Jake slams the door.

"Okay, lock it," he calls up to Nova who is getting this god-awful headache now up on this stepstool so close to the sun.

She sticks the little key into the little lock and tries to turn it, but it won't turn. Shit. That's the one thing she forgot to do yesterday, check the goddamn key. But what is she supposed to be anyway, a goddamn hired hand? But she'll have to tell him, won't she? Won't she? Won't they have to go get some bungee cords or something? Nova turns, shielding her eyes from the sun, but now Jake has disappeared back into the house. He comes out waving *The Scarlet Letter.* "Hey! You almost forgot this!" he yells. He tosses it into the front seat. Like Nova is really going to read *The Scarlet Letter* on this trip. Shit! She's not a hired hand, she's a project.

For the second time that day, Nova has the sense that time has stopped, that she is in one of Jake's photographs. She looks out at the rolling meadow and the little stone farmhouse and the blue line of mountains beyond, where she grew up. She jumps down lightly. When Jake hugs her, she can feel all his ribs.

"Ready?" he says.

She gets in the car.

The next morning, they are on Interstate 81 outside of Chambersburg, Pennsylvania, when the top of the Thule pops up and Jake's clothes start flying out, slowly at first, like something in a dream, scattering all over the interstate behind them. Strangely enough, Nova sees the whole thing, entirely by chance, because she has pulled the passenger-side mirror down to tweeze her face a little bit, those chin hairs. So she just happens to see Jake's red and black checkered L.L. Bean wool shirt out of the corner of her eye as it sails lazily through the air to land on the windshield of a red Chevy Blazer two cars behind them blinding the driver only momentarily but long enough to make her swerve back and forth, back and forth, in larger and larger arcs, the Blazer rocks now until it runs off the road into the median hitting one of those great big rocks like you find in Pennsylvania. Nova puts the tweezers back into her makeup case, which she puts back into her purse. She doesn't say one word to Jake but turns in her seat to watch as his clothes fly through the air faster and faster and all the cars behind them begin to weave and then there's a rattling sound from the top of the Volvo as his printer busts loose to land squarely on the hood of the Subaru wagon just behind them, and his tennis racket bounces off the hood of the little yellow Acura breaking the window and causing the Acura to veer into a silver pickup in the other lane, which hits a Jeep Cherokee, which explodes.

All the cars are running into each other now, out of their nice white lines, crumpling like toy cars. Smoke rises into the sunny air. The dogs start barking.

The Cherokee is burning. Now a Mustang convertible, which has slammed into it, is burning too.

Nova knows this is all her fault.

"Oh no! Oh my God! Oh shit!" Now Jake sees it too, he drives right off the road, they are bumping along over big old rocks and then they are in the trees.

Nova never, ever told. She left Jake, who really was too sensitive for this world. She heard he's been dead for a couple of years now. That day on I-81 has come to seem like a film to her, a DVD that she can play at will in her mind's eye, slow or fast, more vivid than anything else in her life before or since. Nova has never made a good thing out of anything, but she's done all right. She gets along okay. They never got to Maine, of course, after the accident, and Nova has never gotten there since. She thinks about it sometimes, though, and it seems so far away to her now, like another country, the country of Thule perhaps with its piney smell and its pointed trees and the freezing water in Blueberry Lake and they are all still there, Jake's whole family and all their dogs and Jake himself, she can still see his swimming blue eyes right now, Lord he was sweet.

Reprinted with permission of Lee Smith. Published in *Southern Review* 43.1 (Winter 2007).

Lee Smith: A Biographical Sketch

Lee Smith is a vivacious and energetic people person. Her quick smile and sporadic giggles simply fill up any room she occupies. She has risen to the pinnacle of the literary profession with her uncanny ability to surprise readers with the depth that hides in the creases of her thoroughly enjoyable storytelling.

When Lee Smith was born in 1944 in Grundy, Virginia, her mother, who was raised across the state in Chincoteague Island, was teaching home economics, and her father, whose family had lived around Grundy for generations, was serving in the U.S. Navy in New Guinea. When he returned, he took over the Ben Franklin Dime Store and later acquired Grundy's Piggly Wiggly grocery. Lee Smith says, "I was raised to get out. My family wanted me to have advantages that were elsewhere." Her parents sent her each summer to visit her Aunt Gay-Gay in Birmingham and her Aunt Millie in Richmond. Smith decided she wanted to become a writer at age nine, the year after she had written a story whose characters, Adlai Stevenson and Jane Russell, had fallen in love and gone out West in a covered wagon to become Mormons. By the time Lee was in high school, her uncle, Vern Smith, was serving in the state legislature in Richmond, so her family sent her there to attend St. Catherine's for her last two years. Then she enrolled at Hollins College, where she roomed with Annie Dillard, who would later receive a Pulitzer Prize for her book *Pilgrim at Tinker Creek.* Working part-time during the school year and full-time in the summers, Lee Smith became a promising journalist for the *Richmond News Leader,* and she had published her first novel, *The Last Day the Dogbushes Bloomed* (1968). After graduating from Hollins, Smith married the poet James Seay, and they moved to Lexington, Virginia, where he taught English at Washington and Lee University and she taught high school French. The next year Seay had a job at the University of Alabama, and Smith worked for the *Tuscaloosa News* while continuing to write and publish novels. In the mid-seventies, Seay moved to Vanderbilt University, and Smith taught at a private girls' school in Nashville.

"The farther I got away from home," Smith says, "the more I realized that the best stories came from my mountain background." While living in Nashville, after her thirtieth birthday, she started to collect diaries and histories from home and to tape record as many of her relatives as she could. In 1976 Seay was hired by the University of North Carolina in Chapel Hill. The couple's divorce was finalized the next year, but Smith remained in the area and taught at Carolina Friends School, UNC Chapel Hill, and North Carolina State University. Smith's first book to be set in the mountains, *Black Mountain Breakdown,* was published in 1980. The year Smith published her third mountain novel, 1985, she married Hal Crowther, a columnist for the *Spectator,* a magazine of the arts. *Fair and Tender Ladies* (1988) was published before Smith retired from NCSU in 1989. Two story collections and three novels followed in the 1990s, and two more novels, including the *New York Times* best seller *The Last Girls,* were published before the story collection *Mrs. Darcy and the Blue-Eyed Stranger* was released in 2010.

Lee Smith: A Selective Bibliography

INTERNET RESOURCES

Smith's website features extensive information regarding her works, including brief reviews of all her books, an interview, a personal biographical statement, and articles written on her life and works from sources such as the *New York Times* and the *Independent Weekly. Southern Environmental Law Center* features a brief video interview with Smith on southern writers. *Faith and Leadership* gives an insightful interview with Smith titled "A Lifetime of Paying Attention." *Wired for Books* has two audio recordings of interviews that are about thirty minutes long. *Indie Bound* features an interview discussing storytelling today, characters in her books, and the use of memory in fiction writing.

SELECTED BOOKS

Mrs. Darcy and the Blue-Eyed Stranger: New and Selected Stories. Chapel Hill, NC: Algonquin, 2011.

On Agate Hill. Chapel Hill, NC: Algonquin, 2006.

Saving Grace. New York: Putnam, 1995.

The Devil's Dream. New York: Putnam, 1992.

Fair and Tender Ladies. New York: Putnam, 1988.

Oral History. New York: Putnam, 1983.

Black Mountain Breakdown. New York: Putnam, 1980.

PROFILES/INTERVIEWS

Cook, Linda Byrd. "A Spiritual Journey: An Interview with Lee Smith." *Southern Quarterly* 47.1 (2009): 74–103.

Parrish, Nancy C. *Lee Smith, Annie Dillard, and the Hollins Group: A Genesis of Writers.* Southern Literary Studies. Baton Rouge: Louisiana State UP, 1998.

Tate, Linda, ed. *Conversations with Lee Smith.* Jackson: UP of Mississippi, 2001.

Tebbetts, Terrell. "*The Last Girls, Family Linen,* and Faulkner: A Conversation with Lee Smith."*Philological Review* 31.1 (2005): 43–65.

LITERARY CRITICISM

Brosi, George, ed. *Appalachian Heritage* 31.1 (2003). Features Lee Smith.

Cockrell, Amanda. "Full-Tilt Boogie: Lee Smith's Girls." *Hollins Critic* 41.1 (2004): 1–15.

Cook, Linda Byrd. *Dancing in the Flames: Spiritual Journey in the Novels of Lee Smith.* Jefferson, NC: McFarland, 2009.

Hill, Reinhold L. "'These Stories Are Not 'Real,' but They Are as 'Real' as I Can Make Them': Lee Smith's Literary Ethnography." *Southern Folklore* 57.2 (2000): 106–18.

Lang, John., ed. *Iron Mountain Review* 4 (1986). Features Lee Smith.

Frank X Walker

Rock Star

my sistah loves rocks
she'll do anything
for a piece of
hard candy
my sistahz
a rock star
passed her on the street
she didn't even see me
through her tinted windows
my sistahz a mountain
when I call up to her
my 'I love you's'
get lost
in the valleys
my sister's on crack
we only see her
between highs and buys
she be all nervous
and shit
rubbing the back of her hand
like it's some kinda
magic lamp
so we all
stand around and wish
all the dope
in the world
would turn into penny candy
'cause my sister got a sweet tooth
an' mamma swears

she'll pull it out
before she give her up
to sugar

Reprinted with permission of Frank X Walker. Published in *Affrilachia* (Old Cove Press, 2000).

❁ ❁ ❁

Statues of Liberty

mamma scrubbed
rich white porcelain
and hard wood floors
on her hands and knees
hid her pretty face and body
in sack dresses
and aunt jemima scarves
from predators
who assumed
for a few extra dollars
before christmas
in dark kitchen pantries
they could unwrap her
present

aunt helen, her sister
took in miss emereen's laundry
every Saturday morning
sent it back
hand washed, air dried,
starched
ironed, folded
and cleaner
than any professional service
she waited patiently
for her good white woman

to die
and make good on her promise
to leave her
a little something
only to leave her first

aunt bertha, the eldest
exported her maternal skills
to suburbia
to provide surrogate attention
to children of money and privilege
and spent every other moment
preaching about
the richness of the afterlife
before the undertaker
took her
to see for herself

housekeepers
washer women
maids
a whole generation
of portable day care centers
traded their days for dimes
allowing other women
the freedom to shop
and sunbathe
the opportunity to school
or work

this curse-swallowing sorority
dodged dicks
and bosses
before postwar women
punched clocks
they birthed civil and human rights
gave the women's movement
legs

sacrificed their then
to pave the way for a NOW
their hard-earned pennies
sent us off to college
and into the world
our success is their reward
we
are their monuments
but they
are our statues of liberty

Reprinted with permission of Frank X Walker. Published in *Affrilachia* (Old Cove Press, 2000).

❁ ❁ ❁

Step(Fathering) on Eggshells

The angry eyes glaring from across the room,
remind me that I hated my stepfather too.
Mine was vain and loud. He sang his foreplay
in the mirror in falsetto, rocked the bed frames

until she cried out,
then strutted the halls in open boxers
like a rooster with a horse's dick.
Now, I have inherited that role. And my dowry,

a second son, sleeps across the hall and measures
me with piercing eyes, so I love his mother
passionately, but with quiet restraint,
so that one day, measuring his own manhood

he might take pride in the length of his temper
and know why he never saw even the head of mine.

Reprinted with permission of Frank X Walker. Published in *Appalachian Heritage* 36.3 (Summer 2008).

Frank X Walker: A Biographical Sketch

On his website, Frank X Walker writes, "As a co-founder of the Affrilachian Poets and the creator of the word 'Affrilachia,' I believe it is my responsibility to say as loudly and often as possible that people and artists of color are part of the past and present of the multi-state Appalachian region extending from northern Mississippi to southern New York. As a writer/observer/truth teller, I choose to focus on social justice issues as well as multiple themes of family, identity and place." Frank X Walker has read his poetry in Derry, Ireland; in Santiago, Cuba; at Cal-Berkeley; at Northwest Florida State College; and to literally hundreds of other audiences. Susan Mead of Ferrum College expressed in this way the magnetic power that Frank X Walker has over audiences: "Frank's gentle countenance in his poetry readings draws the audience in to listen closely and truly absorb what he has to offer. When he reads his own work, his cadence and hand gestures illuminate the underlying meanings and vivid images of those places and people of whom he writes."

Born in 1961 in Danville, Kentucky, Frank X Walker grew up in the housing projects there, the son of parents who had both grown up on farms. He went from there to the University of Kentucky, where he took creative writing classes from Gurney Norman. From 1985 until 1995 he served as program director for the University's Martin Luther King, Jr., Cultural Center, and the following year he graduated from UK and was hired to direct the Black Cultural Center at Purdue University. Frank X Walker returned to Kentucky after that school year to become the executive director of the Governor's School for the Arts, a position he held for an eight-year period of immense creativity both on the job and beyond. In 1991, in a conversation with Gurney Norman, he coined the term "Affrilachia," and the following year wrote a poem with that title.

Frank X Walker subsequently became fascinated by the historical figure, York, the slave who participated in the Lewis and Clark Expedition, and began writing poems in York's voice while enrolled in Spalding University's low-residency MFA program. After he graduated in 2003 the University Press of Kentucky published *Buffalo Dance: The Journey of York,* and Frank X Walker embarked upon an academic career as interim director of the African/American Studies Program and English professor at Eastern Kentucky University. In 2005 he was the recipient of a seventy-five-thousand-dollar Lanham Literary Fellowship in Poetry. During the 2006–7 school year, while he was a visiting professor at Transylvania University, his third poetry collection, *Black Box,* was published. In 2007 Northern Kentucky University hired Frank X Walker as writer-in-residence, and he founded *Pluck! The Journal of Affrilachian Arts and Culture.* The following year the University Press of Kentucky published *When Winter Come: The Ascension of York.* In 2010 Frank X Walker accepted a job with the University of Kentucky as director of the African American and Africana Studies Program and associate professor in the Department of English. The university also agreed to sponsor his journal, *Pluck!* That year *Isaac Murphy: I Dedicate This Ride* was published, a collection of poetry in the voice of a pioneering African American jockey. Frank X Walker has received two honorary doctorates and has held board positions on the Kentucky Humanities Council, Appalshop, and the Hindman Settlement School.

Frank X Walker: A Selective Bibliography

INTERNET RESOURCES

The *Poetry Society of America* website features Walker's poem "Burning Albatross." *National Public Radio*'s website includes a brief essay from the "This I Believe" series. Walker has a personal website with an artist statement, biographical statement, brief summaries and reviews of his books, and a trailer of a documentary titled *Coal Black Voices. The Tuckaseegee Reader* has an interview and an excerpt of Walker's writing.

SELECTED BOOKS

Isaac Murphy: I Dedicate This Ride. Lexington, KY: Old Cove Press, 2010.
When Winter Come: The Ascension of York. Lexington: UP of Kentucky, 2008.
Black Box. Lexington, KY: Old Cove Press, 2005.
Buffalo Dance: The Journey of York. Lexington: UP of Kentucky, 2003.
Affrilachia. Lexington, KY: Old Cove Press, 2000.

PROFILES/INTERVIEWS

Norman, Gurney. Interview with Frank X Walker. In "Affrilachian: Bluegrass Black Arts Consortium." *Ace Magazine* 12 Nov. 1993.

LITERARY CRITICISM

Brosi, George, ed. *Appalachian Heritage* 39.4 (2011). Features Frank X Walker.
Lang, John. "*When Winter Come: The Ascension of York.*" *Southern Quarterly* 47.3 (Spring 2010): 189–92.
———, ed. *Iron Mountain Review* 25 (2009). Features Frank X Walker.
Turpin, Anita J. "The Dramatic Voices of Frank X Walker." *Journal of Kentucky Studies* 22 (Sept. 2005): 96–103.

Crystal Wilkinson

Sixteen Confessions of Lois Carter

1

My mother never approved but she came to like Roscoe, even after trying hard not to. When Roscoe had his gall bladder surgery Mother came over and helped me out around the house. In the kitchen, with just the two of us washing up the supper dishes, Mother patted my hand and told me that Roscoe was a good person. "He's gonna be fine," she said to me, "don't you worry." And she looked in on Roscoe before she left. She stood in the middle of the floor, near the bed but not too close, and stared at him. I have never known if she was wishing Daddy alive at that moment or if she was having some silent "make up" session with Roscoe. He was snoring lightly underneath the covers, sleeping off the anesthesia. She whispered, "I love you," to me like a secret, gathered her gloves and purse and went.

2

My brother hasn't spoken to me in years, not since Roscoe. And I've given up trying. Jimmy lives in Knifley with his wife and kids. I both miss him and hope never to lay eyes on him again. I hear about him through my sisters. They like the wife but Jimmy ain't changed a bit. This marriage is one issue he can't be budged on. I look at old pictures sometimes and remember us playing tag out in the back yard. His hair straight as a poker, long as a girl's. As a big sister, it was my duty to hold him down and make him let me comb and brush his hair. He was my baby doll. We played hide-and-go-seek. He loved me then. When all us kids worked down at the store, it was me whose skirt tails he clung to. I wore an apron when I worked the cold cuts. I've made many a bologna or hog's head cheese sandwich with Jimmy moving in and out of the front flap of my apron, his jaws beet-red. He would run up and give me kisses when I bent down to stock the low shelves. Jimmy used to call me Lewis instead of Lois when he was little. He don't call me nothing now. Nothing I'd want to hear.

3

Roscoe and I met in 1969. We were both seniors. Integration was cutting its baby teeth. Mostly we stayed to ourselves within groups of our own color unless it was something that involved the girls just being with black girls or the boys being together. There was no mixing of the sexes except to speak nervously in the hallway. We didn't know much about the colored kids and they didn't know much about us. They both intrigued and frightened me. I had never gone to school with black kids before.

Roscoe was in my science class. Mrs. Kiesler was our teacher. Old as dirt. Pink cat-eyed glasses. A thin, haggardly look. Her hair was long and gray. She kept it up in a mound of extended beehive looking like one of those holy-roller women from up off the ridge where my mother grew up. Big, high hair and two sprigs of curlicues at each cheek, right in front of her ears. It was her goal to stump all of us, especially the blacks but Roscoe always had the right answer. He already knew all there was to know about photosynthesis and mollusk traits and invertebrates and zygote division. And he knew how to use the microscope without squeezing one eye shut or going cross-eyed. "Very good, Roscoe," Mrs. Kiesler said aloud one day more enthusiastically than she meant to when Roscoe was the only person in the class who could name the three types of amphibians. She couldn't help herself. Science was her passion and Roscoe's attention to her lessons overwhelmed her. I was proud. I tried to keep my joy to myself but I couldn't. I loved him even then.

4

My sister, Thelma, and me talk pretty near every week. She's a hairdresser over in Danville. She can't have children, so she doted on mine and now has moved on to the grandkids. My other sister? Well Irene and me are cordial. I see her on Christmas, Easter and Thanksgiving. We call to check in and make sure nobody's sick or nobody's dead or dying. We see each other mostly at funerals, reunions and during the holidays but she never let their kids spend the night. Not even once. Something we've never talked about, not even once, but I think about it all the time. Sometimes when I'm in Thelma's chair getting my hair washed and set and she's talking up a storm, I wish Irene was there too. Three sisters cutting up. What's more sisterly than getting your hair done but it never happens.

5

My parents worked hard building up their store. Had me stocking cans of cling peaches and green beans before I could even read the labels. It was the kind of store where you can get hamburger and eggs on credit. All the little black kids use to come in and get pop, potato chips, nabs and nickel candy after school and I couldn't hardly work for staring at them, trying to figure out how their hair stayed that way or how long it took their mothers to put all those little rainbow plastic barrettes in their hair. They were different, yeah, but not in the ways my parents thought. In those days I wanted to be on their side of the counter, just to see what it was like. Now I know. Well no, I guess I'll never know, exactly, but I do know what it feels like to be different.

My father eyed them like he thought they were going to steal something but all the snacks and the things that children loved were right there in front of the counter. In the aisles where my father lurked, peering over at the children, were the grown up produce: Quaker oats, Wonder bread, Carnation milk, Ivory soap, little boxes of Tide detergent, Close-up toothpaste, a few ladies products (as my mother called them) and rows and rows of canned fruits and vegetables. The children would buy their candy and stand around and talk. My father would shoo them out of the store. "Ya'll go on home, now." Then mumble, "Damn little darkies," under his breath. Mother wouldn't be so obvious but after they were gone she would pull out her cleaning rag and wipe down everything she had seen them touch.

6

My father died when I was fourteen. My mother always said he was turning over in his grave. At night when I pray, I ask God to help make my father understand and let him know I'm all right. I love my daddy still. In a perfect world, I see us sitting at the supper table eating pot roast and cornbread as the sun sets on a Sunday evening. Afterwards, me and Mother tending the kids, Roscoe and Daddy out on the porch talking about sports or cars or a basketball game. But that is in my dream world. In my real world even if my father was alive I don't think those things would happen. Not on this planet anyway.

7

Five or six kids came in the store one time and in the shuffle, they left one of the little ones behind. He was crying but was able to tell us his name and where he lived. My mother insisted I walk him home. It was right at springtime, those days when it's cold in the mornings and warm enough in the afternoon to get rid of your sweater. His name was Syrus. I said his name over and over not really to comfort him but to hear its strange sound roll off my own tongue. His name wasn't Bill or Johnny or Luke. Syrus. Syrus took my hand when we were outside the store and walking across the backfield. He seemed scared.

His hand was warm, warmer than my little brother's and moist. I looked at our hands together, his just a few shades darker than mine and I remember noticing but thinking both our hands were just *hands*. Who cared about skin?

8

My mother-in-law cleans up for us every weekend but I don't need her to cook. I can cook as good as any woman. But she cooks anyway and I let her. But I hate it. Every Sunday after church, after we've changed out of our church clothes, she rearranges my kitchen to suit her needs and she lies on my couch while the turkey is cooking or the chicken is frying, the oil in her press-and-curl easing into my couch. Her sweet tea is too sweet. She tastes all the food and puts the spoon back. She is killing Roscoe with all that pork. She still puts it in everything. What I hate more than all of this is that I feel as if I can't say a word. It won't go over well.

9

Miss Pearline, she looks at me sometimes and I can see it in her eyes that she's saying: *You took my son from me!* She's always been accepting, even when all this started and I stayed with her and Mr. Givens when my own mother said, "It just ain't right. I can't have no daughter of mine seeing no niggra. What would your Daddy say, Lois?"

Been a blue million years now and that still gives me the shakes just thinking about it. But on days when I'm in the kitchen with Miss Pearline and it's clear that I've been brought up to make gravy one way and she's been brought up to make it another, I can see it in her eyes that she wishes her son had married a black woman.

10

Even now, when I'm up in age, people from all over come up to me when I'm out and say, "Ain't you one of them Carter girls?"

At the onset their smiles are wide, remembering my folks and Carter's Grocery but just as soon as they recognize me as the one who did *that*, their smiles drop. They clear the mucus from their throats and move on about their business. I don't say a word. Too tired to fight back these days. But I hope to God they don't think I don't notice it at all.

11

I caught Miss Pearline once. I saw her once hugging the neck of one of Roscoe's old girlfriends, one of the black ones. She hugged her neck tight like she wanted her to be her son's wife so bad. When she pulled away, I caught her crying. She cried a grieving cry. We were at a church over in Lexington. I was just about the only white woman there. I looked out across the congregation and caught another white woman's eye but I never said hello to her. I somehow felt like everybody would know why I did. Not that it would matter but I didn't want to call more attention to myself. After the benediction, Roscoe went to the restroom and I made the long walk through the crowd toward our car. I saw Miss Pearline hugging that woman, like she was something precious lost. Maybe it was all for some other reason. Something I don't know. Maybe I'm being paranoid but I'm sure I'm right. If it wasn't like I saw it, I wish somebody could prove me wrong.

12

Me and Roscoe were an accident waiting to happen. He was my lab partner and I was the dumb one. He covered my butt every time. One time we were down in the library like all the other kids in our class, working side by side, and I walked over to read the directions over his shoulder. It wasn't cologne exactly but Roscoe smelled sweet and I could feel the heat as he unexpectedly turned around at the same time I leaned. Our heads nearly butted, but inside, my mind was made up before I even knew what I was thinking about.

I had kissed other boys but nothing more. A bunch of us had gotten together to study over at Susan Beard's house. Her parents hadn't even balked at Roscoe being among us. The basement was where Susan's bedroom was. Their basement was paneled and there was a sitting room at the bottom of the steps: couch, chair, coffee table, and a large dinette table with chairs that we gathered around to study. The Beard parents left the house to pick up groceries. The other kids left. Susan Beard went to take a shower for her date. Roscoe was about to leave. But we brushed together again before he left and we ended up on Susan Beard's couch. After the kiss, everything else was quick—clothes not off but shifted, no music, no romance; no 'I love you's' whispered into each other's ears. We spent the next three days pretending it never happened at all.

On our wedding night Roscoe confessed that it had been his first time, too, and how he had left so quickly because he thought something had happened to him when he climaxed. What about me? I laughed but never told him that I thought I was going to bleed to death. That first night I had prayed to God that by morning my parents wouldn't find me dead in my bed.

13

Me and Roscoe still have sex every Thursday morning. Early. Even before the sun peeks up and turns red. If I were to be honest with myself, I am still startled by Roscoe when I wake up next to him. I always keep the bathroom light on so I can clearly see his dark skin glistening in the sheer light of morning against my own. I touch the short, tight curls against his scalp. Look into his eyes, warm black pools. All this surprises me even after thirty some odd years. Roscoe and me. We've come through too much to talk about any of that out loud, but a woman can have a private thought if she wants to.

14

Our grandchildren, we have three now, are blessed because they are a mixture. I can look at them and see Roscoe clear as day but I can see myself too, my mother even. The eldest has my mother's green eyes and my red hair. I am glad. Not because she's light-skinned but because I overhear them talk about being black. They don't ever talk about being white. Glad some of them can't deny their other side. Can't deny me. Makes me happy. Happier than it should.

15

I am a chameleon. I move in and out of all my selves. With Thelma at the beauty shop I'm a white woman, just a plain white woman. In there we are all the same. We laugh and cut up and have fun but when I'm at Shirley's or Frieda's, I'm somebody different all together. When we sip our iced tea and lemonade and play Tonk and talk about our men, I think they forget that I'm white. I like those times; that's when I'm at my happiest, laughing and having fun with my girls. Both sets of them. I live one life over there, one over here. I live my life straddled. Never standing too straight or tall in either world. The two hardly ever mix. I love my girls, though, both sets. Roscoe hates to come home to a hen party or to come home to find me gone to one, but he knows I know where home is.

16

When Mother died, people came from all over, bringing baskets of food and flowers, looking at Roscoe and me like we were the reason she was dead. My brother got drunk at the wake and called Roscoe out of his name, something the others didn't have enough liquor in them to do. Roscoe and me left. The whole place smelled of dying roses and made me sick to my stomach. I dream about that. Only in my dream Mother is alive, and she steps out from behind my brother and puts her finger to her lips for me to be quiet. Even in death, she is the peacemaker. Or maybe she is urging me not to talk about it. And I don't talk about it anymore. No use. I dream that over and over, but I'm not sure why. If Mother knew me at all, she would know that I have spent what seems like a lifetime holding my tongue.

Reprinted with permission of the Toby Press. Published in *Water Street* (2005).

Crystal Wilkinson: A Biographical Sketch

Crystal Wilkinson teaches in the BFA in Creative Writing program at Morehead State University, and—with her partner, artist Ron Davis—runs the Wild Fig Bookstore in Lexington, Kentucky, and edits *Mythium: A Journal of Contemporary Literature Celebrating Writers of Color.* In demand as a workshop leader, she is best known as the author of two books of delightful short stories.

Wilkinson was born in 1962 and raised by her grandparents on Indian Creek in Casey County, Kentucky. Some who meet Crystal Wilkinson face-to-face are surprised at how thoroughly her childhood reflects old-fashioned mountain ways. Some people unconsciously associate her dark, African American skin with urban life, but Wilkinson's experience, though increasingly uncommon, is representative of generations of African American mountain folk. Wilkinson's grandfather raised tobacco, corn, and sorghum on a small farm, and her grandmother was a domestic worker, primarily in the homes of Casey County teachers. Wilkinson skipped the second grade, which allowed her to be in the same class with the only other two African American students in the county school system, both her cousins. In the third grade, when she had finished reading all the books available to her, she assembled the tales she had written into books using her grandmother's sewing machine. Wilkinson usually spent summers in nearby Stanford, Kentucky, where she stayed with aunts, uncles, and cousins. When she turned sixteen, she secured a job on the Casey County Library's bookmobile. The next year, 1980, she enrolled at Eastern Kentucky University, where she felt terribly out of place. Black students often made fun of her country talk and ways, yet it was difficult for the shy African American to find acceptance among the white students who shared her rural upbringing. Her loneliness perhaps contributed to her falling deeply in love and then giving birth to a son, Gerald, during midterms of her second semester. The baby's father and a friend of Wilkinson's watched Gerald while she attended class, and Wilkinson received a BA in journalism in 1985.

Moving to Lexington, the single mother with a college degree landed jobs at Arby's and Walgreen's, and as a hospital clerk and a custodian. Finally she obtained a job at the *Lexington Herald Leader,* followed by another in public relations for the city of Lexington. In 1989, when Gerald was eight, Wilkinson gave birth to twin girls. By this time, she was thoroughly engaged in her passion—writing. In 1994 she received a writing grant from the Kentucky Foundation for Women, and other grants and workshops followed. In 1997 she began teaching writing at the Kentucky Governor's School for the Arts, and in 2000 her first book, *Blackberries, Blackberries,* was published, a collection of stories set in a community reminiscent of Indian Creek where she was raised. As a result of having a book in print and being an excellent presenter and workshop leader, her calendar filled up. Gurney Norman, a writing teacher at the University of Kentucky and former Kentucky Poet Laureate, dubbed her the "Godmother of Creative Writing in Lexington." She became assistant director of the Carnegie Center for Literacy and Learning, and in 2001 she enrolled in the low-residency MFA program at Spalding University. She graduated in 2003 and was hired to teach creative writing at Indiana University. That year she also published her second book, *Water Street,* set in a community reminiscent of Stanford, Kentucky. In 2005 Crystal Wilkinson returned to Kentucky, accepting a faculty position at Morehead State University.

Crystal Wilkinson: A Selective Bibliography

INTERNET RESOURCES

A brief excerpt from *Water Street* can be found on the Toby Press website. Wilkinson also has a blog titled *Write with Your Spine,* where she shares her reflections on reading, writing, and publishing. The website *Torch: Poetry, Prose and Short Stories by African American Women* features a short story, brief biography, and interview with Wilkinson.

SELECTED BOOKS

Water Street. New Milford, CT: Toby Press, 2002.

Blackberries, Blackberries. New Milford, CT: Toby Press, 2000.

PROFILES/INTERVIEWS

Wilkinson, Crystal E. "On Being 'Country': One Affrilachian Woman's Return Home." In *Back Talk from Appalachia: Confronting Stereotypes.* Ed. Dwight B. Billings, Gurney Norman, and Katherine Ledford. Lexington: UP of Kentucky, 1999. 184–86.

LITERARY CRITICISM

Brosi, George, ed. *Appalachian Heritage* 34.2 (2006). Features Crystal Wilkinson.

Locklear, Erica Abrams. "Consenting to Create: The Affrilachian Movement." *CrossRoads: A Southern Culture Annual* 4 (2009): 169–85.

Wilson-Young, Joy. "*Water Street.*" *Arkansas Review: A Journal of Delta Studies* 36.2 (2005): 136–37.

Meredith Sue Willis

Elvissa and the Rabbi

Elvissa rhymes with Louisa and her hobby was New York City. If you had asked her as a teen in the early 1980s why New York, she would have smiled and shrugged and maybe described a view overlooking all the lights of the city. She was raised in West Virginia near the Ohio River in a suburb where everything was new: houses, high school, church. Her friends were mostly the children of corporate families from over the country, and the handful of native West Virginians she knew had no interest in where they came from.

Elvissa's mother, however, had grown up in Webster County and was the first of her family to attend college. She rarely spoke of her past and almost never visited her family, so Elvissa learned that transplants can thrive if they are put in an auspicious location. She learned another thing from her mother, the importance of having something private, something just your own. Her mother's hobby was Elvis Presley. She kept a closet in the spare bedroom full of memorabilia, and she named her son Edward Elvis and her daughter Elvissa.

So, like her mother, Elvissa kept a cult. She collected Statues of Liberty and maps of the New York City subway system and postcards of the New York skyline. Except for this oddity, she seemed to be perfectly matched to her life: she was elected junior varsity cheerleader, class secretary, homecoming princess. She was active at church and liked to read. She learned from books how to be protected when she had sex, which she only did with one boyfriend in high school and two at college. Like her mother, she had dark-honey good looks and a musical voice. It smoothes things in life when you can walk into a room and people enjoy looking at you.

She went to college in Ohio, where she joined a sorority full of girls who were blonde, pretty, and did service at a local nursing home. The only thing that distinguished Elvissa from the others was that she came from West Virginia, which is not nearly as exotic to Ohioans as it is to, say, New Yorkers. After graduation, Elvissa told her boyfriend she was going to New York, and he assumed she meant for the summer. He said it would be good for them to be apart for a few months and test their love. It never occurred to him that Elvissa might love New York more than she loved him and his brand-new management position with IBM.

Since everyone was going into business in those days, the easiest jobs to get were in social service. Elvissa moved into an apartment with the cousin of one of her sorority sisters, and then she went to a private employment agency run by a heavyset woman named Gertrude Stein. "No relation" said Miss Stein, glaring into Elvissa's Kappa Kappa hello-spirit smile. "No relation at all to the writer, who I am told was a lesbian and extremely lazy, whereas I built this agency up from nothing with my own bare hands. The problem with young women today is that you don't know the meaning of hard work, and you don't know how to sell yourselves." Miss Stein predicted that Elvissa had no chance of getting a job without her help.

Since Elvissa had come to the agency precisely to get help, she smiled and said, "I guess you're right! Just tell me what to do!"

Miss Stein saw she had a winner. "You've got a pretty face" said Miss Stein. "Use it! Smile at them! Be pleasant! Carry yourself with pride! Don't be afraid to use your figure to your advantage. I don't mean blouses cut down to here, I just mean, don't hide it." She began to smack her palm on her desk. "Tell them your good qualities! Don't hide yourself behind a wet blanket!"

Elvissa took a bus from Miss Stein's to the West Side Community Center, which was on the ground floor of a mixed-income housing project, walking distance from the apartment where she was staying. The program coordinator at West Side, Lorelei Lopatkin, was about the same age as Miss Stein and like Miss Stein had a faintly European turn of phrase, not quite an accent. Miss Lopatkin, however, wore a blouse with deep décolletage. She spoke from the beginning as if it were settled that Elvissa would be hired. "You see, my dear, it's a lovely, low-key position. You have only to think up some games for the Puerto Rican children and then help them with their homework during the school year." She made tea for Elvissa and went on explaining. "The day clients, of course," said Miss Lopatkin, "are the Sixty-Plus Club. Some of them are younger if they are on disability or out of work, but we never check ages. We have a fine, intellectually stimulating group of day clients. Such gorgeous, self-motivated people, I can't tell you. What we do is, we give them their heads! Like a fine racehorse, do you understand? This is, for them, the best therapy of all—that they should organize everything for themselves."

After Elvissa had worked at the center for only a few days, she noticed that Miss Lopatkin didn't leave her office. She drank tea and talked on the telephone. The Sixty-Plussers came in to drink tea with her. She liked Elvissa to sit down too. "You are young now, dear," she said, "but you won't always be. You must learn to conserve energy."

Elvissa loved the West Side Center, which seemed like all of New York rolled into one. There were people of all ages and all colors and all income levels taking exercise classes, singing classes, English classes. The little Puerto Rican kids, most of whom were actually from Mexico and the Dominican Republic, were so much fun that she could never could remember to feel sorry for them. And the Sixty-Plussers didn't seem that old. True, a few of them had canes or walkers, but mostly the center was a club for them. Tiny, elderly Martin read the large-type edition of the *New York Times* and knew tremendous amounts about history and politics. He kept trying to convince Elvissa to be a communist. "These are the last days of capitalism, sweetheart," he said. "Mark my words."

"Leave her alone," said the equally tiny and elderly Mr. Bernstein. "She's a lady!" Mr. Bernstein wore a three-piece suit and a little black skullcap and spent time on the phone with his stockbroker.

The women made a special pet of Elvissa. They sat in the small lounge with a view of the front door and the day care playground. "You speak so clearly," said Lois, who had white bangs and was married to Martin the communist.

Lois's friend Rose had black hair and a large, theatrical voice. "My God, you're right," said Rose. "Her voice is like bells ringing. And do you see her hair? Have you ever seen hair like that, which I know is natural. It's natural, isn't it, pumpkin?"

"Mine was that color when I was that age," said Ruthie, the nervous one who wore tight jeans and high heels.

"Well, it isn't anymore," said Rose.

"Shh!" said Lois. "Don't be mean."

"I'm realistic. Ruthie knows, don't you, Ruthie?"

"You're only as old as you feel," said Ruthie.

Elvissa said, "I always wanted dark hair. My favorite fairy tales were about the dark-haired heroines."

"So articulate, too," said Lois. "I am a retired schoolteacher. I have experience in this area. Few young people articulate their words today."

"Now, pumpkin," said Rose, "Tell us again where in the South are you from?"

"Well, not really the South. West Virginia."

"1 had a cousin," said Ruthie, "a branch of the family that moved to Richmond and sold shoes, and I'm told they did very well. I never went there myself."

"Richmond is in Virginia. I'm from *West* Virginia, actually. I grew up right across the river from Ohio."

"I guess that's why you don't have a southern accent," said Lois. "Just between you and me, I've never liked that drawl they have."

"You aren't married, are you, Ellie?" said Rose. "I want you to meet my niece's son."

Lois said, "She'll find plenty of boys on her own. I think you should put her in the musical."

The Sixty-Plus Club was in the middle of a production of *Fiddler on the Roof* but Rose, who was directing, thought Elvissa would make everyone else look old. So Elvissa happily typed up scripts with corrections and cuts, made production schedules, designed the poster, and carried flyers to the local boutiques and bodegas.

Miss Lopatkin said, "Ellie, you must remember! It is most therapeutic if they do it all themselves!"

She loved the production, especially the man who was playing Tevye and never seemed to get out of character. He let his beard grow long, and he wore a vest all the time and would throw his arms in the air in the middle of a card game and sing, "YaYaYaYaYa! If I were a ri-ich man!"

Within a month, Elvissa knew half a dozen Yiddish words and was embarrassed that she had ever asked Lois why Mr. Bernstein wore the little black hat. One morning, she was at the file cabinet behind the door in the office and overheard the women walking by.

Ruthie said, "Ellie is such a nice girl. She's Jewish?"

"Of course not," said Rose, "don't be an idiot."

Lois said, "You don't have to be Jewish to be a nice girl."

"It's just too bad. It's a shame. She's such a nice girl."

Ellie thought it was a shame too, that she didn't have the long dark hair, that she wasn't Jewish.

After work, she did the things that can only be done in New York. She went to poetry readings and free concerts by Juilliard students. She went to the museums that were pay-what-you-will, and she sat in Central Park and listened to the steel-drum bands. If some unsavory or mentally unbalanced man approached her with lewd propositions, she took him as part of the entertainment and shook her head no, learning to smile less or more depending on how long she wanted the entertainment to last.

Inspired by *Fiddler,* she took an acting class at a drama studio over the Orange Julius on Broadway. For one of the first assignments, the class was to observe a person unlike yourself and mimic the walk and the gestures. The next morning, on the way to work, she followed a woman who walked slowly but with grace. She had slightly bowed legs and a wonderful stick carved with the head of an ibis. She wore her hair in a chignon that was equal parts black and white, and she was dressed in a white blouse with colored embroidery, black skirt, and black leather single-strapped shoes in excellent repair.

The woman unlocked the dark gates of a small corset shop. The window was full of nylons in boxes and garter belts and brassieres and even a pink Merry Widow corset. That evening, Ellie saw her again in the bright summer evening, on a bench on the island in the middle of Broadway. Her feet dangled and she talked to a friend. Her hands seemed to be swirling paint in the air.

Ellie hurried home and practiced in front of the mirror, learning to walk as if she carried an old burden. She set up pillows on the bed so she could practice dangling her legs. She crossed her ankles as the corset seller did and worked on the fluid gesture that begins with the palms turned up, slides into a shrug and rolled eyes.

She loved imitating the corset shop lady; she loved her acting class; she loved Martin and Lois and the story of their courtship as idealistic young communists. She loved Mr. Bernstein, who didn't seem to have learned she wasn't Jewish because he always reminded her to light candles on Friday night. She adored the production of *Fiddler,* which was at once wildly sentimental and profoundly true. She felt on the verge of understanding something important.

Her boyfriend came to visit. It was the end of summer, and she realized as soon as she saw him that letting him come was a mistake. He seemed physically a stranger to her, his sweat and his breath foreign. But she was the one who had changed, making broad gestures with her hands. He felt the difference, but to him it was an erotic stimulus. He made little hissing noises and said, "Where have you been all my life?" and put his hands on her waist. He was eager to see New York, wanted to go first class all the way and so didn't care to eat sausage sandwiches and sugared nuts from street vendors. He overspent, and for the first time in her life she made love because she felt it had been paid for. When she told him she had decided to stay in New York, his first response was that it would be a while before he could get a transfer.

Ellie said, "I don't think you understand. I don't want to marry you. I want to live in New York. By myself. Not with you."

He accused her of having fallen in love with someone else. She said it was the city she loved. He didn't believe her. She explained about sitting on the steps of the Museum of Natural History and watching a man twist balloons into elephants and giraffes. Her boyfriend did not understand. He hung his head, and his eyes looked bruised.

The last thing he said to her was, "I wish I was the kind of guy—" and then he smacked his fist into the palm of his hand and stalked off to his flight gate.

He called and wrote and sent flowers and telegrams. He believed that you can have what you want if you are enterprising enough. He asked her father to plead his case, and her father called and talked about the weather and everyone's health, and then reported on an article he'd read about the use of cocaine in New York. Finally he wondered if something might be influencing her judgment. And before she could process what he was saying, he put her mother on the phone.

She forestalled her mother by saying, "Mom, when you first went away from home, did you fit in?"

Annie Jo laughed. "Why, you know the answer to that, honey! I had to learn everything from scratch. Your dad and his family taught me everything I know."

"You made yourself fit."

"After a while I did."

"Well," said Ellie, "I'm making myself fit here."

To ensure that her boyfriend got the point, she started dating Rose's grand-nephew, but it was actually his friend Robert Lipitz, a medical resident at New York Hospital, that she ended up marrying. Robert was so exhausted from his rotations through the hospital that he fell asleep in movies and on benches in museums. She loved this about him. She also loved his mother, Barbara, and his father, Irwin, a dermatologist, who said medical residencies were summer camp today compared to when he did it.

Barbara jumped in and cried, "It's a trick of memory! You're remembering the good old days!"

"The good old days!" cried Irwin. "You call that the good old days!"

Ellie would meet Robert on his midnight break at an all-night coffee shop. He came with stubbly cheeks, white coat spattered with brownish dots of she dared not ask what. He told tales of failed suicides with bone-pierced lungs and livers, alleged perpetrators whose shoulder muscles had been torn apart by police artillery.

The first time they ordered burgers, she was still ignorant enough to be horrified to see his special arrive with bacon and cheese. "Oh," she cried, "they made a mistake, Robert! Do you want to trade? I've got a plain one—"

He looked blank. "No, I confess. I knew it was an artery clogger."

"Oh," said Ellie. "I guess you're not religious, then. I mean, observant."

Robert made a choking sound as he bit into dinner. "You thought I kept kosher? My mother would, pardon the expression, *plotz.* She rebelled against all of that stuff a long time ago. I think maybe in her family the *grandparents* rebelled?"

"Does that mean they—you—don't believe in the Jewish faith?"

Robert looked toward heaven. "My mom and her entire family are atheists. My dad believes in Israel. He goes to reform temple on the High Holy Days."

"It's complicated, then," said Ellie. "What about you?"

The waitress brought his chocolate egg cream. "I was in a temple once. No, I'm joking. I was bar mitzvahed. I'm glad I was bar mitzvahed. Even my mother wanted me to do that, but I haven't been back since. It's a lot of hoo-hah."

She adored the Lipitz family gatherings. They tried to explain Judaism and politics to her. Irwin was a louder, hairier version of Robert, and Barbara dressed like an upscale beatnik. Barbara and Irwin had monumental arguments about the state of Israel, which Irwin supported financially and emotionally and Barbara insisted was a religious theocracy, antifeminist, no different from the Ayatollah Khomeini's theocracy in Iran or the one the right wing was trying to establish in the United States.

Ellie loved the way they argued and the way Robert pronounced consonants in the middle of a word. She was entranced by how he said "Chinese" with an "s" sound at the end instead of a "z." She loved the dark silky hair on his arms and chest, and his high forehead with receding hair. She wanted to make herself sharp and smart like his mother, and when they moved in together, she argued more and stated her opinions more directly.

They got married because they had a chance at a cheap hospital-owned apartment with a little terrace. Robert's mother found a left-wing rabbi who was delighted to perform the ceremony without any details like Ellie converting. His name was Rabbi Stein, no relation to either Gertrude, and Ellie liked him enormously. He was divorced with teenage children and had been a part of the civil rights movement. He had a small beard and gave her books on Judaism as the religion of liberation.

Ellie liked Rabbi Stein's version of Judaism so much that she decided to convert. When she told the day clients at the center, they stared at her as if a tree had sprouted from her forehead. Rose in particular, who was still a little miffed about the great-nephew, said, "And why would a person like yourself want to become a Jew?"

Lois, knitting a red sweater for a grandchild, said, "She's doing it for the boy, of course. He's a Jewish boy, right, Ellie?"

Rose said, "Marry a Jewish boy if you love him, I understand that. But why be such a masochist as convert?"

"I don't know," said Ellie. "I'm sort of attracted to—the religion."

This caused such an unusual silence that she felt she had broken some kind of taboo. Ruthie crossed and recrossed her slim legs in tight jeans and finally said, "I hope you aren't going to cut off your gorgeous hair and put on a *shmata*."

"It's going to be a reform conversion," said Ellie.

Rose shook out her *New York Times* Living section and made a harrumphing noise. "I hope you don't expect people to think you're Jewish."

"Rose!" said Lois. "This is a happy thing! She wants to be close to her husband and his family. You should give her best wishes."

"*Mazel tov*," said Rose from behind the newspaper.

Miss Lopatkin was less interested in the conversion and more in talking about marriage. "Let's order in lunch," she said. "One thing I know is Jewish men. I married three of them." The children in the after-school program, of course, had always assumed that Ellie, like the other white ladies they knew, was already Jewish.

Robert heard of an interesting fellowship in Columbus, Ohio. Something large and dark crossed Ellie's sky. "Columbus?" she said. "But I just got to New York!"

"And I've never lived anyplace else!" said Robert, trying to be humorous. "Okay, okay," he added. "We'll stay another year."

She could tell that Robert, like her old boyfriend, thought that her love affair with New York was a passing phase. There was no question that he thought her Jewishness was. He said things like, "Are you still studying with the Hipster Rabbi? Did he tell you to buy me a black hat?"

Ellie, always amiable to the best of her ability, smiled and kissed his forehead, but meanwhile she inquired of Rabbi Stein which practices were most crucial, should you decide to practice. Rabbi Stein pointed out the downsides of Judaism and Jewish practice for a convert with a recalcitrant spouse. He interpreted old things for today. "The business with not picking up the wheat you drop in the field, and not harvesting the corners of the field," he said, "this was an early social service program: the widows and orphans were supposed to come and take the leftovers."

She loved Judaism for its cleverness, for being Rabbi Stein's religion, for being the underlying tradition of the Lipitzes and the Sixty-Plus Club, for being associated with New York. She loved the way the whole structure did not hang from a single book. In the religion she grew up in, you either accepted it all—

Mary getting pregnant without sex, Jesus coming back to life—or you didn't, in which case you went to Hell. Rabbi Stein's Judaism, on the other hand, had a lot of multiple interpretations; this rabbi said but that rabbi said something different; there was exegesis and storytelling, the explaining of texts by scholars and then texts explaining the explanations all the way to Rabbi Stein explaining to Ellie.

Robert perceived her experiments with Judaism as nuttiness. As a second-year resident, he was busier than ever, so she had plenty of nights to read and attend services while he was on call at the hospital. He didn't mind Rosh Hashanah or Yom Kippur, although he didn't care to fast himself, but he was appalled when she purchased some bundles of branches at the Korean grocery and built a little *sukkah* on their terrace. The beginning of the end was when he borrowed a friend's cottage in the Catskills for the weekend, and Ellie told him she had been trying not to travel on Friday night or Saturday.

Robert said, "You're joking, aren't you? About not traveling on *Shabbos?*"

She looked out the window at the view of high-rises and a slice of East River and Queens. "I want to see what it feels like."

"You can't!" said Robert. "There is no possible way you can know what it feels like. You're about as Jewish as a pork chop!"

He went away without her and was miserable, and Ellie was miserable in New York. On Saturday afternoon, she borrowed a car from another resident and drove to the Catskills to join him, but got lost and didn't find the cabin till almost midnight. They had a tearful and sensual reunion, but she had arrived so late that Robert didn't realize she had broken the Sabbath for him, and she didn't say anything. Thus she did not tell the one thing that might have saved their future together, whether out of perversity or pride, or because she wanted him to think she was really Jewish.

It became clearer and clearer that Ellie was choosing Judaism over Robert. He stormed around the living room, waving his arms, seeming to fill three times the space he usually did. She felt vaguely that her own mother would have found a way to please him and keep kosher as well, but she was still a beginner in life, and not clear about what she really wanted. Through his rages, she kept a coolly insufferable little smile on her lips, and Robert accepted a fellowship in Denver.

She said, as directly and clearly as possible, "Oh, Robert, let's stay in New York and learn to be Jews together!"

"I already know how to be a Jew," said Robert sadly. "I don't have to learn."

Telling Robert's parents about the separation was hard. Barbara shouted, "It's my fault. I should have got a judge for your wedding. If I hadn't introduced you to that hypocritical son-of-a-bitch Stein you wouldn't have gone crazy with the atavistic religious bullshit."

"Maybe she'll change her mind," said Irwin. "Maybe she'll change her mind and go to Denver."

They all cried: Irwin, Barbara, Robert, and Ellie, and Ellie loved them all more than she ever had. She saw Robert off at the airport, and thought for a while that she might change her mind and go with him. But Rose, who was directing *Hello, Dolly!* at the center, had a small stroke, and Ellie took over until she could get back on her feet. Then there were complaints about the quality of Miss Lopatkin's energy expenditure at work, so she took early retirement, and the director gave Ellie the job. By this time, months had passed and Robert had met a formerly Lutheran nurse who hated everything associated with religion.

The hardest thing of all was how to tell her own mother and father, which she didn't do until after *Hello, Dolly!* and the promotion and the nurse. She made a special trip home late in October. She rented a car, drove down slowly through Appalachian foliage splendor and thought about what to tell them and how. She started with the ham at dinner. "It looks great," she said, "but I'm becoming more of a vegetarian. The way animals are treated, in the meat factories. You know."

Her mother gave her a bright little smile. "I thought maybe you weren't eating pork because you were becoming Jewish."

"Well," she said, "to tell the truth, it's both things. I've gotten more interested in—Judaism. I converted. You knew that, didn't you?"

Her mother kept the little bright smile. "We wondered when we saw that rabbi at your wedding."

Her father wiped his mouth and stared over her head out the window. The light fell on the semiabstract design of pink and gray flowers on the plates. The light fell on the little explosion lines etched at the corners of her parents' eyes and mouths.

Her mother said, "I hope you aren't going to church on Sunday to try and convert people."

"Oh, no! That's one of the things I really like about Judaism—they believe—we believe other religions are fine for other people!"

Her father cleared his throat. "I'm not prejudiced but that's a little weird, if you ask me. How can you take a religion seriously if you don't believe it's the best one?"

"It *is* the best one, for Jews."

Her mother burst out, "But, honey, what I don't understand is why you would want to reject Jesus."

"It's not rejection! He was a great teacher. We just don't think he's the—" and her mouth stuck between Redeemer and Savior, and in the end, she couldn't say the Christian words at all. "We just don't think he's *moshiach*."

They all three seemed to stare at the foreign word, as if it had landed resoundingly on the table as firm and pink as the ham.

Finally, Annie Jo said, "Messiah?"

Ellie nodded.

Her father said, "Well, I'm no theologian. I just try and do what the Bible says. That's enough for me."

Her mother said, "But why do you have to change? I mean, it's one thing for Robert and his family—"

"We think the world of Robert and his people," said Ed.

"Oh, yes! We think the world of Robert, but I don't understand why you have to change."

"Mom, you left your family and changed."

Their father snorted. "Annie Jo *had* to change. When Annie Jo went to college, she thought a flush toilet was something to wash your feet."

Annie Jo had grown up with teasing from brothers far more cruel than her husband. "Ed, you always get that wrong," she said. "I thought you all were dirty for having dogs in the house and that little spring of water was for the dogs to drink from."

Ellie had heard this exchange before. Both her parents chuckled and smiled into one another's eyes. "But Mom, you gave up your family. And I have to tell you another change too. Robert and I are separated."

"These things happen to the best of families," said Ed. "Are you going to get back together?"

"We're definitely separated. He's in Denver, and I stayed in New York."

Ed shook his head. "You should go out there and try to talk to him, you should try to work it out. After you went to all that trouble to become Jewish."

"It's not a misunderstanding. We're getting a divorce."

Her father glanced at her mother. "Young people need to think things over sometimes. Your mother went back home for a while, after we first got married."

This was news, that Annie Jo had ever gone back to the Critchfields.

Annie Jo said, "Well, I knew I'd come back."

Their father reached over and grasped her mother's hand. Ellie felt tears in her own eyes.

"Robert and I got married too soon," she said. "Before I was sure who I was."

Her father said, "If you're really getting a divorce, then you don't have to stay Jewish."

"No, I think I'm more interested in being Jewish than I am in being married. I might even go back to school and become something like, I don't know, a rabbi."

Annie Jo frowned and clenched her hands. "I just think you're just embarrassed," she said. "By us."

"It doesn't have anything to do with you. You don't have to reject one thing because you're drawn to something else."

"Then why," said Annie Jo, "why, if you're not embarrassed, did you stop using your own name?"

"Now, honey," said Ed to Annie Jo. "She just took her husband's name. There's nothing wrong with Lipitz for a last name—"

"I don't mean her last name! I mean why do they all call her that nickname like her name was Ellen instead of her real name?"

Her father said, "Maybe in New York your old boy Elvis Presley isn't as popular as back home."

"Are you ashamed of what I named you?" asked Annie Jo. "Does being Jewish mean you have to give up the name I gave you?"

Elvissa was shocked by the anger that came over her. "Why did you name me after Elvis Presley anyhow? Why didn't you give me a real name if you wanted me to keep the name you gave me? Why didn't you name us after some of the Critchfields? Why didn't you take us to visit the Critchfields?"

"Well, those Critchfields—" said her father.

"I should have," said Annie Jo. "I wish I had. There's nothing wrong with my family, they're just good old country people."

"You can still take me," she said, surprising herself, and wondering if this was what she wanted, why she took extra vacation days.

And that was how it came about that Elvissa spent the rest of her vacation driving through West Virginia with her mother meeting relatives. But that's another story. The end of this story is that Elvissa went back to New York and continued to study with Rabbi Stein, who asked her to call him Mike, a nickname for Myron, and she asked him to call her Elvissa, and explained why. She never became a rabbi, but she did marry Rabbi Mike Stein. She continued to work at the West Side Center, and she had two children, and her children grew up knowing New York as that most commonplace of wonders, home. And Elvissa took them to West Virginia every summer.

From time to time Elvissa Mackey Lipitz Stein has a dream in which she and her husband and children, and his children by his first wife, and Robert and his parents and wife, and Elvissa's parents and her brother, and a whole crowd of Stems and Mackeys and Lipitzes and Critchfields, all go up on Critchfield Mountain to celebrate an open-air meal under a pink sky. Sometimes it's a *seder,* and sometimes it's a vegetarian Easter feast. The Lipitzes are there, and crowds of people she knows, and everyone talks, but it comes out as music instead of words. Elvissa always wakes from the dream with a gratifying sense that everything fits together. She never remembers exactly how it fits, but she has a profound belief that it does fit, and that the most important thing in the world is that she knows.

Reprinted with permission of Ohio University Press. Published in *Out of the Mountains: Appalachian Stories* (2010).

Meredith Sue Willis: A Biographical Sketch

Meredith Sue Willis is a writer, a writing teacher, a community activist, and an organic gardener who has published several books in each of four major categories: literary novels, youth novels, short story collections, and books about the writing process.

Willis's paternal grandparents ran a country store in Wise County, Virginia, and her father, Glenn Willis, finished college while intermittently working in the mines. He became a teacher in Shinnston, West Virginia, where he married Lucille Meredith Willis, a fellow teacher whose mother was a mining camp midwife and father was a coal miner. Meredith Sue Willis was born in 1946 and grew up in Shinnston, working in the summers at her family's Dairy King and becoming active in the Baptist church. At fifteen she wrote her first short story, a horror piece about a mountain boy who is afraid of a rickety old bridge. After being voted Most Likely to Succeed by her high school peers, she entered Bucknell University, where, she says, she met her first atheist, tasted alcohol for the first time, and after a year—much to the chagrin of her parents—decided to drop out and spend a year as a VISTA volunteer in a low-income African American neighborhood of Norfolk, Virginia. There she wrote for an application to study at Columbia University's undergraduate college, not realizing that it only accepted men at that time. Her request was forwarded to Columbia's sister school, Barnard College. Willis graduated Phi Beta Kappa and magna cum laude from Barnard in 1969 while also becoming active in Students for a Democratic Society and participating in the dramatic 1968 sit-in at Columbia University. She worked for a year as a recreation therapist at New York's Bellevue Hospital before enrolling at Columbia University School of the Arts, where she earned an MFA degree in 1972.

After Columbia, Willis became involved in the Teachers and Writers Collaborative of New York City, an association that continues to thrive today. This became a full-time job, and Willis writes, "[W]e printed comic books by the kids and made plays and movies—it was pretty wild and lots of fun. I did that right up into the early eighties, although the anarcho-creative aspect of it gradually was replaced by pedagogy." In the twelve years of courtship before they married in 1982, Willis's boyfriend, Andrew Weinberger, finished his medical training and subsequently served at the Fort Hamilton Induction Center in New York City. Meanwhile, the couple moved across the Hudson River to New Jersey, and Willis's first two novels were published by Scribner. The third appeared in 1985, the year their only child, Joel, was born. As Joel became more self-sufficient in the 1990s, Willis took on additional "writer-in-the-schools" contracts as well as teaching for New York University, where she continues as an adjunct assistant professor of creative writing. In the 1990s, Willis published her first story collection, a couple of youth novels, and two books about writing: *Blazing Pencils* (1991) and *Deep Revision* (1993). She also published the final novel in her Blair Ellen Trilogy, *Trespassers* (1997), which depicts her protagonist sitting in at Columbia in 1968.

In this millennium, Meredith Sue Willis continues to be active in the South Orange / Maplewood Community Coalition on Race, a group that encourages racial and cultural neighborhood integration. She still works in the schools and at NYU. Willis has also written two more literary novels, another youth novel, two more story collections, and another book about writing.

Meredith Sue Willis: A Selective Bibliography

INTERNET RESOURCES

Willis has a short story featured in the online version of *Two Hawks* (Spring 2009). The *West Virginia Culture and History* website features an interview. Willis also has a personal website with commentaries and an extensive bibliography.

SELECTED BOOKS

Out of the Mountains: Appalachian Stories. Athens: Ohio UP, 2010.
Ten Strategies to Write Your Novel. Millburn, NJ: Montemayor Press, 2010.
Re-visions: Stories from Stories. Maplewood, NJ: Hamilton Stone Editions, 2010.
Dwight's House and Other Stories. Maplewood, NJ: Hamilton Stone Editions, 2004.
Oradell at Sea. Morgantown: West Virginia UP, 2002.
Trespassers. Maplewood, NJ: Hamilton Stone Editions, 1997.
In the Mountains of America. San Francisco: Mercury House, 1994.
Higher Ground. New York: Scribner, 1981.
Only Great Changes. New York: Scribner, 1985.
A Space Apart. New York: Scribner, 1979.

INTERVIEW

Morgan, Karen. "Meredith Sue Willis: Circling Out, Centering In." In *Appalachia and Beyond: Conversations with Writers from the Mountain South.* Ed. John Lang. Knoxville: U of Tennessee P, 2006. 195–210.

LITERARY CRITICISM

Brosi, George, ed. *Appalachian Heritage* 34.4 (2006). Features Meredith Sue Willis.

Herring, Gina. "Politics and Men: What's 'Really Important' about Meredith Sue Willis and Blair Ellen Morgan." *Appalachian Journal* 25.4 (1998): 414–22.

Lang, John, ed. *Iron Mountain Review* 12 (1996). Features Meredith Sue Willis.

Sullivan, Ken. "Gradual Changes: Meredith Sue Willis and the New Appalachian Fiction." *Appalachian Journal* 14.1 (1986): 38–45.

Part 3

Work and the Economy

Barbara Kingsolver

Homeland

I

My great-grandmother belonged to the Bird Clan. Hers was one of the fugitive bands of Cherokee who resisted capture in the year that General Winfield Scott was in charge of prodding the forest people from their beds and removing them westward. Those few who escaped his notice moved, like wildcat families through the Carolina mountains, leaving the ferns unbroken where they passed, eating wild grapes and chestnuts, drinking when they found streams. The ones who could not travel, the aged and the infirm and the very young, were hidden in deep cane thickets where they would remain undiscovered until they were bones. When the people's hearts could not bear any more, they laid their deerskin packs on the ground and settled again.

General Scott had moved on to other endeavors by this time, and he allowed them to thrive or perish as they would. They built clay houses with thin, bent poles for spines, and in autumn they went down to the streams where the sycamore trees had let their year's work fall, the water steeped brown as leaf tea, and the people cleansed themselves of the sins of the scattered-bone time. They called their refugee years The Time When We Were Not, and they were forgiven, because they had carried the truth of themselves in a sheltered place inside the flesh, exactly the way a fruit that has gone soft still carries inside itself the clean, hard stone of its future.

II

My name is Gloria St. Clair, but like most people I've been called many things. My maiden name was Murray. My grown children have at one time or another hailed me by nearly anything pronounceable. When I was a child myself, my great-grandmother called me by the odd name of Waterbug. I asked her many times why this was, until she said once, to quiet me, "I'll tell you that story."

We were on the front-porch swing, in summer, in darkness. I waited while she drew tobacco smoke in and out of her mouth, but she said nothing. "Well," I said.

Moonlight caught the fronts of her steel-framed spectacles and she looked at me from her invisible place in the dark. "I said I'd tell you that story. I didn't say I would tell it right now."

We lived in Morning Glory, a coal town hacked with sharp blades out of a forest that threatened always to take it back. The hickories encroached on the town, springing up unbidden in the middle of dog pens and front yards and the cemetery. The creeping vines for which the town was named drew themselves along wire fences and up the sides of houses with the persistence of the displaced. I have heard it said that if a man stood still in Morning Glory, he would be tied down by vines and not found until first frost. Even the earth underneath us sometimes moved to repossess its losses: the long, deep shafts that men opened to rob the coal veins would close themselves up again, as quietly as flesh wounds.

My great-grandmother lived with us for her last two years. When she came to us we were instructed to call her Great Grandmother, but that proved impossible and so we called her Great Mam. My knowledge of her life follows an oddly obscured pattern, like a mountain road where much of the scenery is blocked by high laurel bushes, not because they were planted there, but because no one thought to cut them down.

I know that her maternal lineage was distinguished. Her mother's mother's father was said to have gone to England, where he dined with King George and contracted smallpox. When he returned home his family plunged him into an icy stream, which was the curative custom, and he died. Also, her mother was one of the Bird Clan's Beloved Women. When I asked what made her a Beloved Woman, Great Mam said that it was because she kept track of things.

But of Great Mam's own life, before she came to us, I know only a little. She rarely spoke of personal things, favoring instead the legendary and the historic, and so what I did discover came from my mother, who exercised over all matters a form of reverse censorship: she spoke loudly and often of events of which she disapproved, and rarely of those that might have been ordinary or redemptive. She told us, for instance, that Great-Grandfather Murray brought Great Mam from her tribal home in the Hiwassee Valley to live in Kentucky, without Christian sanction, as his common-law wife. According to Mother, he accomplished all of this on a stolen horse. From that time forward Great Mam went by the name of Ruth.

It was my mother's opinion that Great-Grandfather Murray was unfit for respectable work. He died after taking up the honest vocation of coal mining, which also killed their four sons, all on the same day, in a collapsed shaft. Their daughter perished of fever after producing a single illegitimate boy, who turned out to be my father, John Murray. Great Mam was thus returned to refugee ways, raising her grandson alone in hard circumstances, moving from place to place where she could find the odd bit of work. She was quite remarkably old when she came to us.

I know, also, that her true name was Green Leaf, although there is no earthly record of this. The gravesite is marked Ruth. Mother felt we ought to bury her under her Christian name in the hope that God in His infinite mercy would forget about the heathen marriage and stolen horses and call her home. It is likely, however, that He might have passed over the headstone altogether in his search for her, since virtually all the information written there is counterfeit. We even had to invent a date and year of birth for her since these things were unknown. This, especially, was unthinkable to my brothers and me. But we were children, of course, and believed our own birthdays began and ended the calendar.

To look at her, you would not have thought her an Indian. She wore blue and lavender flowered dresses with hand-tatted collars, and brown lace-up shoes with sturdy high heels, and she smoked a regular pipe. She was tall, with bowed calves and a faintly bent-forward posture, spine straight and elbows out and palms forward, giving the impression that she was at any moment prepared to stoop and lift a burden of great bulk or weight. She spoke with a soft hill accent, and spoke properly. My great-grandfather had been an educated man, more prone in his lifetime to errors of judgment than errors of grammar.

Great Mam smoked her pipe mainly in the evenings, and always on the front porch. For a time I believed this was because my mother so vigorously objected to the smell, but Great Mam told me otherwise. A pipe had to be smoked outdoors, she said, where the smoke could return to the Beloved Old Father who gave us tobacco. When I asked her what she meant, she said she meant nothing special at all. It was just the simplest thing, like a bread-and-butter note you send to an aunt after she has fed you a meal.

I often sat with Great Mam in the evenings on our porch swing, which was suspended by four thin, painted chains that squeaked. The air at night smelled of oil and dust, and faintly of livestock, for the man at the end of our lane kept hogs. Great Mam would strike a match and suck the flame into her pipe, lighting her creased face in brief orange bursts.

"The small people are not very bright tonight," she would say, meaning the stars. She held surprising convictions, such as that in the daytime the small people walked among us. I could not begin to picture it.

"You mean down here in the world, or do you mean right here in Morning Glory?" I asked repeatedly. "Would they walk along with Jack and Nathan and me to school?"

She nodded. "They would."

"But why would they come here?" I asked.

"Well, why wouldn't they?" she said.

I thought about this for a while, entirely unconvinced.

"You don't ever have to be lonesome," she said. "That's one thing you never need be."

"But mightn't I step on one of them, if it got in my way and I didn't see it?"

Great Mam said, "No. They aren't that small."

She had particular names for many things, including the months. February she called "Hungry Month." She spoke of certain animals as if they were relatives our parents had neglected to tell us about. The cowering white dog that begged at our kitchen door she called "the sad little cousin." If she felt like it, on these evenings, she would tell me stories about the animals, their personalities and kindnesses and trickery, and the permanent physical markings they invariably earned by doing something they ought not to have done. "Remember that story," she often commanded at the end, and I would be stunned with guilt because my mind had wandered onto crickets and pencil erasers and Black Beauty.

"I might not remember," I told her. "It's too hard."

Great Mam allowed that I might think I had forgotten. "But you haven't. You'll keep it stored away," she said. "If it's important, your heart remembers."

I had known that hearts could break and sometimes even be attacked, with disastrous result, but I had not heard of hearts remembering. I was eleven years old. I did not trust any of my internal parts with the capacity of memory.

When the seasons changed, it never occurred to us to think to ourselves, "This will be Great Mam's last spring. Her last June apples. Her last fresh roasting ears from the garden." She was like an old pine, whose accumulated years cause one to ponder how long it has stood, not how soon it will fall. Of all of us, I think Papa was the only one who believed she could die. He planned the trip to Tennessee. We children simply thought it was a great lark.

This was in June, following a bad spring during which the whole southern spine of the Appalachians had broken out in a rash of wildcat strikes. Papa was back to work at last, no longer home taking up kitchen-table space, but still Mother complained of having to make soups of neck bones and cut our school shoes open to bare our too-long toes to summer's dust, for the whole darn town to see. Papa pointed out that the whole darn town had been on the picket lines, and wouldn't pass judgment on the Murray kids if they ran their bare bottoms down Main Street. And what's more, he said, it wasn't his fault if John L. Lewis had sold him down the river.

My brothers and I thrilled to imagine ourselves racing naked past the Post Office and the women shopping at Herman Ritchie's Market, but we did not laugh out loud. We didn't know exactly who Mr. John L. Lewis was, or what river Papa meant, but we knew not to expect much. The last thing we expected was a trip.

My brother Jack, because of his nature and superior age, was suspicious from the outset. While Papa explained his plan, Jack made a point of pushing lima beans around his plate in single file to illustrate his boredom. It was 1955. Patti Page and Elvis were on the radio and high school boys were fighting their mothers over ducktails. Jack had a year to go before high school, but already the future was plainly evident.

He asked where in Tennessee we would be going, if we did go. The three of us had not seen the far side of a county line.

"The Hiwassee Valley, where Great Mam was born," Papa said.

My brother Nathan grew interested when Jack laid down his fork. Nathan was only eight, but he watched grownups. If there were no men around, he watched Jack.

"Eat your beans, Jack," Mother said. "I didn't put up these limas last fall so you could torment them."

Jack stated, "I'm not eating no beans with guts in them."

Mother took a swat at Jack's arm. "Young man, you watch your mouth. That's the insides of a hog, and a hog's a perfectly respectable animal to eat." Nathan was making noises with his throat. I tried not to make any face one way or the other.

Great Mam told Mother it would have been enough just to have the limas, without the meat. "A person can live on green corn and beans, Florence Ann," she said. "There's no shame in vegetables."

We knew what would happen next, and watched with interest. "If I have to go out myself and throw a rock at a songbird," Mother said, having deepened to the color of beetroot, "nobody is going to say this family goes without meat!"

Mother was a tiny woman who wore stockings and shirt-waists even to hoe the garden. She had yellow hair pinned in a tight bun, with curly bangs in front. We waited with our chins cupped in our palms for Papa's opinion of her plan to make a soup of Robin Redbreast, but he got up from the table and rummaged in the bureau drawer for the gas-station map. Great Mam ate her beans in a careful way, as though each one had its own private importance.

"Are we going to see Injuns?" Nathan asked, but no one answered. Mother began making a great deal of noise clearing up the dishes. We could hear her out in the kitchen, scrubbing.

Papa unfolded the Texaco map on the table and found where Tennessee and North Carolina and Georgia came together in three different pastel colors. Great Mam looked down at the colored lines and squinted, holding the sides of her glasses. "Is this the Hiwassee River?" she wanted to know.

"No, now those lines are highways," he said. "Red is interstate. Blue is river."

"Well, what's this?"

He looked. "That's the state line."

"Now why would they put that on the map? You can't see it."

Papa flattened the creases of the map with his broad hands, which were crisscrossed with fine black lines of coal dust, like a map themselves, no matter how clean, "The Hiwassee Valley's got a town in it now, it says 'Cherokee.' Right here."

"Well, those lines make my eyes smart," Great Mam said. "I'm not going to look anymore."

The boys started to snicker, but Papa gave us a look that said he meant business and sent us off to bed before it went any farther.

"Great Mam's blind as a post hole," Jack said once we were in bed. "She don't know a road from a river."

"She don't know beans from taters," said Nathan.

"You boys hush up, I'm tired," I said. Jack and Nathan slept lengthwise in the bed, and I slept across the top with my own blanket.

"Here's Great Mam," Nathan said. He sucked in his cheeks and crossed his eyes and keeled over backward, bouncing us all on the bedsprings. Jack punched him in the ribs, and Nathan started to cry louder than he had to. I got up and sat by the bedroom door hugging my knees, listening to Papa and Mother. I could hear them in the kitchen.

"As if I hadn't put up with enough, John. It's not enough that Murrays have populated God's earth without the benefit of marriage," Mother said. This was her usual starting point. She was legally married to my father in a Baptist Church, a fact she could work into any conversation.

"Well, I don't see why," she said, "if we never had the money to take the kids anyplace before."

Papa's voice was quieter, and I couldn't hear his answers.

"Was this her idea, John, or yours?"

When Nathan and Jack were asleep I went to the window and slipped over the sill. My feet landed where they always did, in the cool mud of Mother's gladiolus patch alongside the house. Great Mam did not believe in flower patches. Why take a hoe and kill all the growing things in a piece of ground, and then plant others that have been uprooted from somewhere else? This was what she asked me. She thought Mother spent a fearful amount of time moving things needlessly from one place to another.

"I see you, Waterbug," said Great Mam in the darkness, though what she probably meant was that she heard me. All I could see was the glow of her pipe bowl moving above the porch swing.

"Tell me the Waterbug story tonight," I said, settling onto the swing. The fireflies were blinking on and off in the black air above the front yard.

"No, I won't," she said. The orange glow moved to her lap, and faded from bright to dim. "I'll tell you another time."

The swing squeaked its sad song, and I thought about Tennessee. It had never occurred to me that the place where Great Mam had been a child was still on this earth. "Why'd you go away from home?" I asked her.

"You have to marry outside your clan," she said. "That's law. And all the people we knew were Bird Clan. All the others were gone. So when Stewart Murray came and made baby eyes at me, I had to go with him." She laughed. "I liked his horse."

I imagined the two of them on a frisking, strong horse, crossing the mountains to Kentucky. Great Mam with black hair. "Weren't you afraid to go?" I asked.

"Oh, yes I was. The canebrakes were high as a house. I was afraid we'd get lost."

We were to leave on Saturday after Papa got off work. He worked days then, after many graveyard-shift years during which we rarely saw him except asleep, snoring and waking throughout the afternoon, with Mother forever forced to shush us; it was too easy to forget someone was trying to sleep in daylight. My father was a soft-spoken man who sometimes drank but was never mean. He had thick black hair, no beard stubble at all nor hair on his chest, and a nose he called his Cherokee nose. Mother said she thanked the Lord that at least He had seen fit not to put that nose on her children. She also claimed he wore his hair long to flout her, although it wasn't truly long, in our opinion. His nickname in the mine was "Indian John."

There wasn't much to get ready for the trip. All we had to do in the morning was wait for afternoon. Mother was in the house scrubbing so it would be clean when we came back. The primary business of Mother's life was scrubbing things, and she herself looked scrubbed. Her skin was the color of a clean boiled potato. We didn't get in her way.

My brothers were playing a ferocious game of Cowboys and Indians in the backyard, but I soon defected to my own amusements along the yard's weedy borders, picking morning glories, pretending to be a June bride. I grew tired of trying to weave the flowers into my coarse hair and decided to give them to Great Mam. I went around to the front and came up the three porch steps in one jump, just exactly the way Mother said a lady wouldn't do.

"Surprise," I announced. "These are for you." The flowers were already wilting in my hand.

"You shouldn't have picked those," she said.

"They were a present." I sat down, feeling stung.

"Those are not mine to have and not yours to pick," she said, looking at me, not with anger but with intensity. Her brown pupils were as dark as two pits in the earth. "A flower is alive, just as much as you are. A flower is your cousin. Didn't you know that?"

I said, No ma'am, that I didn't.

"Well, I'm telling you now, so you will know. Sometimes a person has got to take a life, like a chicken's or a hog's when you need it. If you're hungry, then they're happy to give their flesh up to you because they're your relatives. But nobody is so hungry they need to kill a flower."

I said nothing.

"They ought to be left where they stand, Waterbug. You need to leave them for the small people to see. When they die they'll fall where they are, and make a seed for next year."

"Nobody cared about these," I contended. "They weren't but just weeds."

"It doesn't matter what they were or were not. It's a bad thing to take for yourself something beautiful that belongs to everybody. Do you understand? To take it is a sin."

I didn't, and I did. I could sense something of wasted life in the sticky leaves, translucent with death, and the purple flowers turning wrinkled and limp. I'd once brought home a balloon from a Ritchie child's birthday party, and it had shriveled and shrunk with just such a slow blue agony.

"I'm sorry," I said.

"It's all right." She patted my hands. "Just throw them over the porch rail there, give them back to the ground. The small people will come and take them back."

I threw the flowers over the railing in a clump, and came back, trying to rub the purple and green juices off my hands onto my dress. In my mother's eyes, this would have been the first sin of my afternoon. I understood the difference between Great Mam's rules and the Sunday-school variety, and that you could read Mother's Bible forward and backward and never find where it said it's a sin to pick flowers because they are our cousins.

"I'll try to remember," I said.

"I want you to," said Great Main. "I want you to tell your children."

"I'm not going to have any children," I said. "No boy's going to marry me. I'm too tall. I've got knob knees."

"Don't ever say you hate what you are." She tucked a loose sheaf of black hair behind my ear. "It's an unkindness to those that made you. That's like a red flower saying it's too red, do you see what I mean?"

"I guess," I said.

"You will have children. And you'll remember about the flowers," she said, and I felt the weight of these promises fall like a deerskin pack between my shoulder blades.

By four o'clock we were waiting so hard we heard the truck crackle up the gravel road. Papa's truck was a rust-colored Ford with complicated cracks hanging like spider-webs in the corners of the windshield. He jumped out with his long, blue-jean strides and patted the round front fender.

"Old Paint's had her oats," he said. "She's raring to go." This was a game he played with Great Mam. Sometimes she would say, "John Murray, you couldn't ride a mule with a saddle on it," and she'd laugh, and we would for a moment see the woman who raised Papa. Her bewilderment and pleasure, to have ended up with this broad-shouldered boy.

Today she said nothing, and Papa went in for Mother. There was only room for three in the cab, so Jack and Nathan and I climbed into the back with the old quilt Mother gave us and a tarpaulin in case of rain.

"What's she waiting for, her own funeral?" Jack asked me.

I looked at Great Mam, sitting still on the porch like a funny old doll. The whole house was crooked, the stoop sagged almost to the ground, and there sat Great Mam as straight as a schoolteacher's ruler. Seeing her there, I fiercely wished to defend my feeling that I knew her better than others did.

"She doesn't want to go," I said. I knew as soon as I'd spoken that it was the absolute truth.

"That's stupid. She's the whole reason we're going. Why wouldn't she want to go see her people?"

"I don't know, Jack," I said.

Papa and Mother eventually came out of the house, Papa in a clean shirt already darkening under the arms, and Mother with her Sunday purse, the scuff marks freshly covered with white shoe polish. She came down the front steps in the bent-over way she walked when she wore high heels. Papa put his hand under Great Mam's elbow and she silently climbed into the cab.

When he came around to the other side I asked him, "Are you sure Great Mam wants to go?"

"Sure she does," he said. "She wants to see the place where she grew up. Like what Morning Glory is to you."

"When I grow up I'm not never coming back to Morning Glory," Jack said.

"Me neither." Nathan spat over the side of the truck, the way he'd seen men do.

"Don't spit, Nathan," Papa said.

"Shut up," Nathan said, after Papa had gotten in the truck and shut the door.

The houses we passed had peeled paint and slumped porches like our own, and they all wore coats of morning-glory vines, deliciously textured and fat as fur coats. We pointed out to each other the company men's houses, which had bright white paint and were known to have indoor bathrooms. The deep ditches along the road, filled with blackberry brambles and early goldenrod, ran past us like rivers. On our walks to school we put these ditches to daily use practicing Duck and Cover, which was what our teachers felt we ought to do when the Communists dropped the H-bomb.

"We'll see Indians in Tennessee," Jack said. I knew we would. Great Mam had told me how it was.

"Great Mam don't look like an Indian," Nathan said.

"Shut up, Nathan," Jack said. "How do you know what an Indian looks like? You ever seen one?"

"She does so look like an Indian," I informed my brothers. "She is one."

According to Papa we all looked like little Indians, I especially. Mother hounded me continually to stay out of the sun, but by each summer's end I was so dark-skinned my schoolmates teased me, saying I ought to be sent over to the Negro school.

"Are we going to be Indians when we grow up?" Nathan asked.

"No, stupid," said Jack. "We'll just be the same as we are now."

We soon ran out of anything productive to do. We played White Horse Zit many times over, until Nathan won, and we tried to play Alphabet but there weren't enough signs. The only public evidence of literacy in that part of the country was the Beech Nut Tobacco signs on barn roofs, and every so often, nailed to a tree trunk, a clapboard on which someone had painted "PREPARE TO MEET GOD."

Papa's old truck didn't go as fast as other cars. Jack and Nathan slapped the fenders like jockeys as we were passed on the uphill slopes, but their coaxing amounted to naught. By the time we went over Jellico Mountain, it was dark.

An enormous amount of sky glittered down at us on the mountain pass, and even though it was June we were cold. Nathan had taken the quilt for himself and gone to sleep. Jack said he ought to punch him one to teach him to be nice, but truthfully, nothing in this world could have taught Nathan to share. Jack and I huddled together under the tarp, which stank of coal oil, and sat against the back of the cab where the engine rendered up through the truck's metal body a faint warmth.

"Jack?" I said.

"What."

"Do you reckon Great Mam's asleep?"

He turned around and cupped his hands to see into the cab. "Nope," he said. "She's sitting up there in between 'em, stiff as a broom handle."

"I'm worried about her," I said.

"Why? If we were home she'd be sitting up just the same, only out front on the porch."

"I know."

"Glorie, you know what?" he asked me.

"What?"

A trailer truck loomed up behind us, decked with rows of red and amber lights like a Christmas tree. We could see the driver inside the cab. A faint blue light on his face made him seem ghostly and entirely alone. He passed us by, staring ahead, as though only he were real on this cold night and we were among all the many things that were not. I shivered, and felt an identical chill run across Jack's shoulders.

"What?" I asked again.

"What, what?"

"You were going to tell me something."

"Oh. I forgot what it was."

"Great Mam says the way to remember something you forgot is to turn your back on it. Say, 'The small people came dancing. They ran through the woods today.' Talk about what they did, and then whatever it was you forgot, they'll bring it back to you."

"That's dumb," Jack said. "That's Great Mam's hobbledy-gobbledy."

For a while we played See Who Can Go to Sleep First, which we knew to be a game that can't consciously be won. He never remembered what he'd meant to say.

When Papa woke us the next morning we were at a truck stop in Knoxville. He took a nap in the truck with his boots sticking out the door while the rest of us went in for breakfast. Inside the restaurant was a long glass counter containing packs of Kools and Mars Bars lined up on cotton batting, objects of great value to be protected from dust and children. The waitress who brought us our eggs had a red wig perched like a bird on her head, and red eyebrows painted on over the real ones.

When it was time to get back in the truck we dragged and pulled on Mother's tired, bread-dough arms, like little babies, asking her how much farther.

"Oh, it's not far. I expect we'll be in Cherokee by lunchtime," she said, but her mouth was set and we knew she was as tired of this trip as any of us.

It was high noon before we saw a sign that indicated we were approaching Cherokee. Jack pummeled the cab window with his fists to make sure they all saw it, but Papa and Mother were absorbed in some kind of argument. There were more signs after that, with pictures of cartoon Indian boys urging us to buy souvenirs or stay in so-and-so's motor lodge. The signs were shaped like log cabins and teepees. Then we saw a real teepee. It was made of aluminum and taller than a house. Inside, it was a souvenir store.

We drove around the streets of Cherokee and saw that the town was all the same, as single-minded in its offerings as a corn patch or an orchard, so that it made no difference where we stopped. We parked in front of Sitting Bull's Genuine Indian Made Souvenirs, and Mother crossed the street to get groceries for our lunch. I had a sense of something gone badly wrong, like a lie told in my past and then forgotten, and now about to catch up with me.

A man in a feather war bonnet danced across from us in the parking lot. His outfit was bright orange, with white fringe trembling along the seams of the pants and sleeves, and a woman in the same clothes sat cross-legged on the pavement playing a tom-tom while he danced. People with cameras gathered and side-stepped around one another to snap their shots. The woman told them that she and her husband Chief Many Feathers were genuine Cherokees, and that this was their welcoming dance. Papa sat with his hands frozen on the steering wheel for a very long time. Then suddenly, without saying anything, he got out of the truck and took Jack and Nathan and me into Sitting Bull's. Nathan wanted a tomahawk.

The store was full of items crowded on shelves, so bright-colored it hurt my eyes to look at them all. I lagged behind the boys. There were some Indian dolls with real feathers on them, red and green, and I would like to have stroked the soft feathers but the dolls were wrapped in cellophane. Among all those bright things, I grew fearfully uncertain about what I ought to want. I went back out to the truck and found Great Mam still sitting in the cab.

"Don't you want to get out?" I asked.

The man in the parking lot was dancing again, and she was watching. "I don't know what they think they're doing. Cherokee don't wear feather bonnets like that," she said.

They looked like Indians to me. I couldn't imagine Indians without feathers. I climbed up onto the seat and closed the door and we sat for a while. I felt a great sadness and embarrassment, as though it were I who had forced her to come here, and I tried to cover it up by pretending to be foolishly cheerful.

"Where's the pole houses, where everybody lives, I wonder," I said. "Do you think maybe they're out of town a ways?"

She didn't answer. Chief Many Feathers hopped around his circle, forward on one leg and backward on the other. Then the dance was over. The woman beating the tom-tom turned it upside down and passed it around for money.

"I guess things have changed pretty much since you moved away, huh, Great Mam?" I asked.

She said, "I've never been here before."

Mother made bologna sandwiches and we ate lunch in a place called Cherokee Park. It was a shaded spot along the river, where the dry banks were worn bald of their grass. Sycamore trees grew at the water's edge, with colorful, waterlogged trash floating in circles in the eddies around their roots. The park's principal attraction was an old buffalo in a pen, identified by a sign as the Last Remaining Buffalo East of the Mississippi. I pitied the beast, thinking it must be lonely without a buffalo wife or buffalo husband, whichever it needed. One of its eyes was put out.

I tried to feed it some dead grass through the cage, while Nathan pelted it with gravel. He said he wanted to see it get mad and charge the fence down, but naturally it did not do that. It simply stood and stared and blinked with its one good eye, and flicked its tail. There were flies all over it, and shiny bald patches on its back, which Papa said were caused by the mange. Mother said we'd better get away from it or we would have the mange too. Great Mam sat at the picnic table with her shoes together, and looked at her sandwich.

We had to go back that same night. It seemed an impossible thing, to come such a distance only to turn right around, but Mother reminded us all that Papa had laid off from work without pay. Where money was concerned we did not argue. The trip home was quiet except for Nathan, who pretended at great length to scalp me with his tomahawk, until the rubber head came loose from its painted stick and fell with a clunk.

III

Before there was a world, there was only the sea, and the high, bright sky arched above it like an overturned bowl.

For as many years as anyone can imagine, the people in the stars looked down at the ocean's glittering face without giving a thought to what it was, or what might lie beneath it. They had their own concerns. But as more time passed, as is natural, they began to grow curious. Eventually it was the water-bug who volunteered to go exploring. She flew down and landed on top of the water, which was beautiful, but not firm as it had appeared. She skated in every direction but could not find a place to stop and rest, so she dived underneath.

She was gone for days and the star people thought she must have drowned, but she hadn't. When she joyfully broke the surface again she had the answer: on the bottom of the sea, there was mud. She had brought a piece of it back with her, and she held up her sodden bit of proof to the bright light.

There, before the crowd of skeptical star eyes, the ball of mud began to grow, and dry up, and grow some more, and out of it came all the voices and life that now dwell on this island that is the earth. The star people fastened it to the sky with four long grape vines so it wouldn't be lost again.

"In school," I told Great Mam, "they said the world's round."

"I didn't say it wasn't round," she said. "It's whatever shape they say it is. But that's how it started. Remember that."

These last words terrified me, always, with their impossible weight. I have had dreams of trying to hold a mountain of water in my arms. "What if I forget?" I asked.

"We already talked about that. I told you how to remember."

"Well, all right," I said. "But if that's how the world started, then what about Adam and Eve?"

She thought about that. "They were the waterbug's children," she said. "Adam and Eve, and the others."

"But they started all the trouble," I pointed out. "Adam and Eve started sin."

"Sometimes that happens. Children can be your heartache. But that doesn't matter, you have to go on and have them," she said. "It works out."

IV

Morning Glory looked no different after we had seen the world and returned to it. Summer settled in, with heat in the air and coal dust thick on the vines. Nearly every night I slipped out and sat with Great Mam where there was the tangible hope of a cool breeze. I felt pleased to be up while my brothers breathed and tossed without consciousness on the hot mattress. During those secret hours, Great Mam and I lived in our own place, a world apart from the arguments and the tired, yellowish light bulbs burning away inside, seeping faintly out the windows, getting used up. Mother's voice in the kitchen was as distant as heat lightning, and as unthreatening. But we could make out words, and I realized once, with a shock, that they were discussing Great Mam's burial.

"Well, it surely can't do her any harm once she's dead and gone, John, for heaven's sakes," Mother said.

Papa spoke more softly and we could never make out his answer.

Great Mam seemed untroubled. "In the old days," she said, "whoever spoke the quietest would win the argument."

She died in October, the Harvest Month. It was my mother who organized the burial and the Bible verses and had her say even about the name that went on the gravestone, but Great Mam secretly prevailed in the question of flowers. Very few would ever have their beauty wasted upon her grave. Only one time for the burial service, and never again after that, did Mother trouble herself to bring up flowers. It was half a dozen white gladioli cut hastily from her garden with a bread knife, and she carried them from home in a jar of water, attempting to trick them into believing they were still alive.

My father's shoes were restless in the grass and hickory saplings at the edge of the cemetery. Mother knelt down in her navy dress and nylon stockings and with her white gloved hands thumped the flower stems impatiently against jar bottom to get them to stand up straight. Already the petals were shriveling from thirst.

As soon as we turned our backs, the small people would come dancing and pick up the flowers. They would kick over the jar and run through the forest, swinging the hollow stems above their heads, scattering them like bones.

Barbara Kingsolver: A Biographical Sketch

Barbara Kingsolver's status as an international literary luminary was reinforced in 2011 when her novel *The Lacuna* won the Orange Prize for fiction. Her Royal Highness, the Duchess of Cornwall, presented the prize at the Royal Festival Hall in London, England, for the outstanding work of the year in the English language. Receiving a European award for a book partially set in Mexico as well as Appalachia reinforced Kingsolver's global thinking, but did not diminish her reputation for acting locally. In the first decade of the twenty-first century she became widely known as a leading advocate for the local foods movement with the publication of *Animal, Vegetable, Miracle* (2007), an account of her family's attempts to eat almost exclusively food grown near their residence. Barbara Kingsolver's stature is such that she not only receives awards but also presents them. In 2000 she created the Bellwether Prize for socially engaged unpublished fiction.

Barbara Kingsolver was born in 1955 in Annapolis, Maryland, while her father was serving as a navy doctor, but the family returned to Kentucky, where both her parents are from, before her second birthday. She was raised in Carlisle, a small northeastern Kentucky town. In 1963, when she was in the second grade, she and her family accompanied her father while he practiced medicine in the Congo and, four years later, in St. Lucia, a Caribbean island. After graduating from Nicholas County High School, Kingsolver entered DePauw University in Greencastle, Indiana, on a music scholarship. She spent her junior year abroad in Athens and Paris, and graduated in 1977 magna cum laude with a double major in biology and English. After a year in France she moved to Tucson, Arizona, where in 1981 she received an MS from the University of Arizona's Department of Ecology and Evolutionary Biology and began her scientific writing career with the Arid Lands Institute. In 1985 she married Joseph Hoffman, a chemist. They had a child, Camille, in 1987, and the next year Barbara Kingsolver released her first novel, the story of a Kentucky woman who moves out West, *The Bean Trees.* It sold over a million copies and was recognized by the *New York Times* and the American Library Association. The following year Kingsolver published a book celebrating dissent, *Holding the Line: Women in the Great Arizona Mine Strike of 1983,* as well as a collection of her stories, *Homeland.* In 1990 her second novel, *Animal Dreams,* was published, and, she and her daughter moved to the Canary Islands. When they returned she and Hoffman divorced. That year, 1992, she published *Another America / Otra America,* a collection of poetry, in English and Spanish.

Barbara Kingsolver's 1993 novel, *Pigs in Heaven,* became a *New York Times* best seller. While on her book tour for this book, she met Steve Hoop, a professor at Emory & Henry College in southwestern Virginia. In 1994 they married, and Kingsolver began spending more and more time on Hoop's farm. In 1996 their daughter, Lily, was born. All eight books Kingsolver has published since *Pigs in Heaven* have been *New York Times* best sellers as well, notably *The Poisonwood Bible* (1998), set in the Congo where she lived when she was seven years old, *Prodigal Summer* (2000), and *Flight Behavior* (2012) both set in the southern mountains. President Bill Clinton bestowed the National Humanities Medal upon Barbara Kingsolver in 2000. In 2011 she became the third annual recipient of the Duke University LEAF Award for lifetime environmental achievement in the fine arts.

Barbara Kingsolver: A Selective Bibliography

INTERNET RESOURCES

HarperCollins Publishers offers browsing ability of Kingsolver's books. *National Public Radio* has an excerpt from and review of *The Lacuna.* The *Telegraph* posted a profile on Kingsolver, discussing several of her books, critics, and politics.

SELECTED BOOKS

Flight Behavior. New York: HarperCollins, 2012.
The Lacuna. New York: HarperCollins, 2009.
Animal, Vegetable, Miracle: A Year of Food Life. New York: HarperCollins, 2008.
Prodigal Summer. New York: HarperCollins, 2000.
The Poisonwood Bible. New York: HarperCollins, 1998.
Pigs in Heaven. New York: Harper Perennial, 1993.
Homeland and Other Stories. New York: Harper and Row, 1989.
The Bean Trees. New York: Harper and Row, 1988.

PROFILES/INTERVIEWS

Epstein, Robin. "An Interview with Barbara Kingsolver." *Progressive* 12.9 (1996): 1–12.
"Messing with the Sacred: An Interview with Barbara Kingsolver." *Appalachian Journal* 28.3 (2001): 304–24.
Perry, Donna, ed. "Interview with Barbara Kingsolver." In *Back Talk: Women Writers Speak Out.* New Brunswick, NJ: Rutgers UP, 1993. 143–69.

LITERARY CRITICISM

Austenfeld, Thomas, ed. *Critical Insights: Barbara Kingsolver.* Ipswitch, MA: Salem Press, 2009.

DeMarr, Mary Jean. *Barbara Kingsolver: A Critical Companion.* Westport, CT: Greenwood, 1999.

Fleischner, Jennifer, ed. *A Reader's Guide to the Fiction of Barbara Kingsolver: The Bean Trees, Homeland and Other Stories, Animal Dreams, Pigs in Heaven.* New York: Harper Perennial, 1994.

Lang, John, ed. *Iron Mountain Review* 28 (2012). Features Barbara Kingsolver.

Leder, Priscilla, ed. *Seeds of Change: Critical Essays on Barbara Kingsolver.* Knoxville: U of Tennessee P, 2010.

Riley, Jeannette E. "The Eco-Narrative and the Enthymeme: Form and Engagement in Environmental Writing." *Interdisciplinary Literary Studies: A Journal of Criticism and Theory* 10.2 (Spring 2009): 82–98.

Snodgrass, Mary Ellen. *Barbara Kingsolver: A Literary Companion.* Jefferson, NC: McFarland, 2004.

Wagner-Martin, Linda. *Barbara Kingsolver.* Great Writers Series. New York: Chelsea House, 2004.

Chris Offutt

Out of the Woods

Gerald opened his front door at dawn, wearing only a quickly drawn-on pair of jeans. His wife's four brothers stood in the ground fog that filtered along the ridge. The oldest brother had become family spokesman after the father's death, and Gerald waited for him to speak. The mother was still boss but everything had to filter through a man.

"It's Ory," the oldest one said. "He got shot and is in the hospital. Somebody's got to fetch him."

The brothers looked at Gerald from below their eyebrows. Going after Ory wasn't a chore anyone wanted, and Gerald was new to the family, married to Kay, the only sister. He still needed to prove his worth. If he brought Ory home, maybe they'd cut the barrier that kept him on the edge of things, like he was nothing but a third or fourth cousin.

"Where's he at?" Gerald said.

"Wahoo, Nebraska. Ory said it would take two days but was easy to find."

"My rig won't make it."

"You can take the old Ford. She'll run till doomsday."

"Who shot him?"

The oldest brother flashed him a mean look. The rest were back to looking down, as if they were carpenters gauging the amount of linoleum needed for a job.

"Some woman," the oldest brother said.

Kay began to cry. The brothers left and Gerald sat on the couch beside Kay. She hugged her knees and bit a thumbnail, gasping in a throaty way that reminded him of the sounds she made in bed. He reached for her. She shrugged from his hand, then allowed his touch.

"Him leaving never made sense," Kay said. "He hadn't done nothing and nobody was after him. He didn't tell a soul why. Just up and went. Be ten years come fall."

"I'll go get him," Gerald whispered.

"You don't care to?"

"No."

"For my brothers?"

"For you."

She snuggled against him, her damp face pressed to his neck. She was tiny inside the robe. He opened the front and she pushed against his leg.

The next day he left in the black pickup. Gerald was thirty years old and had never been out of the county. He wore a suit that was snug in the shoulders, and short in the leg. It had belonged to his father, but he didn't figure anyone would notice. He wished he owned a tie. The dogwoods and redbuds had already lost their spring color. The air was hot. Four hours later he was in Indiana, where the land was flat as a playing card. There was nowhere to hide, no safety at all. Even the sun was too bright. He didn't understand how Ory could stand such open ground.

Illinois was equally flat but with less green to it. Gerald realized that he was driving through a season, watching spring in reverse. The Illinois dirt was black as manure and he pulled over to examine it. The earth was moist and rich. It smelled of life. He let it trickle between his fingers, thinking of the hard clay dirt at home. He decided to stop and get some of this good dirt on the way back.

He drove all day and crossed the Mississippi River at night. At a rest area, he unrolled a blanket and lay down. He was cold. Above him the stars were strewn across the sky. They seemed to be moving down, threatening to press him against the ground. Something bright cut across the night, and he thought someone had shot at him until he realized it was a shooting star. The hills at home blocked so much sky that he'd never seen one. He watched the vast prairie night until fading into sleep.

The eerie light of a flatland dawn woke him early. The sun wasn't visible and the world seemed to glow from within. There were no birds to hear. He could see his breath. He drove west and left the interstate at Wahoo and found the hospital easily. A nurse took him to a small room. Everything was white and the walls seemed to emit a low hum. He couldn't place the smell. A man came into the room wearing a white coat. He spoke with an accent.

"I am Dr. Gupte. You are with the family of Mr. Gowan?"

"You're the doctor?"

"Yes." He sighed and opened a manila folder. "I'm afraid Mr. Gowan has left us."

"Done out, huh. Where to?"

"I'm afraid that is not the circumstance."

"It's not."

"No, he had a pulmonary thromboembolism."

"Is that American?"

"I'm afraid you will excuse me."

Dr. Gupte left the room and Gerald wondered who the funny little man really was. He pulled open a drawer. Inside was a small mallet with a triangular head made of rubber, perfect for nothing. A cop came in the room, and Gerald slowly closed the drawer.

"I'm Sheriff Johnson. You the next of kin?"

"Gerald Bolin."

They watched each other in the tiny room under the artificial light. Gerald didn't like cops. They got to carry a gun, drive fast, and fight. Anybody else got thrown in the pokey for doing the same thing.

"Dr. Gupte asked me to come in," the sheriff said.

"He really is a doctor?"

"He's from Pakistan."

"Run out of your own, huh."

"Look, Mr. Bolin. Your brother-in-law got a blood clot that went to his lung. He died from it."

Gerald cleared his throat, scanned the floor for somewhere to spit, then swallowed it. He rubbed his eyes.

"Say he's dead."

The sheriff nodded.

"That damn doctor ain't worth his hide, is he."

"There's some things to clear up."

The sheriff drove Gerald to his office, a small space with a desk and two chairs. A calendar hung from the wall. The room reminded Gerald of the hospital without the smell.

"Ory was on a tear," the sheriff said. "He was drinking and wrecked his car at his girlfriend's house. She wouldn't let him in and he broke the door open. They started arguing and she shot him."

"Then he got a blood clot."

The sheriff nodded.

"Did he not have a job?" Gerald said.

"No. And there's some money problems. He went through a fence and hit a light post. He owed back rent at a rooming house. Plus the hospital."

"Car bad hurt?"

"It runs."

"Did he own anything?"

"Clothes, a knife, suitcase, a little twenty-two pistol, a pair of boots, and a radio."

"What all does he owe?"

"Twelve hundred dollars."

Gerald walked to the window. He thought of his wife and all her family waiting for him. They'd given him a little money, but he'd need it for gas on the ride back.

"Can I see her?" he said.

"Who?"

"The woman that shot him."

The sheriff drove him a few blocks to a tan building made of stone. Near the eaves were narrow slits to let light in. They went through heavy doors into a common room with a TV set and a pay phone. Four cells formed one wall. A woman sat on a bunk in one of the cells, reading a magazine. She wore an orange jumpsuit that was too big for her.

"Melanie," the sheriff said. "You have a visitor. Ory's brother-in-law."

The sheriff left and Gerald stared through the bars. Her hair was dark purple. One side was long, the other shaved. Each ear had several small gold hoops in a row that reminded Gerald of a guide for a harness. A gold ring pierced her left nostril. She had a black eye. He wanted to watch her for a long time, but looked at his boots instead.

"Hidy," he said.

She rolled the magazine into a tube and held it to her good eye, looking at Gerald.

"I come for Ory," Gerald said, "but he's died on me. Just thought I'd talk to you a minute."

"I didn't kill him."

"I know it."

"I only shot him."

"A blood clot killed him."

"Do you want to screw me?"

Gerald shook his head, his face turning red. She seemed too young to talk that way, too young for jail, too young for Ory.

"Let me have a cigarette," she said.

He passed one through the bars, and she took it without touching his hand. A chain was tattooed around her wrist. She inhaled twin lines of smoke from her mouth into her nose. The ash was long and red. She sucked at the filter, lifting her lips to prevent them from getting burned. She blew a smoke ring. Gerald had never seen anyone get so much out of a single cigarette.

"Wish it was menthol," she said. "Ory smoked menthol."

"Well."

"What do you want," she said.

"I don't know. Nothing I don't guess."

"Me neither, except out of here."

"Don't reckon I can help you there."

"You talk just like Ory did."

"How come you to shoot him?"

"We had a fight, and he like, came over drunk. He wanted something he gave me, and I wouldn't give it back. It was mine. He busted the lock and started tearing everything up, you know, looking for it. I had a little pistol in my vanity and I like, got it out."

Melanie finished the cigarette, and he gave her another one, careful not to look at the ring in her nose. Behind her was a stainless steel toilet with a sink on top where the tank should be. When you washed your hands, it flushed the toilet. He thought of the jail at home with its putrid hole in the floor and no sink at all.

"What was it he was wanting so bad?"

"A wig," she said. "It was blond and he liked me to wear it. Sometimes I wore it in bed."

"You shot him over a wig."

"I was scared. He kept screaming, 'Give me back my wig.' So I, you know, shot him. Just once. If I knew he'd get that blood clot, I wouldn't have done it."

Gerald wondered how old she was but didn't want to insult her by asking. He felt sorry for her.

"He give you that eye?"

"The cops did. They think me and Ory sell dope but we don't, not really. Nothing heavy. Just to, like, friends."

"Why do you do that?" he said.

"Deal?"

"No. Cut your hair and stick that thing in your nose."

"Shut up," she said. She began yelling. "I don't need you. Get away from me. Get out of here!"

The sheriff came into the common room and took Gerald outside. The sky was dark with the smell of rain. He wanted to stand there until the storm swept over him, rinsing him of the jail. He underwent a sudden sense of vertigo, and for a moment he didn't know where he was, only that he was two days from anything familiar. He didn't even know where his truck was.

"She's a hard one," the sheriff said.

"I don't want no charges pressed against her."

"That's not up to you."

"She didn't kill him."

"I don't know about Kentucky," the sheriff said, "but in Nebraska, shooting people's a crime. Look, there's been a big wreck on Ninety-two and five people are coming to the hospital. They need the space. We got to get your brother-in-law to a funeral home."

"Can't afford it."

"The hospital's worse. It charges by the day."

"What in case I take his stuff and leave."

"The county'll bury him."

"That'll run you how much?"

"About a thousand."

"That's a lot of money."

The sheriff nodded.

"Tell you what," Gerald said. "I'll sell you his car for one dollar. You can use it to pay off what all he owes. There's that radio and stuff. Plus I'll throw in a hundred cash."

"You can't buy a body."

"It ain't yours to sell or mine to buy. I just want to get him home. Family wants him."

"I don't know if it's legal."

"He ain't the first person to die somewhere else. My cousin's aunt came in on a train after getting killed in a wreck. They set her off at the Rocksalt station. She was in a box."

The sheriff puffed his cheeks and blew air. He went to his office and dialed the courthouse and asked for a notary public. Half an hour later the car belonged to the city of Wahoo. It was a Chevelle and for a moment Gerald wondered if he'd made a mistake. They were pretty good cars.

The sheriff drove them to the hospital. Gerald pulled the money out and started counting.

"Keep it," the sheriff said.

"Give it to Melanie. She wants menthol cigarettes."

"You and Ory aren'ta whole lot alike, are you."

"I never knew him that good."

"The only man I saw give money away was my daddy."

"Was he rich?"

"No," said the sheriff, "Daddy was a farmer."

"You all worked this flat land?"

"It worked him right back into it."

Gerald followed the sheriff into the hospital and signed several forms. An orderly wheeled in a gurney with the body on it, covered with a white cloth. He pushed it to an exit beside the emergency room. Three ambulances drove into the lot and paramedics began moving the injured people into the hospital. The orderlies left the gurney and went to help. A state police car stopped behind the ambulances.

"I have to talk to them," the sheriff said. "Then I'll get an ambulance to drop the body down at the train station."

The sheriff left the car and walked to the state trooper. Nobody was looking at Gerald. He pushed the gurney into the lot and along the side of the building. A breeze rippled the cloth that covered Ory. Gerald held it down with one hand but the gurney went crooked. He let go of the cloth and righted the gurney and the wind blew the cloth away. Ory was stretched out naked with a hole in his side. He didn't look dead, but Gerald didn't think he looked too good either. He looked like a man with a bad hangover that he might shake by dinner.

Gerald dropped the tailgate of his pickup and dragged Ory into the truck. He threw his blanket over him and weighted the corners with tire tools, the spare, and a coal shovel. He drove the rest of the day. In Illinois, he stopped and lay down beside the truck. Without the blanket he was cold, but he didn't feel right about taking it back from Ory. Gerald thought about Ory asking Melanie to wear the blond wig. He wondered if it made a difference when they were in bed.

He woke with frost on him. A buzzard circled high above the truck. He drove into the rising sun, thinking that he'd done everything backward. No matter when he drove, he was always aimed at the sun. Mist lifted above the land as the frost gave way. At the next exit, Gerald left the interstate for a farm road and parked beside a plowed field.

He carried the shovel over a wire fence. The dirt was loose and easy to take. It would make a fine garden at home. His body took over, grateful for the labor after three days of driving. A pair of redwing blackbirds sat on a power line, courting each other, and Gerald wondered how birds knew to go with their own kind. Maybe Ory knew he was in the wrong tree and that's why he wanted Melanie to wear a wig. Gerald tried to imagine her with blond hair. He suddenly understood that he wanted her, had wanted her at the jailhouse. He couldn't figure why. It bothered him that he had so much desire for a woman he didn't consider attractive.

He climbed in the back and mounded the dirt to balance the load. As he traveled south, he reentered spring. The buds of softwood trees turned pale green. Flocks of starlings moved over him in a dark cloud, heading north. By nightfall, he crossed the Ohio River into Kentucky. In four hours he'd be home. He was getting sleepy, but coffee had stopped doing him any good. He slid into a zone of the road, letting the rhythm of motion enter his body. A loud noise made him jerk upright. He thought he'd had a flat until he saw that he'd drifted across the breakdown lane and onto the edge of the median. He parked and lay down in the bench seat. He was lucky not to have been killed. The law would have a hard time with that—two dead men, one naked and already stiff, and a load of dirt.

When he woke, it was light and he felt tired already. At a gas station he stared at the rest room mirror, thinking that he looked like the third day of a three-day drunk. The suit was ruined. He combed his hair with water and stepped into the sun. A dog was in the back of his pickup, digging. Gerald yelled, looking for something to grab. The dog saw him and jumped off the truck and loped away. Gerald shoved dirt over Ory's exposed hand. A man came behind him.

"Shoo-eee," the man said. "You waited long enough didn't you."

Gerald grunted. He was smoothing the dirt, replacing the weights along the blanket's edge. The man spoke again.

"Had to take one to the renderers myself last week. Got some kind of bug that killed it in three days. Vet said it was a new one on him."

"A new one."

"I put mine in a garbage bag. Keeps the smell in better than dirt."

"It does."

"Did yours up and not eat, then lay down and start breathing hard?"

"More or less."

"It's the same thing. A malady, the vet called it."

"A malady."

Gerald got in the truck and decided not to stop until he was home. The stench was bad and getting worse. He wondered if breathing a bad smell made your lungs stink. The land started to roll, the crests rising higher as he traveled east. The sun was very hot. It seemed to him as if summer had arrived while he was gone. He'd been to winter and back.

Deep in the hills, he left the interstate for a blacktop road that turned to dirt, following the twists of a creek. He stopped at the foot of his wife's home hill. Kay would be up there, at her mom's house with all her family. They would feed him, give him whiskey, wait for him to tell what happened. He brushed off his suit and thought about the events, collecting them in sequence. He told the story in his head. He thought some more, then practiced again. Ory had quit drinking and taken a good job as manager of a department store. He'd gotten engaged to a woman he'd met at church, but had held off telling the family until he could bring her home. She was nice as pie, blond headed. He was teaching her to shoot a pistol and it went off by accident. She was tore all to pieces about it. He'd never seen anyone in such bad shape. All she did was cry. It was a malady.

Gerald drove slowly up the hill. Later, he could tell the truth to the oldest brother, who'd tell the rest. They'd appreciate his public lie and he'd be in with the family. He parked in the yard beside his mother-in-law's house. Dogs ran toward the truck, then kids. Adults stepped onto the porch and Gerald could see them looking for Ory in the cab. Kay came out of the house. She smiled at him, the same small smile that she always used, and he wondered how she'd look in a wig.

He got out of the truck and waited. Everything was the same—the house, the trees, the people. He recognized the leaves and the outline of the branches against the sky. He knew how the light would fall, where the shadows would go. The smell of the woods was familiar. It would be this way forever. Abruptly, as if doused by water, he knew why Ory had left.

Reprinted with permission of the author. Published in *Out of the Woods: Stories* (Simon and Schuster, 1999).

Chris Offutt: A Biographical Sketch

Chris Offutt's hallmark is versatility. Not only has he written books in three different genres, he is also in demand as a television script writer, having written shows for both HBO and Showtime; he has written comic books and a film script as well.

Chris Offutt was born in Lexington, Kentucky, in 1958. Soon, however, his father, Andrew J. Offutt, a science fiction writer and insurance salesman, moved his young family to a house built by L. P. Haldeman, the creator of the Kentucky Firebrick Company, in one of the most remote places in northeastern Kentucky, at least twenty miles from any county-seat town. Chris Offutt grew up as the only kid in the small, impoverished community of Haldeman, Kentucky, who lived in a nice big house and whose father drove first a Mercedes and then a Volkswagen. Early on, Offutt got used to proving he was just as tough as his neighbors, but he also was the son of a writer, a voracious reader who started keeping a journal when he was ten years old. Offutt quit high school at the age of seventeen and started hitchhiking around the country, finding jobs wherever he could. Sporadically, he attended Morehead State University, graduating in 1981 with a degree in theater and a minor in English. After graduation he continued his odyssey around the United States and Europe. In 1982 he sold everything he owned and lived in Paris for a year that he considers important in his development as a writer. His favorites among his more than fifty jobs in America were as a dishwasher at the Grand Canyon, a tour guide in the Everglades, and a family photographer in New England.

Offutt began settling down when he married Rita Lily, and was accepted into the MFA program at the University of Iowa. His son Sam was born in 1990, the year he graduated. Success as a writer came almost immediately. His first story collection, *Kentucky Straight,* was published in 1992, the year son James was born, and a few months later, his first memoir, *The Same Year Twice* (1993), was released. The following year the American Academy of Arts and Letters presented Offutt with its Jean Stein Award. In 1996 Offutt collected both a Whiting Writers Award and a Guggenheim Foundation Award for fiction, and was named one of Granta's 20 Best Young American Novelists. The next year, Offutt's first novel, *The Good Brother,* was released. During the 1990s, Offutt continued to travel around the country, teaching not only at the University of Iowa but also at the University of New Mexico and Wesleyan University in Connecticut. For the 1998–99 school year, Offutt left the University of Montana and returned to his alma mater, Morehead State University, to teach. While there his second short-story collection, *Out of the Woods,* was published.

During the first decade of the new millennium, Offutt lived mostly in Iowa City, but also in Texas, accepting temporary jobs both in acting and teaching. He published a memoir of his return to Kentucky to teach, *No Heroes* (2003); was awarded a Lannan Foundation grant; and created a screenplay based on his story collection *Out of the Woods.* He wrote episodes of *True Blood* for HBO, and episodes of *Weeds* for Showtime. He also published his first comic book. During that decade, Chris Offutt and Rita Lily were divorced, and a few years later he married Gloria Branham, who gave birth to a daughter. In 2010, Offutt's "Tough Trade" episodes were produced by Lionsgate for television syndication. In 2011 Chris Offutt accepted a faculty position at the University of Mississippi. His first film, *The Trapper,* was also produced that year. He continues to write and market both stories and novels, as well as screenplays for both premium channels and networks.

Chris Offutt: A Selective Bibliography

INTERNET RESOURCES

National Public Radio has a recording of Offutt reading the short story "A Good Pine." Offutt's author page by *Simon and Schuster* offers live links to the first chapter of his books *The Good Brother* and *No Heroes. Indie Bound* features an interview titled "Looking Back, Looking In." *WordSmitten* offers a briefer interview with Offutt on the role and voice of writers. The *New York Times* has a biographical sketch on Offutt titled "At Home with Chris Offutt: Learning Not to Trespass on the Gently Rolling Past."

SELECTED BOOKS

No Heroes: A Memoir. New York: Simon and Schuster, 2002.

Out of the Woods: Stories. New York: Scribner, 1999.

The Good Brother. New York: Simon and Schuster, 1998.

The Same River Twice: A Memoir. New York: Simon and Schuster, 1993.

Kentucky Straight: Stories. New York: Vintage/Alfred A. Knopf, 1992.

PROFILES/INTERVIEWS

May, Charles. "Interview: Chris Offutt: Iowa, October 2000." *Appalachian Heritage* 30.1 (2002): 4–17.

Palmer, Louis H., III. "Chris Offutt Comes Home." *Appalachian Journal* 26.1 (1998): 22–31.

LITERARY CRITICISM

Bilger, Burkhard. "Homeland Insecurity: Chris Offutt's Memoir Explores Returning, as Well as Leaving, Home." *New York Times Book Review* 7 July 2002: 24.

Burroughs, Franklin. "Landscapes of the Alternate Self." *Southern Review* 30.1 (1994): 143–55.

Gerlach, John. "Narrative, Lyric, and Plot in Chris Offutt's *Out of the Woods*." In *The Art of Brevity: Excursions in Short Fiction Theory and Analysis*. Ed. Per Winther, Jakob Lothe, and Hans H. Skei. Columbia: U of South Carolina P, 2004. 44–56.

Petersen, Robert C. "Chris Offutt." In *American Short-Story Writers since World War II: Fifth Series*. Ed. Richard E. Lee and Patrick Meanor. *Dictionary of Literary Biography*. Vol. 335. Detroit: Gale, 2007.

Schafer, William J."Kentucky Straight / Kentucky Bent." *Appalachian Journal* 21.1 (1993): 50–55.

Wieck, Carl."Chris Offutt, The Good Brother." In *Still in Print: The Southern Novel Today*. Ed. Jan Nordby Gretlund. Columbia: South Carolina UP, 2010. 119–34.

Ron Rash

Blackberries in June

On those August nights when no late-afternoon thunderstorm rinsed the heat and humidity from the air, no breeze stirred the cattails and willow oak leaves, Jamie and Matt sometimes made love surrounded by water. Tonight might be such a night, Jamie thought. She rolled down the window and let air blast away some of the cigarette smoke that clung to her uniform and hair. She was exhausted from eight hours of navigating tables with hardly a pause to stand still, much less sit down, from the effort it took to lift the sides of her mouth into an unwavering smile. Exhausted too from the work she'd done at the house before her shift at the restaurant. The radio in the decade-old Ford Escort didn't work, so she hummed a Dixie Chicks song about chains being loosened. That's what she wanted, to be unchained in the weightlessness of water. She wanted to feel Matt lift and hold her so close their hearts were only inches apart.

In a few minutes the road fell sharply. At the bottom of the hill she turned off the blacktop onto what was, at least for now, more red-clay washout than road. The Escort bumped and jarred as it made its way down to the lake house. Their house, hers and Matt's. Barely a year married, hardly out of their teens, and they had a place they owned, not rented. It was a miracle Jamie still had trouble believing. And this night, like every night as she turned in to the drive, a part of her felt surprise the house was really there.

But it was, and already looking so much better than in June when she and Matt had signed the papers at the bank. What had been a tangle of kudzu and briars, a yard and garden. Broken windows, rotted boards, and rust-rotten screens replaced. Now Jamie spent her mornings washing years of grime off walls and blinds. When that was done she could start caulking the cracks and gashes on the walls and ceilings. Matt reshingled the roof evenings after he got off, working until he could no longer see to nail. As he must have this night, because the ladder lay against the side of the house. In another month, when the shingles had been paid for, they would drive down to Seneca and buy paint. If things went well, in a year they'd have enough saved to replace the plumbing and wiring.

Matt waited on the screened-in porch. The light wasn't on, but Jamie knew he was there. As she came up the steps, his form emerged from the dark like something summoned out of air. He sat in the porch swing, stripped to his jeans. His work boots, shirt, and socks lay in a heap near the door. The swing creaked and swayed as she curled into his lap, her head against his chest. Her lips tasted the salty sweat on his skin as his arms pulled her closer. She felt the hardness of Matt's arms, muscled by two months of ten- to twelve-hour days cutting pulpwood. She wished of those hard muscles a kind of armor to protect him while he logged with her brother, Charlton, on the ridges where the Chauga River ran through Big Laurel Valley.

You best get a good look at your husband's pretty face right now, Charlton had said the first morning he came to pick up Matt. Feel the smooth of his skin too, little sister, because a man who cuts pulpwood don't stay pretty long.

Charlton had spoken in a joking manner, but she'd seen the certain truth of it in her brother's face, the broken nose and gapped smile, the raised, purple ridges on his arms and legs where flesh had been knitted back together. Jamie had watched Charlton as he and Matt walked to the log truck with its busted headlights and crumpled fender and cracked windshield. A truck no more beat-up and battered than its owner, Jamie had realized in that moment. Charlton was thirty years old, but he moved with the stiffness of an old man. Dr. Wesley in Seneca said he needed back surgery, but Charlton would hear nothing of it. Her sister-in-law, Linda, had told Jamie of nights Charlton drank half a bottle of whiskey to kill the pain. And sometimes, as Matt had witnessed, Charlton didn't wait until night.

The porch swing creaked as Jamie pressed her head closer to Matt's chest, close enough so she could not just hear but feel the strong, sure beat of his heart. First get the house fixed up, Jamie thought. Then when that was done she and Matt would start taking night classes again at the technical college. In a year they'd have their degrees. Then good jobs and children. It was a mantra she recited every night before falling asleep.

"Want to get in the lake?" Matt asked, softly kissing the top of her head.

"Yes," Jamie said, though she felt, to use her mother's words, tired to the bone. In some ways that was what made their lovemaking so good, especially on Saturday nights—finding in each other's bodies that last ounce of strength left from their long day, their long week, and sharing it.

They walked down the grassy slope to where a half-sunk pier leaned into the lake. On the bank they took off their clothes and stepped onto the pier, the boards trembling beneath them. At the pier's end the boards became slick with algae and water rose to their ankles. They felt for the drop-off with their feet, entered the water with a splash.

Then Jamie was weightless, the water up to her breasts, her feet lifting from the silt as she wrapped her arms around Matt. The sway of water eased away the weariness of eight hours of standing, eased as well the dim ache behind her eyes caused by hurry and noise and cigarette smoke. Water sloshed softly against the pier legs. The moon mirrored itself in the water, and Matt's head and shoulders shimmered in a yellow glow as Jamie raised her mouth to his.

They slept late the next morning, then worked on the house two hours before driving up the mountain to her grandmother's for Sunday lunch. Behind the farmhouse a barn Jamie's grandfather had built in the 1950s crumbled into a rotting pile of tin and wood. In a white oak out by the boarded-up well, a cicada called for rain.

"Let's not stay more than an hour," Matt said as they stepped onto the front porch. "That's as long as I can stand Linda."

Inside, Jamie's parents, Charlton, Linda, and their children already sat at the table. Food was on the table and the drinks poured.

"About to start without you," Linda said sharply as they sat down. "When young ones get hungry they get contrary. If you had kids you'd know that."

"Them kids don't seem to be acting contrary to me," Matt said, nodding at the three children. "The only person acting contrary is their momma."

"I'm sorry," Jamie said. "We were working on the house and lost track of time."

"I know you all are trying to save money, but I still wish you had a phone," her mother said.

Grandma Chastain came in from the kitchen with a basket of rolls. She sat down at the table beside the youngest child.

"Say us a prayer, Luther," she said to her son.

For a few minutes they ate in silence. Then Charlton turned to his father.

"You ought to have seen the satin back me and Matt killed Wednesday morning. Eight rattles and long as my leg," Charlton said. "Them chain saws have made me so deaf I didn't even hear it. I'm just glad Matt did or I'd of sure stepped right on it."

"Don't tell such a thing, Charlton," Grandma Chastain said. "I worry enough about you out in them woods all day as it is."

"How's your back, Son?" Jamie's mother asked.

It was Linda who answered.

"Bothers him all the time. He turns all night in bed trying to get comfortable. Ain't neither of us had a good night's sleep in months."

"You don't think the surgery would do you good?" Grandma Chastain asked.

Charlton shook his head.

"It didn't help Bobby Hemphill's back none. Just cost him a bunch of money and a month not being able to work."

When they'd finished dessert, Jamie's mother turned to her.

"You want to go with me and Linda to that flower show in Seneca?"

"I better not," Jamie said. "I need to work on the house."

"You and Matt are going to work yourselves clear to the bone fixing that house if you're not careful," her mother said.

Jamie's father winked at Jamie.

"Your momma's always looking for the dark cloud in a blue sky."

"I do no such thing, Luther Alexander," her mother said. "It's just the most wonderful kind of thing that Jamie and Matt have that place young as they are. It's like getting blackberries in June. I just don't want them wearing themselves out."

"They're young and healthy, Momma. They can handle it," Charlton said. "Just be happy for them."

Linda sighed loudly and Charlton's lips tightened. The smile vanished from his face. He stared at his wife but did not speak. Instead, it was Grandma Chastain who spoke.

"You two need to be in church on Sunday morning," she said to Jamie, "not working on that house. You've been blessed, and you best let the Lord know you appreciate it."

"Look at you," Linda said angrily to Christy, the youngest child. "You got that pudding all over your Sunday dress." She yanked the child from her chair. "Come on, we're going to the bathroom and clean that stain, for what little good it'll do."

Linda walked a few steps, then turned back to the table, her hand gripping Christy's arm so hard the child whimpered.

"I reckon we all don't get lucky with lake houses and such," Linda said, looking not at Matt but at Jamie, "but that don't mean we don't deserve just as much. You just make sure your husband saves enough of his strength to do the job Charlton's overpaying him to do."

"I reckon if Charlton's got any complaints about me earning my pay he can tell me his own self," Matt said.

Linda swatted Christy's backside with her free hand.

"You hush now," she said to the child and dragged her into the bathroom.

For a few moments the only sound was the ticking of the mantel clock.

"You don't pay Linda no mind," Charlton said to Matt. "The smartest thing I done in a long while is let go that no-account Talley boy and hire you. You never slack up and you don't call in sick on Mondays. You ain't got a dime from me you ain't earned."

"And I wouldn't expect otherwise," Matt said.

"Still, it's a good thing Charlton's done," Jamie's mother said as she got up, "especially letting you work percentage." She laid her hand on her son's shoulder as she reached around him to pick up his plate. "You've always been good to look after your sister, and I know she'll always be grateful, won't you, girl?"

"Yes, ma'am," Jamie said.

The bathroom door opened and Christy came out trailing her mother, her eyes swollen from crying.

"We ought to be going," Matt said, pushing back his chair. "I need to get some more shingles on that roof."

"You shouldn't to be in such a rush," Grandma Chastain said, but Matt was already walking toward the door.

Jamie pushed back her chair.

"We do need to be going."

"At least let me wrap you up something for supper," Grandma Chastain said.

Jamie thought about how much work they had to do and how good it would be not to have to cook.

"Okay, Grandma," she said.

Matt was in the car when she came out, the engine running and his hands gripping the steering wheel. Jamie placed the leftovers in the backseat and got in beside Matt.

"You could have waited for me," she said.

"If I'd stayed any longer I'd of said some things you wouldn't want me to," Matt said, "and not just to Linda. Your mother and grandma need to keep their advice to themselves."

"They just care about me," Jamie said, "about us."

They drove back to the house in silence and worked until dusk. As Jamie cleaned the blinds she heard Matt's hammer tapping above as if he was nailing her shut inside the house. She thought about the rattlesnake, how it could easily have bitten Matt, and remembered twelve years earlier, when her mother and Mr. Jenkins, the elementary school principal, appeared at the classroom door.

"Your daddy's been hurt," her mother said. Charlton was outside waiting in the logging truck, and they drove the fifteen miles to the county hospital. Her father had been driving a skid loader that morning. It had rained the night before and the machine had turned over on a ridge. His hand was shattered in two places, and there was nerve damage as well. Jamie remembered stepping into the white room with her mother and seeing her father in the bed, a morphine drip jabbed into his arm like a fang. If that skidder had turned over one more time you'd be looking at a dead man, her father had told them. Charlton had quit high school and worked full-time cutting pulpwood to make sure food was on the table that winter. Her father eventually got a job as a night watchman, a job, unlike cutting pulpwood, a man needed only one good hand to do.

"I get scared for you, for us," Jamie said that night as they lay in bed. "Sometimes I wish we'd never had the chance to buy this place."

"You don't mean that," Matt said. "This place is the best thing that might ever happen to us. How many chances do young folks get to own a house on a lake? If we hadn't seen Old Man Watson's sign before the real-estate agents did, they'd have razed the house and sold the lot alone to some Floridian at twice what we paid."

"I know that," Jamie said, "but I can't help being scared for you. It's just like things have been too easy for us. Look at Charlton. Him and Linda have been married ten years and they're still in a trailer. Linda says good luck follows us around like a dog that needs petting all the time. She thinks you and me getting this house is just one more piece of luck."

"Well, the next time she says that you tell her anybody with no better sense than to have three kids the first five years she's married can't expect to have much money left for a down payment on a house, especially with a skidder to pay off as well."

Matt turned his head toward her. She could feel the stir of his breath.

"Linda's just jealous," he said, "that and she's still pissed off Charlton's paying me percentage. Linda best be worrying about her own self. She's got troubles enough at home without stirring up troubles for other people."

"You mean Charlton's drinking?"

"Yeah. Every morning this week he's reeked of alcohol, and it ain't his aftershave. The money they waste on whiskey and her on makeup and fancy hairdos could help make a down payment, not to mention that Bronco when they already had a perfectly good car. Damn, Jamie, they got three vehicles and only two people to drive them."

Matt placed his hand on the back of Jamie's head, letting his fingers run through her cropped hair, hair shorter than his. His voice softened.

"You make your own luck," Matt said. "Some will say we're lucky when you're working in a dentist's office and I'm a shift supervisor in a plant, like we hadn't been planning that very life since we were juniors in high school. They'll forget they stayed at home nights and watched TV instead of taking classes at Tech. They'll forget how we worked near full-time jobs in high school and saved that money when they wasted theirs on new trucks and fancy clothes."

"I know that," Jamie said. "But I get so tired of people acting resentful because we're doing well. It even happens at the café. Why can't they all be like Charlton, just happy for us?"

"Because it reminds them they're too lazy and undisciplined to do it themselves," Matt said. "People like that will pull you down with them if you give them the chance, but we're not going to let them do that to us."

Matt moved his hand slowly down her spine, letting it rest in the small of the back.

"It's time to sleep, baby," he said.

Soon Matt's breathing became slow and regular. He shifted in the bed and his hand slipped free from her back. First, get the house fixed up, she told herself as she let her weariness and the sound of tree frogs and crickets carry her toward sleep.

Two more weeks passed, and it was almost time for Jamie to turn the calendar nailed by the kitchen door. She knew soon the leaves would start to turn. Frost would whiten the grass and she and Matt would sleep under piles of quilts Grandma Alexander had sewn. They'd sleep under a roof that no longer leaked. After Charlton picked up Matt, Jamie caulked the back room, the room that would someday be a nursery. As she filled in cracks she envisioned the lake house when it was completely renovated—the walls bright with fresh paint, all the leaks plugged, a porcelain tub and toilet, master bedroom built onto the back. Jamie imagined summer nights when children slept as she and Matt walked hand in hand down to the pier, undressing each other to share again the unburdening of water.

Everything but the back room's ceiling had been caulked when she stopped at one-thirty to eat lunch and change into her waitress's uniform. She was closing the front door when she heard a vehicle bumping down through the woods to the house. In a few moments she saw her father's truck, behind the windshield his distraught face. At that moment something gave inside her, as if her bones had succumbed to the weight of the flesh they carried. The sky and woods and lake seemed suddenly farther away, as if a space had been cleared that held only her. She closed her hand around the key in her palm and held it so tight her knuckles whitened. Her father kicked the cab door open with his boot.

"It's bad," he said, "real bad." He didn't cut off the engine or get out from behind the wheel. "Linda and Matt and your momma are already at the hospital."

She didn't understand, not at first. She tried to picture a situation where her mother and Linda and Matt could have been hurt together—a car wreck, or fire—something she could frame and make sense of.

"Momma and Linda are hurt too?" Jamie finally asked.

"No," her father said, "just Charlton." His voice cracked. "They're going to have to take your brother's leg off, baby."

Jamie understood then, and at that moment she felt many things, including relief that it wasn't Matt.

When they entered the waiting room, her mother and Linda sat on a long green couch. Matt sat opposite them in a blue plastic chair. Dried blood stained his work shirt and jeans. He stood up, his face pale and haggard as he embraced her. Jamie smelled the blood as she rested her head against his chest.

"We were cleaning limbs," Matt said, "and the saw jumped back and dug into his leg till it got to bone. I made a tourniquet with my belt, but he still like to have bled to death." Matt paused. "Charlton shouldn't have been running that saw. He'd been drinking."

Matt held her close a few more moments, then stepped back. He nodded toward the corner where Linda and her mother sat.

"You better say something to your momma and Linda," he said and released her arms. Jamie let go too. It was only then that she realized the key was still in her closed right hand. She slipped it into her uniform pocket.

Her mother stood when Jamie approached, but Linda stayed on the couch, her head bowed.

"Pray hard, girl," her mother said as she embraced Jamie. "Your brother is going to need every prayer he can get."

"You seen him yet, Momma?" she asked. Jamie smelled the Camay soap her mother used every night. She breathed deep, let the smell of the soap replace the smell of blood.

"No, he's still in surgery, will be for at least another hour."

Her mother released her and stepped back.

"I can't stand myself just sitting here," she said and nodded at Jamie's father standing beside the door marked SURGERY. "Come on, Luther. I'm going to get us all some doughnuts and coffee and I need you to help carry it." She turned to Jamie. "You stay here and look after Linda."

Jamie sat in the place her mother had left. Linda's head remained bowed, but her eyes were open. Jamie looked up at the wall clock. Two-twenty-three. The red minute hand went around seven more times before Jamie spoke.

"It's going to be all right, Linda," she said. It was the only thing she could think to say.

Linda lifted her head, looked right at Jamie. "You sound pretty sure of that. Maybe if it was your husband getting his leg took off you'd think different."

Linda wasn't thirty yet, but Jamie saw something she recognized in every older woman in her family. It was how they looked out at the world, their eyes resigned to bad times and trouble. I don't ever remember being young, Grandma Alexander had once told her. All I remember is something always needing to be done, whether it was hoeing a field or the washing or feeding hungry children or cows or chickens.

The elevator door opened and Jamie's parents stepped out, their hands filled with paper bags.

"You think this couldn't have happened to Matt," Linda said, raising her voice enough that Jamie's parents came no closer. "You think it happened because Charlton had been drinking."

"I don't think any such thing," Jamie said.

Linda looked at her in-laws.

"I got three young ones to feed and buy school clothes for, and a disability check ain't going to be enough to do that."

"We'll do everything we can to help you," Jamie's father said and offered Linda a cup of coffee. "Here. This will give you some strength."

"I don't need strength," Linda said, her voice wild and angry. "I need the money Charlton overpaid Matt. Money that should be ours. Money we need worse than they do."

Linda looked at her father-in-law.

"You know Charlton paid hourly wages to everybody else who worked for him."

"I earned every cent he paid me," Matt said. He had left his seat and stepped closer, standing next to Jamie now. "I been there every day and I've cut plenty of days dawn to dark. It's bad what's happened to Charlton, and I'm sorry it happened. But me and Jamie don't owe you anything." Jamie placed her hand on Matt's arm, but he jerked it away. "I ain't listening to this anymore."

"You owe us everything," Linda shouted as Matt walked toward the elevator. "If Charlton hadn't taken you on you'd never have been able to make a down payment on that lake house." Linda looked at Jamie's parents now, tears streaming down her face. "A lake house, and the five of us in a beat-up doublewide."

The surgery room door opened, and a nurse glared at them all briefly before the door closed again.

Jamie's mother sat down on the couch and pressed Linda's head to her bosom. "We're all going to do everything possible to get you all through this, and that includes Matt and Jamie," she said.

Linda sobbed now, her face smeared with mascara. Minutes passed before she raised her head. She tried to smile as she brushed tears from her cheeks and slowly lifted herself from the couch. Jamie's father gripped Linda's upper arm when her knees buckled.

"I know I look a sight," Linda said. "I best go to the bathroom and tidy up so Charlton won't see me like this." She looked at Jamie. "I'm sorry," she said.

Jamie's father walked Linda to the restroom and waited by the door.

"Come here, girl," her mother said to Jamie.

Jamie didn't move. She was afraid, almost as afraid as when she'd seen her father's face through the windshield.

"I need to call the restaurant, let them know what's going on."

"That can wait a few minutes," her mother said. "We need to talk, and right now."

Jamie remained where she was.

"I know you're put out with Linda," her mother said, "and I don't blame you. Grieving don't give her no excuse to talk that way to you and Matt." She paused, waited for Jamie to meet her eyes. "But you know you got to help them."

Jamie turned and stared at the wall clock. She thought how only two hours earlier she had been caulking the back room of the lake house.

"Me and your daddy will do what we can, but that won't be near enough. Your daddy says even if the skidder's sold, it'll bring no more than two thousand dollars. We're not talking about just Linda here. We're talking about your niece and nephews."

"Why are you saying this to me, Momma?" Jamie asked. "Matt's going to have to find another job now, and there's no way he'll make the kind of money

Charlton paid him. We need all the money we got just to make the payments on the lake house, much less fix it up. We'll have tuition to pay as well come spring."

The elevator door opened. Jamie hoped it was Matt, but a chaplain got off and walked past them toward the intensive care unit.

"You've been blessed, Jamie," her mother said. "Linda's right. Charlton never let anyone but Matt work percentage. You could give Charlton the difference between what Matt got paid and the six dollars an hour anybody else would have got."

"But we'd have to sell the lake house," Jamie said. "How can you ask me and Matt to do that?"

"The same way I'd have asked your brother to quit high school. Only I never had to ask. He knew what had to be done and did it without me saying a word to him. Seventeen years old and he knew what had to be done." Her mother laid her hand on Jamie's. "That lake house, you had no right to expect such a place so young. You know it was a miracle you got it in the first place. You can't expect miracles in this life, girl."

The bathroom door opened and Linda came out. She and Jamie's father walked toward them.

"Maybe not, Momma," Jamie said, her voice low but sharp, "but when they come a person's got a right to take them."

"You got to do what's best for the whole family," her mother said, speaking quietly as well. "You got to accept that life is full of disappointments. That's something you learn as you grow older."

There had been complications during the surgery, and Jamie was unable to see Charlton until after seven-thirty. His eyes opened when she placed her hand on his, but he was too drugged to say anything coherent. Jamie wondered if he even understood what had happened to him. She hoped that for a little while longer he didn't.

When Jamie and Matt got back to the lake house it was dark, and by then things had been decided, but not before harsh words had been exchanged.

"Come on," Matt said, reaching for her hand after they got out of the Escort. "Let's go down to the lake, baby. I need one good thing to happen in my life today."

"Not tonight," Jamie said. "I'm going on in."

She changed into her nightgown. Matt came in soon afterward naked and dripping, work clothes and boots cradled in his arms. Jamie stepped out of the bathroom, a toothbrush in her hand.

“Put those clothes out on the porch,” she said. “I don’t want to smell that blood anymore.”

Jamie was in bed when he came back, and soon Matt cut out the light and joined her. For a minute the only sounds were the crickets and tree frogs. The mattress’s worn-out springs creaked as Matt turned to face her.

“I’ll go see Harold Wilkinson in the morning,” he said. “He knows I did good work for Charlton. I figure I can get eight dollars an hour to work on his crew, especially since I know how to run a skidder.”

He reached out and laid his arm on Jamie’s shoulder.

“Come here,” he said, pulling her closer.

She smelled the thick, fishy odor of the lake, felt the lake’s coldness on his skin.

“They’ll be needing help a long time,” Matt said. “In two, three years at most we’ll have jobs that pay three times what we’re making now. Keeping this house is going to save us a lot of money, money we can help them with later.”

Matt paused.

“You listening to me?”

“Yes,” Jamie said.

“Linda’s parents can help too. I didn’t hear your momma say a word about them helping out.” Matt kissed her softly on the cheek. “They’ll be all right. We’ll all be all right. Go to sleep, babe. You got another long day coming.”

But she did not fall asleep, not for a while, and she woke at first light. She left the bed and went to the bathroom. Jamie turned on the faucet and soaked a washcloth, wrung it out and pressed it to her face. She set it on the basin and looked at the mirror. A crack jagged across the glass like a lightning bolt, a crack caulk couldn’t fill. Something else to be replaced.

Reprinted with permission of Picador. Published in *Chemistry and Other Stories* (2007).

Ron Rash: A Biographical Sketch

Ron Rash's second novel, *Saints at the River* (2004), received outstanding regional recognition, winning the fiction book of the year award from both the Southern Independent Booksellers Association and the Southern Book Critics Circle, as well as an unprecedented second Weatherford Award as the outstanding work of Appalachian fiction. His 2007 story collection, *Chemistry and Other Stories,* and his novel *Serena* (2008) gained national attention as finalists for the PEN/Faulkner Award for fiction. Rash's 2010 story collection, *Burning Bright,* enjoyed international recognition as the winner of the Frank O'Connor Award, given to the outstanding story collection of the year in the English language. Clearly, in half a dozen years, Ron Rash's stature has grown from regional to international in scope.

"How could I not grow up believing words were magical? How could I not want to be a writer?" Ron Rash asked the reporter from Western Carolina University where he teaches, after telling her the story that begins, "It was a warm summer evening, and my grandfather, still dressed in his work clothes, was smoking a Camel cigarette as he lingered at the kitchen table after a hard day's work." Rash goes on to tell that he noticed that his grandfather's "reading" of *The Cat in the Hat* differed from his mother's, and from the way he had read it earlier. This was the first time Rash realized that his grandfather, who had grown up deep in the mountains in Watauga County, North Carolina, couldn't read or write.

Eureka Mill (1998) is the title of Ron Rash's first poetry book and also the name of the textile plant in Chester, South Carolina, where both his parents got jobs when their family left the mountains. Not content with the life of a mill worker, Rash's father pursued his education after hours until he became an art professor at Gardner-Webb University in Boiling Springs, North Carolina. Ron Rash was born in Chester in 1953, but moved to Boiling Springs when he was seven and graduated from Gardner-Webb in 1976. There he is still remembered as a competitive long-distance runner often seen running around the campus and the small town. He traveled less than one hundred miles away to receive an MFA from Clemson University in 1979. There he met his wife, also a student at the time; they remained in Clemson and began to raise a son and daughter while Rash taught at Tri-County Technical College nearby. It wasn't until 1994, when Ron Rash was forty years old, that his first book, a story collection titled *The Night the New Jesus Fell to Earth and Other Stories from Cliffside, North Carolina,* was published. Four years later, *Eureka Mill* appeared. In 2000 he published a story collection and gathered his poems about Watauga County,

North Carolina, in *Among the Believers.* His first novel, *One Foot in Eden,* and another poetry collection, *Raising the Dead,* followed just two years later.

The next year, 2003, Ron Rash was offered a distinguished professorship at Western Carolina University, in the mountains about seventy miles north of Clemson. He maintains his Clemson home as well as an apartment near campus. Since coming to Western, his last four novels have been published, but Ron Rash has not forsaken the origins of his writing and has continued to publish in poetry and story. In 2011, when Rash's reputation allowed him to choose practically whichever publisher he wished, his poetry collection *Waking* was released by the Hub City Press, a small press out of Spartanburg, South Carolina. This is emblematic for a humble writer who is more comfortable in the shadows than the spotlight and who said, after telling the story about his grandfather, "I think one of the reasons I write is that it is an act of gratitude that the people who came before me sacrificed so much."

Ron Rash: A Selective Bibliography

INTERNET RESOURCES

The *HarperCollins Publisher* website offers a brief biography and bibliography of Rash's works that allows readers to browse inside his novels. The *New York Times* and *Salon* both have reviews of *Serena* online. An interview titled "Language Can Be Magical" is posted on the *Southern Scribe* website.

SELECTED BOOKS

The Cove. New York: Ecco / HarperCollins, 2012.

Waking. Spartanburg, SC: Hub City Press, 2011.

Burning Bright: Stories. New York: Ecco / HarperCollins, 2010.

Serena. New York: Ecco / HarperCollins, 2008.

Chemistry and Other Stories. New York: Picador, 2007.

The World Made Straight. New York: Henry Holt, 2006.

Saints at the River. New York: Picador, 2005.

One Foot in Eden. Charlotte: Novello Festival Press, 2002.

Raising the Dead. Oak Ridge, TN: Iris Press, 2002.

Casualties. Beaufort, SC: Bench Press, 2000.

The Night the New Jesus Fell to Earth and Other Stories from Cliffside, North Carolina. Beaufort, SC: Bench Press, 1994.

INTERVIEWS/PROFILES

Bjerre, Thomas Ærvold. "'The Natural World Is the Most Universal of Languages': An Interview with Ron Rash."*Appalachian Journal* 34.2 (2007): 216–27.

Brown, Joyce Compton. "Ron Rash: The Power of Blood-Memory." In *Appalachia and Beyond: Conversations with Writers from the Mountain South.* Ed. John Lang. Knoxville: U of Tennessee P, 2006. 335–53.

Marion, Jeff Daniel. "Interview with Ron Rash." *Mossy Creek Reader* 9 (2000): 18–40.

LITERARY CRITICISM

Baldwin, Kara. "'Incredible Eloquence': How Ron Rash's Novels Keep the Celtic Literary Tradition Alive." *South Carolina Review* 39.1 (2006): 37–45.

Brosi, George, ed. *Appalachian Heritage* 30.4 (2003). Features Ron Rash.

Brown, Joyce Compton, and Mark Powell. "Ron Rash's *Serena* and the 'Blank and Pitiless Gaze' of Exploitation in Appalachia." *North Carolina Literary Review* 19 (2010): 70–88.

Graves, Jesse. "Lattice Work: Formal Tendencies in the Poetry of Robert Morgan and Ron Rash." *Southern Quarterly* 45.1 (2007): 78–86.

Higgins, Anna Dunlap. "'Anything but Surrender': Preserving Southern Appalachia in the Works of Ron Rash." *North Carolina Literary Review* 13 (2004): 49–58.

Lang, John, ed. *Iron Mountain Review* 20 (2004). Features Ron Rash.

Charles Wright

Appalachian Farewell

Sunset in Appalachia, bituminous bulwark
Against the western skydrop.
An Advent of gold and green, an Easter of ashes.

If night is our last address,
This is the place we moved from,
Backs on fire, our futures hard-edged and sure to arrive.

These are the towns our lives abandoned,
Wind in our faces,
The idea of incident like a box beside us on the Trailways seat.

And where were we headed for?
The country of Narrative, that dark territory
Which spells out our stories in sentences, which gives them an end
and beginning . . .

Goddess of Bad Roads and Inclement Weather, take down
Our names, remember us in the drip
And thaw of the wintry mix, remember us when the light cools.

Help us never to get above our raising, help us
To hold hard to what was there,
Orebank and Reedy Creek, Surgoinsville down the line.

Reprinted with permission of Charles Wright. Published in *Scar Tissue* (Farrar, Straus, and Giroux, 2006).

❁ ❁ ❁

Get a Job

Just over sixteen, a cigarette-smoking boy and a bit,
I spent the summer digging ditches,
And carrying heavy things
                                        at Bloomingdale School site.
I learned how a backhoe works, and how to handle a shovel,
And multiple words not found in the dictionary.
Sullivan County, Tennessee, a buck twenty an hour,
1952.
     Worst job of my life, but I stuck it out.

Everyone else supported a family, not me.
I was the high school kid, and went home
Each night to my mother's cooking.
                                                            God knows where the others went.
Mostly across the line into Scott County, Virginia, I think,
Appalachian appendix, dead end.
Slackers and multipliers, now in, now out of jail, on whom I depended.
Cold grace for them.
                                        God rest them all road ever they offended,

To rhyme a prominent priest.
                                                  Without a ministry, without portfolio,
Each morning I sought them out
For their first instructions, for their laying on of hands.
I wish I could say that summer changed my life,
                                                                      or changed theirs,
But it didn't. Apparently, nothing ever does.
I did, however, leave a skin there.
A bright one, I'm told, but less bright than its new brother.

Reprinted with permission of Charles Wright. Published in *Appalachian Heritage* 32.2 (Spring 2004) and reprinted in *Scar Tissue* (Farrar, Straus, and Giroux, 2006).

❁ ❁ ❁

Nostalgia

Always it comes when we least expect it, like a wave,
Or like the shadow of several waves,
                                                            one after the next,
Becoming singular as the face

Of someone who rose and fell apart at the edge of our lives.

Breaks up and re-forms, breaks up, re-forms.
And all the attendant retinue of loss foams out
Brilliant and sea-white, then sinks away.

Memory's dog-teeth,
                                    lovely detritus smoothed out and laid up.

And always the feeling comes that it was better then,
Whatever *it* was—
                                    people and places, the sweet taste of things—
And this one, wave-borne and wave-washed, was part of all that.

We take the conceit in hand, and rub it for good luck.

Or rub it against the evil eye.
And yet, when that wave appears, or that wave's shadow, we like it,
Or say we do,
                  and hope the next time.

We'll be surprised again, and returned again, despite the fact
The time will come, they say, when the weight of nostalgia,
                                                                        that ten-food spread
Of sand in the heart, outweighs
Whatever living existence we drop on the scales.

May it never arrive, Lord, may it never arrive.

Reprinted with permission of Charles Wright. Published in *A Short History of the Shadow: Poems* (Farrar, Straus, and Giroux, 2002).

❁ ❁ ❁

What Do You Write About, Where Do Your Ideas Come From?

Landscape, of course, the idea of God and language
Itself, that pure grace
                    which is invisible and sure and clear,
Fall equinox two hours old,
Pine cones dangling and doomed over peach tree and privet,
Clouds bulbous and buzzard-traced.
The Big Empty is also a subject of some note,
Dark dark and never again,
The missing word and there you have it,
                                        heart and heart beat.
Never again and never again,
Backdrop of back yard and earth and sky
Jury-rigged carefully into place,
Wind from the west and then some,
Everything up and running hard,
                              everything under way,
Never again never again.

Charles Wright: A Biographical Sketch

Charles Wright is one of America's most distinguished contemporary poets. He has been awarded many of the most prestigious honors in poetry, culminating in the Pulitzer Prize that he won in 1998.

Charles Wright was born in 1935 at Pickwick Dam, Tennessee, where his father, an engineer, worked for the Tennessee Valley Authority. During Wright's first year, his family moved to Corinth, Mississippi, then Hiwassee Dam, North Carolina, and on to Knoxville. His family was among the first to arrive at Oak Ridge, Tennessee, and stayed there during World War II. When he was ten, they moved to Kingsport, Tennessee. He went to boarding school and then to Davidson College, where he majored in history, graduating in 1957. He served in the U.S. Army at an intelligence office in Verona, Italy, and it was there that he first became interested in poetry through the work of Ezra Pound. He also became a big fan of Italian movies—especially those by Federico Fellini, Michelangelo Antonioni, and Mario Monicelli—and has reflected in recent years that their abrupt beginnings and rapid movement from one image to the next may have been an early influence on his poetry. After Wright was discharged from the army he enrolled in the MFA program at the University of Iowa and graduated in 1963. A Fulbright Fellowship allowed him to return to Italy, where he studied at the University of Rome for the next two years. In 1968 another Fulbright made it possible for him to spend a year at the University of Padua. The next year Wright married Holly McIntire, an artist and television actress, and he began teaching at the University of California at Irvine. Their son, Luke, was born, in Irvine, and Wright's first book—a poetry collection, *The Grave of the Right Hand* (1970)—was published by Wesleyan University Press. His second poetry collection, *Hard Freight* (1973), was nominated for the National Book Award, and in 1978 his translation of *The Storm and Other Poems* by the Italian poet Eugenio Montale won the PEN Translation Prize.

Wright's sixth poetry collection, *Country Music* (1983), won the National Book Award, and in that same year he left California to become a professor at the University of Virginia. Before the end of the decade he published two more poetry collections, a book of criticism, and another translation of Italian poetry. In the 1990s he published six books of poetry and one of literary criticism. In 1992 the Academy of American Arts and Letters awarded him its ten-thousand-dollar Award of Merit in Poetry, and then, the next year, he won the one-hundred-thousand-dollar Ruth Lilly Poetry Prize. *Chickamauga* (1995) is set on the battlefield where Wright's great-grandfather was said to have taken a bullet in the mouth while yelling "Charge."It won the Lenore Marshall Poetry Prize from the Academy of American Poets. *Black Zodiac* (1997) won the

Pulitzer Prize in Poetry and the National Book Critics Circle Award. In 1999 Charles Wright was elected a chancellor of the Academy of American Poets.

Charles Wright published seven more poetry collections in the next decade, including *Scar Tissue* (2007), which won Canada's most lucrative international literary award, the Griffin Poetry Prize. In 2010 Wright published *Outtakes*. In May of that year he retired from the University of Virginia, and he and Holly began spending even more time at their cabin near Troy, Montana, just west of Glacier National Park.

Charles Wright: A Selective Bibliography

INTERNET RESOURCES

Seven of Wright's poems are available on the *Poetry Foundation* website along with a recording of a poem being read, a biographical sketch, and an interview on the topic of "the inexhaustible power of words" by NewsHour. The *Paris Review* offers an in-depth interview.

SELECTED BOOKS

Bye-and-Bye: Selected Late Poems. New York: Farrar, Straus, and Giroux, 2011.
Sestets: Poems. New York: Farrar, Straus, and Giroux, 2010.
Scar Tissue: Poems. New York: Farrar, Straus, and Giroux, 2007.
Buffalo Yoga: Poems. New York: Farrar, Straus, and Giroux, 2005.
A Short History of the Shadow: Poems. New York: Farrar, Straus, and Giroux, 2002.
Negative Blue: Selected Later Poems. New York: Farrar, Straus, and Giroux, 2001.
Appalachia. New York: Farrar, Straus, and Giroux, 1999.
Black Zodiac: Poems. New York: Farrar, Straus, and Giroux, 1998.
The World of the Ten Thousand Things: Poems, 1980–1990. New York: Farrar, Straus, and Giroux, 1990.

PROFILES/INTERVIEWS

Bourgeois, Louis. "An Interview with Charles Wright." *Carolina Quarterly* 56.2–3 (2004): 30–36.
Denham, Robert D., ed. *Charles Wright in Conversation: Interviews, 1979–2006.* Jefferson, NC: McFarland, 2008.
Young, David. "Charles Wright: Language, Landscape, and the Idea of God." in *Appalachia and Beyond: Conversations with Writers from the Mountain South.* Ed. John Lang. Knoxville: U of Tennessee P, 2006. 121–37.

LITERARY CRITICISM

Denham, Robert D. *The Early Poetry of Charles Wright: A Companion, 1960–1990.* Jefferson, NC: McFarland, 2009.

Lang, John. "The Energy of Absence." *Six Poets from the Mountain South.* Baton Rouge: Louisiana State UP, 2010. 157–94.

———, ed. *Iron Mountain Review* 8 (1992). Features Charles Wright.

McClatchy, J. D. "Ars Longa." *Poetry* 175.1 (1999): 78–89.

Moffett, Joe. *Understanding Charles Wright.* Columbia: South Carolina UP, 2008.

Slicer, Deborah. "Do What the Clouds Do: Charles Wright's Ambivalent Relationship with Nature and Landscape." *Isle: Interdisciplinary Studies in Literature and Environment* 13.2 (2006): 167–78.

Spiegelman, Willard. "Landscape and Identity: Charles Wright's Backyard Metaphysics." *Southern Review* 40.1 (2004): 172–96.

Part 4

Cultural Traditions

Darnell Arnoult

Learning Strategy at English Field

C.P.'s Outlaws versus the Martinsville Oilers.
Hot dogs and popcorn fill Friday night air
along with moths that flutter and flirt
with danger in the field lights.
Mothers ask questions of fathers
who talk to each other.
Their deep gravelly voices face the playing field—
they judge ball speed, weigh batting stance,
third baseman's charge, pitcher's windup, the balk,
short's scoop and fire to first.
They call for double plays, measure the power
of the catcher's legs, how fast his mask comes off.
Weaver, policeman, sander, insurance man,
mailman, doctor, lawyer, teacher,
foreman, yardman, fixer, preacher.
Their sons are scattered across a diamond
cupped in advertisements for WMVA, STP,
Blacky's Texaco, First Baptist Church, Red Man
Chew, Dixie Pig Pit-Cooked Bar-B-Q.
A fastball smacks the glove on third
then rockets to first—policeman to preacher.
A mother jumps on the concrete bleacher.
Claps and fidgets and does a hip walk in her seat.
She prays for a third out.

I am a girlfriend. A cheerleader. A rising senior.
I think I am listening and watching
to learn the game of baseball. If not for my boyfriend,
I would have no interest in the game.

An initiate spectator, I have not grasped
the mental energy of baseball:
telepathy between pitcher and catcher,
tension between the batter and pitcher,
pitcher and basemen, basemen and runner,
stealer and pitcher, catcher and batter.
SA-*wing batter! Swing!*
I only faintly appreciate the music of a hard ball
kissing the sweet spot of a wooden bat,
the dance of a runner in a pickle,
the warrior scrimmage as the third-base runner
goes for the steal and the catcher defends home.
I foolishly think I am learning baseball:
pass balls on third strikes, pop flies, fielder's choice,
fastballs, curveballs, spitballs, grease balls,
high balls, low balls, inside, outside, bunts,
line drives, foul tips, steals, the sacrifice—
sacrifice fly, sacrifice bunt, sacrifice play on the runner.
So many sacrifices.
My boyfriend's mother shares her popcorn.
I clap when she claps. Yell when she yells.
Fidget when she fidgets. Smile when she smiles.
I watch her son, the third baseman.
He rests between batters, his right hip
shoved out to be a resting place
for the back of his gloved hand.
He spits absently and watches the pitcher approach the rubber.
He is cocky. He's also cute and a good kisser.
I forgive his arrogance for love. For his sake
I watch and learn and get my mind
around what I can in the little time I have left.
Come August he'll say no to college baseball.
I'll turn in my pompoms a year early.
I'll work half-days and he'll join the Marines.
The Cards will play the Braves in a three-game series.
Our honeymoon nights will be spent in Atlanta Stadium.
Our honeymoon days will be spent dodging rhinos
in his parents' Galaxy 500 at Lion Country Safari

and riding the roller coaster at Six Flags Over Georgia—
a preview of things to come.
I will throw up whatever I eat. I will lose before I gain.
By May I'll be a mother finishing senior English
and he'll make Lance Corporal and move us to Lejeune.
Our old paths will be unrecoverable
except through our son and daughter.

Fourteen years later, I shift my attention
from the memory of a third baseman
to the shortstop-gone-catcher
who, in the hesitation of play,
pushes out his right hip to make a resting place
for the back of his gloved hand.
He spits absently and pulls his mask over his face.
A girl somewhere in the stands
writes his name over and over in her notebook.
He squats as the pitcher addresses the rubber.
I am out of my seat as he pops up.
Out of his crouch, he flings off his mask,
backs up first.
Other players' fathers nod to me,
acknowledge a job well done.
Unlike the catcher's grandmother, I am forced out
of my element. I bridge the distance
between fidgeting mothers and voyeuristic fathers.
I am chastised by the blind tournament umpire,
my ex-mother-in-law in it right alongside me.
She shares her popcorn, watches and judges
her grandson—and me. Conspires in my strategy.
I am here, in the bleachers, willing a win
across distance only a mother can fathom.

❁ ❁ ❁

Outrageous Love

How long
did I wait for
him to come love me? Lord!
I was starving! But hard as his
heart was

it was
food to me. Why
I had to bite my way
to that poor blinded and bleeding
thing. A

demon
I was. Must have
smelled the blood. On some nights
between cold sheets and closed eyes I'd
feel the

dark soft
ringlets, as if
his head already lay
on that pillow there waiting for
my love

to touch.
I'd feel that man's
skin beneath my hands, his
curls sliding between my fingers.
My hands

traveling
his neck, his chest,
his belly. Trace and taste
sweet bites of ribs, of tender thigh,
morsel

of neck
meat. Must have cast
a mighty spell on him
gobbling him up like that in dreams.
He came

to me
on a Sunday.
The mountains moved closer.
I heard a whippoorwill at noon.
He knocked.

I knew
It was him and
there he stood. Said he was
eaten up by melancholy.
Eaten

by a
sorrow. Me on
his mind all the time. He
didn't show his heart to any
body.

Truly
I have married
meat and bread. As sure as
this banquet passes my lips, love
is food.

Reprinted with permission of LSU Press. Published in *What Travels with Us* (2005).

❁ ❁ ❁

Pilgrimage

Alongside Bull Mountain Road
great Uncle Edgar's maple
catches fire come October
and burns until winter
turns it to finger-like embers.

Flatlanders look out in awe,
breathless at red and rust
textured vistas that are general
as postcards to me.
No spectacle there.

I take no annual trek
on snaking scenic roads.
My pilgrimage is here
among steel girders
and prestressed walls.

My eyes close on the cusp of November.
Ignited above fading grass
blazes old Edgar's maple phoenix.
There, panoramas ashen
against one single violent beauty.

Reprinted with permission of LSU Press. Published in *What Travels with Us* (2005).

❁ ❁ ❁

Work

You wake up knowing you'll work.
You don't worry that circumstances will hurt

your chances to choose your labor. It seems
your choice is made. Reams

of fabric undergird your life. But fate may
lead you down a surprising path. One day

you may wake up and find you had more choices
than you knew. You leave your bed, your home, with voices

carried in your head of who you leave behind. Here
you live out your path with collective memory. Veneer

line—I worked one for three months between Lejeune
and college. After two babies. Worked to the tune

of minimum wage, ten-hour days, and culled furniture. Once I went
into the deafening grind and buzz of the machine room. My only factory stint.

Never set foot in a towel mill. But that doesn't matter.
I dream my mother's and grandmother's dreams. Dreams of clatter

and snap, of doffers and fixers, of motion. I dream thread streaming from
    cotton icicles
mounted on frames. Spinning dripping cones feeding hungry looms that
    pulse and ripple

as they weave. Shuttles throwing thread. Clack-thump. Clack-thump.
Humming sirens sing fiber into endless reams of cloth. Clack-thump.

Whir. Whir. Whir. Fibrous colors drape the architecture
of my sleep. Clacking and whirring lift louder and louder to rapture.

Reprinted with permission of LSU Press. Published in *What Travels with Us* (2005).

Darnell Arnoult: A Biographical Sketch

Darnell Arnoult writes poetry, stories, and novels that are strongly grounded in working-class Appalachian and southern life. Her down-to-earth writing and teaching have won her legions of loyal admirers. Born in 1955 in Martinsville, Virginia, she and her family moved to nearby Danville so she could go to second grade in a Catholic school. She spent much of her early childhood in a house that doubled as her Baptist mother's beauty shop and her Catholic father's architecture office. When she was eight, her mother was diagnosed with schizophrenia after telling a motorcycle policeman, "Only God can write me a ticket." The next year her father went bankrupt and "took to the road." While her mother was hospitalized, Darnell attended a Catholic boarding school for a year in Lynchburg. Then she and her mother moved in with her grandmother, who came from a farm near the crest of the Blue Ridge in Floyd County, Virginia. They lived on the outskirts of Fieldale, a mill town founded by Marshall Field, the department store magnate, located about five miles into the hills from Martinsville. There she attended public schools, including George Washington Carver High School, where she was a cheerleader and class president. Following her junior year she married her sweetheart and gave birth to their son. After graduation her husband became a Marine, and she joined him at Camp Lejeune where their daughter was born. Looking back on that time, Arnoult considers her first husband to be heroic. "He took on helping me care for my sick mother and also my alcoholic father, who developed terminal cancer when I was twenty-one." After completing his service with the Marines he encouraged Arnoult to apply for admission to the University of North Carolina in hopes of obtaining basketball tickets, and the family moved there.

After a short stint as a UNC student, Darnell Arnoult's divorce sent her scrambling to make a living as a single mother and resulted in an eight-year gap in her education. She worked at a variety of jobs, and says, "I used to drop my kids off at school, sit in my car in the McDonald's parking lot and work on my poems for an hour before going to clean two or three houses a day." In 1990 she finally graduated from UNC with a major in American Studies and was hired by Duke's Center for Documentary Studies. Soon her poems and short stories began being published, and she started teaching writing at Duke Continuing Studies. During that time she also attended North Carolina State University, again working with her writing mentor, Lee Smith, with whom she had studied years earlier at UNC.

On April Fool's Day in the year 2000 Arnoult married metal artist and cowboy William Brock, and they moved to Smith County, Tennessee. While she lived there, one of her friends called her the "Mary Kay of creative writing," because she even held writing workshops in living rooms. In 2005 Louisiana State University Press published *What Travels with Us,* a book of poems that together present a portrait of Fieldale, Virginia. It became the Southern Independent Booksellers poetry book of the year and the only poetry collection to win a Weatherford Award from the Appalachian Studies Association during the years that poetry was considered in the same category with fiction. During the following year, Arnoult's novel, *Sufficient Grace,* was published by Simon and Schuster, and in 2009 she received an MFA from the University of Memphis. Later that year Darnell Arnoult became writer-in-residence at Lincoln Memorial University and the director of their Mountain Heritage Literary Festival.

Darnell Arnoult: A Selective Bibliography

INTERNET RESOURCES

The *Writer's Almanac* offers the poem "Psychology Today." Arnoult's website includes the opening scene of *Sufficient Grace. Southern Literary Review* posted an interview with Arnoult, and the *Table Rock Writer's Blog* offers a brief review of Arnoult's poems.

SELECTED BOOKS

Sufficient Grace. New York: Free Press/Simon and Schuster, 2006.
What Travels with Us: Poems. Baton Rouge: Louisiana State UP, 2005.

PROFILES

Browning, Maria. "Longshot Miracles." *Independent Weekly* 28 June 2006.
"Darnell Arnoult." *Contemporary Authors Online.* Detroit: Gale, 2007.
"Darnell Arnoult." *Gale Biography in Context.* 28 Oct. 2011.

LITERARY CRITICISM

Brosi, George, ed. *Appalachian Heritage* 35.1 (Winter 2007). Features Darnell Arnoult.

Pinckney Benedict

Pig Helmet and the Wall of Life

Pig Helmet needed to see the Wall of Life.

I call him Pig Helmet because he's the sort of fellow that, in olden times, you'd have been one of the Civilized People trying like hell with fire and boiling oil and molten lead and such, to keep him and his kind out, and he'd have been one of the dreaded barbarians, he'd have been the lead barbarian in fact, climbing over your city walls by means of an improvised ladder, with his snarling face painted a furious blue, and something large and heavy and sharp-edged clutched in his massive fist, and wearing a pig for a hat. The head and hide of a boar, thick and knobby and naturally tough, hardened further by curing and the cunning attachment of metal plates and studs and rings, with the great toothy maw of the feral hog sloping down over his heavy brow, its tusks like upthrust sabers and its dead piggy eyes glinting dully above his own. Pig Helmet.

Pig Helmet is a cop. He's employed by the county sheriff's department, and he lives down at the end of my road with his diminutive, pretty wife. Before that he was a "contractor" in Iraq and Afghanistan, where the money was good and the action was better, but his wife worried too much with him away. We tried to look after her as much as possible, my own wife and I, but we were no substitute for the ministrations of Pig Helmet, as you can imagine. He's a dutiful and attentive husband. Before that work, he was a bail bondsman, a bounty hunter (he hates that term, silly movie bullshit he calls it), and one time a guy that had jumped bail threw acid in his face, trying to blind him, to avoid capture.

The acid missed his eyes but crisped him pretty good otherwise, and the left side of his head is kind of a nightmare. The teeth show through permanently on that side, and the flesh is rippled and brown like old melted candle wax. He keeps pretty much to himself does Pig Helmet, has some acreage and a few animals like we all do around here, following his hobbies in his off-hours, hand-loading cartridges and felling trees on his place and then turning the stumps into sawdust with his stump grinder.

He loves the stump grinder. When I cut down a tree, he'll bring the stump grinder over to my place and grind the stump into the ground, leaving nothing but a hole and a few roots and a mound of soft, warm sawdust. He'll grind stumps for hours with apparent satisfaction. Sometimes in the fall he'll bring over the loin from a deer he's shot, and that's good eating. His wife's vegetable garden always produces plenty of tomatoes for them and for us.

Pig Helmet is not a fellow much given to self-pity, as you can imagine, or even to much at all in the way of self-regard, but he had recently been through a bad experience, and he was feeling down and lost and deeply in need of an encounter with Life that would restore him to a proper sense of himself, which is to say, no particular sense of himself at all, except for a kind of exuberant well-being of the sort that would allow him, as of old, to grind a stump or love his wife or swing a truncheon with a deep-seated sense of pleasure.

The bad experience that he underwent can briefly be described as follows: OxyContin addict, alcohol, family Monopoly game gone bad, shotgun deployed, multiple homicide. Topped off with suicide-by-cop. When Pig Helmet arrived in his cruiser at this lonely place to which he had been called, way out in the wilds of the western end of the county, the OxyContin addict was sitting shirtless and blood-spattered on the porch of the little frame house where he had just killed his brother, a cousin, his grandmother (can you imagine?) and an uncle. The house wasn't an unpleasant looking place, a neatly tended bungalow, with a pretty trumpet vine twining around the porch railing. The door stood wide open behind the OxyContin addict, the screen door too, the room behind it black as pitch; and he still had the scattergun in one hand, wouldn't turn it loose no matter how loudly Pig Helmet yelled for him to do so. Most people, people even marginally in their right minds, do what Pig Helmet tells them to do when he raises his voice at them.

This guy just smoked his cigarette down to the filter and then kind of lazily (this is how Pig Helmet described it to me) stood up and swung the muzzle of the gun around to cover Pig Helmet. So Pig Helmet took him down, double-tapped him right in the center of his chest with the .45 caliber service pistol he carries, and the guy sat down again, hand still wrapped around the stock of the shotgun, and he died right there on the porch. Pig Helmet wouldn't have felt bad about shooting the guy, he said, if there had been some utility in it; but the people beyond that open door were already dead as it turned out, and so there was nobody to rescue. There weren't even any shells in the shotgun anymore. The OxyContin addict had used them all up on his Monopoly opponents and the grandmother, who hadn't even, to all appearances, been involved in the game at all.

"Fucking mess," Pig Helmet said, and I believe him.

So when he saw the sign for the Wall of Life down at the county fairgrounds, he was in the mood. He didn't anticipate any trouble on account of the shooting because the homicides in the bungalow had been so brutal, and everybody agreed that the OxyContin addict had needed killing. It was a good shoot. Being on administrative leave pending a formal inquiry, Pig Helmet had the leisure to do what he wanted, and he didn't feel much like hand-loading any ammunition, and he didn't feel like grinding stumps, and he knew that his wife's sympathy and worry, while affectionately meant (she's an affectionate woman with Pig Helmet at least, though cripplingly shy around others, even those of us who have known her for years) would just make him feel worse. So he took himself off to see what the Wall of Life was all about.

Pig Helmet on duty, wearing his Nomex gloves and his bulky body armor and his brown sheriff's office uniform with its broad Sam Browne belt across his barrel body and his thick utility belt (flex cuffs, pepper spray, billy club, taser on the left side, service pistol on the right, plus radio and tactical flashlight and knife and other assorted gadgetry), can be a pretty unsettling sight. He's a big fellow, as I say, a man mountain, well over six feet tall, two hundred fifty pounds if he's an ounce, with a head shaved bald and gleaming and broad as the Dome of the Rock in Jerusalem. And he's got that nasty confusion of his face on the left side, which a person can grow used to, and even fond of, but not in a short period of time.

Now, you know what the Wall of Life is, even if you don't think you do. It's just like the Wall of Death, the county fair attraction where a rider on an old motorbike roars around the inside of a big wooden cylinder, centrifugal force sticking him perpendicular to the sides. The crowd stands on a catwalk at the top of the cylinder, looking in while the guy on the sputtering motorbike apparently defies gravity below them.

At the bigger, better shows, there are a couple, maybe even three motorbikes on the wall at one time, crossing one another's paths, cutting down toward the bottom of the cylinder and then shooting back to the top again, to cause the crowd to draw back in alarm, fearful that a biker will shoot out onto the catwalk and knock them over and kill them. Sometimes a pretty girl will stand at the bottom of the cylinder, in its center, gesturing toward the motorcyclists as they circle above her head, showing her faith in them, that they will not come unstuck from the walls and crash down on top of her. That's the Wall of Death.

The Wall of Life was just like that, only it was an evangelical preacher and his family who did the riding, and it was the preacher's daughter who stood in the bottom. The Wall of Life was this preacher's ministry, like an old time tent revival meeting but on motorcycles, and he went from town to town, fairground to fairground, setting up the Wall, running for a couple three days until the crowds let down, preaching at the people that came to see him ride and shout.

When his work in one place was done, he and his family would tear down the Wall of Life into a series of short arcs that stacked neatly one inside the next, and stow them aboard the aged Fruehauf tractor-trailer his ministry moved in. There was a huge portrait of the Wall on the side of the trailer, the great wooden cylinder and crude human figures speeding along on motorcycles inside, with a giant Jesus stretching his hands out on either side, like he wanted to catch the little riders if they flew out. After he packed up his stuff, the preacher and his family would shove off for the next place he felt called to.

Pig Helmet wasn't a particularly religious man. Like most of the rest of us he grew up in a Baptist household, and he had been saved at a certain point in his boyhood because it was expected of him, and he had given testimony at various times for much the same reason, but none of it—as he has told me—touched his heart very much. As soon as he moved out of his parents' house, he stopped going to church, more through indifference than any animosity toward the institution. When he met and started courting the pretty girl who would become his wife, he took up going again, because it was what she wanted, it was one of the few places where she came out of her shyness a little and felt at ease among people; and her beauty and kindness and gentleness toward him did touch his heart, and so he went.

Pig Helmet has told me about a tribe of savage Germans whom he particularly admires, that lived back in Roman times. These Germans, it seems, were converted to Christianity sometime after the reign of the Emperor Constantine. This is the sort of thing Pig Helmet knows about, though to look at him—the truculent set of his jaw, the heavy forehead, the glittering left eye that peers out from within the folds of scar tissue—you would never expect it. He reads a lot of nonfiction books about obscure tidbits and peculiarities of history, and other books about the oddities scattered throughout the galaxy: singularities and quarks and quantum theory and gravitons and the like. He says these things just naturally catch his interest.

In the book about Christianity, when these great big hairy Teutonic warriors were baptized, when the Roman priests led them down into the cold rushing water of the river that ran near their home village up in the Black Forest, they willingly pledged themselves to Christ and dunked themselves under. All except their sword arms. Their right hands, palms horny and hard with callus from years of wielding their long blades, those they kept dry above the fast-flowing current. The rest of them might belong to gentle Jesus, but their strength and their killing skills—they still belonged to the god of battle.

Pig Helmet told me that was what he always felt like: some kind of a half-breed monster, a chimera, part one thing and part another and nothing that was whole. He had felt that other piece of him—the sword arm, held up above the current—when the OxyContin addict brought the shotgun to bear, the muzzle yawning wide and dark, and when Pig Helmet, without so much as thinking or deciding, sent a pair of 230-grain Speer Gold Dot jacketed hollow points into the guy's chest at nine hundred feet per second.

He had stood there for a moment, pistol in his hand, the pistol reports, so closely spaced they might have been a single sound, echoing off the clapboard side of the tidy bungalow. He'd been around death plenty of times, working for the creepy little bail bondsman in Craig County, in the Middle East, and while serving mental hygiene warrants and issuing subpoenas and such for the sheriff's office; and he could sense it now, boiling off the punctured corpse of the mutt with his shotgun, percolating out of the dark doorway of the bungalow behind the slumped body.

Death dwelt in the house, he knew, and probably had for years, for decades, just waiting on this day, on this combination of drugs and rage and cheating, to take down everyone inside. He could tell it was there, crouched inside the doorway like a lurking beast, but he couldn't see it.

He said he might as well have been naked out there in that little yard, with a couple of dusty chickens pecking in the thin grass around his feet, and the branches of the trees creaking and talking in the light wind that had sprung up. That empty doorway, with its moronic dead guardian, it called to him. It yearned for him. All of his body armor, his pistol and his taser and his years of training—worth nothing. He knew that, if he walked into that place alone, he was finished. When backup arrived, he would be gone. He could cross the yard and step over the OxyContin addict and past the threshold and on into the dark. He even took a step or two in that direction.

And then—this is his take on it—a miracle happened. A woman called his name. At the time, he thought it was his wife. It was definitely a woman's voice. And it wasn't his regular name that she called, it was his secret name, a name no one knew him by. It was a name that he himself didn't know he owned, or that owned him, until the second he heard the woman's voice speak it. He wouldn't tell me what it was, no man should know that about another man, but he said the moment he heard it, he knew it as inescapably his. It was like she was saying it into his ear. He imagined that his wife must be praying for him, a thing she did regularly throughout the day when he was on duty, and that her prayer was what halted his progress toward the door of the bungalow. He imagined that the name she called him was how she referred to him when she spoke with God.

So he found himself at the Wall of Life. After the search of the bungalow revealed the extent of the slaughter (Pig Helmet couldn't bring himself to go inside even after other units from the sheriff's office arrived), after the arrival and departure of the county coroner, after the ambulances had borne the body bags away—after all that, as he drove homeward, he passed the county fairground, and he saw the tractor-trailer with its garish illustration on the side, and beyond that the squat cylinder of the Wall of Life itself. That word, *Life,* written in letters of orange flame on both the semi-trailer and the Wall, captured and held his eye. Death clung to him. It was on his clothes, his hands, in his nostrils. *Life.*

He pulled the cruiser into the near-empty parking lot, paid the old lady at the foot of the stairs that led to the catwalk along the top edge of the Wall. As he handed her his money, he thought briefly of the grandmother who had died, cowering in one of the narrow back rooms, her hands held up beseechingly before her. The other deputies had described her to him in almost loving detail. "The show's already in progress," the old lady at the Wall told him in a voice like the chirp of a bird, and he nodded at her. The board stairs under his feet trembled with the unmuffled roar of the motorcycles, and the entire Wall shook with their passing.

There were maybe half a dozen spectators atop the Wall. It was the first show of the day, a light crowd. In the evening, under the unearthly glow of the sizzling sodium lamps, there would be more. The few who were there at the catwalk's railing drew back when they caught sight of Pig Helmet ascending the stairs. He was used to that reaction to his size and his marred face and his uniform, so he hardly noticed. A couple of the people held dollar bills out over the void, so that the motorcycle riders would come up near the edge of the Wall and snatch them. With Pig Helmet's arrival, the dollars and the riders were forgotten. Pig Helmet strode to the edge of the platform and looked down.

Easy enough to imagine what he saw as he looked into the well, which was poorly lighted, just a few strings of dingy Christmas bulbs clinging to the safety railing against which Pig Helmet leaned his weight. What else could a man like Pig Helmet see? The stench of exhaust flooded his nose, but it seemed to him to be the smell of burning cordite. He was looking into the muzzle of a great gun. It was the muzzle of the OxyContin addict's shotgun. It was the muzzle of every gun he had ever stared down. It was the muzzle of his own service pistol, pointed straight at his face.

Easy enough to imagine, too, what it was like for the preacher and his people, his family, when Pig Helmet appeared above them, his Neanderthal head silhouetted against the light of the lowering sky, exposed teeth gritted, his expression (what they could see of it in the dim light) filled with mortal terror, the other spectators on the catwalk drawing back from him, their offerings suddenly out of reach.

Near catastrophe as one motorcyclist, flames crackling from the straight exhaust pipe of his aging Indian bike, dove unexpectedly low on the Wall, nearly colliding with his younger brother, while their father, the preacher, fought to avoid running over them both. The preacher was shouting out above the roar of the engines the text of the gospel of James—he had just gotten to "There is one lawgiver, who is able to save and to destroy. Who art thou that judgest another?"—and he lost his place momentarily, dread and fascination drawing his attention upward to Pig Helmet's looming head and shoulders, the gleam of his shaved skull, the puckered flesh of his scars. His speed chopped as he braked to avoid his boys, his bike wobbled nauseously, and he nearly toppled off the Wall and to the floor.

Pig Helmet's vision quickly adjusted to the changed light. Now he saw more clearly. In white letters two feet high, just below the lip of the wall all the way around, ran the legend "In my name shall they cast out devils. They shall speak with new tongues. They shall take up serpents." Pig Helmet was standing just opposite the word *serpents,* so he could only see the end and the beginning of the quote, . . . *shall take up serpents. In my name they shall* . . . , but he was a good enough student of the gospels from his youth up to know what was hidden from his gaze. The floor of the well seemed to be alive. It was moving, shifting, shining in the blasts of fire from the motorcycle exhausts: iridescent scales, eyes, flickering tongues. It was a snake pit. Adders, vipers, harmless bright green ribbon snakes like blades of grass, the undulating lozenge pattern of diamondback rattlesnakes, the warning sizzle of their tails drowned out in the cacophony of the bikes.

Standing in the midst of the snakes, ankle deep in them, her feet bare, was a young girl, her face turned upward toward Pig Helmet, her expression delighted as though she was glad to see him. In each of her small, pale hands she grasped, just below the spearpoint head, a struggling pit viper. Her eyes were wide and bright, and Pig Helmet realized that she was not looking at him at all. She was gazing past him at something just over his shoulder with that rapturous look on her face.

Her eyes weren't unfocused or dazed. They had the concentrated aspect of the eyes of someone who has caught sight of something precious and vanishing—a lover who has spotted the ghost of a long-dead darling, a sniper to whom a target has just offered himself up for a head shot—and who can hardly bear the intensity of the vision, but who doesn't dare to look away lest it be lost forever. There was something behind him, above him, Pig Helmet knew, but he couldn't bring himself to turn around, to see what it was. The girl was seeing it enough for both of them.

The men on the motorcycles, the preacher and his sons, had speedily recovered their composure, and they swung back into rhythm, racing their bikes in swift ellipses around the interior of the well, now at the top, now at the bottom, weaving across one another's paths at measured intervals, as though they were performing an intricate dance. They were a handsome family, fine-boned and slender, their faces similar, old, young, younger, like the same man appearing in a series of photographs taken through the years. The preacher found his voice again, this time calling on the psalms, as though perhaps to ward off Pig Helmet with his perpetual unintended sneer, whom the preacher might have suspected of being not altogether human, not altogether benign. "Yea, though I walk through the valley of the shadow of death, I will fear no evil," he called out to the crowd on the catwalk.

Pig Helmet saw that the girl wasn't quite as young as he had first taken her to be. She was exquisite, her head tilted, her hair light as silk, her back slightly arched, her breasts pressing against the thin white cotton of her shirt. From his vantage point above her, Pig Helmet could see down into the neck of her blouse, could see the small hollow at the base of her throat, the sheen of perspiration that collected there. He could see the soft swelling of her breasts, the lacy edges of her bra. He loved his wife very much. And, in that instant, he wanted simultaneously to protect the girl in the snakepit from all the death that was in the world and to screw her silly. Her lips were moving, revealing glimpses of her healthy gums, her small even teeth, her glistening tongue. He couldn't hear her voice, but he knew that she must be praying. He wondered what her prayer was.

The preacher's voice was still audible, and the crowd had begun offering their dollar bills again. "Thou preparest a table before me in the presence of mine enemies," the old man declared. Pig Helmet had a couple of dollars in his wallet, and he thought about holding them out so that one of the riders would snatch them from his hand, and perhaps his fingers would brush against Pig Helmet's fingers, and in that brief contact Pig Helmet would feel what he needed to feel, would know what he wanted to know. *Life.*

It occurred to him that he might even, under the guise of holding out his offering, grab a passing motorcyclist by the wrist. Who among us, faced with that moment of failed equilibrium, the man teetering or the edge of the icy step, the woman the heel of whose shoe has caught in a steel grating, hasn't entertained, however temporarily, that temptation to reach out and, gently, almost lovingly, *push?* Just to see the expression on the face of the one who might have been rescued but who has been doomed instead. Pig Helmet told me it was like that feeling. Would the rider be jerked from his bike and swing there, dangling by the wrist in Pig Helmet's grasp until Pig Helmet dropped him into the writhing snakes? Would the weight of the man and the hurtling bike jerk Pig Helmet's shoulder clean out of its socket, might he be dragged bodily off the catwalk and into the well?

The motorcycles were running in unison, stacked like the rungs of a ladder as they raced around the Wall, and the girl had begun singing, her voice a thin piping that barely reached Pig Helmet's ears. A woman near him on the catwalk had begun clapping her hands together and shouting "Hallelujah" while the men beside her looked slightly chagrined. The boards thrummed like a vast heart beneath Pig Helmet's feet, and the voice of the preacher, in constant flux from the Doppler effect as he came near and went past and away again, beat at Pig Helmet's ears. "I shall dwell in the house of the Lord forever," he called. The snakes flopped and coiled at the girl's feet.

Pig Helmet no longer felt as though he was looking down, into the cylinder. He suddenly knew himself to be looking up. It came to him that he was staring into the barrel of an incalculably large telescope, one with greater power even than the ones they mount on the high ridges, far from the cities and their polluting lights. He knew himself to be watching through it something distant and ancient, something akin to the circuit of the planets, old, young, younger, near, far, farther, around and around in their endless courses, and the weak little Christmas lights were the surrounding stars, and the girl, the infinitely desirable girl clad in white at the very center of it all, singing and praying, and now she's even laughing, laughing breathlessly, her mouth wide with joy, her eyes half-closed, her nostrils flared, a viper grasped tight in each hand, her feet sunk in the unfathomable twinings of the serpents—At what is she laughing?

At him. At Pig Helmet. He's speaking, he's crying out in the command voice he's been taught to use on suspects, in the irresistible voice with which he directed the OxyContin addict to put down the shotgun. He doesn't understand the words he's saying. They're bubbling out of him like water from a busted spigot. The woman next to him is swaying, gaping at him worshipfully, shouting "Hallelujah! Hallelujah!" for all she's worth.

They're the girl's words that pour out of him, Pig Helmet knows, the words she was speaking earlier but that he couldn't hear. The words of her prayer.

Her body is shivering and shaking, pulsing like a quasar in one of Pig Helmet's peculiar books, a quasar at the far distant end of the universe. The girl in the pit, the stout woman on the catwalk beside him, they're dancing the same dance, binary suns, quivering as though they're demented with some awful fever. Pig Helmet's hands are spread wide. He cannot understand the words of the prayer, but in the midst of them he hears her say, once, clear as a bell, his secret name. It wasn't his wife at all who called him. He tries to make it be his wife, who has known him in his most intimate moments, and who wants nothing more in the world than to save him, to keep him safe and beside her forever. But no matter how hard he tries, it is this girl who knows the name, who calls to him in his most secret places.

"Put down the weapon." It was a prayer, what he had said to the OxyContin addict. He knew that. "Lay down on the ground." It was a prayer. There was no way for the OxyContin addict to divine what Pig Helmet truly wanted. Pig Helmet didn't hold the key to his understanding. The words of Pig Helmet's heart must have sounded like gibberish in his ears, and it didn't matter how loudly Pig Helmet spoke them, or how beseechingly he meant them. He couldn't imagine the OxyContin addict's secret name; he couldn't save him. We are so distant from one another, impossible to know. "Don't make me shoot you." An unheard prayer.

Pig Helmet's hands are open. The motorcycles continue to circle above him, hanging precariously over his head—who knows what astonishing force keeps them there?—but the screaming of their engines is muted, it no longer reaches his ears, his brain. He speaks in tongues, and spittle flecks his fleshy lips.

He's reaching outward, upward, straining toward the whirling constellation of men, motorbikes, snakes, voices. He's reaching for the girl who knows his name, and she has stopped dancing. She stretches out her slender arms toward him, her skin shining with sweat. She stands on tiptoe among the snakes. He's a tall man, but she's far away. Faster and faster the motorcycles go, and her prayer rises continuously from his lips, unmediated. The Wall of Life is an intricate machine built by men to show him this girl at the other end of space. The door of the little bungalow yawns behind him, and the slain OxyContin addict is the doorman, he's the concierge with the disconcerting smile, holding the portal wide, gesturing Pig Helmet inside with a generous sweep of the scattergun. It's an easy door to enter, the door to that house.

What lies before Pig Helmet's eyes is likewise a door, a hard entrance, a long narrow tunnel of infinite length. Pig Helmet thrusts his killing hand, his unbaptized hand, out toward the girl. She is far away and getting farther, but she extends her hand toward him as well, and her lips shape his true name. If Pig Helmet is strong enough, if he strains far enough, if the motorcycles spin fast enough, and if he keeps stretching out his unclean hand forever, he will reach her.

Reprinted with permission of Pinckney Benedict. Published in *Miracle Boy and Other Stories* (Press 53, 2010).

Pinckney Benedict: A Biographical Sketch

Pinckney Benedict is one of America's premier short-story writers. His playful attitude toward writing is endearing, and his thematic depth and stylistic virtuosity are impressive. He was born in 1964 and grew up on a seven-hundred-acre cattle farm located in Greenbrier County, West Virginia. This farm was established by his grandfather, a Procter and Gamble executive, and run by his father, a second-generation Republican elected official. As a boy, Pinckney Benedict's favorite reading matter was a comic-book series titled *Weird Wars*. At the age of thirteen, he was enrolled in the prestigious Hill School in Pennsylvania, and, from there, went to Princeton University to study to be a classicist because, he says, he had "discovered that classical literature was full of the things I like: bawdy jokes and sexual escapades and monsters and wars." Then he discovered *The Stories of Breece D'J Pancake*, a short-story collection depicting West Virginia's lower classes, which, he says, "changed my life [. . .] I knew not only *that* I wanted to write. I also suddenly knew *what* I wanted to write." He took courses under Joyce Carol Oates, a leading American literary figure, and went on to the University of Iowa Writers Workshop, widely viewed as the country's most selective creative writing program. Before he left Iowa he had a story collection, *Town Smokes* (1989), later declared a notable book of the year by The *New York Times Book Review*.

Pinckney Benedict's first academic job after Iowa was at Oberlin College, and in the summer of 1989 he taught at the Appalachian Writers Workshop at Hindman, Kentucky. There he met Laura Philpot, who, at the time, was living in St. Louis and working for Busch Creative, a subsidiary of Anheuser-Busch. Benedict later recalled, "Here was this beautiful, smart woman, a writer who was making good money and had an unending supply of Budweiser. I knew I had to get that deal locked in before she wised up." They married in 1990. For the next several years, Benedict accepted short-term appointments at a variety of universities and published another story collection, *Wrecking Yard* (1992), and his first novel, *Dogs of God* (1995), both also deemed "notable" by the *Times*. In 1998 he landed a tenure-track job at Hollins University in Virginia.

Then in 2002 he contracted what he terms "a wickedly aggressive cancer," which he has said was "the best thing that ever happened to me." The cancer went into remission, and since then his career, which had been marked by meteoric rise in reputation and seriousness, took a decidedly whimsical turn. In 2006 he accepted a job as a full professor at Southern Illinois University, devoted bountiful time to his two children, and began working on graphic fiction alongside more traditional forms of writing. In 2009 Pinckney and Laura

Benedict began publishing an annual periodical, *Surreal South,* but he didn't publish another book until 2010 when *Miracle Boy and Other Stories* was released. He drives a Can-Am Spyder sportster, and his favorite gun in his extensive collection is "a pimped-out heavy barrel Bushmaster AR15 Carbine." He recently summed up his attitude about writing and life on a Facebook post: "The impulse to make up stories is a strange, largely worthless, self-aggrandizing, atavistic, and mostly ancillary function [. . .] that I seem to be wired for. [. . .] That it has led to any kind of job or career or living or life is astonishing to me and shows the true generosity at the heart of the world."

Pinckney Benedict: A Selective Bibliography

INTERNET RESOURCES

The *Rumpus* offers an interview with Benedict. *Charlotte Viewpoint* offers an interview titled "Breaking the Curse of Literary Fiction." *Red Room* has a biography of Benedict.

SELECTED BOOKS

Miracle Boy and Other Stories. Winston Salem, NC: Press 53, 2010.
Dogs of God. New York: Nan A. Talese / Doubleday, 1993.
The Wrecking Yard. New York: Nan A. Talese / Doubleday, 1992.
Town Smokes. Princeton, NJ: Ontario Review Books, 1987.

PROFILES/INTERVIEWS

Brosi, George. *Appalachian Heritage* 38.1 (2010). Features Pinckney Benedict.

LITERARY CRITICISM

Douglass, Thomas E. "Pinckney Benedict." *Appalachian Journal* 20.1 (1992): 68–74.
Freeman, Angela B. "The Origins and Fortunes of Negativity: The West Virginia Worlds of Kromer, Pancake, and Benedict." *Appalachian Journal* 25.3 (1998): 244–69.
Holbrook, Chris. "The Regional Claim." *Appalachian Journal* 20.4 (1993): 368–73.
Miller, Jim Wayne. "New Generation of Savages Sighted in West Virginia." *Appalachian Heritage* 16.4 (1988): 28–33.
Vice, Brad. "Pinckney Benedict." In *American Short-Story Writers since World War II: Fourth Series.* Dictionary of Literary Biography 244. Ed. Patrick Meanor and Joseph McNicholas. Detroit: Thomson Gale, 2001. 27–33.
Williams, John Alexander. "Unpacking Pinckney in Poland." *Appalachian Journal* 20.2 (1993): 162–75.

Silas House

Total Immersion

After Liz tells her, Charma doesn't say anything for a long moment. She is sitting on the couch, smoking a cigarette with one hand and patting the baby's back with the other. "Saved?" she says, as if completely baffled. The word comes out in one great plume of smoke. The baby is sprawled out asleep across the top of her legs. "Tell me you're kidding, Mother."

Liz balances on the edge of her chair and pulls off her panty hose. Her big toe has broken through, just as always. "Why would I kid over such a thing, Charma? You don't kid over stuff to do with the Lord—that's dangerous."

Charma laughs. Her laugh is clear and pretty. Men melt for it. "You are the worst sinner I know, Mother. People actually refer to you as 'The Whore of Black Banks.'" Charma laughs some more. She shakes her head, carelessly flicks her cigarette toward the ashtray.

"Just that one woman," Liz says. She pulls her legs up under herself and rubs her feet.

"Because you were having an affair with her husband!" Charma plays with the baby's thin hair. He is four months old and his scent has spread across the whole room. The whole house smells like Johnson's baby bath. "You're still having an affair with him. How are you going to handle that, now that you've took up going to church?"

Liz looks out the window, even though it is covered by sheers so thick they can't be seen through. The sunlight is very bright there, causing them to glow. They look electric and alive. "I guess I'll just have to quit him."

"Yeah right," Charma says. She is always saying this, and she has a certain way of emphasizing "right" that drives Liz crazy. Liz feels like jumping up from the chair and leaning across the coffee table to smack her daughter's face.

"When hell freezes over, you'll quit him." Charma picks up the remote and aims it at the television, a signal that she is finished with this conversation.

"It'd be nice to come home from church and have somebody be tickled that I got saved," Liz says. "Most daughters would love for their mothers to join church."

"I would, too, if I didn't think it was just another one of your phases." Liz gets up and goes to her room. She moved in with Charma four months ago when her landlord kicked her out. She has a good-paying job at the yarn factory, but she has never been able to save money. She blows her paycheck every weekend because she can't be with her boyfriend, Bruce, then. He has to be with his wife, Lanie, who wears a 1980s hairdo—she even has bangs—and saucer-sized dabs of rouge. So Liz spends her money at the honky-tonks and has people over for grill-outs on Sundays. She buys family packs of ribeyes and baking potatoes. Plus she has that big debt to the collection agency and they take a chunk of that out of her check. She wouldn't live with Charma if she had anywhere else to go. They get along fine as long as they never see one another.

Her room is small and dark. There are clothes all over the floor and the remnants of last night's supper—a combo from Long John Silver's—are strewn out on the nightstand. She sits down at her vanity table and looks in the mirror. She is finally starting to show her fifty years. People have never been able to guess how old she is. She was thirty before she ever got carded at the liquor store. But now her face is lined with her mistakes. Her eyes seem drawn at the corners and her mouth is starting to pinch and grow smaller.

She always thought she would feel different when she got saved. But she doesn't. She always imagined that she would feel so clean—inside and out—and that a light would radiate from her face. She had thought it would feel as if God had reached down and grabbed her beneath the ribs to pack her around as if she was floating, her feet dangling just over the floor. She has thought about going to church for the last year or so. She knows this is the only way she can ever get away from Bruce. He is a force of nature. Black wavy hair and blue eyes and a tender voice that whispers when he is trying to charm her. His breath is always hot and sweet. He keeps a Cert in his mouth all the time, even when he is smoking. He goes on trips to the riverboats in Cincinnati where he and his wife gamble. He plays the tables but Lanie only offers herself to the slot machines. She is too conservative to risk playing 21. On these trips, Bruce sneaks into the fancy shops on the riverboats and buys Liz expensive outfits with his winnings. He brings them to her in plastic covers like you get at the drycleaners. She can never understand how he sneaks these things past Lanie.

She and Bruce cannot go to public places like the riverboats or the racetrack or even the Shoney's right here in town. They can only go to secret places. They spend a lot of time on the lake in Bruce's bass boat. It is red and has what Bruce calls a "meadowflake" finish. The meadowflakes glisten in the sun. They fish for a while and then Bruce always says he finds it incredibly sexy that Liz is willing to bait her own hook and take her own fish off the line. She loves catching bluegills, she loves the way he looks at her when she reels one in. She knows how much he loves that little squeal she lets curl from her mouth, knows how excited he gets by seeing her bent over the side of the boat to slide the fish into their basket. After they have fished for a few minutes he speaks to her in that low, breathy way and she always finds herself lying back on the scratchy boat-carpet. With his weight upon her, sometimes she can feel the water moving beneath them—even through all that fiberglass—and it is like being in a dream. It is like floating.

All this will have to change. She will not go to church and have an affair. She was raised to know better than that, anyway. When she rededicated her life today, her sister, Avalene, who had forced her to go to church with her, said this: "Liz, you was always the biggest sinner ever was. And most of the time the biggest sinners make the biggest Christians."

Avalene is right. Liz will give her all to serving the Lord. She will be baptized next Sunday and will invite everyone she knows. She will start praying to receive the Holy Ghost so she can shout and dance around the altar. She will sing with the choir and eventually teach Sunday school and go on retreats with the young people to Gatlinburg. She thinks it is funny, how the church-people all say "young people," as if "teenagers" is a bad word they can't fit their mouths around. The young people will like her because she will not be a prude. When they ask her if she thinks rock n roll is bad, she will lean forward and say "Of course not" with a great air of confidentiality. Because really, she doesn't think it's bad. Sometimes music like that makes her feel even more in touch with God. Sometimes when she is dancing she feels like she is celebrating life, and that has to be a good thing. But she can't think about that right now. She will sort all of that out later. Because she knows that dancing is against the church. So is rock n roll. Still, the teenagers will think of her as the cool Sunday school teacher. She will never call them "the young people" to their faces.

She wonders how she can still have her Sunday grill-outs. All her friends like to drink. They sit out on Charma's back deck and drink beer. Liz always fills the baby's plastic pool with ice and bottles of Michelob. The baby is too young for the pool anyway, and Liz has no idea why Charma has bought it. This is something that she is known for—the ice-filled baby pool—and she likes doing something no one else does. After they eat her salads and her steaks and drink her beer, they like to sit around and play poker. They cuss and sometimes get drunk and often get into fights. But then everyone comes back again and they are all the best of friends. She hates the thought of losing them, but a Christian woman cannot have that going on. Maybe she can talk some of them into going to church with her.

She looks at herself a while longer and decides that she will feel differently after she is baptized. Right now she feels exactly the same. At church she had felt a moment of pure ecstasy when she knelt at the altar to pray. There were many hands on her, women who prayed out loud in great breathless pleadings. The women cried and begged the Lord to forgive Liz her sins. The choir started up and they played a real fast song—"God's not dead oh no no no He's still alive Oh God's not dead, he's still alive"—and some of the women started shouting and speaking in tongues and Liz thought she could feel the Holy Ghost running up and down her back, like warm water. She couldn't help but to cry and it seemed she had never had such a cleansing cry before. When she sat in her room alone and cried over Bruce—knowing that he was off somewhere with his wife—her tears always seeped out slow and hot, but at church her whole body had shuddered and the tears had felt cool on her face. She had tasted their salt on her lips.

"Mother?" Charma shouts, slapping her palm against Liz' door. Liz hates being called Mother. Every other girl she knows says "mommy," but not Charma. Even when she was little, she addressed her in such a way. And to other people she just called her mother "Liz," as if they are not a drop of kin. "What are you doing in there?"

Liz starts to throw the door open but thinks better of it. A Christian woman has to have a good demeanor. Avalene calls it "letting your light shine." Avalene gave her advice all the way home from church today. She said how Liz had to stop wearing so much makeup and never wear pants and let her hair grow out and stop cussing and most importantly she had to let her light shine. Liz musters up a smile when she opens the door.

Charma greets this with a smug laugh, so quiet that Liz would not even recognize it except for the lift of Charma's shoulders. "Can you watch the baby this evening? Roger Lanham wants to take me to the theater."

Charma always says "theater," too. She will not say "the movies."

"I was planning on going to church tonight, Charma."

"Well, can't you take him? It'd be good for him to go." Charma lights a cigarette off the burning embers of her last.

"He's four months old, honey. If he got anything out of church at all, it'd be the Sunday school."

"Well fine, then!" Charma yells and stomps away. At the end of the hall she turns around and says, "See, you haven't changed a bit. Same old selfish Liz."

"All right then," Liz says. This has always been their problem. Liz has never known whether she was the child or the boss. She feels more like Charma is her sister than daughter. Charma seems to go out every night now. She is a good-looking girl, and she has this big fine apartment which the father of her baby pays for every month. He does this because he is a federal lawyer and doesn't want his wife to know that Charma has had a child by him. He even drew up a contract that Charma signed, saying she would remain silent unless he didn't pay child support and the rent. Charma tells all her friends that she is "set for life." Last week she wanted a new living room suite and a big-screen television. When the lawyer refused to buy it, she said she'd call his wife. He reminded her of the contract but Charma simply blew a line of smoke across the telephone receiver and spoke calmly. "That paper might hold up in court, but she'll still know." Next day, the Furniture-Town van pulled in and unloaded her order.

Liz watches her own daughter twist her way down the hall and feels as if they don't know each other at all. Perhaps comparing their relationship to sisterhood is all wrong. They are simply two people who have been forced to go through life together.

Liz takes the baby to church that night. Avalene comes and picks them up. It is a hot night but the air conditioner doesn't work and Avalene doesn't want her hair messed up, so she won't roll down the windows and Liz sweats in her new dress, which she bought at the Fashion Bug today. All her dresses for honky-tonking were either too short or too low-cut.

Liz glances back at the baby, who is content—he loves riding in cars—and then cracks the window. She lights a cigarette and blows the smoke toward the stream of air that is whistling in.

"What are you doing?" Avalene says. They are stopped at a red light so she is able to glare at Liz for a long moment.

Liz doesn't know what she is talking about.

"You're smoking! We'll go to church smelling like smoke, Liz. Just throw that pack out, now honey. That craving will be took from you. You won't want things of the world anymore."

"I doubt smoking will send me to Hell, Avalene," Liz says, watching for the light to change, since Avalene is not.

"But it will, honey," Avalene says, as if she is certain not only of this, but of everything. "Your body is a temple."Liz lets the cigarette drop out of the little space at the top of the window but doesn't throw out her pack.

Everyone at the church is happy to see her. Actually, they look stunned, as if they never expected her to come back and their big smiles and laughter seems to be out of speechlessness more than anything. All of the woman rub her back in a perfect circle. Liz notices that they all look tired and pale. Maybe it is because they are not wearing makeup. But there is something in their eyes that makes her long for them. She wants to wrap her arms around the women and tell them that she loves them. She doesn't know why; maybe this is part of being a Christian. It seems like something Christ would do.

The baby seems to love church. He bounces on Liz's lap when the choir sings. Everybody plays with him and runs a finger over his soft hair. The ladies in front of her all ask to hold him, and she lets them. He is happy against their big, warm breasts. Liz cannot follow the preacher tonight. He paces all over the church, hollering and stomping. The crowd nearly drowns him out with their amens. He is talking about the Rapture. She catches something about Jesus Parting the Sky and the Twinkling of An Eye. She remembers Zelda, her best friend at work, once telling her that in a Pentecostal church, there are only three sermons. "The rapture, the holy ghost, and the offering," Zelda said. She feels bad for letting Zelda talk this way.

When the sermon is over, she feels as if she has been in a daze. She is only brought awake when the altar call starts. She loves to hear them sing, especially the fast songs when they pound the tambourines and everybody starts speaking in tongues. She can't help moving about in her seat. The music is good enough to dance to.

That night, she calls Bruce. He has told her to never call his house and really she ought to wait to talk to him at work tomorrow. He is her supervisor and she can go into his sound-proof office anytime she wants. She likes it there not only because of him but also because you can't hear the grind of the yarn machines while there. It is like walking out of a storm into a safe place. But she can't wait to talk to him. Luckily he answers the phone.

"Bruce?"

He whispers. She can picture him hunkering into himself as he talks. She can hear a television playing in the background and wonders if he and Lanie have been lying on the couch together, watching the news. Bruce watches CNN all the time. He cannot get enough of it. He says it is important to stay informed.

"I told you to never call me here."He's mad.

"I'm sorry, but I have to talk to you. Can't you act like you're out of smokes or something? Meet me at the Dairy Mart?"

"Ten minutes," he says and hangs up.

Charma is still not back, and Liz had not thought of this before calling Bruce, so she just loads the baby up and heads out. He is asleep anyway and won't know a thing. Bruce will just have to get in the car with her. He does. He pulls in and simply slides from his car to hers. She thought that maybe that same old feeling wouldn't come to her upon seeing him, but it does. She still feels that sizzle in her stomach. He is still good-looking to her. The only thing is that she realizes for the first time that he knows he is good looking, too. And she realizes that this is exactly why she has always been so attracted to him. Conceit is something that is appealing to her.

It is as if he had been expecting her call, because he is fixed up. He is wearing dress shorts and boat shoes. And he is wearing a shirt she bought for him, a green polo shirt with that little horse emblem over his heart. Her favorite shirt that she bought him is one that he never, ever wears. It says FISHERMEN DO IT IN THE WATER. She wonders what he has done with it and bets Lanie has sold it in one of those huge yard sales she is famous for. She probably won't let him wear such a thing. Lanie is Presbyterian. Liz doesn't know much about that denomination, but Bruce says they worry a lot about what other people think.

"Where have you been, all decked out?" she asks.

"We went to the steak house this evening."

Another place they can't go. The only place they ever eat is at the boat dock. Greasy hamburgers wrapped in wax paper. Or in the break room at work. Nabs and a Pepsi, or sometimes a bag of popcorn they put in the microwave. Every time she smells microwaved popcorn, she thinks of him. It is the same with the air on the lake and Eternity for Men cologne. These smells are her connection to him, and she will never be able to rid herself of him in this way. By way of scent, he will always be with her.

"What is it?" he asks. "I don't have much time."

She lights a cigarette. Although she knows this act won't go along good with what she is about to say, her nerves need the nicotine. "I got saved this morning. I'm going to start going to church."

"Church? Have you lost your mind? You're not ready for that."

"I have to do something. I've got to have some kind of life. I'm not going to have one with you—you're never going to leave her."

"I can't, Liz. You know that." He looks around to make sure that no one can see them. Her Mustang has tinted windows, so nobody can. "What's the use leaving her if she gets everything? Would you want a man with nothing?"

Liz looks at her cigarette and throws it out the window. "I've never had anything before. Why should now be any different?" She holds onto the steering wheel very tightly, as if she is driving around a sharp curve. "It don't matter now, anyway. I want you to come to my baptism."

Bruce makes a sound like his words are caught in the back of his throat. Then he assembles them properly. "Now I know you've lost your mind."

Liz doesn't feel anything at all. She feels empty. There is not even that yearning of wanting to be filled up by something. She looks straight ahead. "I'm going to try to do right, Bruce. We have to quit this."

Bruce flips down the visor and looks at himself in the mirror. "You're not church-going material, Liz. You're just not made that way."

She starts the car and checks the rearview mirror, which she has adjusted so she can see the baby. He is still sound asleep. After a long silence of Bruce just staring at her, she says, "Get out, Bruce. I'm done."

"We'll talk about this more, at work," he says, not even looking at her now. Scanning the parking lot. The lights from the store are bright and his face looks very pale in their glare. She thinks of his brown shoulders, speckled by water. Sometimes they go up into a cove and skinny dip. They lie back naked on the boat and the sun catches in the little wet orbs on his slick skin. She shakes this image out of her mind.

"There's nothing else to say," she says, and with her foot on the brake, slides the gear down into reverse. "Go on."

He doesn't argue, but he lets out one of those sighs that used to unnerve her. It used to send her into a frenzy, thinking she had upset him. But now she doesn't care. She is at peace with the world. He gets out and shoves his hands deep into the pockets of his Duck Head shorts. He stands there only for a second before looking around quickly, making sure no one has seen him. She sits there with the car running even after he has driven away.

That week, Liz avoids Bruce at work. She ignores him when he taps her on the shoulder and tells her to come to his office. When he walked by, the musk of his cologne trailed behind. She even ignores him in the break room, where he stands by the microwave, waiting for his corn to pop. But she has to make herself not look at him. He always wears Dockers to work, and they look so good on him. She has always liked to see him in dress socks and penny loafers. She tries to not think about all that, though. She focuses on her yarn line and lets the noise of the factory force Bruce out of her head.

On break, she talks about church to the rest of the girls. None of them can believe it. They want to know what they will do about Saturday nights, when they all get together and go to The Spot, where they each take turns buying pitchers of Michelob and are the most popular table of women in the whole place. They want to know how they can talk to her like they used to. They all claim to respect her decision, though—even Zelda—and she thinks they are genuinely happy for her.

Avalene bought her a whole garbage bag full of skirts at the Catholic store in town, and Liz wears them to work. She doesn't feel right in pants any more. It is what Avalene called "being condemned." Avalene said, "If wearing eye makeup and pants condemns you, then you ought not do it. That feeling of being condemned is God whispering in your ear. Doubt is just God, warning us."

The closer it gets to Sunday, the more nervous Liz becomes, as if the baptism were an impending job interview that she is not prepared for. Avalene talks about it all the time. She verses Liz in all the ways of the church, as their mother never had taken them growing up and none of Liz's ex-husbands ever wanted to go. Avalene told her that it is the freshest feeling, when you rise up out of that water. "It really feels just like they say—as if your sins have been washed away," she says. The Pentecostals practice total immersion, and this is the main thing Liz dreads. She can't stand being under water. It smothers her to death. Once she had been on a pontoon at the lake, everybody drunk and somebody had pushed her in as a joke. Although she is a good swimmer, when she went under, she lost it. She came up hyperventilating so hard that a bunch of men had to jump in and pull her out. She had done it with one of the men that night, right up on the bank while everybody else partied. She remembers him moving on top of her, throbbing and breathing hard. She wonders now if anyone had seen them, and is amazed that she had never even cared before.

Still, she wants this. She wants a change, and in a town like Black Banks, this is the most you can change. There are only two kinds of people here: sinners and Christians. She wants to try a new crowd.

She is happy when the preacher calls to tell her that the church has decided it will be best to use the river. In the winter, they use the baptistery that they had built in the church, but during the hot months they like to use the river. She can picture it, all of the people standing on the bank singing and slapping tambourines. She loves the feel of river water, as it is always moving. Pushing on, not letting anything stand in its way.

On Friday she calls everyone she knows to invite them to her baptism. Most of them say they will be there, but a lot of them have excuses, too. Excuses Liz herself has used many times to escape similar situations. She is no fool. Everyone sounds genuinely shocked at the prospect of her going to church, too. One of her honky-tonk friends laughs out loud when Liz invites her. "Lord, Liz, if you start going to church, the roof will cave in!" she says. Liz can't help herself—she hangs up on her.

And now, on the very morning of her baptism, Charma says she is not going. The baby is crying, but she stands at the stove, stirring eggs and bouncing him on her hip. She talks over his cries. "I'm not going to go there and watch you make a fool out of yourself, Mother." She shifts the baby to her other hip. "Because you know good and damn well that come next month, you'll be right back at the Spot. You'll be down on the lake with Bruce. You are not going to change, and we both know that."

"Can't you give me the benefit of the doubt?"

Charma doesn't look at her. With one hand she pours the eggs out onto a plate. Behind her morning light falls in the window in a white glare, so that Liz cannot see her face. "I've never understood that phrase," Charma says.

"Can't you believe in me this once, Charma Diane?"

From halfway across the kitchen, Charma throws the plate onto the table. When it hits, the eggs bounce off and scatter off the edge and onto the floor. "When did you ever believe in me?"

Liz wants to tell Charma that she is right. She knows that she was never a good mother. Marrying one man after another, sleeping with men she brought home from the honky-tonk. People always at the house, drinking liquor and smoking dope right in the living room. Once she had been sitting in a man's lap and taking a shot of bourbon he had poured for her and just as she brought the glass down, she saw Charma standing in the hallway, watching her. She was only four years old, and she had dragged the bedspread from her room. "I had a bad dream," Charma said, but instead of going to her, instead of packing her back to bed and tucking her in, Liz had shouted, "Go back to bed! Quit spying on me." And Charma had simply turned around and shuffled back down the hallway, the bedspread trailing along behind her. Liz thinks now of how Charma must have felt, lying there in the darkness, afraid, listening to her mother's laughter in the living room. Liz is more ashamed of that moment than any other in her life and she wants to ask for Charma's forgiveness, but she can't find the right words. She knows if she doesn't say it exactly right, Charma will just laugh at her, or get even madder.

Without another word, she stands and takes her purse, which is hanging from the back of the chair, and puts it on her shoulder. She walks outside and waits on the porch for Avalene. She is dying for a cigarette, but she doesn't smoke one. She concentrates on the blue mountains in the distance until Avalene's car coughs its way up the road.

It is an impossibly perfect day. It looks like something out of a movie. The sky is just right—completely blue—and a little breeze moves through the willows lining the river. The people are all standing on the bank and seem very far away. The preacher puts one hand into the small of her back and whispers, "Take a deep breath." Before doing so, she scans the crowd one more time. She doesn't know who she expects to see, but there is not one single person she knows besides Avalene, who is bawling into a ragged Kleenex. None of her girlfriends, not even Zelda. Had she really thought Bruce would be there? He is at home watching CNN while Lanie is at the Presbyterian Sunday service. Worst of all, Charma is not here. She had hoped she might come up out of the water and see Charma, approval stamped across her face.

"Liz?" The pastor says. "Take a deep breath."

He caps his hand over her mouth and then "In the name of the father and the son and the Holy Ghost," and he is leaning her back. It is like being dipped during a dance. She is underwater for what seems a very long time, but she is not afraid. She feels like she could lie there in that water from now on. She can hear the river moving beside her ears. She can taste the water that seeps in between the pastor's big fingers. She is under so long that she has time to open her eyes. And all she can see is light, slanting down onto the river's surface.

Reprinted with permission of Silas House. Published in *Night Train Magazine* (Fall 2003).

Silas House: A Biographical Sketch

Silas House first received national attention as a mail carrier who was a novelist; then he became known as a voice for country working people, and later as an environmental activist. For a while he was concentrating on plays and movie scripts, and then he expanded his career to include writing youth novels. In addition to these accomplishments, Silas House is a published poet, short-story writer, music writer, and public radio commentator as well as a passionate public speaker on a variety of topics.

From his birth in 1971 until 2010 Silas House lived his entire life in Lily, a town in Laurel County, Kentucky. Now he lives in Berea, less than fifty miles north. His first Lily home was a trailer on Robinson Creek, but when he was nine he moved into a house in the valley below with his mom, a "lunch lady" at his elementary school, and his father, who worked in a fiberglass factory that blew up the year after he retired, killing seven employees. Their new home was close to his Aunt Dot's country store, where storytellers gathered, as well as the Lily Holiness Church, which they attended. House has noted, "I believe that one of the main reasons I'm a writer is that I went to church so much, and the only permissible thing to take with me was a little tablet and pencil." In the summers he stayed with kinfolks deeper into the coalfields in Leslie County, the home of his mother's people. In high school he worked as a cook at restaurants and continued working while commuting first to Sue Bennett College and then to satellite campuses and eventually the main campus of Eastern Kentucky University. During this time he lived in a trailer in Lily with a cousin who shared his love of dancing, partying, fishing, and camping.

Silas House graduated from EKU in 1994 and soon married, moving into a home on Slate Ridge in Lily. In 1995 his first daughter, Cheyenne, was born, and a story by Silas appeared in *Appalachian Heritage.* The following year Silas was hired by the post office as a rural mail carrier. In 1997 Silas went to hear Lee Smith read in Hazard, and she encouraged him to attend the Appalachian Writers Workshop at Hindman, which he did that summer, sleeping in a tent in lieu of paying for a room. Another daughter, Olivia, was born in 1998, and his first novel, *Clay's Quilt,* was published by Algonquin in 2001, when he was twenty-nine. The next year Algonquin published his second book in what would become a trilogy about an Eastern Kentucky family, *A Parchment of Leaves.* On the basis of that success, Silas quit his job at the post office and enrolled in the low-residency MFA program at Spalding University. He received the degree in 2003, and the next year signed contracts to teach at both his alma maters—EKU and Spalding—jobs that allowed him to still live in Lily. *The Coal Tattoo,* the third novel in his trilogy, was published in 2004.

In 2005 House was hired as writer-in-residence at Lincoln Memorial University. There he established the Mountain Heritage Literary Festival, and also became more and more deeply involved in the struggle against mountaintop removal coal mining. In 2009 he published a youth novel, *Eli the Good,* and *Something's Rising: Appalachians Fighting Mountaintop Removal,* coauthored by Jason Howard. In 2010 Silas House divorced and was hired to teach at Berea College. For the first time in his life he moved away from Lily, Kentucky. During the 2011-2012 school hear he interrupted his teaching career at Berea to be the interim director of the Loyal Jones Appalachian Center. His fifth novel, *Same Sun Here* (coauthored with Neela Vaswani), was published in the spring of 2012.

Silas House: A Selective Bibliography

INTERNET RESOURCES

Ashley Judd includes a recording of a speech by Silas House on her website. Silas House's website includes information about all of his work, teaching resources, and links to his other activities online. *Reading Groups Guide* offers a biography of House and interview by Marianne Worthington. Darnell Arnoult's website *Dancing with the Gorilla* offers an interview with House, and *Southern Scribe* presents a profile on House titled "Kentucky's Literary Light."

SELECTED BOOKS

Same Sun Here (with Neela Vaswani). Somerville, MA: Candlewick Books, 2012.
Eli the Good. Somerville, MA: Candlewick Books, 2009.
Something's Rising: Appalachians Fighting Mountaintop Removal (with Jason Howard). Lexington: UP of Kentucky, 2009.
The Hurting Part: Evolution of an American Play. Louisville, KY: Motes Books, 2008.
The Coal Tattoo. Chapel Hill, NC: Algonquin, 2004.
A Parchment of Leaves. Chapel Hill, NC: Algonquin, 2002.
Clay's Quilt. Chapel Hill, NC: Algonquin, 2001.

PROFILES/INTERVIEWS

Brosi, George, ed. *Appalachian Heritage* 32.2 (2004). Features Silas House.

LITERARY CRITICISM

Freund, Hugo. "Ballads, Sisters, and Curses: The Uses of Traditional Appalachian Culture in the Novels of Silas House." *Tennessee Folklore Society Bulletin* 62.1 (2006): 11–19.

Lang, John, ed. *Iron Mountain Review* 26 (2010). Features Silas House.

Reynolds, Jennifer Adkins. "Turn Your Radio On: Music in the Novels of Silas House."*Journal of Kentucky Studies* 24 (2007): 157–64.

Summerlin, Donna. "Gender, Race and Religion in Silas House's Appalachian Trilogy." *Appalachian Journal* 37.1/2 (2009): 76–99.

Maurice Manning

XLIX

O boss of ashes boss of dust
you bother with what floats above
the chimney what settles to the ground
you wake the motes from sleep you make
them curtsey in a ray of sun
they hold their tiny breath as if
they're waiting for the little name
of the dance that's coming next then they
will take their places Boss if I
were smaller I would join them O
I'd cut a rug or two I'd slap
my hand against my shoe if that's
the kind of fuss you're raising Boss
you know I never know for sure
I only know you bother me
from time to time you've caught my breath
a time or two you've stirred me up
before which makes me want to tell
you Boss I wouldn't mind it if
you bothered me a little more

Reprinted with permission of Houghton Mifflin Harcourt. Published in *Bucolics: Poems* (2007).

❁ ❁ ❁

That Durned Ole Via Negativa

You ever say a word like *naw,*
That *n, a, double-u* instead

of *no?* Let's try it, *naw.* You feel
your jaw drop farther down and hang;

you say it slower, don't you, as if
a *naw* weighs twice as much as *no.*

It's also sadder sounding than
a *no.* Yore Daddy still alive?

a friend you haven't seen might ask.
If you say *naw,* it means you still

cannot get over him. But would
you want to? *Naw.* Did you hear it then,

that affirmation? You can't say *naw*
without the trickle of a smile.

The eggheads call that wistful, now –
O sad desire, O boiling pot

of melancholy pitch! Down in
that gloomy sadness always is

a hope. You gittin' any strange?
That always gets a *naw,* and a laugh.

I've had that asked of me. It's sad
to contemplate sometimes, but kind

of funny, too. It makes me think
of *git* and who came up with that,

and the last burdened letter hitched
to *naw,* that team of *you*s and yoked

together—the you you are for now
and the you you might become if you

said yeah, to feel the sag of doubt
when only one of you is left

to pull the load of living. My,
but we're in lonesome country now.

I wonder if we ever leave it?
We could say yeah, but wouldn't we

be wiser if we stuck it out
with naw, and know the weight of what

we know is dragging right behind us,
the squeak and buck of gear along

with us, O mournful plea, O song
we know, by heart, by God, by heart.

Reprinted with permission of Houghton Mifflin Harcourt. Published in *The Common Man: Poems* (2010).

❁ ❁ ❁

The Dream of a Mountain Woman Big Enough for Me

I had a pretty good'un last night,
a dream. I'm calling it The Dream

of a Mountain Woman Big Enough
for Me, a heavy title, I know,

but I like a little bigger woman,
and mountain women are something else,

because they're from the mountains, and big!
Well, anyway, in the dream I told

her everything. I told her, I like
the things that come into the world

already made, like a birdsong or
the purple on a pokeweed stem,

the humble things that humble all
the rest. You take the wind that slips

across the hill—nobody made it,
nobody taught it how to blow!

I'm telling you I like a wind!
My arms were stuck out like a scarecrow's.

She squinted her eyes and nodded slow,
then she stared right through me, smiled, and said,

You couldn't never tell me enough—
It was almost a whisper, more breath than sound,

and I knew exactly what she meant—
she wanted me to hush; so I hushed

my foolish talk and dropped my arms,
but accidentally I brushed my hand

against her leg and somehow it
got stuck, and neither of us knew

what caused it or why we couldn't get
unstuck, so I started singing that song,

the thighbone's connected to the—I paused—
the Lord. The what? she said. The Lord

told me to make you happy. Well,
she said, well ain't that somethin'—'spose

you connect your hand-bone to my back.
Now, words like that will fill a man

with hope. I told you mountain women
are something else, you never know,

not even in a poor man's dream
that doesn't get too far—my hand

was inches from her back and creeping
closer when I woke up. If the dream

had lasted longer, though, she had
one heck of a question to ask of me—

And did you tell the Lord you would?
She would have breathed it out like that,

our faces almost touching. If
the dream had ended there, before

I had a chance to answer? Lord knows
if I'd ever want another dream.

Maurice Manning: A Biographical Sketch

When Maurice Manning was named one of three finalists for the Pulitzer Prize in poetry in 2011 for his collection *The Common Man,* while still in his forties, it was just another indication of the dramatic trajectory of his career. He was in his thirties when his very first book of poetry, *Lawrence Booth's Book of Visions,* was selected for the Yale Series of Younger Poets in 2001.

Maurice Manning was born in 1966 and grew up in Danville, Kentucky, but he was well aware of his family's roots in the mountains of eastern Kentucky. His maternal great-great-grandmother, Laura Hiatt Baker, died at the ripe old age of 109 when Manning was eight, and his great aunt on his father's side, Clara Burchell, lived to be 108. His grandmother lived to be 94. Manning's father grew up in a log cabin in Tyner, Kentucky, and lived "almost a 19th Century life as a youngster." Manning writes, "The fact that my family's roots go back to the earliest days of Kentucky has always been a source of inspiration and mystery for me. It is a world of its own, and it is the taproot of everything I try to do with poetry. My feet may have been mostly in Danville when I was growing up, but my spirit has always lingered in Clay County." In elementary school he was a shoeshine boy at a barber shop where he listened to the stories of elders, and later he had a paper route. Manning worked for a wholesale grocery company that made deliveries out in the country during the summers of his college years, and this also strengthened his connection to rural Kentucky. He went back to work for that company after graduating from Earlham College in 1988 and then took a job with the Christian Appalachian Project teaching adult literary and GED preparation. He recounts that the first night that GED classes were offered at Paint Lick Elementary School, over one hundred students showed up.

In 1990 Manning began working toward an MA in English at the University of Kentucky. There he took a class from Wendell Berry and got to know Berry's fellow Stegner scholars, Gurney Norman and James Baker Hall. He also began corresponding with James Still. For four years after receiving his MA, Manning lived in Richmond and Berea, Kentucky, while working for Kentucky Educational Television in Lexington. He began his MFA work in 1996 at the University of Alabama, and completed that degree in 1999. A writing fellowship landed him at the Fine Arts Work Center in Provincetown, Massachusetts, for the next academic year, and then he was hired as a professor by DePauw University. It was while there that Yale University Press published *Lawrence Booth's Book of Visions.* In 2004 Manning was hired to teach at Indiana University, and that year Harcourt published A *Companion to Owls: Being the Commonplace Book of D. Boone, Long Hunter, Back Woodsman, &c.* Since

2006 he has also taught for the low-residency MFA program at Warren Wilson College. Harcourt published *Bucolics* in 2007, and in 2009 the Fellowship of Southern Writers gave Manning its poetry award. *The Common Man* was published in 2010. During the 2011–12 school year, Manning enjoyed a Guggenheim Fellowship, which has allowed him to work on another poetry book while staying with his wife, Amanda, on their farm not far from Danville. He joined the faculty of Transylvania University in the fall of 2012.

Maurice Manning: A Selective Bibliography

INTERNET RESOURCES

The *Cortland Review* offers five of Manning's poems. The *Poetry Review* has the poems "A Blasphemy" and "Sad and Alone" and an article. *National Public Radio* offers two of Manning's poems from the collection *Bucolics*. *Reading between A and B* has the poems "A Wavering Spindle of Forsythia" and "Moonshine." The *Sycamore Review* offers an interview with Manning titled "Quantum Cowboys and Honky Tonk Heroes: A Conversation with Maurice Manning."

SELECTED BOOKS

The Gone and the Going Away. New York: Houghton Mifflin Harcourt, 2013.

The Common Man. New York: Houghton Mifflin Harcourt, 2010.

Bucolics. Boston: Harcourt, 2007.

A Companion for Owls: Being the Commonplace Book of D. Boone, Long Hunter, Back Woodsman, &c. Boston: Harcourt, 2004.

Lawrence Booth's Book of Visions. Yale Series of Younger Poets 95. New Haven, CT: Yale University Press, 2001.

LITERARY CRITICISM

Campion, Peter. "Sincerity and Its Discontents in American Poetry Now." *Poetry* 191.5 (2008): 417–24.

Edwards, Lynnell. "Pastoral without Nostalgia." *American Book Review* 31.5 (July/Aug. 2010): 27.

Lang, John, ed. *Iron Mountain Review* 26 (2011). Features Maurice Manning.

Pettingell, Phoebe. "Reading Minds." *New Leader* 87.5 (Sept./Oct. 2004): 36–38.

Taylor, John. "*Lawrence Booth's Book of Visions.*" *Poetry* 180.2 (May 2002): 99–101.

Sharyn McCrumb

Abide with Me

A plaque, a photo, a cardboard likeness. Well, they will find none of those things here. Oh, they exist, and I have them still, but they are packed away in the other house, buried with the life I have now escaped, as surely as Liam has escaped his.

I cannot honestly say that Liam loved the mountain house. Perhaps he did, for all I know, but he was never here very much. I was trying to please him when I chose it, but he may have let me buy it as much for the tax advantages as to spend time in this place. "But you grew up in these hills, "I said once, as he looked down from our limestone terrace at the newly-landscaped ridges studded with what he called "stone and glass excrescences," built by the other summer people. He shuddered a little. "I'm not from here," he said. "Not from this place."

Well, naturally it has changed here since he was a raw-boned mountain boy. But at least it is close to heaven. One cannot argue with that.

He did come from these mountains, long ago before I knew him. Back when he was not Liam, the exalted racing champion, but plain old Billy, a north Georgia dirt track driver—before the fame and the money bronzed his life until the only mountains around him were the barriers of handlers and managers and buffers between him and everything else. When I chose this stone and glass eyrie on a cliff top, I thought I had found the best of both worlds for us: an elegant home in an exclusive enclave with other people from our social stratum, and all around us the enfolding hills he always said he missed so much. I don't know what else he could have wanted.

Sometimes I would stand outside under a blanket of stars and wonder if he might be up there, looking down on me in some form of heroic transfiguration. There must be scores of people out there who would believe that implicitly, but I was not one of them. Or else I fancied that he might be there beside me, if only I could have turned around quickly enough. If there is a hereafter, he ought to spend it watching over me, instead of staying out there with them. Surely now that he's dead, it can be my turn at last.

The local people come by sometimes to deliver flowers (on his birthday, never on mine, or on the anniversary of a race he'd won). Sometimes they bring me letters from strangers that were put by mistake into their mailboxes. As I stand on the threshold, I can see them peering past me, down the hall, into the glass-walled great room, looking for the contrails of Liam's fame: a model of the race car; a bronze plaque; a photo of him with a president or film star; a life-size cardboard effigy of Liam himself, arms folded, staring bleakly into the camera with that look I could never quite decipher. Now, though, I think I have worked out the meaning of that somber expression, so different from those first posed publicity pictures they took of him, when he was just beginning the journey that has brought me here and him—nowhere.

Back then—and ten years hardly seems a long time, looking back—Liam in a royal blue firesuit mugs at the camera with an aw-shucks grin, still marveling at his good fortune and happy to bask in the light of his new-found celebrity. He is a chosen one, ready to pay any price for that ride. A decade later, the face in the frame is a solemn man in black and gold, with mournful eyes and a chiseled face infinitely more handsome through time and experience, but minus the joy he took with him when he started. I see nothing of the jubilant boy in the face of this somber successor. Now he is like a one-star general who has seen the war, not from a desk in the Pentagon, but from a blood-soaked battlefield. The youthful smile is gone; supplanted by the weary resignation of one who has to live with his wishes granted.

It isn't fun anymore. He knows it, but the rest of them don't. You can die out there. He knows that, too. He has a scar for every time that lesson was repeated. The younger ones drive dirt track in Podunk on weeknights under playful *nommes de guerre,* too impatient for the clatter of their own heartbeats to wait for the real race on Sunday. But through the week Liam goes to practices and crew conferences, meetings and banquets; he signs his name a few hundred more times, always with a weather eye on the inexorable approach of Sunday next.

At daybreak in the hours before the race, I pretend to be asleep as I listen to him throwing up in the bathroom. Later, when he steps out of the motor home into a field of microphones and camera lights, he makes bland remarks in a toneless voice, and they will take his numbness for courage.

But he knew. He knew.

The people who come to pry probably know about that last trophy, too. The one he did not win. The victor that day, that West Coast boy with the bland, perfect face of a plastic doll, won the race that Liam never finished, and afterward he brought the brass monstrosity to me as an offering, kindly meant, or perhaps a sacrifice to some nemesis so that he should not be the next one . . . the next one. There is always a next one.

I accepted the trophy; because to do so was easier than explaining why the thing meant nothing to me. It meant a great deal to the winner. That was the point. I took it, and, mindful of Biblical precedent, I kissed his cheek. I did not say, "Why don't you go back out there to the eternal sunshine and lose yourself in the movies? Be famous for your face; it's good enough for that. What business have you out there, playing hole and corner with death every Sunday afternoon? The road is a circle, all right. Don't you know where it leads?"

I came here to the mountain house a few weeks after it happened. After the carefully choreographed public memorial service, after decorous press releases and days of business meetings that melded into one long ordeal of signing pieces of paper.

I work in the garden now in the cool of the evening. It gives me something to do with my hands while I think, turning over in my mind all the things I never actually said. "Why don't you quit then? Surely we have enough money for that. Why don't you walk away . . . while you can?" Unspoken. Useless, really. Because he couldn't walk away. Back to being nobody. Or maybe he just loved it. Even when his hands shook so much he could barely put on his driving gloves, he would not have turned back.

The closest I ever heard him come to expressing regret came once when I walked him to the car at Darlington, and he murmured, "I just wish it could be fun again."

The service was lovely. The governor said a few words. The president sent a telegram. Inside the church were the same sleek people one might expect to find at a film premiere or aboard someone's yacht off St. Thomas. Outside on the church lawn, standing vigil in the rain, were the others: the truck drivers, the store clerks, and all those pitiful women who loved whatever image of Liam they had conjured from that face on the key chain, the coffee mug. And somewhere, caught between the celebrities and the people in the rain, was Liam. At the close of the service, a black pop star, blonder than I am, sang "Abide With Me" in a throaty gospel contralto. I think he would have liked that old hymn. I found it in a hymn book as I planned the service with the bishop, the rabbi, and the Air Force chaplain. Even in death, Liam must be all things to all people. . . . One verse intrigued me.

> Come not in terrors, as the King of Kings,
> But kind and good, with healing in Thy wings . . .

"We don't usually sing that verse," the cathedral's music director told me, but I requested it anyhow.

Afterward, I came away to this house in Liam's mountains, bent on solitude. I brought no one with me. The television stayed dark in the corner by the stone fireplace. When I ventured outside, it was only to instill perfection in the garden.

Once while I was pulling creeper vines out of a bed of pink impatiens, I found myself thinking, "I wonder where Liam has gone," and when I remembered that he had died, the question did not quite resolve itself.

The first time I saw the boy it was nearly dusk. I knew that he didn't belong to one of the families up here. He looked all right—they all wear jeans and tee shirts nowadays—but there was an exotic look about his wiry frame, his black hair and dark almond eyes that made me think "local." I judged him to be about fourteen. In another time he wouldn't have been out of place on this mountain in buckskin and moccasins, but now in faded levis and battered sneakers, he simply looked like one of the cove dwellers scouting for odd jobs among the summer people.

He squatted on his haunches beside the flower bed, watching me work with clinical interest. I turned to ask him what he'd come about, and it was then that I noticed his tee shirt: Davey Allison—Rising Star. It was a crisp unfaded black, the yellow star and the black and red-orange 28 car bright as new. Davey Allison.

"You shouldn't be wearing that shirt out and about," I told him. "It's probably worth something."

He raised his eyebrows. "Huh?"

"Davey Allison. The Rising Star? He died ten years ago at Talladega. The shirt is a collector's item. It ought to be kept in a box—not worn."

"You know about racing?"

His tone of incredulity nettled me. "I should," I said, stabbing at the creeper vine with my trowel.

He watched me in silence for a few moments, and then without a word he bent forward and began to pull more vine tendrils from the bed of impatiens. If he had pressed sympathy on me, or asked about Liam, if he'd said anything at all, I might have snubbed him and sent him on his way, but the companionable silence was oddly comforting, as if a friendly collie had ambled up to keep me company.

"I was married to Liam Bethel," I said at last, still intent upon the encroaching weeds. "I suppose you knew that."

He shrugged. "Knew you lived somewhere up here."

"And you don't."

He smiled. "My people have been on this mountain a long time," he said.

I knew he was a local. NASCAR tee shirts are not worn up here on the hill.

Summer people may watch the races on big-screen TVs, but they do not wear their hearts on their sleeves—or on their shirts.

"Do you mind how things have changed up here?" I asked him once.

He shrugged. "I don't think these people really want to be here."

I was puzzled. Surely if you spend a million dollars on a home . . .

But he went on. "In the gift shops now they play Navajo flute music. They decorate their homes in desert colors as if they thought north Georgia bordered New Mexico. It's not that they're here that I mind. It's that they want to make here somewhere else."

"But we don't really live here," I reminded him. "We only come for a while to get away from real life."

In those dark Indian eyes I caught a flicker of Liam's bleak-eyed stare. "They come up here," he said softly, "they shouldn't change it and take it away from them has loved it like it was."

After a few more evenings of weeding and comfortable silence, I learned that the boy's name was Eddie. I didn't quite catch his surname, but it sounded German; anyhow it ended with macher. I didn't like to ask again. Once I tried to give him a handful of dollar bills for his help in the garden, but he only smiled and waved it away. By then I was glad of his company and had only been looking for a way to cement the bargain. Liam would not have offered him money. He knew these people, but I can only guess at what motivates them to do anything.

Perhaps Eddie's people were better off than I had at first supposed. I had an idea that they might be silkscreen printers—these hills are full of jackleg craftsmen. Every day he wore a different racing shirt—Dale Earnhardt, Neil Bonnett, Tim Richmond—all looking like new. His family manufactures these reproductions of racing legends, I thought, and I wondered if I ought to have a word with them about trademark infringement, but I was too tired to care, really. What does it matter if they sell a few bootlegged tee shirts of dead drivers here in the back of beyond?

One day, though, when he was decked out in Fireball Roberts, I felt an unaccountable spurt of irritation. "Don't you have a Liam Bethel shirt?" I said.

He shrugged. "Wouldn't be right to wear one here. You up here and all."

"I wouldn't mind," I said, although I didn't know that until I heard myself say it. "Just don't wear some cheap reproduction. Come inside."

We kept caps, shirts, and race trinkets in a drawer up here to give away in case, say, the TV repairman turned out to be a fan of racing. From the guest room bureau I dug out an old shirt commemorating Liam's first Cup win at Bristol. "Here," I said. "Have it. You were his neighbor."

He thanked me solemnly, and went away soon after. It was only then that I remembered the curious sense of honor these local people had. If you ever did them the slightest good turn, they would be forever your vassal, and they would go to any length to repay a kindness. I hoped if the boy felt compelled to return a favor that it would come in the form of tomatoes from the family garden, and nothing more valuable or troublesome than that.

A day or two later, in the gray evening when the deer venture out of the woods, Eddie returned, empty-handed, but still in my debt, it seemed.

"Come on. I want to show you something!" he said, fairly dancing with excitement.

Inwardly, I sighed. What had he to show me? A litter of pigs? A prize watermelon? A hundred newly-bootlegged copies of Liam's victory shirt? But I went with him anyhow, because I had grown tired of pulling up creeping vines from my flower bed. No matter how many times I ripped out the invader's new shoots, more would have taken their place by the next time I weeded.

In the gathering twilight we walked away from the soaring glass houses on manicured lawns, over to the other side of the mountain and into the woods, following no path that I could discern, but Eddie's pace never slowed. The sun was nearly gone, and in the night air the chill deepened.

"Is it much farther?" I asked, but he simply gestured forward and quickened his pace, so I stumbled on after him, knowing that without him I could not find my way back.

Long minutes passed, punctuated only by the sound of twigs snapping as I hurried to keep up with this boy who neither stumbled nor slowed. I could see the stars again now, for the pines thinned as we reached the edge of the ridge.

We stood on the edge of a precipice, where an outcropping of rock formed a ledge overhanging the valley below. I was disoriented and did not know in which direction we had come. Should this be the side of the mountain that overlooked the village crossroads below or was it the wilderness side that gave out onto trees and a rock-studded stream? In any case, neither of those vistas spread out before me.

I saw a forest stretching to the mountains across the valley, but far below us lay a circular field ablaze with lights. I could make out an oval of red Georgia mud, encircled by a rickety grandstand of the sort one saw at high school baseball fields forty years ago. Within the oval was an assortment of haulers, campers, pick-up trucks, and here and there a garishly painted stock car.

A dirt track.

Well, they are common enough in north Georgia, but I had not known that one existed so close to our enclave. Surely some of the residents up here would have complained about it. Liam used to say that he attended the Residents'

Meeting to make sure that they were not planning to hand out smallpox-infected blankets to the locals. Of course, they would do no such thing, but I did think that they would object to a dirt track in the proximity of their luxury homes.

Eddie had knelt down on the ledge at my elbow, and was pointing excitedly at the spectacle below. Mud flew and cars slid forward: a race had begun. I watched the rainbow of cars circle the track for a moment, and the one that pulled ahead as it took the corner at full speed caught my eye. Red and silver. Liam's number. The paint scheme identical, even down to the sponsors' logos.

Rage struggled with amazement. Was this what he had come to show me? This cheap imitation, this flagrant image theft, a greater sacrilege than a few knock-off tee shirts?

"You can't do this!" I said, shouting into the silence, for the sounds of the track did not carry all the way to the mountaintop. I kept staring down at the track below while I screamed the words into the wind. Copyright infringement . . . lawyers . . . fraud . . . "I won't allow it!"

I shook with fury, grieving widow now suddenly keeper of the flame. Of the business at least. Ready to call lawyers to this solitary mountaintop, as one might summon dragons.

I would have said more, but all the while I had been watching those cars weaving and cornering around the track in a pavane on wheels. The way they took the corners at full speed, but never got loose. The way they passed, a tap on the bumper here and there, but no one spun out. No one hit the wall. How many races had I seen over the years? Five hundred? A thousand? Watching at first only to see if Liam would walk away, but finally understanding the rhythms of the dance. At last able to judge the skill of the dancers themselves. I had seen them all, and without consciously trying to train my eye, I was able to tell good from great. I could discern style. I cannot explain it. A horse show judge will tell you that before a rider is halfway across a ring he will know the novice from the expert, even at a walk. After a while you just know.

As I knew now.

The pink 51. The red 25. The black and red-orange 28. The black number three. Oh, yes. And there among them Liam's red and silver Chevy. All of them driving like no backwoods dirt track driver ever could, in perfect control, with surgical precision at breathless speeds—reaction time a blink, a heartbeat. A hundred things to watch all at once, swoop and glide, cut and corner, but never, never slowing down in the river of air.

It was them. Neil. Tim. Davey. Dale. Liam. Impossible, but just slightly less impossible than the notion that anyone else could drive like that with such perfection . . . And I looked and a whirlwind came out of the north . . . Like angels in chariots. Out here in the middle of nowhere.

I had found him.

I gulped air to keep from crying out, as I turned to ask Eddie where I was, and how I could make my way down off this mountain to where they were. To Liam. But the boy was backing away from me, shaking his head, hurt by my outburst. I had rejected his gift. He held up his hands, imploring me not to follow, and turned back toward the dark woods. I stumbled after him, crying out for him to stop, not to leave me alone on the mountain. But he was gone in an instant, and when I could no longer hear the sound of his footfalls in the bracken, I turned back to the ledge, thinking that I would find my own way down to the valley. I would follow the lights.

But they, too, were gone.

I knelt down and crawled to the very edge of the precipice, leaning as far over as I dared, straining for a glimpse of what had been so clear before. All I saw from the rock outcrop was a dark and silent plain, black with an unbroken sea of trees. Cold and silent under the distant stars.

Abide With Me. I have walked this mountain every day since then, at dawn, at twilight, even sometimes at midnight when the dew soaks my shoes and the night mist turns my hair to sodden strings. But Eddie never came back, and though I have walked those woods a hundred times, with that old hymn circling in my head, keeping time with my heartbeat, I have never found the rock ledge or that place in the valley where heaven's morning breaks and earth's vain shadows flee.

A plaque, a photo, a cardboard likeness. I have all these things still. And a stone and glass house on a mountain, close to heaven.

Reprinted with permission of Sharyn McCrumb. Published in *Appalachian Heritage* 32.4 (Fall 2004).

Sharyn McCrumb: A Biographical Sketch

Sharyn McCrumb is a prolific novelist whose clever lines and plot twists have captivated a large popular audience. Her deep underlying themes and her thoroughly researched settings have enthused literary critics whose analyses have appeared not only in journals but also in a book, *From a Race of Storytellers: Essays on the Ballad Novels of Sharyn McCrumb* by Kimberly M. Holloway (2003).

Sharyn McCrumb was born in 1948 in Wilmington, North Carolina, and lived in the state until she was in her thirties. The product of a father from the mountains and a mother from a plantation on the coastal plain, McCrumb went to first grade in Chapel Hill while her father was working on a doctorate, and from grades two to nine she lived in Burlington, where he was a school principal. She wrote her first story there at the tender age of eight. The protagonist was a boy who owned a horse and lived on a Wyoming ranch, and the plot centered upon the visit of a UFO. Her high school years were spent in Greenville, where her father headed the Elementary Education Department at East Carolina University. McCrumb double majored at the University of North Carolina in Spanish and communications and first taught Spanish in her mother's home county and then was a reporter for the *Smoky Mountain Times* out of Bryson City. In the 1980s she completed an MA in English at Virginia Tech, and has continued to live in the Virginia mountains since that time.

Sharyn McCrumb's first book rolled off the presses in New York in 1984, published by Avon. By the end of that decade, McCrumb had risen to the top of the mystery genre, winning virtually every award in that field. However, she refused to be limited or defined by that focus. The same year that two of her mysteries were published, 1990, Scribner's published her first trade novel in hardback. *If Ever I Return Pretty Peggy-O* took for its title the name of a traditional mountain ballad and became the first of her "ballad novels." In the 1990s, four more followed, including *She Walks These Hills* and *The Rosewood Casket,* both of which were *New York Times* best sellers. Two more ballad novels appeared in the first decade of the twenty-first century, including *Ghost Riders* (1983), which won a national Audie Award for "best recorded book."

When race car driver Dale Earnhardt was killed in 2001 Sharyn McCrumb was fascinated by the outpouring of emotion, noticing a parallel between the pilgrimages that NASCAR fans were making and those recounted in Geoffrey Chaucer's fourteenth-century classic, *The Canterbury Tales,* which she studied in graduate school. She contacted her old friend Jane Hicks, a NASCAR fan as well as an upper East Tennessee poet, quilter, and teacher of gifted children.

They began attending races together, and McCrumb also became a fan. *St. Dale* (2005) became the novel depicting the Earnhardt pilgrimages. *Once around the Track* (2007) followed. McCrumb returned to ballad novels in 2010 with *The Devil amongst the Lawyers,* followed by *The Ballad of Tom Dooley* in 2011.

Sharyn McCrumb sees herself as part of the bardic tradition of the Appalachian South that aspires to transmit cultural values and historical heritage in an entertaining way. She has read her work all over the United States and at Oxford University in England and the University of Bonn in Germany. Back in her home state, the Library of Virginia has named her a Virginia Woman of History for her contribution to literature.

Sharyn McCrumb: A Selective Bibliography

INTERNET RESOURCES

Appalachian Voices features an interview with McCrumb that draws connections between her work and environmental issues in Appalachia. The *News and Observer* has an article describing her mission to create authentic southern fiction. McCrumb's website features a bibliography of all her works, interviews as well as numerous essays and discussion questions, including a link to an essay, "The Harmonies behind her Ballad Books." *Southern Scribe* posted an interview with McCrumb titled "A Sense of Place."

SELECTED BOOKS

The Ballad of Tom Dooley. New York: Thomas Dunne Books, 2011.
Faster Pastor (with Adam Edwards). Ingalls Publishing Group, 2011.
The Devil amongst the Lawyers. New York: Thomas Dunne Books, 2010.
Once around the Track. New York: Kensington, 2007.
St. Dale. New York: Kensington, 2005.
Ghost Riders. New York: Dutton, 2003.
The Songcatcher. New York: Dutton, 2001.
The Ballad of Frankie Silver. New York: Dutton, 1998.
Foggy Mountain Breakdown and Other Stories. New York: Ballantine/Random House, 1997.
The Rosewood Casket. New York: Dutton, 1996.
She Walks These Hills. New York: Scribner, 1994.

PROFILES/INTERVIEWS

Jentsch, Nancy K., and Danny L. Miller. "Lighting the Fuse: Wilma Dykeman and Sharyn McCrumb as Appalachian Activists" In *Beyond Hill and Hollow: Original Readings in Appalachian Women's Studies.* Athens: Ohio UP, 2005. 75–94.

LITERARY CRITICISM

Brosi, George, ed. *Appalachian Heritage* 32.4 (2004). Features Sharyn McCrumb.

Holloway, Kimberley M., ed. *From a Race of Storytellers: Essays on the Ballad Novels of Sharyn McCrumb.* Macon, GA: Mercer UP, 2003.

Jennings, Rachel. "Celtic Women and White Guilt: Frankie Silver and Chipita Rodriguez in Folk Memory." *MELUS: The Journal of the Society for the Study of the Multi-Ethnic Literature of the United States* 28.1 (2003): 17–37.

Lang, John, ed. *Iron Mountain Review* 22 (2006). Features Sharyn McCrumb.

Rubin, Rachel. "'What Ain't Called Melungeons Is Called Hillbillies': Southern Appalachia's In-between People." *Forum for Modern Language Studies* 40.3 (2004): 259–78.

Willis, Meredith Sue. "The Ballads of Sharyn McCrumb." *Appalachian Journal* 25.3 (1998): 320–28.

Part 5

Institutions

Kathryn Stripling Byer

Mountain Time

News travels slowly up here
in the mountains, our narrow
roads twisting for days, maybe years,
till we get where we're going,
if we ever do. Even if some lonesome message
should make it through Deep Gap
or the fastness of Thunderhead, we're not obliged
to believe it's true, are we? Consider
the famous poet, minding her post
at the Library of Congress, who
shrugged off the question of what we'd be
reading at century's end: "By the year 2000
nobody will be reading poems." Thus she
prophesied. End of that
interview! End of the world
as we know it. Yet, how can I fault
her despair, doing time as she was
in a crumbling Capitol, sirens
and gunfire the nights long, the Pentagon's
stockpile of weapons stacked higher
and higher? No wonder the books
stacked around her began to seem relics.
No wonder she dreamed her own bones
dug up years later, tagged in a museum somewhere
in the Midwest: American Poet—Extinct Species.

Up here in the mountains
we know what extinct means. We've seen
how our breath on a bitter night
fades like a ghost from the window glass.

We know the wolf's gone.
The panther. We've heard the old stories
run down, stutter out
into silence. Who knows where we're heading?
All roads seem to lead
to Millennium, dark roads with drop-offs
we can't plumb. It's time to be brought up short
now with the tale-teller's *Listen:* There once lived
a woman named Delphia
who walked through these hills teaching children
to read. She was known as a quilter
whose hand never wearied, a mother
who raised up two daughters to pass on
her words like a strong chain of stitches.
Imagine her sitting among us,
her quick thimble moving along these lines
as if to hear every word striking true
as the stab of her needle through calico.
While prophets discourse about endings,
don't you think she'd tell us the world as we know it
keeps calling us back to beginnings?
This labor to make our words matter
is what any good quilter teaches.
A stitch in time, let's say.
A blind stitch
that clings to the edges
of what's left, the ripped
scraps and remnants, whatever
won't stop taking shape even though the whole
crazy quilt's falling to pieces.

❁ ❁ ❁

Precious Little

The passageway down which they had
just gone was bright as the eye of a needle.
—Eudora Welty, *Losing Battles*

So we'd gathered to talk about writing,
remembering great ones who'd recently gone
from our midst and the various ways
they had followed each voice through

the needle's eye into the clearing of art,
when a novelist slouched
on the front row opined
that the only real subject is battle

and how men survive it.
I seethed while my student poets,
all of them women, sat waiting for someone
to challenge his vision of literature,

belligerent canon
where warring tribes battle it out
in their epics and blood-spattered novels.
"Miss Welty" I countered, "stayed

clear of the battlefield, if you recall.
She sat down every day at the same desk
and made language raise the world up
from the grave of our common amnesia."

He barely acknowledged
my comment. He wanted to flirt
with my students. He shrugged at me,
stood up and showed off the fit

of his tight jeans. My god,
what a chasm he opened up right there
between us: we stared like combatants
across the trench, loading our weapons,

his now on full frontal display,
along with a first novel already lobbed
to reviewers by Random House. As for me,
middle-aged poet, what were mine?

Precious little. The shot I recalled
having seen months ago of a woman my age
holding up to the camera a photo of daughter
or sister or good friend who'd disappeared

into the rubble of felled towers, the same woman
I had seen sifting through ruins in Fallujah
and Kabul, even now cringing
when she hears the gunfire in Baghdad,

a woman who stares back at me
when I'm dusting my daughter's face
framed on the shelf,
smiling out at a day that's been gone

for so long I can barely remember it,
nothing much going on, no bombs,
no fireworks, just late summer afternoon
and the dogs asleep under the oak tree.

Reprinted with permission of LSU Press. Published in *Coming to Rest: Poems* (2006).

Kathryn Stripling Byer: A Biographical Sketch

The lyrical quality of Kathryn Stripling Byer's poetry has inspired composers to set several of her poems to music that has been performed in North Carolina, Georgia, New York, and Hungary. "Singing must have seemed the only way [that mountain women] could travel," Byer wrote in *Bloodroot: Reflections on Place by Appalachian Women Writers,* edited by Joyce Dyer, "[. . .] they were able to sing their way through their solitude and into a larger web of voices, voices that I have come to see as connective tissue stretching across these hills." When Byer was ten, her paternal grandmother died. Born in Dahlonega, Georgia, this grandmother had come to the flat southern part of the state to teach Latin, and stayed."Had she tried to sing her way out of her solitude and back home?" Byer wondered. "Sometimes I think that all the poems I have written since I came to the mountains have been an attempt to find a song that would sail her away, out of the sad story in which she had become trapped, back to the mountains where she belonged and longed to be."

Kathryn Stripling Byer was born in 1944 and grew up on a South Georgia farm. She graduated from Wesleyan College in Macon, Georgia, in 1966 and received her MFA from the University of North Carolina at Greensboro in 1968. There she studied under Allen Tate and Fred Chappell. That year she accepted a job at Western Carolina University, and two years later married James Byer, a young man whose family roots went way back on the Obed River watershed in East Tennessee, and who also taught English at Western. In 1978 their daughter, Corinna, was born. As the young Byer couple walked in the mountains not far from campus, Byer writes that she "found my imagination being stirred by those trails, by the leaf mold and dirt of them, their shifting light, their windy sounds, their atmosphere of mystery and solitude . . . voices seemed to rise right up out of the leaf mold." When she was walking in the Smokies with her husband, the voice of a mountain woman came to her, and the poems this voice inspired became her second chapbook, *Alma,* in 1983.

Byer's first poetry collection manuscript, *The Girl in the Midst of the Harvest,* was chosen for the national Associated Writing Programs Award Series in 1986. She returned to the mountain voices with the first of five books from Louisiana State University Press, *Wildwood Flower* (1992), which won the Lamont Prize from the Academy of American Poets. *Black Shawl* followed in 1998, inspired initially by an abandoned home she found on the Kanati Fork Trail in the Great Smoky Mountains National Park. That year she retired from Western Carolina University, having served as a professor, the director of the writers' program, and poet-in-residence. In 2002 *Catching Light* won the Southern Independent

Booksellers Association award in poetry. Then in 2005 Kathryn Stripling Byer succeeded her former professor, Fred Chappell, as poet laureate of North Carolina, the first woman ever chosen. She held that post for five years, working tirelessly to promote poetry and the poets of the state. During that time LSU Press published a fourth collection, *Coming to Rest* (2006). Her fifth collection, also from LSU Press, is *Descent*, published in 2012.

In 2007, after Kathryn Stripling Byer won the poetry award from the Fellowship of Southern Writers, she told Nicole Cartwright Denison in an interview, "Our writers must lead the response against the depredation of our landscape and environment by reminding our communities that they must love these places enough to fight for them."

Kathryn Stripling Byer: A Selective Bibliography

INTERNET RESOURCES

The *Cortland Review* has a wide collection of Byer's poems. The *Dead Mule School of Southern Literature* has "Spade," "Crone's Quilt," and "Exit to C.E.R.E.S." The *Blue Moon Review* offers "Closer." *Story South* has "The Still Here and Now," "Chicago Bound," "Night Fishing," and "Halloween Again." *Red Room* offers Byer's poems "Coastal Plain," "Women Respond to War," and "Full Moon," and reviews of Byer's work by *Appalachian Heritage*, The *Hollins Critic*, and *Foreword Magazine*. Kathryn Stripling Byer has an extensive website of her own that provides more resources and promotes other poets.

SELECTED BOOKS

Descent: Poems. Baton Rouge: Louisiana State UP, 2012.
Coming to Rest: Poems. Baton Rouge: Louisiana State UP, 2006.
Wake: Poems. Sylva, NC: Spring Street Editions, 2003.
Catching Light: Poems. Baton Rouge: Louisiana State UP, 2002.
Black Shawl: Poems. Baton Rouge: Louisiana State UP, 1998.
Wildwood Flower: Poems. Baton Rouge: Louisiana State UP, 1992.
The Girl in the Midst of the Harvest. Lubbock: Texas Tech Press, 1986.

INTERVIEW

Smith, Lee. "Kathryn Stripling Byer: Singing the Mountain." In *Appalachia and Beyond: Conversations with Writers from the Mountain South.* Ed. John Lang. Knoxville: U of Tennessee P, 2006. 293–311.

LITERARY CRITICISM

Chappell, Fred. "Windy-voices: Kathryn Stripling Byer's Poetry." *Shenandoah* 55.1 (2005): 64–82.

Harvley-Felder, Irene. "Word Choice." *Our State* 73.5 (2005): 46–53.

Lang, John. "Kathryn Stripling Byer: 'Laying Up Treasures on Earth.'" In *Six Poets from the Mountain South.* Baton Rouge: Louisiana State UP, 2010. 125–56.

———, ed. *Iron Mountain Review* 18 (2002). Features Kathryn Stripling Byer.

Richman, Ann F. "Singing Our Hearts Away: The Poetry of Kathryn Stripling Byer." In *Her Words: Diverse Voices in Contemporary Appalachian Women's Poetry.* Ed. Felicia Mitchel. Knoxville: U of Tennessee P, 2002. 38–48.

Smith, James. "Not Always a 'Piece of Cake': Harrowing Humor in the Poetry of Kathryn Stripling Byer." *North Carolina Literary Review* 17 (2008): 66–73.

Elizabeth Cox

The Last Fourth Grade

1

I know almost nothing about prisons, but I know enough to hold my glance at the level of an inmate's eyes, and to keep my expression absent of pity. I know how to look straight at people, with no judgment. I learned this particular sensitivity in the fourth-grade class of Mrs. Natalie Johnson. She instructed us to look people in the eye, especially if they were poor or had some misshapen feature. She said it was unkind not to do so. But Mrs. Johnson is an inmate in the Virginia Prison for Women. I have come to visit her, bringing books and a long loaf of bread, and I have been told that I will be escorted to a room with tables, a pot of tea, and privacy.

The blunt hedge around the prison is cut like the work of a cheap barber. Cut by someone who cares nothing about hedges, but who is aware of an effect that comes across as neat, and with an obvious order. Scraggly bushes grow in the dirt beside the office door entrance. I must go through the office into a part of the building where doors close behind me.

The walls hold a burnt smell, or worse, a smell that tries to be clean—disinfectant and old stone. This particular prison has the smell of a school, and I wonder if Mrs. Johnson notices the similar odor.

I am thirty-one, and until a few days ago I had not heard from Mrs. Johnson. Then I received a note asking me to visit her here. I don't know how she knew I had moved back into town, and I wonder if she has thought of me through the years. I have thought about her often.

2

In the fourth grade I wrote a poem about the death of my father, and read it at Writing Time. After class, Mrs. Johnson walked to my desk at the back of the room and told me my poem was good. "Very nice," she whispered. She asked if she could have a copy for herself. I said I didn't mind. She smelled like talcum powder and soap.

That night I copied the poem in a careful, neat hand. I gave it to her the next morning. She thanked me and asked how my mother liked reading it.

"Fine," I said, though I had not shown the poem to my mother.

3

I went to the trial of Mrs. Johnson, and even testified on her behalf. Many of my classmates told the court that she was a good teacher, and that they loved her. I told the judge that she was the best teacher I'd ever had. After the guilty verdict, Mrs. Johnson left the courtroom, a policeman on either side, and I tried to think of ways to rescue her. While she was in prison, I sent postcards. I sent them until I graduated from high school.

At the trial, her arms and legs grew spindly, and as the factual account asserted itself in the newspapers, Natalie Johnson's stout figure changed into a bent, stooped oldness that reached beyond her years. She turned sixty the year she went to prison—only a few years before she would have retired from Vena Wilburn Elementary School.

During the months of the trial, I drew maps, and pretended to be doing this for Mrs. Johnson, as if she had assigned it. Mrs. Johnson loved maps. She pulled them down like a shade over the blackboard and made us see the roads, the mountains, the dark and light terrain of different countries. She pointed out cities and rural areas, then told stories about people who lived in odd parts of the world. We never knew if the stories she told were made-up or true, but her teaching gave us a way to move inside the maps. She made the lines and boundaries come alive. She traced with her finger, and let us trace with our fingers, the routes that led to historical discovery, or wars that brought life-and-death boundaries to our minds. She said, as she let the large map roll back up above the blackboard, "I love maps. I love all kinds of maps." She let us draw maps of America and color them, drawing in states and boundaries, shading the mountains and making rivers wide and blue.

Before the year was up, every fourth grader felt the contagious affection she had for maps. At recess we drew rivers and mountains and shapes of countries on one another's arms or backs. We wore maps, and drew them, and believed in their importance to our understanding of geography and history.

I also collected Luna moths and pinned them to a board. I pretended this, too, had been homework assigned by Mrs. Johnson. I kept trying to picture the way Mr. Johnson might have looked before he died.

4

Natalie Johnson brought students into her home twice a year. In the fall she entertained us the week before Christmas vacation with popcorn and cider; in the springtime, around Easter, she served cookies or cake, with lemonade and ice cream. Her husband, Harry, read the class fantastic stories: fairy tales or tales that scared us into laughter. Everyone called Mr. Johnson "Harry," though Mrs. Johnson was always "Mrs. Johnson."

Harry Johnson had a clear melodic voice and he spent days before our visit choosing stories he thought we would like. Sometimes he made up a story himself. Mrs. Johnson felt proud of her husband and bragged about how much fun he was. She said she had loved him since she was a little girl not much older than we were. She said she had loved him forever, but she blushed when she said it.

Before being promoted into Mrs. Johnson's fourth-grade class, everyone knew they would have a special time at her house—in the fall, and again in the spring. As years went on, though, and as Harry grew older, his stories took on a slightly risqué tone. The year before I was in fourth grade a few of the stories had been categorized as too bold for young ears, and in places even suggestive.

At our first party in the fall, after one of these more bawdy stories, Mrs. Johnson mentioned to her husband the inappropriateness of the subject matter, and we thought we were about to hear our teacher have a fight with her husband. "You're too prim," he told her, and left the house. Mrs. Johnson looked helpless and teary. At the trial she testified to these facts. And as she spoke about Harry, she began to cry, saying she had only wanted him to be more careful about choosing the stories.

The day after our fall visit, Mrs. Johnson read to us a story about Arabian nights. She wanted us to forget about Harry. But many of us had already told our parents about Harry Johnson, and though the parents whispered to one another, no one took action. Natalie Johnson was beloved, she was trusted. Almost everyone in town had been her fourth-grade student.

A few months passed and the class was wondering if the spring party would be canceled. Their parents told them not to mention a party but to let Mrs. Johnson decide. During the last week in March, she sent permission notes to our homes, and our parents signed them.

My mother said she would pick me up at five-thirty and take me to Denny's. Daylight saving time had not yet begun, so the light died around five. She told me to wait outside on the steps. She knew that in the past Harry Johnson sometimes drove children home in his big van.

5

When we arrived, Harry was in his reading chair and had pillows propped all around the room where children could sit or lean back. He looked happy and suggested that we go to the kitchen and bring our food back to the living room. We loved eating in the Johnsons' living room, because we couldn't eat in our living rooms at home.

When Harry introduced himself, Jeffrey Bohm said, "We already know you. We met you before Christmas." He sounded rude when he said it.

"Of course you did," said Harry. "I remember you." Then he told Jeffrey something that Jeffrey had wanted for Christmas, so Jeffrey would know he remembered.

Harry's eyes were sweaty, watery, and his face slightly flushed, but he was smiling. Still, I was glad I would not ride in the van with him and asked my friend Mary Alice if she wanted to ride with me and my mama to Denny's.

"I can't," said Mary Alice. "I have to go home the way my note says to—in the van."

Harry Johnson urged Mary Alice to sit near him. He said she had pretty hair and that he liked to touch it. "It feels like silk," he said. Mary Alice smiled, and I wished he had said those words about my hair. Mary Alice already had a father who said nice things to her, and my father had been dead a year. I was thinking of another poem I could write, about how much my father loved my hair, when Harry told us to sit down. Mrs. Johnson said she would bring more lemonade and cake in a little while. Ice cream would come last. We always had two stories, but when the second story was told we got ice cream.

The first story was about a frog, and a princess who was looking for a prince. When the beautiful princess kissed the frog everyone made sniveling noises, then Harry stopped the story to ask if anyone had ever been kissed, and when four people raised their hands he said, "Mary Alice, what about you?" And she said, "No, just my parents." So Harry told us, "Maybe before this day is over *everybody* can be kissed." Then Mrs. Johnson came in and he finished the story, but I don't think she heard him ask those questions. She was just bringing in the ice cream.

As he began the second story we could hear her washing dishes. We could hear her rattling glasses and plates, so Harry called out for her to close the kitchen door because some of us couldn't hear with all that noise. But no one was having trouble hearing. When she closed the door, Harry scooted down on the floor with us, near me and Mary Alice, and he pulled Mary Alice onto his lap. I had never seen anyone drunk except on TV, but I knew that Mr. Johnson was acting strange.

Mary Alice looked at me. Her eyes scanned the room to see reactions, but Harry said, "Now I'm going to hold Mary Alice on my lap and I'm going to put her into what's called an armlock. Some of you boys know what this is because you've seen wrestling on TV." The boys nodded, but we still didn't know what was happening.

Jeffrey Bohm said, "Let me do it. I can do it."

Mr. Johnson spoke roughly. "Now, Jeffrey, sit down and watch how Mary Alice tries to get loose." Mary Alice wiggled trying to get out of Mr. Johnson's arms, and her wiggling made his eyes shine. He held her tighter.

"Hey, no fair," said Jeffrey. "You're holding her too tight. That's not fair." Others seemed to be frightened, because Mary Alice herself looked as if she were about to cry. Her bottom lip quivered. So he let Mary Alice go and said, "Okay, Jeff-boy, come over here and we'll see how you do."

Jeffrey took a position on his hands and knees, as a wrestler would. "This is how it's *supposed* to be," he said.

I could see a bulge in Mr. Johnson's pants, and his eyes looked glazed. He was looking at me. He even reached to pull me onto his lap, but I slipped out of his grasp and followed Mary Alice into the bathroom. "I hate him," said Mary Alice. "I want to go home."

"I do too," I said.

"When your mama comes I'm going with you."

We heard some scuffling and someone yelled. When Mary Alice and I came out of the bathroom, Jeffrey was standing up hitting Mr. Johnson in the head. Harry Johnson was kneeling, holding on to Jeffrey's pants. He wouldn't let go. Mrs. Johnson stood at the kitchen door. "Harry! What are you doing!"

Harry sat back on the floor. His pants now looked wet. Mrs. Johnson gathered us up like chickens, and we hurried into the kitchen. She blocked the kitchen door with a chair and then turned to us. "I'm sorry. I shouldn't've brought you here today. Mr. Johnson, he isn't well. He's sick, I think he's sick." She kept her voice very calm, so we began to feel calm within ourselves. She said we could take a walk and she would show us some bird's nests, maybe an owl, and if we walked all the way to the pond we could see some funny-looking fish.

Jeffrey clung to Mrs. Johnson, and Mary Alice and I walked along beside him. Jeffrey could not stop trembling, and Mrs. Johnson comforted him every few seconds. Her voice sounded deep, as from a cave. "Don't you worry, Jeffrey. You are just fine now. Don't you worry." She stroked his head and back. "You didn't do anything wrong, and Mrs. Johnson won't take you back there again."

I tried to comfort Mary Alice in the same way, my hand on her back.

On the way to Denny's my mother asked us about the party and said how nice Mrs. Johnson was to invite us to her house. She said that since the

Johnsons never had any children of their own, they thought of the fourth grade as their special children. "They must like having young voices in that stuffy old house." My mother pulled into the Denny's parking lot.

"It's not stuffy," I said, in defense of my teacher.

6

A few days after this incident, Harry Johnson was found dead in the backyard of his house. At her trial Mrs. Johnson claimed that he had shot himself. She said he hadn't meant to but was cleaning his gun and it went off. She looked at the jury, people she knew, people who knew Harry, and she tried to make an excuse for him. "He probably didn't know what he was doing. He was so drunk. During that last year, seems he was always drunk."

But what happened, Mrs. Johnson finally confessed, was that she had come from teaching one afternoon and found Harry with pictures on the kitchen table: photographs of children in underwear or nude. His camera was on the table beside her car keys, and when she came in, though she barely remembered the exact moment, she would see forever the vacant, stupid expression on his face.

Natalie Johnson took the gun from in their hall cabinet, and she shot Harry in the chest. She could not stand to be around him. She could no longer bear the thought of him in her house, or alive. Until that moment, she had not known she was as capable of murder as she was of love. She said all these words at the trial, and I remembered her words, the way I remembered about maps and countries.

Harry had been shot three times.

Mrs. Johnson confessed, "I shot him, then shot him again. I don't know how many times." She tried to stand in the witness chair, but the prosecutor laid a hand on her shoulder. "I didn't know what else to do," she said. "I couldn't hear those sweet voices in the schoolroom without thinking of Harry."

She hated him with her whole heart.

7

Mrs. Johnson's letter asking me to visit her in prison said: *I know you probably have not thought about me in many years, but I remember you. I remember everyone in that last fourth-grade class from the year Harry died.*

I had thought about her often, and had thought about visiting her in prison. I didn't know what I could say, so I dropped the idea. I couldn't imagine what she wanted to say to me now, but I decided to go. I wanted to see her.

She was sitting in a large room with windows. Her hair was thin and very white. She had lost weight, but she didn't look as gaunt as I had expected. Her face looked pale from lack of sunlight.

“I’m Carey Hammond,” I said, using my maiden name.

She raised one arm and started to rise.

“Well, it’s Bowles now, though I’m probably going to be Hammond again soon. I divorced my husband a month ago, and moved back here.”

She asked me about my husband, my life. She was hungry for news.

As I drew closer, I couldn’t help seeing the hardness that had crept into her face, the lines and rough skin that had replaced her plump, soft body. I wondered if she still smelled like powder, like Chanel No. 5, which we all knew was her favorite perfume.

“I have a daughter,” I told her. “She’s nine.”

“She must be in the fourth grade.” Mrs. Johnson smiled. “Does she live with you?”

“She’s with me during the week but goes to her father on weekends.”

“Oh, I was hoping you might bring her by.” Mrs. Johnson looked embarrassed at the suggestion. “I guess that wouldn’t be appropriate,” she explained, “but I’d love to see her. Does she look like you? You were such a thin, wiry child.”

“I’ll bring a picture next time,” I said. “Maybe I’ll even bring Soskia.”

“Soskia?”

“My husband’s family is from Czechoslovakia.” I thought of the shape and boundaries of that country as I said it.

We sat at a small table near a window, where someone had placed two cups and some tea, with Ritz crackers on a paper plate.

“I have some jam in my room, but I forgot to bring it.” She called her cell a “room,” and I was surprised that she could keep food there. I must have looked surprised.

“I’m a teacher here at the prison,” Mrs. Johnson said. “I teach reading and writing to women who never learned, or who didn’t do so well in school. Sometimes I teach geography, maps.” She smiled. “I get special privileges because I help to rehabilitate. I don’t know who I am unless I’m teaching.” She chuckled, so I did too. I was glad I had come by.

“I want to tell you something,” she said. Her hands grew nervous, her fingers wiggling like worms. “Since I’ve been in this place, I’ve thought a lot about Harry, and what he did. And you might be surprised to know that I realize now what really happened.” She turned to look at me. I couldn’t read her mood.

“Harry was a good man until the year of that last fourth grade,” she said.

“Yes, ma’am,” I said, falling into an old student habit of polite agreement.

“Sometimes I believe Harry is still in the house, sitting in his chair,” she said sadly. “And I write poems to him—the way you did to your father. I still have that poem you wrote for your father. Did you know that?”

"No, ma'am." I felt that I had been jerked up, then let down again softly. She removed her glasses and squeezed with her thumb and finger the bridge of her nose. She put her glasses back on. "Would you like for me to show you *my* poems sometime?"

I nodded without giving consent.

8

I had felt closer to my father after his death than when he was alive. The poems I wrote made me feel close to him. When he was alive, he traveled on business most of the week, so my mother and I seemed to live alone. In fact, Mary Alice thought my parents were divorced. "He's gone all the time," Mary Alice said. "Why is he gone all the time?"

"That's his job. He has to go. But when he's home, he's real nice." And he was. On the nights he was home, he tucked me in bed, and I felt that the house was safe in a way I never felt when he was traveling. He brought presents from places like Ohio and Washington and Texas and he showed me those places on a map in my room. We put pins in the map so I could see where he would be going the next week, and I liked it better if the states were close-by. He called us every night, usually just before bedtime, and asked me something about my homework. Sometimes he told me to memorize a poem so that when he got home I could say it to him. He liked when I knew something by heart.

So when the car he was driving crashed into another car, and my mother told me he would not be coming home, and that we would be going to his funeral, I wrote poem after poem, hoping he would see that everything I was writing was "by heart." And when I wrote them down, I felt he was alive, and near me. I never showed anyone those poems, except one I showed to Mrs. Johnson.

9

Soskia could hardly wait to see my fourth-grade teacher.

"Is she old?" she kept asking. She had dressed in her best Sunday outfit, and I tried to tell her that the place we were going was a prison and that it wouldn't look like other buildings where she had been. I told her that people were locked up because they had done something they weren't supposed to do, and Soskia asked what my teacher had done. I said that I would explain when she was a little older.

"When I'm ten?" Soskia asked.

"Older than ten," I told her.

The day was gray with a light drizzle, and the prison appeared especially dreary. I tried to distract Soskia with gifts we had brought for Mrs. Johnson. I gave instructions about politeness. "Don't mention Mrs. Johnson's clothes," I said, “because in prison you have to wear an orange outfit. Everybody has to wear the same thing.”

“Why?”

“They just do. It’s a rule.”

“Will she like my dress? Will she think it’s pretty?”

“Yes.”

Soskia turned as we went into a section where doors closed behind us with a metal lock. We walked toward the room where Mrs. Johnson waited. She had put on a sweater over her orange clothes, and she looked almost normal, sitting at the table with some tea and a plate of crackers. I had brought some snacks to put out. Soskia seemed shy when she saw Mrs. Johnson, but she wasn’t shy for long.

“Soskia.” Mrs. Johnson said the name with immediate affection. “Look how dressed up you are. I feel like we’re about to have a party.”

Soskia grinned and sat in the chair that Mrs. Johnson had pulled out for her. I asked Soskia if she wanted to open the bag and offer Mrs. Johnson one of the cinnamon buns we had brought. We put out food, and Mrs. Johnson spoke in tones that made the moment seem celebratory. Soskia began to tell Mrs. Johnson about her dog—a puppy—and how it liked to chew up shoes. She told her the puppy’s name and said she had gotten it just a few days ago. She said we couldn’t stay long, because we had to get back to the puppy.

Mrs. Johnson knew all the right questions to ask. Then she told Soskia that she had been my teacher many years ago. “And I remember when your mother was the same age as you are now.” Soskia looked at me as though Mrs. Johnson might be teasing, so I nodded and said it was true.

“My daddy doesn’t live with us anymore.” Soskia’s face looked quite thoughtful. “He lives in Maryland, and I go to see him on weekends. Mama says he can’t live with us in the house anymore.”

“Well.” Mrs. Johnson buttoned her sweater, then lifted a piece of paper from her pocket. “Maybe I should show you this.” She unfolded the paper to reveal large block handwriting on unlined paper. The lines were crooked and went down the page in a diagonal. I recognized it as the poem I had written to my father.

“Sometimes,” said Mrs. Johnson, “if somebody in the family is gone, or not in the house”—she made the situation sound regular—“people, especially children, find it a good idea to write something to that person. Even if you don’t give it to them. You can write a poem or draw a picture, then when you see the person again, if you want to, you can give it to him. Or you can put it in an envelope and mail it. If you want, I can help, so you can surprise your daddy.”

Soskia surged forward with excitement. She wanted to begin that very moment. Mrs. Johnson obliged by asking the guard for paper and a pencil. In moments she was leaning over Soskia, guiding her hand across the page. I watched, remembering the smell of talcum powder and soap. My poem lay open on the table, and I could see the blocky letters and the lines that went down in a slant.

10

We visited Mrs. Johnson every Sunday for six months. She never again brought up the subject of Harry. Still, I felt uneasy, without knowing the source of my uneasiness. One Sunday, Soskia got home late from an afternoon with her father, so that our visit was whittled down to only thirty minutes. That was the day Mrs. Johnson looked angry as we walked into the visitors' room.

"Well," she said. "Glad you could come." She moved to pull out something from a book bag she carried. "I wanted you to see some pictures of Harry. Soskia has never seen my Harry."

"Who's Harry?" Soskia asked.

"He was my husband." Then she paused, holding her mouth tight, pursing it. "Your *mother* remembers him. Don't you remember him?" She looked hard at me. "Your mother *liked* him." I had never seen the particular face she showed to us now, this odd expression. I almost didn't recognize her.

"No." I spoke defensively. "I liked *you,* not him. At the trial, I spoke for *you.*"

"That's not what I mean, dear," she said. "I mean you and Mary Alice, all you little girls—you wanted to make Harry pay attention to you." Her hands were folding and unfolding a ratty piece of paper. "You know what you did."

I asked Soskia to go to find a nurse. We called the people who worked in the prison "nurses."

"Mrs. Johnson, what's wrong?" I said. "Why are you doing this?"

"You and Mary Alice, some of the others, too, you had your flirty ways, your teasing girly voices."

"What are you talking about? Are you saying we *wanted* Harry to do what he did?" I couldn't believe Mrs. Johnson had lived so long with this idea. "You think we *wanted* him to touch us?"

Mrs. Johnson had become unglued. She wasn't listening to me. "Your sweet-smelling hair," she said. She put down the piece of paper and began to wring her hands, as if she were washing them. "And you sat with your little dresses open, legs sprawled out like *whores.* You let him see your little-girlness. What was he supposed to do? He couldn't help himself." She spread the pictures of Harry on the table. "I should never have brought you into the house."

I stood up, wanting to leave. "But you *did* bring us there. You put us in the room with him." I was furious and rushed toward the door, so I didn't see the moment her face changed, but I heard the sound she made, like a breath-cry. When I turned around to say one more thing, her face was buried in her arms.

Her voice came out muffled, full of tears. "I *closed* that kitchen door," she said. "I closed that door and washed my dishes, making noise so I couldn't hear. I didn't *want* to hear. I was *glad* when he told me to close that door." She looked up, her face wet. "I stood at the sink, and washed and washed, then I heard Jeffrey yelling." She paused, then looked straight at me. "As long as everyone was quiet, as long as there wasn't any noise, just Harry's story-voice, I could keep on washing. But when Jeffrey started to yell, I had to come through the door and see."

She strained to get up, pushing on the sides of the chair. She almost fell, and I caught her, helped her to stand. "He never touched you, Carey, did he? Did he?"

"Don't talk," I said.

"I thought he was getting better," she continued. "I thought it might help to have children in the house. He always wanted children of our own, you know." Her eyes grew huge, and she looked at me without actually seeing. "Then when I found the photographs, then I had to do what I did, you see. He never would have stopped."

"Don't," I said, reaching for her arm.

"Mama?" Soskia stood at the door. I didn't know how much she had heard, or how much she understood. She hadn't gone for a nurse.

"Soskia! Go!"

Mrs. Johnson was still talking, not yelling but speaking in a soft, singsong voice. I tried to comfort her.

"Don't say anything nice to me," she said. "That door has been in my mind, and now I've opened it. I know what I was thinking while I washed all those little plates and dried them, taking a *long* time. I think part of me thought that if Harry got caught, if he went far enough to get caught, *then* he would stop. Then he would stop. I wanted to save my Harry."

"We're all right," I told her. "The whole fourth grade came out all right. Mary Alice is a lawyer, and Jeffrey owns a large business in Richmond. Everyone in that last fourth grade came out all right."

"Well," she said, but her eyes had changed color. They had turned black, completely pupils. I felt that I could see all the way to the bowels of her soul. She sat down again, as if she had fallen into her chair. Something seemed over, and in a few days I would realize that what was over was her own life.

On Thursday morning when the guard came to Mrs. Johnson's "room," she was found dead on her cot. She had died of a heart attack during the night. The warden asked if I could come identify the body. Not knowing whom to call, they called me. When I arrived, I found Soskia's pictures and writing taped to the wall over her bed.

11

The weeks are long without her.

Soskia and I went to the funeral with a town full of old fourth graders. Now, on Sundays, we sit and talk about her. I didn't tell anyone about the door Mrs. Johnson's words opened in *me*. I didn't say how I had envied the attention Mr. Johnson paid to Mary Alice, how I wanted that attention for myself. I didn't tell how Harry Johnson met me at the door that day, how he slipped his hand beneath my dress and rubbed my back and bottom, my legs. I was aware of pleasure I had not felt before, though I knew this was a wrong kind of pleasure. He had lifted me up and whispered something in my ear that I didn't understand, so I laughed and touched his cheek. For one moment, I felt like he was a father, though not mine. Mine was dead. I could see Mrs. Johnson standing behind him, smiling a false, hard smile. She put her hand on his shoulder, and he put me down.

Yesterday, Soskia mentioned that she could still bring back the smell of Mrs. Johnson, and asked if she was "remembering the smell, or was Mrs. Johnson really close-by." I told her I thought she was close-by. I told her that sometimes a teacher is so strongly imprinted on our minds that we carry that teacher with us through the years. Soskia asked what I remembered when I thought about Mrs. Johnson.

"That's easy," I said. "I learned about maps and far-off countries. Maybe I even married your dad because of what she taught me about other places. She kept my father alive for me when I needed him." "What about you?" I asked. "How do you remember her?"

Soskia took my question seriously, "Well, I think about how weird she was the last time I saw her. But mostly, I remember how she taught me to draw, you know, pushing my hand over the page until I could feel how to do it myself. But what I think about most is the way she would hum in my ear. She hummed real quiet while I was trying to do something, and when she did that, hummed, I could do it right."

"The humming," I said. "I had forgotten."

"And now, when I have to do something real hard, and if I think I can't do it"—Soskia looked out over the yard—"I hum to myself, so quiet my ear can hardly hear the sound—and it's like a little road I go on, that takes me straight to the top. And I can do anything."

Natalie Johnson had taught her fledglings with a hum. I myself had forgotten. With a steady sound she had borne us like water toward the sea, her head wide with secrets. Her last fourth grade was Soskia: art lessons, writing, maps. Boundaries Mrs. Johnson herself could not keep. Harry and his hands rose like wings beneath little dresses, and Mrs. Johnson swept her house clean.

Reprinted with permission of Elizabeth Cox. Published in *Bargains in the Real World* (Random House, 2001).

Elizabeth Cox: A Biographical Sketch

In 2011 the Fellowship of Southern Writers presented Elizabeth Cox the Robert Penn Warren Award for fiction writing at their biennial conference in Chattanooga, Tennessee, her home town. This award was especially meaningful to her because she has been an admirer of Warren's work since before she went to college. Cox is a widely published poet and the author of a story collection, and she has published four novels.

Elizabeth Cox, who goes by "Betsy," grew up on the hundred-acre campus of the Baylor School, where her father, "Hub" Barks, was headmaster. From the window of her bedroom, she could see the Moccasin Bend of the Tennessee River, Williams Island, Lookout Mountain, Signal Mountain, and Elder Mountain. She told Fred Brown and Jeanne McDonald, for their book *Growing Up Southern: How the South Shapes Its Writers*, that "the river taught me how to move, the island taught me how to be alone, and the mountains taught me how to remain." She was the only sister of two brothers, and lived on the campus of what was then an all-boys secondary school. "I learned to be an extrovert, but my real strength is in being contemplative and interior," she told Brown and McDonald. She kept the poems she wrote as a child in a secret black book.

Cox began college at the University of Tennessee, but when her boyfriend, James Cox, entered medical school at the University of Mississippi, she married him and transferred there. That same year James Meredith enrolled as the first black student to attend previously all-white classes in Mississippi, an event that attracted National Guard troops and impressed upon Cox the complexity of race, a topic she has frequently addressed in her subsequent writing. After graduating from Ole Miss in 1964 she worked as a special education teacher in Memphis, Raleigh, and Fort Knox. She moved to Durham in the 1970s, still teaching special education, and then enrolled in the MFA program at the University of North Carolina at Greensboro, where she studied poetry under Fred Chappell. While she was there, the first short story she wrote, "Land of Goshen," was cited for excellence by both the Pushcart Prize and *Best American Short Stories*. Also while at Greensboro, Cox and her husband separated, and she began her life as a single mother. She received her MFA in 1979 and began teaching for Duke University Continuing Education, which, in 1983—after she earned a fellowship to attend the Yaddo Writers Colony—made her a lecturer in the English Department, a position that changed to Full Professor of the Practice of Writing before she left. In 1986 her first novel, *Familiar Ground*, was published by Atheneum. In the 1990s Elizabeth Cox taught creative writing at the University of Michigan and then Boston, where she took teaching positions at MIT, Tufts, Boston University, and the Bennington Writing Seminars. There she met and married C. Michael Curtis, also a native of the South, who had worked for the *Atlantic Monthly* since 1963 and been the magazine's fiction editor beginning in 1982. While living in Boston, Cox retained her deep ties to the South by teaching at Duke in the summers until 2002. In 1992 Cox published *The Ragged Way People Fall Out of Love*. In 1998 another novel, *Night Talk*, won the Lillian Smith Award, given to work that promotes harmony between the races. In 2001 her first story collection, *Bargains in the Real World: 13 Stories*, was published. The novel, *The Slow Moon*, followed in 2007.

Currently, Cox and Curtis live in Spartanburg, South Carolina, and share a faculty post at Wofford College.

Elizabeth Cox: A Selective Bibliography

INTERNET RESOURCES

Cox has a website that includes the text of some of her poems and an extensive bibliography of interviews and reviews by well-known newspapers such as the Washington *Post*, the *New York Times*, and the *Chicago Tribune*. The *Identity Theory* offers an interview with Cox in which she discusses the idea of "southern writers" and her experience as a professor.

SELECTED BOOKS

The Slow Moon. New York: Random House, 2007.
Bargains in the Real World: 13 Stories. New York: Random House, 2001.
Night Talk. St. Paul: Graywolf, 1997.
The Ragged Way People Fall Out of Love. New York: North Point, 1991.
Familiar Ground. New York: Atheneum / Simon and Schuster, 1984.

PROFILES/INTERVIEWS

Johnson, Sarah Anne. "Tips from a Master Storyteller: Fiction Writer Elizabeth Cox on Setting Characters in Motion and Finding the Right Rhythm in Her Narrative Structures." *The Writer* 121.12 (2008): 20–23.
Reames, Kelly. "Interview with Elizabeth Cox." *Mississippi Quarterly* 52.2 (1999): 307–21.

Chris Holbrook

All the Ills

The sidewalk in front of the Hazard Regional Hospital is strewn with cigarette butts. Some of the smokers are visitors, I grant you. But some wear gowns and robes. Some have drip bags hooked to their arms. They lean against those hat rack-looking carts, puffing away. The air is too still to clear the smoke. It hangs a few feet above their heads in a darksome cloud. What people won't do to theirselves.

They stand off a hair when I walk by. They nod and blow their smoke and watch me with side-turned eyes. The thought of their staring makes my neck itch. I catch myself swatting flies, feeling for bites. I can feel the sweat starting, running down my shirt collar, making a chill. I don't let on though. I'd as soon eat dirt as give these like the satisfaction.

I notice one old boy sitting on the steps with his head in his hands. He has a cast on his left wrist and two black eyes and a bandaged left ear. I know him for a Holyfield from Quicksand Creek that I used to take calls on the first Friday of every month. It'd be him drunk and falling down and dripping blood: Why, I sure hate you-all had to come all this way out here, and Now, I'll not lie to you, I have had some little to drink.

Then it'd be his old woman laying bunged up in the back room, her holding a butcher knife, cussing him in one breath and begging us not to take him off in the next. Oh, look what he done to me! and Oh, he's all I got! and Oh, he didn't go to! It's untelling which one would be worse off—her with her head stove in or him cut open—both too lit to feel it. And then it's Oh, my nerves! and Oh, my back! and Oh, this bad cough, it's like to kill me! And the younguns standing there taking it in, grinning like fools for the commotion, none but the littlest still with sense and shame enough to hide behind the furniture and cry. Lord have mercy!

I stand a minute on the steps and stare hard at him. He doesn't move a muscle, just holds his head and sucks his cigarette, the smoke rolling around his ears. But I know he's seen me. I know he knows I'm there. And I think, You better hang your head, you sorry trash. You better not look up.

The lobby is worse yet. It's all the ills of east Kentucky. Old folks with black lung. With crippling arthritis. With heart disease like Daddy has. It's what you'd expect from the lives they've led, the hard kind of work they've done, what they've made do with or without. Them you can feel for. But then too it's people my age with emphysema or liver disease from too much pills and smoking and drinking. And worse yet it's the young people. Some of these boys, and girls too, in here shot or stabbed or car-wrecked, or else putting on for the disability checks. Blissed-out on that methamphetamine. It's sick-making to look at them. It's television to blame and these sorry parents. And I blame the Welfare. I don't go to make no judgments though.

I pass among them, let them look me over—the haircut, the uniform jacket, the badge, the bulge of my holstered .38. Each step I take my stomach turns more sour. I want to be off alone on some far ridge top with clear air to breathe and nothing but trees around me.

I consider riding out Highway 15 to my house. I could surprise Angie and my little girl, maybe take us all out to Cliff Hagan's Steakhouse. It seems like a good idea until I think about it. Until I think about the reception I got last time. You're not supposed to come without calling. You're not supposed to come without calling.

Don't you think that made me hot? It nine going on ten in the morning and Angie standing there in that housedress still, barring the door. I told her it's my damn house whether I live there or not and I'll come and go as I please.

You're not supposed to come without calling. You're not supposed to come without calling. That whiny voice. Oooh, I'd liked to smacked her. I feel a burning in my chest, and I have to tell myself, "No, Brody. You're doing yourself no good."

Daddy's room is on the third floor, down the hall from Intensive Care. I pass by the elevators in favor of the stairs, and by the time I've walked up I feel calm again. I need to tell Daddy I've fed his dogs and put out hay for his cattle and that one old mule he keeps and made sure there's water for everything.

I see Katrina the minute I step into the hallway. She looks so much like Mommy it's a shock to me. She's standing outside Daddy's room wiping her eyes with a tissue, her and that husband of hers, that Pete, and two of her younguns, I can't even name them for sure. And there's half a dozen of that church crowd with them—Betty Goble and Marvin Justice and that Viola Owens. The Trace Fork Church of Zion. You can't catch a cold without them putting you on the prayer list. I'd about forgot about Daddy rededicating himself to the Lord.

I'd about put it out of my mind.

My first thought is to sneak off before I'm spotted, but before I can, Katrina spots me. Standing there talking to Pastor Justice, Katrina's all tears and meekness, her cheeks red as apples. But when she sees me, it's like a switch being thrown. Her face cools. She crosses her arms on her chest and rolls her eyes like Oh, Lord give me strength. There's never no mistaking Katrina's feelings.

I have no choice. I march right up, put my arm around her shoulders, and say, "Hello, stranger."

"Stranger, yourself," she tells me. But then she hugs me and says, "God bless." The way she says it, I believe I'd just as soon been told to go burn in hell. It's a wonder her tongue don't break off in her head.

"Where's the rest of the clan?" I ask. "Where's Johnny? Where's Missy and her bunch?"

She doesn't answer, just sighs and shakes her head. But I never expected no more answer. I know where they're at, our brother and sister. Off trying to decide whether they love Daddy more or hate him. I don't say it.

"I reckon Daddy's had a time," I say.

Her face peakens. Her eyes mist over. "It's a pity," she says. "Lord love its heart. Laying there in sickness." She dabs her eyes with her wadded tissue.

"He's a tough one," I say.

"We've been praying for him," she says.

"Well I know he appreciates it."

"The prayer of the upright is the Lord's delight," she says. She pauses to slip the tissue into her dress pocket. When she looks at me again her eyes are dry and stern. "Of course they's a many we've prayed for and it not took. A many that have backslid and forsooken vows and turned deaf ears to the Lord's good word."

I think a minute about what she said and how she meant me to take it. There's any number of cutting replies I could make. About that husband of hers. About them kids. And Katrina's not above reproach her own self. But then I say to myself, "No, Brody. What's the use?"

I just smile. "I know it's told in his recovery," I say. "Your-all's prayers. It's the Lord's blessing you-all being here."

She frowns and makes to shoo me off, but her face has reddened a little. I know I've hit her where she lives. I go off down the hall while she's still yet wondering about my sincerity.

I get a cup of coffee in the cafeteria and sit at a corner table to wait. It's not hardly noontime yet. I've been up since a quarter till five and already it feels like the day will never be gone. The older I get it seems like the earlier I rise. Daddy used to say he'd got to where he was rising up almost before he laid down. His legs bothered him, sciatica and arthritis. It's a blessing I don't have no more wrong with me than this heartburn. It's coffee kills me. But I won't give up my coffee.

The dinner crowd increases as a quarter after comes on. I see that Miller boy come in as I'm getting up to leave. I know all about his troubles, about his wife's baby coming too early and there being complications and them not able to go home yet. He's wearing his uniform, so I know he's just come in from patrol. He's a young-looking man still, the most of his hard duty still yet before him.

My first term in office, I did stops on drunk drivers and speeders. I did traffic control at high school ball games. I headed up funeral processions. Once in a while I went in with the DEA or the state police to burn out a pot patch or arrest somebody dealing out of their home, but it was mostly boresome.

Even so I'd come home and tell Angie how rough I had it. Oh, it's such a trial. I don't believe I can take it, the way people are. She'd rub my neck and say, Poor baby. The truth is I was just putting on.

Then I got my first bad case. It was this young high school girl that got abducted. We found her half a mile up a holler, raped and beat to death. From the way her face looked . . . I got sick that day.

We found who done it sitting parked in a creek bed not far from the scene. I remember his face and eyes were bloody from where she'd gouged him with her fingernails. There was blood and filth on his clothes and on the interior of his pickup. I remember it was a green Chevy with a camper top and a trout sticker on the tailgate. He never made no protest when we took him, never made no sign we were even there until one of the deputies slipped and fell in the creek, and then he laughed. Him just killed a girl and able to laugh at somebody falling in mud. No more conscience than a cur dog.

As I walk by the Miller boy's table, I put my hand on his shoulder and squeeze. He looks up at me. He's not been in uniform a full year. He knows me, but not so well as to be familiar.

Next week I'll slip an envelope in his mailbox, seventy-five or a hundred, whatever I can scrape up. He won't know who did it, not directly, but he'll remember that he saw me in the hospital and that I was respectful to him and concerned. It ain't because he's a state police. It ain't because he's a Miller and his family can carry half of Clear Creek at election time. I'll do it because of what kind of fix he's in, because it's a way to behave. I don't have no ulterior motives.

The church crowd is gone by the time I wind back around to Daddy's room. It's just Katrina now, hovering about the doorway, wiping her eyes. I just nod and go on in the room. He's laying in his bed so still you'd think he was asleep if not dead. His eyes are open, though, and blinking. He's lost so much weight I almost wonder if it's him laying there. His arms are sticks. His body's just a wrinkle in the sheets.

I call, "How are you?" He doesn't answer or move. The back of his left hand is laid across his forehead. His right hand is pressed palm down on an open Bible, one finger pointing, like he's marking a line for reading.

I step into the room. "Daddy," I say. "It's Brody?"

He lowers his arm to cover his eyes, but still he doesn't speak. I look at the bedpan on the side table, at the monitors reading out how much life he has in him. It's so quiet in the room I can hear the air whistling through his nose tube.

"I got the rest of your hay in," I say. "I've watered and fed."

He looks up then, but not at me. His eyes are moist like he's been crying. "I ain't doing no good," he says. His voice is so weak I can barely hear him.

"I got the rest of your hay in," I say again.

"It's God's love struck me down," he says. "Struck me down in my arrogance."

I wonder at the change in him. Two weeks ago we were mowing hay together. His biggest complaint was being tired and out of breath. It's not just his health he's lost but his nerve. And I wonder if it's his illness or the church that's robbed him most.

"I had that Sizemore boy come in and trim that old jenny's hooves," I say. I move close to the bed, leaning down to put my hand on the bed rail. It's raised so he won't fall out on the floor in his weakness. His eyes focus on my chest. "They were growed out so much she couldn't hardly walk," I say.

He gives a start, like he's just now seeing me. I watch the sense come back into his face. After a moment he nods weakly. "I thank you," he says, and I know it's something like his old self I'm talking to again.

We speak of weather and livestock and the chores left waiting him at home. Katrina comes in after a while, though she stands close to the doorway still. The look on her face is pure misery. I can't help but feel the least bit kindly to her. Her and me are the only ones that didn't take sides against him years ago. I give her that.

I'm not laying no blame on Missy or brother John. Lord knows I don't fault Mommy for leaving out. She'd had enough of his meanness, more than enough. But I never could hold him in complete account for how he acted. It was what-all he'd went through. Korea. When he was drinking, he used to recall it all to us, Mommy and us children, gather us around and describe how a man's body would look after he'd been dead awhile, how it would swell and turn black and burst open, how it would smell. He'd tell about boys close as brothers getting killed right next to him, shot or blowed up or burned alive. He'd talk about how many he killed and what way he killed them. We'd set there and listen, afraid to move lest he bare his hand. Of course it may be he'd have drunk like he did no matter what.

When I make to leave he offers his hand to shake. I try and be gentle when I take it. It's cold and bloodless-looking and trembly. I feel the least bit ill touching it. He looks at me funny for a second. I start to smile, but then I see the look come on his face, the look I know well, the look that says he's about to knock fire out of me. It's funny how I feel for a second, almost like I wish he would, but there's barely enough strength left in him to raise his head, or enough will either. I squeeze his hand, shaking it for real, squeeze until his knuckles pop. I manage to leave without saying anything more. At least I've got that much sense.

All up and down the hall are patients' rooms, some with doors standing open. I hear low moans, some weeping. I try not to look in. I'm thirsty, but the first fountain I pass has a tobacco cud clogging the drain. I feel myself start to shake. Just the sight of that foulness makes me want to tear hell out of whatever I can put my hands on.

By the time I get down to the lobby, I'm so mad I can't hardly see straight.

For some reason I think about the times—there's been a few—when I've gone on calls to the houses of people I've knowed. I'd go in and see piled-up trash or beer cans strewed on the floor or half-gone bottles of liquor or pills. It's embarrassing is what it is, going in on somebody you're used to seeing out in their garden every day or at the grocery store or the barber's and finding out how bad-off in truth they really are. It's disheartening.

It's something like that feeling I got seeing Daddy in that bare, scrubbed room with an oxygen tube clipped to his nostril and a feeder tube in the vein of his arm. I feel myself getting mad at him, like him laying there is through some fault of his own. That don't make no sense, I know. It ain't no crime being sick in the hospital.

I think about Angie telling me I couldn't see nothing but the bad in people. Even if that's so, who is she to say it? The time she brought that church crowd to our house. To pray for our union. To bring God's counsel to our union. I only regret I left out that night. I only regret I didn't throw them each one out a window. My own damn house.

I head for a pay phone. That child is as much mine as hers, I think. I've still got some rights in her regard. Something funny happens when I pick up the phone. I can't think of my own number. I press the coin return. Drop the change into the slot once more. I tap the three-number prefix, then stop. I don't know whether to laugh or cuss. Who forgets their own phone number?

I stand holding the receiver so long my ear gets numb. I begin to think about who-all has handled it before me, about who-all has breathed onto the mouthpiece. When I move it away I see the oily smear of thumbprints on the black plastic. I'm about sick to my stomach when I finally get my memory again. I repeat the number to myself as I dial. I listen to the rings. I count up to twelve before I finally hang up. I know she's there. I know she's not answering of a purpose. She knows it's me calling.

I walk outside among the smokers. I see that Holyfield still sitting on the steps, his ride not come yet. I stare at the back of his neck, rattle the change in my pocket. His head bends almost to his ankles, like me just standing there is a weight pressing him down. And then he does something I don't expect. He looks up at me, looks me straight in the eye, like he's about to tell me something.

Of a sudden then his cigarette drops and sparks against the sidewalk. He hops up and jake-legs it down the sidewalk, shaking his head in a way that makes me want to go after him and ask what it is he thinks he means. These others all stare at me now, and I'm glad of my polished shoes, my uniform jacket, my badge.

I'm in my pickup and driving out Highway 15 before I even realize where I'm headed. My brain is spinning. Is it too much to ask? Some more understanding? After what-all I give her, is it too much to expect? Some more consideration? She never wanted, nor our baby neither, not for a blessed thing. For her to up and leave me like she did. Not no more consideration of me than a dog.

Just before the turnoff to my house, I make myself pull off onto the road shoulder. I'm wound up still, thinking what I'd like to say to Angie, what I'd like to do. It's an effort to hold myself still, to try and think calm. I shut the pickup off. There's so little traffic this time of morning I can hear the creek running nearby. I tell myself I have to think what is it that really matters here.

I think about Daddy living out these last years as alone as he's been, half his children not speaking to him. I'm not near as old as he was when Mommy left out. I ain't a fool. I see the path I'm on. I see where it is I'm headed.

I think about Angie. It's heartbreaking to me now to think how close we once were. We just need to calm down. We just need to look at things in a different light. Ain't no problem don't have a solution. If I could just sit down with her, explain things to her the way I have it lined out in my mind. I ain't saying I never done her wrong. I ain't saying that. But I ain't a bad man. I ain't a bad man at heart. I can change my ways. I can change my ways and I will.

For some reason I think about my baptism, those solemn witnesses lining the creek bank, waiting to shout and sing at the moment of my salvation. I remember still being head under in that mucky water, coming up for my first breath as a member of the body of Christ. My soul saved, my sins washed clean for good and all. I listen to the creek running. I think about that good feeling I once had, thinking I was saved, thinking I was redeemed. I feel myself start to calm.

By the time I start the pickup again, I've figured what I need to say. I feel better driving the little distance up the branch road. Things seem better now that I've reasoned it out. I pause a minute after I pull in the driveway. I notice how rutted it is from where the gravel has washed away. What it needs is paving. It's something I should have done long ago. I look the place over. It occurs to me how the yard could be leveled and made bigger with a couple hours' dozer work. There'd be room enough, maybe, for a deck or a brick patio. I could put in a gazebo at the far end like Angie always wanted. A grape arbor even. It's a wonder to me I've not done all this before. This could be a showplace. I could come home of a night and get my tension out doing improvements.

I walk by the Taurus I bought new last year and that Angie got in the settlement. I start to get mad when I notice how grimed over it is with tree sap and road grit. Then I tell myself it's just a car. It don't mean a thing. The fact I'm still making payments on it don't mean a thing. Angie does the best she can. I walk toward the house, thinking generous thoughts.

Angie flings the door open before I can even knock. What I want is to hug her and tell her how pretty she is and how much I've missed the sight of her, despite all. But I can't get the words out. I can't speak. All I can do is stand there, looking surly, I know.

"Well?" she asks.

Something flares up in me at the sound of her voice. I feel a little gurgle deep in my stomach. I taste something sour at the back of my throat. I feel myself getting mad again. I try to keep calm as I answer. What comes out, comes out wrong. "It's nice to see you too," I say.

The skin draws so tight across her forehead I can see the veins standing out at the temples. Her jawline bunches up with muscle. Her teeth flash. And her eyes. It's a look of pure hatred she gives me with her eyes. And then she starts in with that mouth. It's Who do you think you are, barging into my house? and What do you think you're about, I'd like to know? and Yip, yip-yip, yip-yip, on and on.

Then it's her bringing up all her old complaints and me bringing up mine and her screaming at me and me screaming at her. I don't know how long it is before I get hold of myself again. Shut up, I tell myself. Just shut up. She winds down pretty soon. It takes two to argue. In a little while she's done.

I take my chance to speak, keeping my voice low and calm, like I would if I was on a call. I catch myself almost calling her ma'am. "I apologize," I say. "I'm sorry. I shouldn't have come without calling. I'm sorry. I know I'm in the wrong." I say that again and again, studying her as I speak.

"I'm not asking for nothing," I say. "Not a thing. I don't deserve nothing and I'm not asking. You don't have to worry about me being after something. I'm not."

I pause to take a breath, to get my words in order. "This situation we're in," I say, "I know it's me that's brought us to it. I know it. It's on me. I know it."

For a minute then she looks at me, like Who is this talking? But her face has softened a little, and I know I've struck a chord. I start to feel myself taking charge. I feel like I know just what to say. "What I come out here for . . . what I mean to say . . . I've thought through some things is all. Believe it or not. I've thought through and I've prayed and I've come to realize some things."

Of a sudden she stiffens up. "If you expect—" she starts.

I lower my voice still more. "I don't expect a thing," I say. "Not a thing. All I'm saying is I want to do better. I want to do right. That's all. That's it. This situation we're in, it's on me. I don't expect a thing. I don't have no delusions."

I pause. I tell myself, be careful. You've said enough now. Be careful.

"That's all I want to say. That's what I come out here for. I love you. I still do. I love that little girl of ours and I love you. I'm always going to. That's all I mean to say." And I hush.

For a minute we stand there staring at one another. She doesn't say anything, but I know I've struck a chord. I know I've got through to something. She'll be thinking about my words, turning them over to find some hidden intent. She'll doubt me being sincere. I've laid the foundation though.

I spy my daughter as I start to leave. She's standing a few feet behind her mother. It's not been a week since I've seen her, but she seems more grown even in that little time. I have to fight myself not to try and speak to her. I know I can't though. Not right now, I can't. I can't undo myself, not now. I make myself leave.

I drive fast out Highway 15. I feel good. It's like I've been dashed in the face with a bucket of cold water. I feel like I've started on a new path. I know it. In my heart I know it. It's like I've come awake somehow.

The pickup starts to fishtail before I even realize how fast I'm going. I drift into a curve. The steering wheel bucks in my hands. I hold the road but come into the following straight stretch on the wrong side of the line, head-on to some old car. I cut hard, hear my tires screech, feel my outside wheels lift from the pavement. I brace for the smack, but then the pickup gives a lurch and somehow I'm four wheels down again and passing the car on my own side of center.

My hands are still gripping hard to the steering wheel when I come to rest on the road shoulder. I sit for a minute while the adrenaline flows out of me. When my heart has slowed a little, I get out and walk around the pickup. There's no damage that I can see, no sign of any mishap, none but my shaking knees. I get back behind the wheel and start to go on. Then something occurs to me. That car. It occurs to me that I know that old car.

I sight my objective two minutes after I begin pursuit. Before he even sees me coming, I'm up hard on his bumper. He slows some but doesn't pull off. It's not until I reach to turn on the siren and don't find the switch that I remember I'm not in my cruiser. I trail him another five miles like that, then turn off behind him onto Quicksand Creek. A mile further when the blacktop road changes to dirt, I flash my headlights and lay on with my horn.

He pulls over. He don't know to do anything else. I count the crowd of heads in the car. It's old Holyfield driving and next to him a young kid and then his old woman and then an older boy and girl in the backseat. Holyfield stares at me in his side mirror as I walk up. He rolls the window down but doesn't get out. He's waiting for me to speak.

"I want to talk to you," I say.

"What is it I done?" he asks.

That gets me. Him questioning me. "Just get out of the damn car," I say.

I reach through the open window and collar him and jerk the door open. He holds on to the steering wheel for a second, but I tumble him out. He hits the ground like a sack of wet manure, then grabs hold of my leg. "Get up," I say. I slap him to get him to turn loose, but he just holds on tighter.

"Get up from there," I hear myself shout, though my voice sounds far off. There's a dull little pain starting at the back of my head. I feel myself getting sick. It's the smell of him—his unwashed hide, the cigarette smoke in his clothes. It's what it reminds me of. A call to Jones Fork for a burned-out trailer—the smell of fabric burning and wood and smoldering metal, of bodies broiling in among melted-together plastic and glass and insulation.I punch Holyfield in the head with my closed fist. Go easy, I tell myself, but it's like my brain and body are in two separate places. Holyfield ducks his head between his shoulders, and I think here's a man used to getting beat. I punch him again, on his shoulder, on the crown of his skull, but despite all, the memories rise up on me. That car crash on Beaver Creek—the one boy smeared across the pavement like a dead dog, the other mangled up inside the wreckage so bad you couldn't hardly tell skin and bone apart from metal. That child on Black Mare . . . What Angie couldn't never understand. What nobody couldn't never understand. It's how the job wears on a man. A law officer is human like anybody else.

When I come to myself, Holyfield is curled up on the ground, and I'm standing astraddle him. I swear it looks like he's grinning at me. Grinning.

I leave him laying there. I'm not mad anymore. I feel weak and sore-muscled. It's a chore just to haul myself into the cab of my pickup. Let's go, I tell myself. Let's go. But the more I try to will myself to drive on, the more I just want to sit still. I think about that look he give me at the hospital. I intend to know what he meant by that.

I'm doing myself no good, I know it. I close my eyes and press my forehead against the steering wheel. I try to think about something else. That last day I worked outside with Daddy. I remember the heat of the morning, the itch of crumbled straw and seed heads in my clothes, the smell of the hay rising in dust clouds off the bales. For a second I have that day in mind. Then I lose it to thoughts of Daddy being sick and in the hospital.

I open my eyes. Holyfield is on his feet again, staring at me, not moving. Get on! I want to shout, Get! Instead, I step out of the truck. I strip off my sheriff's jacket, my badge, unclip my .38, and lay them wrapped together on the seat. I'm surprised at how much lighter I feel. Holyfield's family is out of the car now. They stand distant, quiet and staring.

Oh sure, now. I'm not fool enough to believe that we can resolve our differences with just a snap of the fingers. Oh no. It will take work between the two of us. Real work. I think about Angie, how much older she looked to me in just a week's time.

The bandage on Holyfield's head is dripping, and there's a ring of stick burrs in his hair. His face is bruised and dirt-smeared. The one eye that's not swollen shut is raised to look at me.

I flex my hands. They have begun to swell. I force my fingers closed, throw a punch to the side of Holyfield's head. I feel a knuckle crack, the pain like a charge of electricity up and down my arm. I punch again with my hurt fist, and for an instant I feel myself relieved of care.

Holyfield doubles up on the ground. I kick him in the ribs with my boot toe, but there's no satisfaction in that. I want to break my hands on him. I want to gouge his eyes out with my thumbs. I grab his hair, pull his head back. I pop short punches at his cheek, at his ear—whatever shows for a target. I don't know how long it is I beat him. It's like hoeing corn or mowing hay. You get into it good you can lose all track of yourself.

Reprinted with permission of the University Press of Kentucky. Published in *Upheaval: Stories* (2009).

Chris Holbrook: A Biographical Sketch

Chris Holbrook is solid; his writing is strong; his worldview is substantial. Holbrook has a rare combination of down-to-earth experience and erudite education. He was born in 1961 and grew up in a family that had lived for generations around Soft Shell, Kentucky, in Knott County, the heart of the coalfields—the kind of place outsiders like to call "gritty." And it does provide ample grist for Chris Holbrook's mill.

Holbrook's father supported his family by living away from home and working in Dayton, Ohio, at a Frigidaire plant and a GM factory, finally obtaining a job near home for Kentucky and West Virginia Gas. His mother worked out of their home as a seamstress, and continued this work through her eighties. On their place were a dozen apple trees and a huge vegetable garden. The first school Holbrook attended had three rooms for first through eighth grades, outhouses, a coal-burning pot-bellied stove, and an outside pump for water. After the schools were consolidated, Holbrook says, "I never enjoyed school as much."

While at Knott County High School, Holbrook worked as a bag-boy at Casey's IGA and bought a Chevy Nova. He says, "[A]s a teenager, my main entertainment was driving all the back roads in the county." He attended the University of Kentucky from 1979 to 1983, and claims that his professors there, Gurney Norman, James Baker Hall, and Ed McClanahan, were the best teachers he ever had. From 1984 until 1986 Holbrook studied at the prestigious Iowa Writers' Workshop, and immediately thereafter enjoyed a residency fellowship at the Fine Arts Work Center at Provincetown, Massachusetts. There he took long walks and attended music concerts. He asserts that the very best show he saw during that time was Jack Casady and Jorma Kaukonen performing together. Returning to Lexington, Kentucky, he had a series of odd jobs and then settled down for a year and a half working at Hillenmeyer's Nursery. In 1989 he got a job back home in Knott County teaching at Alice Lloyd College. Two years later Holbrook married the former Mary Elizabeth Healy, who had come to Hazard right out of Harvard to work with the Jesuit Volunteer Corps. During his fourteen years teaching at Alice Lloyd, Gnoman Press, one of the finest small literary presses of the late twentieth century, published Holbrook's first story collection, *Hell and Ohio* (1995). In 2003 Chris and Mary Elizabeth Holbrook and their daughter, Erin, then seven years old, moved to Lexington, Kentucky, and Chris took the job he still holds as an English professor at Morehead State University, the Kentucky university closest to the coalfields. In 2009 the University Press of Kentucky published Holbrook's second story collection, *Upheaval.* Two years later, Mary Elizabeth Holbrook completed her doctorate in accounting, took a job as an associate professor at Eastern Kentucky University, and the couple adopted a son, Michael John.

In an interview with Crystal Wilkinson that appeared in the *New Southerner* in 2009, Holbrook admitted, "Clearly, I'm very slow with my writing. I'll spend several months on a story. [. . .] The work itself comes to me slowly, and the ideas for the stories come to me slowly. [. . .] I have to get every line pretty much there before I can go on. And I actually revise as I'm writing." What this tedious process has produced is deeply authentic, powerful stories that convey the realities of present-day life in the Appalachian coalfields with candor yet quiet respect for both the land and the people.

Chris Holbrook: A Selective Bibliography

INTERNET RESOURCES

The *New Southerner* offers Crystal Wilkinson interviewing Holbrook on writing, activism, and his heritage.

SELECTED BOOKS

Upheaval: Stories. Lexington: UP of Kentucky, 2009.
Hell and Ohio: Stories of Southern Appalachia. Frankfort, KY: Gnomon, 1995.

LITERARY CRITICISM

Worthington, Marianne."Constancy and Change: The Appalachian Community in the Short Stories of Chris Holbrook and Elaine Fowler Palencia." *Journal of Kentucky Studies* 21 (Sept. 2004): 128–34.

Jeff Daniel Marion

Codas

"What you see is what you get."
Such codas we learned from exotic
sources, say the carnival barker lining
his olive-skinned girls on stage outside the tent,
their little hoochie-koochie twists
and bumps luring us in to the hope
of some imagined Casbah. "Just a hint,
boys, of what you'll see inside." Room led to room
like every mystery, until our pockets emptied
of loose change, and we still had not seen it all.
So it was with my father's junkhouse,
so much to see and so little
time to take it all in: rows of jars
loaded with rubber washers, gaskets,
nuts and bolts, brass wood screws,
steel ball bearings so shiny I could feel
the silky roundness of them turning
between my fingers, a few slipped to school
for trade as we scrawled with shoetip
the ovals and rings in the dust of marble
season. How did he know what had been moved
and placed back so carefully, a PT boat
piston cut in half and fashioned
into an ashtray (his relic from the war
years of working for Alcoa in Detroit), only two
ball bearings taken from the jar and clacking
in my pocket? At ten I believed it was
the immaculate order in the mind of God,
His eye on each and every sparrow. "Son,

you don't need to be messing with the things
in my house." And so I learned not to tamper,
to look but not to touch. Until I turned fourteen
and he handed me his .22 automatic rifle:
at the dump site I watched him
drop rats on the run, never more than
a single shot. He lined five beer bottles
against the red clay bank. "First you shoot
the lip off, then the neck, and last you take
the easy gut shot." Long ago I had heard
the legend around town: "Boy, your old man
could shoot the hairs off a chigger's ass."
Our first trip into the field,
"See that rabbit hiding over behind the cedar—
take him when I flush him out." I stared
and stared and finally saw the tip of one ear
peeking through the cedar. Gut shot, he flopped
down the bank. My father turned his back
to me, lifted the rabbit by its hind legs,
and stilled its spasms with one quick blow
to the head. He thought I did not see
and through all the years we never spoke
of it. But today, standing in his junkhouse
ten years past his dying, I lift from memory
that old tattered scrap "what you see
is what you get," look at all these treasures
he laid up, and bow to every moment of his mercy.

Reprinted with permission of Wind Publishing. Published in *Father* (2009).

❁ ❁ ❁

Song for Wood's Barbeque Shack in McKenzie, Tennessee

Here in mid-winter let us begin
to lift our voices in the pine woods:

O sing praise to the pig
who in the season of first frost
gave his tender hams and succulent shoulders
to our appetite:

praise to the hickory embers
for the sweetest smoke
a man is ever to smell
its incense a savor
of time bone deep:

praise for Colonel Wood and all his workers
in the dark hours who keep watch
in this turning of the flesh
to the delight of our taste:

praise to the sauce—vinegar, pepper, and tomato—
sprinkled for the tang of second fire:

praise we now say for mudwallow, hog grunt, and pig squeal,
snorkle snout ringing bubbles of swill in the trough,
each slurp a sloppy vowel of hunger,
jowl and hock, fatback and sowbelly, root dirt and pure
piggishness of sow, boar, and barrow.

Reprinted with permission of Celtic Cat Publishing. Published in *Ebbing and Flowing Springs* (2009).

❁ ❁ ❁

The Dying Art

"You're in the zone of particularity,"
the radiologist said to the intern,
staring at the moon-disk screen,
socket and bone of my hip
his lunar landscape. The needle eased
into the narrow groove, left its message
to heal, rise from the table and walk.

Restored and reprieved but with no physician's
skill, I'll take up the fountain pen to probe
that zone of particularity, the address
of both letters and poetry.

Email won't suffice—I want
that handwritten page, ink as blue
as this morning's April sky, cursive letters
sweeping across the distances to some
mailbox, long-awaited words alighting,
perched in a safe nest.

So it's been called the dying art,
attempts to revive it as fruitless
as trying to raise the dead.

Nobody's got the time now;
let instant messaging pop up on screen
or text message, or even better
call on cell while scanning
grocery shelves, evening's dinner
and conversation just arm's length away.

Didn't Emily say so long ago
"These are my letters to a world
that did not write to me"?

What I need to say is in that narrow
valley, the zone of what I had no chance
to say to all those long gone.

It's not their answers I seek,
but my need to remember,
and in so doing raise the dead,
let words rise and walk into flesh
before I cross into their country,
shade among shades,
with no forwarding address.

Reprinted with permission of Texas Review Press. Published in *The Southern Poetry Anthology.* Vol. 3. *Contemporary Appalachia* (2010).

Jeff Daniel Marion: A Biographical Sketch

Jeff Daniel Marion is a bard, clearly one of the most distinguished contemporary Tennessee poets and one who has gained significant national attention. His *Ebbing and Flowing Springs: New and Selected Poems and Prose, 1976–2001* won the 2004 Independent Publisher's Award in poetry, and in 2011 he received the Fellowship of Southern Writers' Award for Appalachian writing.

Jeff Daniel Marion was born in 1940 in Rogersville, Tennessee. Two of his father's brothers married two of his mother's sisters and lived on nearby farms. He was the only child of those three sibling marriages. His father was an ink specialist at Rogersville Card and Label Company, and Marion feels that his father's habit of attention to detail aided his own developing qualities as a writer. His grandmother's blindness, he believes, attuned him to the use of words to create vivid and accurate mental images. When he was three years old, his father moved his family to Detroit temporarily while working in an Alcoa defense plant. Marion recalls during that time "lying on the floor, looking at a magazine with a pencil in my hand, and I had this overwhelming desire to write that came over me like hunger pangs." Ever since, he says, writing "is my deepest longing—it's a longing to connect . . . and that's part of what teaching is as well."After receiving a BA in English from the University of Tennessee, he taught in Knoxville and Rogersville for a couple of years and then returned to UT for an MA in English.

In 1966 Marion began teaching at Carson-Newman College, located in Jefferson City, Tennessee, about forty miles down the Holston River from his hometown of Rogersville. Except for a year in Mississippi, he served Carson-Newman until his retirement. There Marion was director of the Appalachian Center; poet-in-residence; the editor of the *Mossy Creek Reader,* a literary journal that he founded; and an English professor. In 1975 Marion launched the *Small Farm,* a poetry journal that brought to light many of the region's most celebrated contemporary writers. The next year, his career as a published poet got off to a running start with the publication of two chapbooks and a poetry collection. Two years later he received the first literary fellowship awarded by the Tennessee Arts Commission. After the *Small Farm* folded in 1980 Marion founded Mill Spring Press, utilizing an old-fashioned hand-set printing press he kept at his cabin on the Holston River. Marion found other publishers for three poetry books in the 1980s and four in the 1990s, along with *Hello Crow* (1992), a children's book from Orchard Press. Still he had time during the school year to be a poet-in-the-schools, not only in Tennessee, but also in North Carolina and Virginia. During the summers he taught at numerous workshops, including as poet-in-residence at the Tennessee Governor's School for the Humanities for about ten years. After his retirement from Carson-Newman in 2002 Marion moved to Knoxville. Three more poetry books have followed, and in 2010 he was appointed the Jack E. Reese Writer-in-Residence for the University of Tennessee Libraries.

"By writing a poem," Jeff Daniel Marion reflects, "I am saying, 'yes' to certain values, to those values of the sanctity of human life, the power and virtue of emotions, and the precise use of language, language as a tool to cut to the truth of human life."

Jeff Daniel Marion: A Selective Bibliography

INTERNET RESOURCES

The *Poetry Foundation* features Marion's poems "78 RPM" and "Reunion." *American Life in Poetry* features Marion's poem "Reunion." *Celtic Cat Publishing* also offers several examples of Marion's work. The *Asheville Poetry Review* includes a critical assessment titled "Better American Poetry," looking at several of Marion's poems, and the *Volunteer Review* offers an interview.

SELECTED BOOKS

Father. Nicholasville, KY: Wind Publications, 2009.

Ebbing and Flowing Springs: New and Selected Poems and Prose, 1976–2001. Knoxville: Celtic Cat Publishing, 2002.

Letters Home. Millwood, VA: Sow's Ear Press, 2001.

The Chinese Poet Awakens. Nicholasville, KY: Wind Publications, 1999.

Lost and Found. Millwood, VA: Sow's Ear Press, 1994.

Vigils: Selected Poems. Boone, NC: Appalachian Consortium Press, 1990.

Miracles of Air. New Market, TN: Mill Springs Press, 1987.

PROFILES/INTERVIEWS

Lee, Ernest. "The Journey a Poem Makes: Interviewing Jeff Daniel Marion." *Appalachian Journal* 31.2 (2004): 194–211.

Marion, Stephen. "Jeff Daniel Marion: Fishing in Language." In *Appalachia and Beyond: Conversations with Writers from the Mountain South.* Ed. John Lang. Knoxville: U of Tennessee P, 2006. 194–211.

LITERARY CRITICISM

Brosi, George, ed. *Appalachian Heritage* 31.4 (2003). Features Jeff Daniel Marion.

Lang, John. "Measures of Grace." In *Six Poets from the Mountain South.* Baton Rouge: Louisiana State UP, 2010. 99–124.

———, ed. *Iron Mountain Review* 11 (1995). Features Jeff Daniel Marion.

Worthington, Marianne. "Epistolary Exchanges: The Personal and Poetic Journey of Jeff Daniel Marion in *Letters Home*." *Journal of Appalachian Studies* 9.2 (Fall 2003): 406–14.

Jayne Anne Phillips

The Bad Thing

We found the kittens in a pile, too young to even stagger, the mother too hungry herself to feed them, or caught by the dogs. We had a big old plastic purse with a blanket inside, and we put them all in there and hauled them around in the wagon. I liked them, they were a little town of their own, part of our gang to defend against the Polish kids that lived right next to the tracks, or the Irish kids in the houses down by the river. Gang warfare, but our gang was only us. We boys kept our pockets full of rocks, small ones to chuck at the dogs. Now and then the City would clean the stray dogs out of the rail yard, put out poisoned meat. We'd see carcasses dropped in the ditch round back of the tracks, like the dogs crawled there on purpose when they knew something was wrong. Some City worker emptied bags of lime over them, shaking the bags with his gloved hands, rolling a wheelbarrow along. Sleep dust for the dogs. We'd see him, and he'd shoo us away, angry, like we'd caught him at murder. But it was just a benediction, like Father Salvadore gave in the shape of the cross after services. Grass grew up over the dogs, high and green, till they were only bones, and the rangy pups who'd survived were big enough to slink after us, compete with the cats for mice and rats, hunt the cats. Those dogs' faces were so scarred they looked painted in thin white lines.

I was a murderer myself. The first time, my dad made me, showed me how. He put that passel of kittens we brought home into a burlap sack like they pour wood pulp into at the sawmill. He made me hold it open and put in the rocks. The rocks were heavy, and I put them under the kittens, like a hard bed. The kittens were so young they barely had their eyes open. The rocks were too hard, so I put in some of the soft rags we kept around for washing cars or cleaning motors, wiping oily grime off carburetors. Even then, we had a car that worked and a car that didn't, for fooling with. My dad told me it was fine to cushion the rocks, and I could let these kittens go a few blocks away but they'd die of starvation or something would kill them, and they would suffer. If I brought them back here, he said, or any other passel of animals so young he couldn't chase them off, we'd have to do all this again, and he'd personally escort me to the riverbank and watch me throw in the bag. Rule one, he said, you don't make a baby and then leave it, unless you're dead yourself. Plenty around here might have been taught this simple rule. That was about all he ever said about my mother. Or any of the other fathers and mothers missing in the neighborhood. One father we knew had died a soldier, and that seemed honorable. Other people should take care of what he was forced to leave, no matter how hard that might be. Here I'd intervened in something, my dad said, and I should be a man and finish it. He struggled to keep us fed and clothed. No one was going to bottle-feed these kittens and find them homes over on Fairmont Hill, where the rich people kept their cats indoors and fed them out of cans. He was right. Where we lived on the alley, so close to the rail yard, people thought cats were diseased vermin, and they shot them and chased them and kicked them. This was the cleanest and strongest those kittens were ever going to be.

So I took them to the riverbank, to the tunnel under the rail bridge. I put the bag on the ground, and I could see the kittens shifting around in the burlap and hear them mewing. They sounded loud in the tunnel, where the air was different, enclosed in a high space, like at church. We kids always went there, but I'd never been there alone. It was deep and shady under the rail bridge in the summer, with the river beside, and you could watch the trains overhead sometimes and see them cross the river. Trains came barreling across from the rail yard over us. Just at the midpoint, a stone support of the same thick rock stood up in the deepest water of the river. It was built to look like the tunnel bridges on either side, but it was only half as big, and bore the most stress. It stood out of the water like a man with a massive weight on his shoulders. As a train reached it, I had to fight not to hold my breath, then the train streaked across to the other side and filled the entire span before it lost itself around the bend of the hill. At dusk you could see town lights come on up and down the riverbank, but the other bank was darkness and trees. There was a brushy mound of island in the middle of the river, not far from the central support of the bridge. Might have been slag at one time because it was treeless, but the river had risen and fallen over it enough times to deposit a rich layer of sediment. The island was green every summer with grass and flowering weeds and brush that died back in winter. Deer swam out to it from the other side of the river. You could see them plain if they were standing on top of the mound, one or two or three of them. They'd look up when a train passed, then fall to grazing again safe from whatever hunted them in the woods.

It was quiet that day. There were no trains. Even the kittens had got quiet. They must have fallen asleep on those soft rags all curled up into one another. There wasn't a sound when I put them in the water.

After that I wouldn't let anyone take kittens from the rail yard until they were well onto their feet, and then we'd let them loose by the river where there were toads and minnows and mice and lizards. They could take their own chances. Death was not the bad thing. Leaving something behind when you gave up or walked away was the bad thing.

Reprinted with permission of Jayne Anne Phillips. Published in *Ploughshares* 29 (Fall 2003).

❁ ❁ ❁

Something That Happened

I am in the basement sorting clothes, whites with whites, colors with colors, delicates with delicates—it's a segregated world—when my youngest child yells down the steps. She yells when I'm in the basement, always, angrily, as if I've slipped below the surface and though she's twenty-one years old she can't believe it.

"Do you know what day it is? I mean do you *know* what day it is, Kay?" It's this new thing of calling me by my first name. She stands groggy-eyed, surveying her mother.

I say, "No, Angela, so what does that make me?" Now my daughter shifts into second, narrows those baby blues I once surveyed in such wonder and prayed *Lord, lord, this is the last.*

"Well, never mind," she says. "I've made you breakfast." And she has, eggs and toast and juice and flowers on the porch. Then she sits and watches me eat it, twirling her fine gold hair.

Halfway through the eggs it dawns on me, my ex-wedding anniversary. Angela, under the eyeliner and blue jeans you're a haunted and ancient presence. When most children can't remember an anniversary, Angela can't forget it. Every year for five years, she has pushed me to the brink of remembrance.

"The trouble with you," she finally says, "is that you don't care enough about yourself to remember what's been important in your life."

"Angela," I say, "in the first place I haven't been married for five years, so I no longer have a wedding anniversary to remember."

"That doesn't matter" (twirling her hair, not scowling). "It's still something that happened."

Two years ago I had part of an ulcerated stomach removed and I said to the kids, "Look, I can't worry for you anymore. If you get into trouble, don't call me. If you want someone to take care of you, take care of each other." So the three older girls packed Angela off to college and her brother drove her there. Since then I've gradually resumed my duties. Except that I was inconspicuously absent from my daughters' weddings. I say inconspicuously because, thank God, all of them were hippies who got married in fields without benefit of aunts and uncles. Or mothers. But Angela reads *Glamour,* and she'll ask me to her wedding. Though Mr. Charm has yet to appear in any permanent guise, she's already gearing up for it. Pleadings. Remonstrations. Perhaps a few tears near the end. But I shall hold firm, I hate sacrificial offerings of my own flesh. "I can't help it," I'll joke, "I have a weak stomach, only half of it is there."

Angela sighs, perhaps foreseeing it all. The phone is ringing. And slowly, there she goes. By the time she picks it up, cradles the receiver to her brown neck, her voice is normal. Penny-bright, and she spends it fast. I look out the screened porch on the alley and the clean garbage cans. It seems to me that I remembered everything before the kids were born. I say kids as though they appeared collectively in a giant egg, my stomach. When actually there were two years, then one year, then two, then three between them. The Child-Bearing Years, as though you stand there like a blossomed pear tree and the fruit plops off. Eaten or rotted to seed to start the whole thing all over again.

Angela has fixed too much food for me. She often does. I don't digest large amounts so I eat small portions six times a day. The dog drags his basset ears to my feet, waits for the plate. And I give it to him, urging him on so he'll gobble it fast and silent before Angela comes back.

Dear children, I always confused my stomach with my womb. Lulled into confusion by nearly four pregnant years I heard them say, "Oh, you're eating for two," as if the two organs were directly connected by a small tube. In the hospital I was convinced they had removed my uterus along with half of my stomach. The doctors, at an end of patience, labeled my decision an anxiety reaction. And I reacted anxiously by demanding an X ray so I could see that my womb was still there.

Angela returns, looks at the plate, which I have forgotten to pick up, looks at the dog, puts her hand on my shoulder.

"I'm sorry," she says.

"Well," I say.

Angela twists her long fingers, her fine thin fingers with their smooth knuckles, twists the diamond ring her father gave her when she was sixteen. "Richard," I'd said to my husband, "she's your daughter, not your fiancée."

"Kay," intoned the husband, the insurance agent, the successful adjuster of claims, "she's only sixteen once. This ring is a gift, our love for Angela. She's beautiful, she's blossoming."

"Richard," I said, shuffling Maalox bottles and planning my bland lunch, "diamonds are not for blossoms. They're for those who need a piece of the rock." At which Richard laughed heartily, always amused at my cynicism regarding the business that principally buttered my bread. Buttered his bread, because by then I couldn't eat butter.

"What is it you're afraid to face?" asked Richard. "What is it in your life you can't control? You're eating yourself alive. You're dissolving your own stomach."

"Richard," I said, "it's a tired old story. I have this husband who wants to marry his daughter."

"I want you to see a psychiatrist," said Richard, tightening his expertly knotted tie. "That's what you need, Kay, a chance to talk it over with someone who's objective."

"I'm not interested in objectives," I said. "I'm interested in shrimp and butter sauce, Tabasco, hot chilis, and an end of pain."

"Pain never ends," said Richard.

"Oh, Richard," I said, "no wonder you're the King of the Southeast Division."

"Look," he said, "I'm trying to put four kids through college and one wife through graduate school. I'm starting five investment plans now so when our kids get married no one has to wait twenty-five years to finish a dissertation on George Eliot like you did. Really, am I such a bad guy? I don't remember forcing you into any of this. And your goddamn stomach has to quit digesting itself. I want you to see a psychiatrist."

"Richard," I said, "if our daughters have five children in eight years—which most of them won't, being members of Zero Population Growth who quote *Diet for a Small Planet* every Thanksgiving—they may still be slow with PhDs despite your investment plans."

Richard untied his tie and tied it again. "Listen," he said. "Plenty of women with five children have PhDs."

"Really," I said. "I'd like to see those statistics."

"I suppose you resent your children's births," he said, straightening his collar. "Well, just remember, the last one was your miscalculation."

"And the first one was yours," I said.

It's true. We got pregnant, as Richard affectionately referred to it, in a borrowed bunk bed on Fire Island. It was the eighth time we'd slept together. Richard gasped that of course he'd take care of things, had he ever failed me? But I had my first orgasm and no one remembered anything.

After the fourth pregnancy and first son, Richard was satisfied. Angela, you were born in a bad year. You were expensive, your father was starting in insurance after five years as a high school principal. He wanted the rock, all of it. I had a rock in my belly we thought three times was dead. So he swore his love to you, with that ring he thee guiltily wed. Sweet Sixteen, does she remember? She never forgets.

Angela pasted sugar cubes to pink ribbons for a week, Sweet Sixteen party favors she read about in *Seventeen,* while the older girls shook their sad heads. Home from colleges in Ann Arbor, Boston, Berkeley, they stared aghast at their golden-haired baby sister, her Villager suits, the ladybug stickpin in her blouses. Angela owned no blue jeans; her boyfriend opened the car door for her and carried her books home. They weren't heavy, he was a halfback. Older sister no. 3: "Don't you have arms?" Older sister no. 2: "He'll take it out of your hide, wait and see." Older sister no. 1: "The nuclear family lives off women's guts. Your mother has ulcers, Angela, she can't eat gravy with your daddy."

At which point Richard slapped oldest sister, his miscalculation, and she flew back to Berkeley, having cried in my hands and begged me to come with her. She missed the Sweet Sixteen party. She missed Thanksgiving and Christmas for the next two years.

Angela's jaw set hard. I saw her reject politics, feminism, and everyone's miscalculations. I hung sugar cubes from the ceiling for her party until the room looked like the picture in the magazine. I ironed sixteen pink satin ribbons she twisted in her hair. I applauded with everyone else, including the smiling halfback, when her father slipped the diamond on her finger. Then I filed for divorce.

The day Richard moved out of the house, my son switched his major to pre-med at NYU. He said it was the only way to get out of selling insurance. The last sound of the marriage was Richard being nervously sick in the kitchen sink. Angela gave him a cold washcloth and took me out to dinner at Señor Miguel's while he stacked up his boxes and drove them away. I ate chilis rellenos, guacamole chips in sour cream, cheese enchiladas, Mexican fried bread and three green chili burritos. Then I ate tranquilizers and bouillon for two weeks.

Angela was frightened.

"Mother," she said, "I wish you could be happy."

"Angela," I answered, "I'm glad you married your father, I couldn't do it anymore."

Angela finished high school the next year and twelve copies each of *Ingenue, Cosmopolitan, Mademoiselle.* She also read the Bible alone at night in her room.

"Because I'm nervous," she said, "and it helps me sleep. All the trees and fruit, the figs, begat and begat going down like the multiplication tables."

"Angela," I said, "are you thinking of making love to someone?"

"No, Mother," she said, "I think I'll wait. I think I'll wait a long time."

Angela quit eating meat and blinked her mascaraed eyes at the glistening fried liver I slid onto her plate.

"It's so brown," she said. "It's just something's guts."

"You've always loved it," I said, and she tried to eat it, glancing at my midriff, glancing at my milk and cottage cheese.

When her father took over the Midwest and married a widow, Angela declined to go with him. When I went to the hospital to have my stomach reduced by half, Angela declined my invitations to visit and went on a fast. She grew wan and romantic, said she wished I taught at her college instead of City, she'd read about Sylvia Plath in *Mademoiselle.* We talked on the telephone while I watched the hospital grounds go dark in my square window. It was summer and the trees were so heavy.

I thought about Angela, I thought about my miscalculations. I thought about milk products and white mucous coatings. About Richard's face the night of the first baby, skinny in his turned-up coat. About his mother sending roses every birth, American Beauties.

And babies slipping in the washbasin, tiny wriggling arms, the blue veins in their translucent heads. And starting oranges for ten years, piercing thick skins with a fingernail so the kids could peel them. After a while, I didn't want to watch the skin give way to the white ragged coat beneath.

Angela comes home in the summers, halfway through business, elementary education, or home ec. She doesn't want to climb the Rockies or go to India. She wants to show houses to wives, real estate, and feed me mashed potatoes, cherry pie, avocados, and artichokes. Today she not only fixes breakfast for my ex-anniversary, she fixes lunch and dinner. She wants to pile up my plate and see me eat everything. If I eat, surely something good will happen. She won't remember what's been important enough in my life to make me forget everything. She is spooning breaded clams, french fries, nuts and anchovy salad onto my plate.

"Angela, it's too much."

"That's OK, we'll save what you don't want."

"Angela, save it for who?"She puts down her fork. "For anyone," she says. "For any time they want it."In a moment, she slides my plate onto her empty one and begins to eat.

Reprinted with permission of Jayne Anne Phillips. Published in *Fast Lanes: Stories* (E. P. Dutton / Seymour Lawrence, 1987).

Jayne Anne Phillips: A Biographical Sketch

In 2010 Jayne Anne Phillips was named one of four finalists for the National Book Award for her novel, *Lark and Termite*. This recognition crowns a distinguished writing career that has been marked by multiple honors and awards and seen her work translated into fourteen languages.

Jayne Anne Phillips is the descendant of two families that have been in what is now West Virginia since the 1700s. She was born in 1952 in Buckhannon to a schoolteacher mother and a contractor father. By the age of nine she had dabbled in creative writing. At West Virginia University she developed her writing skills and graduated with an English degree magna cum laude in 1974. Then her life took a dramatic turn. She took off for California and worked as a waitress and at other temporary jobs there and in Colorado, basically immersing herself in working-class life. In 1976 Truck Press published four hundred copies of a strikingly innovative twenty-four-page chapbook of one-page prose pieces with her parents' wedding picture on the cover. It received two of the most respected small press prizes, a Pushcart and a Fels Award. This first chapbook was also instrumental in her winning her first National Endowment for the Arts grant and gaining admission into the prestigious Iowa Writers' Workshop at the age of twenty-five. While at Iowa, another chapbook, *Counting*, was published and won the St. Lawrence Award. Phillips's first academic job took her back to California, to Humboldt State, for the 1978–79 school year. While she was there, her first book, *Black Tickets*, a story collection, was published. Writing in the *Los Angeles Times* in 2011 Susan Salter Reynolds said, "Most readers can recall times of perfect synchronicity—when [a particular] book was the necessary enzyme, the catalyst, the missing piece. *Black Tickets* [. . .] was, for more than one earnest English major, such a book." Raymond Carver, who is widely viewed as an American master of the short story, enthused that Phillips's work was "unlike any in our literature." Nobel Laureate Nadine Gordimer of South Africa called Phillips "the best short story writer since Eudora Welty."

This dramatic success resulted in a writing fellowship at the Fine Arts Work Center of Provincetown, Massachusetts, followed by a Bunting Fellowship at Radcliffe College and, in 1982, an assistant professorship at Boston University. Jayne Anne Phillips's first novel, *Machine Dreams* (1984), was nominated for the National Book Critics Circle Award, and the *New York Times Book Review* declared it one of the twelve best books of the year. In 1985 Phillips married Mark Stockman, a Harvard-educated cardiologist. The next year she was named writer-in-residence at Brandeis University, and while there, another story collection, *Fast Lanes* (1987), was released. Harvard University lured her back into teaching in 1990 and again in the 1993 and 1994 school year when Houghton-Mifflin published her second novel, *Shelter.* In 1996 Brandeis University again appointed her writer-in-residence, and in 2000 a third novel, *Motherkind,* was published by Alfred A. Knopf. She credits writers' colonies, like Yaddo and McDowell, for enabling her to write during her years of active teaching and raising her two boys and two more that her husband brought to their family from a previous marriage. In 2007 Phillips was hired by Rutgers University to found, design, and run a new MFA program in creative writing, and she is immensely proud of the dramatically diverse program she has created there. The success of *Lark and Termite,* which also was a finalist for the National Book Critics Award, France's Prix de Medici Etranger, and the Heartland Prize, bodes well for her continued productivity as a writer and teacher.

Jayne Anne Phillips: A Selective Bibliography

INTERNET RESOURCES

The *Narrative* has short clips of several of Phillips's works and interviews. Phillips's website includes nine essays, a bibliography of her works, and brief reviews. *National Public Radio* has an excerpt from *Lark and Termite,* a review of the novel, and a statement of inspiration for the book. The *Bombsite* gives an extensive interview with Phillips, which explores themes in her writing and her style, and how she balances writing with her home life.

SELECTED BOOKS

Lark and Termite. New York: Knopf, 2009.
MotherKind: A Novel. New York: Knopf, 2000.
Shelter. New York: Houghton Mifflin, 1994.
Black Tickets. New York: Delacorte / Seymour Lawrence, 1989.
Machine Dreams. New York: Dutton Adult, 1984.

PROFILES/INTERVIEWS

Disheroon-Green, Suzanne. "Jayne Anne Phillips." In *The History of Southern Women's Literature.* Ed. Carolyn Perry, Mary Louise Weaks, and Doris Betts. Baton Rouge: Louisiana State UP, 2002. 594–98.

Johnson, Sarah Anne. "The Sound of a Novel: Jayne Anne Phillips, Author of *Lark and Termite,* Painstakingly Writes by Ear—Finding a Way into a Story through a Voice Not an Idea." *Writer* Nov. 2009.

Lyons, Bonnie, and Bill Oliver. "The Mystery of Language: An Interview with Jayne Anne Phillips." *New Letters* 61.1 (1994): 114–29.

Rhodes, Kate. "Interview with Jayne Anne Phillips." *Women's Studies: An Interdisciplinary Journal* 31.4 (2002): 517–20.

LITERARY CRITICISM

Brosi, George, ed. *Appalachian Heritage* 37.1 (2009). Features Jayne Anne Phillips.

Durrans, Stephanie. "Dissolving Borders: Towards a Community of Memory in the Fiction of Jayne Anne Phillips." In *Narratives of Community: Women's Short Story Sequences.* Ed. Roxanne Harde. Newcastle upon Tyne, England: Cambridge Scholars, 2007. 57–75.

Gaskins, Avery F. "Middle-class Townie: Jayne Anne Phillips and the Appalachian Experience." *Appalachian Journal* 19.3 (1992): 308–16.

Glenday, Michael K. "The Secret Sharing: Myth and Memory in the Writing of Jayne Anne Phillips." In *American Mythologies: Essays on Contemporary Literature.* Ed. William Blazek and Michael K. Glenday. Liverpool, England: Liverpool UP, 2005. 63–78.

Godden, Richard. "No End to the Work? Jayne Anne Phillips and the Exquisite Corpse of Southern Labor." *Journal of American Studies* 36.2 (2002): 249–80.

Afterword

On Teaching with This Book as a Text

by Morgan Cottrell and Kate Egerton

We have designed *Appalachian Gateway* to bring contemporary Appalachian writing to a widening circle of readers. Many of those readers will encounter this material in a college or high school classroom, and this afterword is intended to support teachers in sharing Appalachian literature with students. For college-level courses in Appalachian literature, *Appalachian Gateway* complements a wide range of classic and contemporary novels ranging from James Still's *River of Earth* to Jayne Anne Phillips's *Lark and Termite,* as well as collections of poetry and short fiction such as Frank X Walker's *Affrilachia,* Pinckney Benedict's *Town Smokes,* or Darnell Arnoult's *What Travels with Us.* The biographical and bibliographic materials on each author can support student exploration and research while also helping teachers prepare courses and lessons featuring contemporary Appalachian writers.

In order to facilitate connections with interdisciplinary courses in Appalachian Studies, as well as courses focused on literature, this collection follows the organizing principles of *The Encyclopedia of Appalachia* (U of Tennessee P, 2006), with sections focused on The Landscape, The People, Work and the Economy, Cultural Traditions, and Institutions. Appalachian literature carries great potential for multidisciplinary work. Students and teachers can pair readings with examples of Appalachian music, cultural artifacts, and texts on history, the economy, and culture. Consider collaborating with colleagues in neighboring disciplines. Directly involving students in research about Appalachian topics and subjects can enrich classroom conversations. Oral presentations, written research papers, or creative works representing their findings are all options for students to share what they have learned about Appalachian culture.

Works in this anthology can also usefully be read in many different combinations, including those focused on secondary themes, formal characteristics, or other relationships. Many of the works included in this volume can be informed by student investigations of topics ranging from health and medicine in Appalachia (Chris Holbrook's "All The Ills," Lee Smith's "Ultima Thule," Jeff Daniel Marion's "The Dying Art," and Jayne Anne Phillips's "Something That Happened") to the Cherokee in the modern world (Robert Conley's "The Plastic Indian" and Barbara Kingsolver's "Homeland");from the effects of mining, timber harvest, and industrial development (Ron Rash's "Blackberries in June," and Robert Morgan's "Brownfield" and "The Bullnoser") to religious traditions (Silas House's "Total Immersion," Pinckney Benedict's "Pig Helmet and the Wall of Life," and Maurice Manning's "XLIX"); from parents and their children ("Jeff Daniel Marion's "Codas," Chris Holbrook's "All the Ills," Frank X Walker's "Step(Fathering) on Eggshells," and Darnell Arnoult's "Learning at English Field") to a nation grappling with war (Mark Powell's "The Beauties of This Earth," Kathryn Stripling Byer's "Precious Little," Darnell Arnoult's "Learning Strategy at English Field," and Robert Morgan's "Vietnam War Memorial").

Many of the authors included in this anthology teach creative writing and are members of a vibrant writing community nurtured through events like the Appalachian Writers Workshop at the Hindman Settlement School in Hindman, Kentucky. Several pieces in this collection that actively consider the writer's role include Nikki Giovanni's "Serious Poems," Charles Wright's "What Do You Write About, Where Do Your Ideas Come From?" and "Appalachian Farewell," and Kathryn Stripling Byer's "Mountain Time" and "Precious Little." Consider using "What Do You Write About, Where Do Your Ideas Come From?" to ask students to write their own poems about place, in a similar vein to George Ella Lyon's "Where I'm From," a poem that has become a widely used writing prompt (Lyon's own website has more information about how students can write their own poems about their origins). Many student writers in Appalachia tell stories about their assumptions that literature happens in other places, and to other people.

The works contained in *Appalachian Gateway* can provide models and inspiration for writers who want to make literature about the things they value most. Beyond these pages, Silas House's *The Hurting Part: Evolution of an American Play* provides another way to look at how stories can transform on the path from the oral tradition into multiple written forms. The print edition of *The Hurting Part,* published by Motes Books, features a short story, a play, and an essay all written about the same family story that inspired House. In addition, an interview with House discusses the way these different works developed. This kind of collection can help students explore the advantages and disadvantages of different storytelling mediums. Transitioning their own creative works into different forms can help students develop a deeper understanding of the event that they are writing about and the importance it holds for the people involved in the story.

Place

Place matters in Appalachian literature, even when one's connection to place is threatened, as in Robert Morgan's "The Bullnoser." Take advantage of this in a classroom setting by starting from the place students are most familiar with—the place they consider their own. This can be their current home, where they are from, or even a place they want to someday inhabit. For students living in the region, reading works from contemporary Appalachian literature can help connect elements of the traditional high school and college canons more firmly to students' lives. Recognizing oneself or one's community in literature can be a powerful experience, and one, we hope, that can open doors to other works. The focus on place in some works of Appalachian literature, such as Jeff Daniel Marion's poem "Songs for Wood's Barbeque Shack in McKenzie, Tennessee," or Nikki Giovanni's "Knoxville, Tennessee," can illuminate the nature of place when these works are read in close conjunction with other works of American literature, or with longer works of Appalachian literature like Silas House's novel *Clay's Quilt* (2001),Lee Smith's *Oral History* (1983), or Ron Rash's *Saints at the River* (2004).

Teachers from outside the region who teach in Appalachia may be nervous about bringing Appalachian literature into the classroom. However, teaching the region's literature can be a great way to connect with students and to draw on students' expertise and experience. Invite students to educate others about Appalachia, beginning with you. Students can illuminate cultural nuances in the literature that might not be understood or recognized by people outside the region, and can improve their close reading skills at the same time. Also, our experience shows that even in a class dominated by students from Appalachia, many students hold conflicting views based on widely different experiences having to do with language, culture, faith, history, and politics. Use these differences to encourage students to broaden their views of Appalachia, its history, and its diversity. Reading and discussing the works of the Affrilachian poets, including Frank X Walker and Crystal Wilkinson, or Cherokee writers like Robert Conley, can be a good way to counteract the stereotype that Appalachian culture is white culture, even in largely homogeneous communities.

Teachers from Appalachia teaching outside the region may be more concerned about student-held stereotypes about Appalachian culture itself. The idea of overcoming these stereotypes can be intimidating, but consider asking students to think and talk about the stereotypes that others hold about the students' own places and cultures. Stories like Pinckney Benedict's "Pig Helmet and the Wall of Life" confront images that many readers find cartoonish or frightening, including a narcotic-addicted murderer and a serpent-handling evangelist, and transcend them in a story overflowing with eerie beauty. This kind of activity can open up the opportunity to discuss stereotypes about Appalachia as you work closely with texts. The vibrancy that comes from an excellent story can demolish the pat, sound-bite-sized assumptions that minimize the complexity and the beauty of human life.

Story

Many of the best contemporary Appalachian stories portray characters who are themselves debating the nature and importance of place and the force of others' expectations in their lives. Matt and Jamie, the young couple at the center of Ron Rash's story "Blackberries in June," are forced to confront their families' views of how they should live, and what kinds of educational and financial success they are entitled to enjoy.

Students from inside and outside the region can identify with generational conflicts and the pain that comes from putting oneself before one's kinfolk. In his poem "Appalachian Farewell"—in envisioning the very act of leaving "these towns our lives abandoned"—Charles Wright invokes the often-stated admonition "never [. . .] get above our raising."For every character who seems bound by the connection to place, there are others in *Appalachian Gateway* who find their origins empowering even as they seem to have left them behind. Elvissa Mackey Lipitz Stein, in Meredith Sue Willis's "Elvissa and the Rabbi," finds, after years in New York, that her mother's rural West Virginia roots are the missing ingredients that make her Jewish, urban life possible.

One rich vein of inquiry involves how the genres and forms in contemporary Appalachian literature continue to change while maintaining connections to oral storytelling, folk song, and other traditional arts, and Appalachian writers often speak about these connections in interviews about their work. Particularly in the high school classroom, where connections between literary study and creative writing can improve students' grasp of literature and language, it can be beneficial to invite students to explore contemporary texts by playing with imitation, adaptation, and retellings. Ask students to write poems about their summer jobs, following Charles Wright's recollections in "Get a Job" about the time he "learned how a backhoe works, and how to handle a shovel, / And multiple words not found in the dictionary."

Language and Dialect

Judging others by their accent and dialect is one of the strongest remaining biases that many Americans find culturally acceptable. People, particularly teachers, correct the pronunciation of others all day long without stopping to consider the meaning behind that act. A person who would never tolerate someone calling a child a "backwards hillbilly" often sees no problem telling a child that "ain't" is never an appropriate word, regardless of the context. Students must also realize that the way they use language factors into the way that they are viewed by other people. Using the word "ain't" or "heared" says something about where the speaker comes from, and can transform the way others will react. It may also bar some people from understanding the speaker in certain contexts.

Appalachian literature provides an opportunity to talk about the complexities of dialect in written language rather than just glossing over them. Students can learn a great deal from exploring the differences between literary works that utilize dialect well, examples of local color writing from the nineteenth century that now sound increasingly artificial and potentially offensive to modern readers, and those that don't do it at all. For instance, "That Durned Ole Via Negativa" by Maurice Manning explores the use of the double negative in a way that is both probing and encouraging. Approaching dialect in this way gives students a chance to understand and appreciate the various ways that language can function. Students can learn a great deal by examining the ways they themselves talk through writing.

About the Editors

GEORGE BROSI grew up in Oak Ridge, Tennessee, and worked for the Council of the Southern Mountains in Berea, Kentucky, in the summer of 1963 between semesters at Carleton College. He graduated in 1965 and was employed by a variety of nonprofit organizations, including the Council again in 1967. In 1971 he married Connie Fearington and moved to a small farm in Tennessee's Sequatchie Valley, working for Save Our Cumberland Mountains and other organizations. Late in the 1970s he moved back to Berea, Kentucky, to become the manager of the Appalachian Book and Record Shop for the Council of the Southern Mountains and then created a family retail book business specializing exclusively in books about the Southern Mountain region. He and Connie continue to run this business. In the 1990s Brosi received a master's in education from Western Carolina University, and then taught at locations ranging from the University of Kentucky to off-campus centers of community colleges. His courses included Appalachian Studies, Appalachian Literature, Kentucky Literature, Native American Literature, American Literature, British Literature, World Literature, and various expository and creative writing courses. Since 2002 Brosi has edited *Appalachian Heritage,* a regional literary quarterly. He is the coeditor of *Jesse Stuart: The Man and His Books* (Jesse Stuart Foundation, 1988) and *No Lonesome Road: The Prose and Poetry of Don West* (U of Illinois P, 2004). In 2003 the Appalachian Writers Association presented him with the award for Outstanding Contribution to Appalachian Literature.

KATE EGERTON teaches English at Berea College, where she specializes in modern and contemporary American and British literature and offers courses in creative and professional writing. She earned her MA and PhD from the University of North Carolina at Chapel Hill. From 2008 to 2010, she served as the president of the Arthur Miller Society, and her critical edition of Miller's play *The Last Yankee* was published by Methuen in January 2011. Her essay on fathers and sons in Pinckney Benedict's short stories appeared in the winter 2010 issue of *Appalachian Heritage,* and she has also published articles in the *Journal of American Drama and Theatre* and the *Arthur Miller Journal.* Her current research on images of Appalachia on the contemporary American stage, including the 2009 musical *The Burnt Part Boys,* was presented at the 2011 meeting of the Appalachian Studies Association.

About the Student Editors

SAMANTHA LYNN COLE is a graduate of Berea College who received her degree in Appalachian Studies. She is from Beattyville, Kentucky, and has read regional literature since early high school. While attending Berea she worked for nearly four years as a student editorial assistant at *Appalachian Heritage* magazine. She also took classes in Appalachian Studies ranging from regional literature to dulcimer making. A writer herself, Samantha has attended the Mountain Heritage Literary Festival at Lincoln Memorial University, as well as the Appalachian Writers' Workshop at Hindman Settlement School. Her poetry has been published in anthologies and regional magazines.

MORGAN COTTRELL, from Roane County, West Virginia, is a senior English Education major at Berea College, where she worked for the Loyal Jones Appalachian Center's Brushy Fork Institute. While in high school she attended the West Virginia Governor's School for the Arts in creative writing. As part of her preparation for a career teaching high school, she is developing curriculum and classroom materials for teaching the works of a range of contemporary West Virginia writers.

Appalachian Gateway was designed and typeset on a Macintosh OS 10.6.8 computer system using CS5 InDesign software. The body text is set in 9/13 ITC Chelteham Std Light and display type is set in ITC Cheltenham Handtooled Std. This book was designed and typeset by Barbara Karwhite and manufactured by Thomson-Shore, Inc.